BLACKOUT

KIT MALLORY

BLACKOUT

KIT MALLORY

BLACKOUT

© 2018 Kit Mallory

Cover and interior design by Rachel Lawston
www.lawstondesign.com

First edition

ISBN (Print): 978-1-9999697-0-7
ISBN (eBook): 978-1-9999697-1-4
ISBN (CreateSpace): 978-1-9999697-2-1

Material from the song "They Will Float Your Body Out To Sea" by Ben Marwood reproduced with permission from Ben Marwood, with thanks.

Contact the author:
Email: kitmallorywrites@gmail.com
Twitter: @kitkattus

CONTENTS

To my grandad, Derek;
adventurer and story-teller.

1

THE BOY WHO STEPPED
OFF THE LEDGE

Mackenzie was late.

This should not have been important. In the ten years the Board had been governing the UK, a number of ambitiously foolhardy people had tried to break into their headquarters. Every one of them had ended up with a bullet in their head, if they were lucky.

Mackenzie, however, had left the headquarters through a fifth-floor window some hours ago and was still bullet-free. This was an achievement worth celebrating. But it was six in the morning on a dark, icy canal towpath on the outskirts of Birmingham, and the enormous man waiting for him up ahead did not appear to be in a celebratory mood.

The man was illuminated by a full moon hanging low in the sky, his hands jammed into his pockets and his breath puffing out white clouds in the freezing air. It wasn't often you met someone who could actually breathe aggressively. This was not the sort of person you kept waiting.

Mackenzie should have been used to them. When you were an illegal Northerner on the wrong side of the Wall you either made the best of the skills you had or you sank, and somehow word had got out that he was all right at what he did. And then sometime over the last couple of years men like this had started materialising behind him in alleyways and saying things like "A friend of mine wants to have a little chat with you," without even a trace of irony. It was difficult to complain about this – it was a long time since he'd been starving, and these days he was considered too useful to get threatened much – but he still had to fight down a yelp of panic every time a hand grabbed him from behind.

He sometimes wondered what his family would have said if they could have known that at seventeen he'd end up widely regarded as the best thief in the South. They would probably have laughed too hard at the idea to be able to say much at all. But he didn't think about that often because doing so brought a hard, painful lump to his throat, and if it was a bad idea to keep a man like this one waiting, it would be an even worse idea to cry in front of him.

He quickened his pace. The sooner this was over with, the better. They were on the edge of the city but they could have been right out in the depths of the countryside for all you could tell; there was no distant roar of traffic, no wayward revellers stumbling home from a night out. Only the frozen, starry night, and the inky water of the canal.

Ten years ago, a bird's eye view of the city would have shown an intricate network laced in the orange glow of streetlights and the red and white lights of cars, snaking through the streets like blood pumping through veins. Now the map had gone dark, and only the brave or terminally foolish ventured out during curfew hours. People like Mackenzie, in fact, and the silent, sullen man who loomed in front of him.

He'd seen this one before. His name was Rafe, or something. Possibly he was one of the less friendly ones, which, all things considered, was quite an accolade.

"You're late," the man probably called Rafe rumbled, as Mackenzie halted in front of him.

"Yeah," Mackenzie agreed. "Sorry about that."

"Thought you weren't coming."

"Well, here I am. It's all good."

Rafe grunted in a way that suggested he did not agree with this analysis. A note of suspicion entered his voice. "You got the stuff?"

"You got my money?"

Rafe reached into his jacket and produced a large envelope. He wasn't the employer, he was just an oversized errand boy with a powerful, mysterious boss. Mackenzie had put great effort into ensuring he'd never laid eyes on the boss or learned their name. With these people, you really didn't want to know the details.

He knew the money would be there but he made a show of peering inside the envelope anyway because you had to keep up appearances. It wouldn't do to look as if you were going soft. That was when people started getting funny ideas, like throwing you in the canal instead of paying you the money they owed you.

He nodded in satisfaction and glanced up at Rafe. The man had small eyes squashed into the centre of a very large round face, and the sort of expression he might have adopted if Mackenzie had just vomited on his shoes.

Mackenzie tried to ignore this. "I got the stuff."

Rafe coughed. "Still got that accent, too."

Mackenzie stopped, his hand halfway to his pocket. He tried to keep his voice steady. "What's my accent got to do with anything?"

Rafe squinted hard at him. "You told anyone about this job?"

"What? Of course not."

"Sure about that?"

Ah. Now he remembered. Rafe was like the worst kind of school bully, except with considerably more weight and weaponry to throw around. It would be a bad idea to antagonise him.

Well, he never had been very good at keeping his mouth shut. "Has it ever occurred to you," he said, "that you might have some trust issues?"

Rafe's brows knitted together. He clenched a massive fist. "You what?"

"Nothing," Mackenzie said hastily. "Never mind. Look, I haven't told anyone. There's no problem here."

"Good," Rafe said. "Best if you keep it that way. 'Cos I'm just sayin', that accent. Cause you problems if the Board ever wanted to ask you any questions."

"Are you threatening me?"

Rafe spat onto the ground between them. Mackenzie made a concerted effort not to step backwards. "Nah," Rafe said. "Just makin' sure everyone knows where they stand."

"Right," Mackenzie said slowly. "Understood."

Rafe raised his eyebrows. "We doin' business, then, or what?"

Inside Mackenzie's jacket, hidden under the leather, were two pockets. He slipped his hand inside the right hand one, pulled out something small and smooth and offered it to Rafe, who shoved it into his own pocket without a flicker of interest. Mackenzie watched with some relief as the man turned and stumped away down the towpath towards the centre of Birmingham, woollen hat pulled over his ears.

The second memory stick, safe in his other pocket and now nestled next to twenty thousand pounds in cash, Mackenzie kept for himself.

He'd taken it on impulse, which wasn't like him at all. Over the last two and a half years he'd developed a rigid set of rules, right down to the socks he wore, and he never deviated from his plan. Get in, get the job done, get out. Keep quiet, keep tidy, and always look before you leap.

But this time had been different. He'd broken into the *Board headquarters*. It had been, frankly, bloody hard work. And when he'd found what he was looking for, this other memory stick had just been. . . sitting there. Someone must have been in the middle of using it. It looked so ordinary, and yet it had been so difficult getting in for the first one that he couldn't help but wonder what might be on this. And, more importantly, whether somebody might pay for it.

He always worked on commission now. He stole to order. He didn't need to do anything else these days.

But. . . he'd been paid a *lot* of money for this job. It would have been a waste to leave it lying around.

The problem now, of course, was that he had no idea what he actually had.

Fortunately, he knew someone who could help him.

2

REBELLION

Skyler perched on a dented refrigerator at the edge of the landfill site, swinging her legs as AJ rummaged through the heaps of scrap metal that surrounded them. There was no point offering to help; it all looked like junk to her. But AJ seemed content to comb through the endless piles in the fading light, swatting away the odd fly and occasionally straightening up in triumph.

She trained her torch on the half-rusted lump in his hand and he inspected it happily. "Brilliant," he said, almost to himself.

Skyler wrinkled her nose. "Looks like someone threw that away for a reason."

He placed the piece of twisted metal carefully in his handcart and resumed his hunt. "No imagination, that's your problem."

"Oh, sure. And this from the guy who told me a screen full of code looks like someone's been mashing their hands on a keyboard."

He waved an airy hand. "It's different. You can *make* something out of this. Something real."

Skyler held the torch and said nothing. She disagreed. The uses for a pile of scrap metal were finite, even to someone with AJ's skills and imagination. But learn enough about code, on the other hand, and you could do anything.

Well. Almost anything.

The last rays of the setting sun had disappeared at the horizon. Her stomach clenched. She had forgotten herself. She had been here too long.

She slid off the side of the refrigerator. "I should get going."

AJ straightened up, a shadow of disappointment crossing his face. "It's not that late. Stay a bit longer. I haven't seen you in ages."

She shifted from foot to foot, biting her lip. "I can't really –"

"Oh, go on. Come back to mine. Just for a bit." He stretched his long limbs and gave her an easy, disarming grin. His black hair flopped into his eyes in a way that he probably thought made him look suave and carefree. "I'll show you what I've been building."

Evidently this was meant to be appealing. She rolled her eyes and picked up her bike. "Another car?" AJ loved motor vehicles and it was a source of great sorrow to him that there were hardly any around anymore. He still liked to fix them up, though – and build his own – which was why he spent half his time rummaging around the scrapyard. He seemed not to care about the awkward questions he'd have to answer if anyone caught him there.

"Nope. A motorbike."

She laughed. "You're kidding."

"I'm not. It's gonna be awesome. Come and see."

Skyler hesitated. It was true that she hadn't spent much time with AJ lately. Things were not as simple between them as they had once been. They'd both been busy growing up, and she wasn't sure they'd been growing in the same direction.

"Oh, go on." He cast his torch over her bike. "That thing's falling apart. Let me take a look at it."

Skyler rattled the bike. "The chain keeps coming off," she admitted.

"Well, that settles it, then. Come on."

She opened her mouth to protest and then shut it again. After all, it was good to be outside, and to be having a conversation with an actual person. And she hadn't been out of the cellar properly for weeks. And she was sick of doing as she was told.

"All right," she said. "Let's go."

AJ cast longing looks at the occasional cars that passed them as they headed back along the main road towards the dilapidated estate where he lived. It was past five o'clock and the roads were so choked with cyclists and buses the cars could only crawl, but presumably the ability to look down their nose at everyone else compensated for the time the drivers wasted actually trying to get anywhere in them.

When Skyler was small, the buses had had adverts for films on the sides of them. Now they bore the Board's insignia, a shield with a stylised flame in the centre, and a variety of slogans: *Sacrifices Today, Opportunities Tomorrow. Putting the Great back in Great Britain.* Her personal favourite was the hand snatching a piece of bread from the clutches of a pouting child, with the legend: *Is Your Child Going Hungry to Feed the Unregistered?* Subtlety really wasn't the Board's style.

The mysterious lumps of metal and the large tyre in AJ's handcart drew curious glances from the passing commuters. Unease prickled on Skyler's skin with every eye that flickered towards them, but he chattered away, filling her in on the gossip from the city's criminal fraternity: who looked like they might be switching alliances, who'd slept with whom, who'd pissed somebody off and needed to watch their back.

If he'd tried to have this conversation with anyone else in the city he'd probably have got his head kicked in. He trusted Skyler, though. And it wasn't like she had anyone to repeat any of this to, anyway.

She wasn't really listening to him. Her attention was on the homeward travellers. Kids in school uniform, adults in suits or paint-splattered overalls: different as they were, they all walked the same way – heads down, footsteps hurried. There was no such thing as a good excuse for being caught out after curfew.

And further down the street, two navy-clad figures, each heavy, measured step in perfect unison. Truncheons hung from their belts – for when a lighter touch was required – and semi-automatic rifles were slung across their chests, for when only the threat of being riddled with bullets would do. The crowds parted around them as though they were radioactive. Skyler felt like she was under a spotlight.

AJ had finally noticed her discomfort. He put a hand on her shoulder. "Don't worry about them."

This was such a ridiculous thing to say that incredulity cut through her unease. "Uh – which bit should I not worry about? The bit where they clock you've probably got an illegal vehicle stashed away? Or the bit where they ask for my ID and lock me up when I can't show them one?"

"They won't –"

"They might."

What had got into AJ? He seemed to think he was untouchable these days – and, by extension, that she was too. He hadn't always been like this. When they'd first met he'd been as scared of the Board as she was. Although he was a legal Southerner with a biometric ID, the brown skin that spoke to his Bangladeshi heritage drew plenty of harassment from the enforcers, and he'd understood exactly how dangerous the South was for an unregistered Northerner. She'd felt safer around him then. She hadn't had to worry that he might make some careless comment that would get her shot.

He slung an arm around her. "They won't give you any trouble while you're with me."

Which was also ridiculous – AJ had been in prison at least three times – except that in the South, the boundary between the law and the criminal underworld's big players was a murky, perilous grey area. Not that AJ would exactly count as a big player.

He'd started talking again. She had no idea what about, but she nodded along as the enforcers passed, so that she wouldn't betray herself by looking too scared or too guilty or too Northern.

The enforcers ignored them. Skyler tried to will away the churning in her stomach.

It was full dark by the time they reached AJ's little two-up, two-down terraced house. He was only nineteen, but he'd lived alone as long as she'd known him. She didn't know where his parents were. Ages ago, in an uncharacteristically introspective mood, he'd told her that his grandparents had been forced to leave the UK during the mass deportations when the Board first came to power, but he wouldn't say much more than that. She didn't mind. She understood not wanting to talk about the past.

In his cluttered living room, he poured himself a glass of whiskey and offered her the bottle. She shook her head.

"Sure?" He topped up his own glass.

She frowned. "How'd you afford that?" The bottle in his hand wasn't homemade.

He grinned. "Been getting paid pretty well lately."

"How so?"

He crouched to inspect her bicycle chain. "I've been doing some work for Redruth." His tone was casual, but he avoided her eyes.

She stiffened. "What kind of work?"

"Just. . . you know." He waved a hand and reached for a little can of oil. "Stuff. You know."

"Not really. Are you sure that's a good idea?"

"It's fine. Why wouldn't it be?"

"Well – how much work are you doing for him?"

"Bits and pieces."

She knew that vague tone. "AJ, please tell me you haven't joined his crew."

"Would it be so bad if I had?"

Shit.

She poked him in the shoulder. He glanced up, a lock of hair falling across his forehead. "What's the matter, Sky?"

And now he was going to play dumb. "What are you doing?" she said. "Why are you working for him?"

He turned back to her bike and picked up a pump. "Your tyres are nearly flat. Look, there's nothing to worry about. He's not so bad."

She swallowed her retort. When AJ thought he knew best there was no arguing with him. "Just – be careful, all right? Please?"

He gave her a winning smile. "You know me."

"Yeah." She stood up. "I should get going."

"Why? You on a tag or something?"

He was kidding, but he couldn't know how close to the truth he was. She tried not to snap at him. "I just need to get back."

"There's no law against having fun, you know, Sky."

His tone was light, but it gave her a prickle of irritation. "There's a law against being out past seven, though, and you know it."

He consulted his watch. "Well, you're not gonna make it in before then anyway. C'mon. You got a job that won't wait a couple more hours?"

"You know what it can be like."

He put his glass down amongst the oil-covered rags and tools, and stood in front of her. "You know, Sky. . . I know we've talked about this before, but – you could always stay here. If you wanted to. There's room."

"Room's one thing. Electricity's something else. You know that." She forced a smile. "I appreciate it. I do. But. . . you know."

AJ handed her bike over and returned her smile ruefully. "That should keep you going for a bit. You gonna come see me again soon?"

She was already halfway out the door. "Sure. Thanks for sorting the bike."

She climbed on and sped off without looking back.

The full moon hung in the sky, turning the world ghostly grey. Skyler pedalled hard through the empty streets and cursed herself. She'd let herself be swayed by the desire to act, for once, like a normal teenager. *Stupid.* Once she got out of the city she'd be safer; the enforcers didn't usually bother patrolling the country lanes. But she might still pay for tonight's recklessness.

She braced herself as she jolted over cracks and potholes, trying to ignore her pulse ticking like a countdown, faster and faster. It was all wrong, being out like this in the dark. She was too small, too exposed, a mouse in a hedgerow, waiting to be caught. Too much like another night, years ago, out in the open blackness. Except the danger was different now.

What would it be like to move in with AJ? It wasn't the first time he'd suggested it. Over the last few years he'd looked out for her, been kind to her in an older-brother type way – although sometimes lately there was an undercurrent to their interactions that made her think maybe he didn't look at her in a very brotherly way anymore.

It was out of the question anyway, of course. AJ's electricity ration only just kept his lights on – standard for a nineteen-year-old with a criminal record and no legitimate income. Even if she could live there legally and claim a ration, it would never keep her in work. There was only one place she could get that.

Yellow squares of light appeared in the distance and her stomach gave a treacherous flip. She plunged, too fast, into a deep pothole and almost threw herself off.

She swore and slammed her feet down on the tarmac. Her hands shook on the handlebars.

She rubbed her hand over her face. *It's okay. You're okay. You should have stayed at AJ's.*

Too late now.

She took a deep breath, climbed off the bike and turned off the road onto a dirt track that led through the fields towards the mansion.

Daniel's estate. She never had been able to think of it as home. Her third winter in that bloody cellar now: no heating, no natural light, just endless damp clothes and never being warm. And Daniel, constantly holding it over her head what a massive favour he was doing her.

Her presence in the cellar was a secret to everyone except Daniel and some of his trusted knuckle-draggers, and there were rules about when she could enter and leave.

He liked to make a big deal out of how much of a risk he was taking giving a home – if you could call it that – to an illegal Northern refugee. As if there was a soul in the city who would have dared ask Daniel Redruth what he kept in his cellar.

The house was obscured by the woodland at the back of the grounds. In theory, it wasn't difficult to get onto Daniel's land. A simple wire fence marked the boundary at the edge of the trees, although anyone who wasn't supposed to be there would soon find out that was where the easy bit ended. Skyler abandoned her bike against the fence and ducked through the wires into the dense, damp, wet-leaf-smelling darkness beyond.

Someone would have seen her coming and, sure enough, when she emerged from the woods there was a person-shaped lump lurking outside, dazzling her with the light from his torch. She didn't know this one's name; they were all the same, and not her allies.

He grunted in recognition. She blinked away the torch beam, saw the baseball bat in his hand, hanging by his side. "You're late," he said. "Supposed to be in by five, ain't you?"

She didn't answer. She headed towards the house and left the man standing in the shadows behind her.

It would have been sensible to be scared. Instead she felt nothing. This happened sometimes. She slipped in through the back door and closed it quietly behind her.

The kitchen, vast and spotless with its granite floor and marble worktops, was empty. She exhaled. Perhaps Daniel was out. Perhaps he wouldn't hear about her transgression, or if he did, maybe he wouldn't care. It was impossible to know.

After all this time she knew exactly how long it took to reach the cellar, how to move so her feet made no sound on the polished floor, like a ghost. She tiptoed through the kitchen and opened the door into the main hallway.

When she'd first arrived here, this was what had stunned her most. The oak floor, polished to a mirror-shine; the sweeping staircase with its finely carved banisters; and suspended from the ceiling, flooding the place with a heavy golden glow, a chandelier laden with candles and crystal shards.

When she was young she'd thought houses like this belonged to film stars and royalty. Instead it turned out they belonged to people like Daniel.

The trapdoor to the cellar lay through a door under the stairs. As she turned the handle, another door clicked open behind her. She whipped round.

Daniel moved towards her, his expression blank. She froze.

He didn't speak. He just grabbed her by the throat and slammed her against the wall.

He wasn't a large man, but he lifted her with one hand. Her head knocked against the wall. She gasped, but there was nowhere for the air to go.

His fingers tightened and bright spots danced in her vision. Behind them was Daniel's face: expensive tan, mild, round blue eyes behind wire-rimmed glasses, hair thinning a little across the top. He didn't look angry but that didn't mean anything. It certainly didn't mean he wasn't capable of strangling her.

She met his eyes through the bursts of darkness in her vision, and waited.

But he waited, too. His hand locked around her windpipe until she let out a small, involuntary choked noise that she hated herself for and then, delicately, he let her go.

"Get downstairs," he said.

She turned away from him. All the way down into the cellar, as she fumbled through the darkness to light a candle, she felt his presence in the hallway above, and she balled her hands tightly into fists to keep them from shaking.

3

A CALCULATED RISK

Skyler stayed awake all night, sitting on her lumpy mattress, wrapped in damp blankets. The mattress had been there when she arrived – new, apparently – and she'd wondered at the time how Daniel had explained to the rest of the household what on earth he was doing with it. But that was before she'd understood that Daniel never had to explain anything to anyone.

She'd told AJ she had work to do and it was true, but it could have waited. It was more that immersing herself in figures and code allowed her not to think about Daniel's hands around her throat. She fell asleep around dawn with her laptop still on her lap.

When she woke, the candle she'd left alight had burned out. She rolled her head painfully from side to side to ease the stiffness in her neck and fumbled for the matches tucked down beside the mattress. When she'd moved in, Daniel had told her she could use the light fitting down here for an extra fee. The convenience would have been outweighed by the sour taste of asking him for a favour, of putting yet another thing within his control. Candles were preferable.

The ladder under the stairs dropped down into a wine store – tens if not hundreds of thousands of pounds' worth, these days. In her pettier moments she sometimes thought about smashing the bottles, but she knew she never would. She didn't hate herself that much.

The room she lived in was through the wine cellar, behind a locked door. Any sense of privacy was an illusion, though; she had a key, but so did Daniel and whoever else he felt like giving it to. The point was that his family wouldn't stumble across her by accident.

She wrapped her blanket tighter round her shoulders and headed for the tiny room at the far end of the cellar which contained a toilet and a sink. That, at least, she could be grateful for – she'd assumed she would have to use a bucket – but of course Daniel was the sort of person who had a bathroom for his damn cellar.

She turned the tap and tried to suppress the flutter of relief when it yielded an icy trickle. At least he hadn't shut the water off this time.

She needed to get outside. It wasn't unusual for her to spend days or even weeks in the cellar without leaving, but today Daniel might well want to come and have another conversation about her curfew, just in case she'd somehow failed to get the point last night. She refused to sit there waiting for him. Besides, she'd finished most of her work. She would go and check her messages.

Outside, she used her sleeve to wipe the dew from her bike saddle and set off into the city. Beads of moisture hung from the bare branches of trees and collected in her hair as she pedalled, but she didn't care. She just needed to be somewhere Daniel couldn't reach her, even if it could only be for a little while.

The morning fog thickened into drizzle as she cut through the Jewellery Quarter with its gleaming shop facades. Ahead of her, a scowling man in white overalls scrubbed furiously at the graffiti scrawled on the red brickwork. He was wasting his time, of course – more appeared every day. Every colour, every word, every squiggle held a meaning: they were messages, communications between members of the city's underworld.

Skyler wove around the other cyclists, horses and carts heading for the Bullring markets. Birmingham had been a big shopping city once, but like everywhere else most of the high street shops had closed. People spent their money on things they needed, not things they wanted. The Jewellery Quarter was an exception, for a small subsection of society who still knew what a disposable income was.

A horn blasted behind her. She jerked her head over her shoulder to see the traffic scrambling out of the way of three large, shiny black four by fours.

She wished she could stop the way her heart pounded, frantic, whenever she caught a glimpse of one of the huge black cars. She pulled over to the pavement with a cluster of other cyclists and waited for the Board cars to pass before setting off again.

Then she rounded a corner and all her muscles locked together.

Greycoats. *Oh, no no no.* Two women, in their black leather boots and trademark long grey jackets: the Board's special agents, deployed to deal with anything the enforcers couldn't resolve with ordinary garden variety brutality. They stepped into an electronics shop and a moment later two customers made a hasty exit. As Skyler passed, she glimpsed the greycoats leaning against the counter, talking to a middle-aged shop worker with a face the colour of putty. She forced herself to keep pedalling. *For God's sake don't give them a reason to notice you.*

By the time she reached the Bullring markets it was clear that it had been the wrong day to come into town. Fear rippled through the marketplace in jerky movements, eyes that flickered from side to side, short, clipped conversations. She should probably turn around. There was no point in a wasted journey, though, and who knew how long the greycoats would be out for?

And she couldn't go back to the cellar yet. She just couldn't.

She pushed her hood down as she climbed off her bike. The drizzle was already soaking into her hair, but the greycoats didn't like it when they couldn't see people's faces, and she couldn't risk looking like she had anything to hide.

She crossed the square as quickly as she dared, weaving around at least fifty people queuing outside a bakery for their bread ration. The ration was supposed to be a token of the Board's generosity – *see, we won't let you starve, aren't you grateful?*

Most of the queue were inspecting their feet in silence. This was sensible. There were often informants in the ration lines; people complained more when they were hungry. Some of these seemed past even that, though. Half of them looked like they were relying on the wall behind them to hold them up. A scrawny girl, no more than five or six, hung off her father's arm – "I'm hungry, Daddy. It's cold. I'm getting wet."

All of which was true, no doubt – the girl's ragged pigtails straggled down her back in sodden, ratty strands, her threadbare coat soaked through. Skyler should have felt bad for her, but she only felt irritation, which was apparently shared by the rest of the queue. People tutted and shifted. A plump-cheeked woman snapped, "Can't you shut her up?"

The girl's father glared at her. "If you don't like it you can always piss off. You look like you could afford to skip a few rations, anyway."

Skyler hurried away as the voices rose behind her. It was almost enough to make her grateful she wasn't entitled to a ration. She pushed through the crowds towards the public toilets, slipped inside and headed to the end cubicle.

The cubicle walls were covered with scribbles and gouges: writing in capital letters, in rounded lower case, in pencil, in biro, in thick marker pen, carved into the paintwork with keys. She scanned it all, mentally separating old messages from new ones.

The one that stood out was scrawled in purple marker on the back of the door. *Looking for a good time?* it read. *Call 611274.* It was not, of course, a real phone number. It was a code.

Mackenzie's code. That was unexpected.

Mackenzie lived in a high rise block near the city centre, one of a cluster that were only a few years old but already decaying. There were hundreds of empty apartments in the blocks, which made them pretty much perfect for someone like him to squat in unnoticed. No lights, of course. Just shadowy stairwells, mould, and dubious red-brown stains on the concrete floor. The occasional hooded figure passed her on the stairs.

She'd considered leaving the visit to another day, and if it had been anyone else she might have done, but Mackenzie hadn't contacted her for well over a year. Whatever he wanted, it was something more than a chat about the weather.

His bedsit was on the twenty-third floor. She banged relentlessly on the door until he answered it, bleary-eyed, in a t-shirt and boxer shorts with his hair sticking up all over the place.

His pale skin, like hers, had the pallor of someone who didn't see enough sunlight, but he'd filled out a bit since she'd last seen him. He was still slim, wiry, but what there was to him was all muscle: the product of all those nights climbing drainpipes and running across rooftops. He had dark hair that fell into bright wary eyes, a thin, bird-like face, and a Yorkshire accent that was going to get him shot if he ever opened his mouth in front of the wrong person. In another life, they'd been in the same year at school.

The bedsit was pristine, his sparse possessions arranged in neat and deliberate order. She went to step inside and he winced. "Oh," she said. "Right. Sorry." She bent to unlace her boots.

He rubbed sleep out of his eyes and pulled on a pair of jeans. "I didn't think you'd come."

"Well. Here I am."

He motioned for her to sit on one of the plastic garden chairs he used as living room furniture. "How are you?"

"I'm fine." She pulled up a chair. "What did you want?"

He sat opposite her. His foot was jumping already. "I got. . . a thing. Not sure what it is."

She waited. He held out a hand and opened his palm.

"It's a memory stick," she said.

"I know *that*. I mean I don't know what's on it. I tried sticking it in that" – he gestured at a sleek laptop on the floor next to his mattress – "but I couldn't get into it."

What was he doing with a laptop? He couldn't have an electricity supply. You needed a permit – and a biometric ID that proclaimed you not only British enough, but Southern enough – to get a ration. The bedsit contained no other electronics aside from a battery-powered radio.

She took the memory stick from him. It was plain, silvery metal, no brand name, no identifiers. "Where'd you get this, Mack?"

"I took it," he said, as if it were obvious.

"Who's it for?"

"No one. I was looking for something else and I found this and – well, I thought. . . Anyway, I took it."

"Where from? When?"

"Last night. I, uh – look, you won't say anything, will you?"

She rolled her eyes. "Who am I gonna tell, exactly?"

"Fair enough. Oh, hell. I. . . took it from the Board headquarters."

"Huh." *That explains the greycoats.*

"You could at least pretend to be a bit impressed."

Actually, she was. But he didn't need her to massage his ego; he knew full well what he'd accomplished. She stood up. "Want me to take a look?"

"Would you? You should get about an hour off the laptop."

"And where'd you get *that*?"

He blushed. "I stole it this morning. On the way home."

"Of course you did."

She sat cross-legged on the floor in front of the laptop and plugged the drive in. Mackenzie wandered over to the other side of the room and switched the radio on.

Well, she wasn't going to get anything off this in a hurry. An image of a padlock appeared on the screen, demanding a password – and that was all she could get. But the password page contained, very small in the top right-hand corner, an emblem that she recognised.

She looked hard at it. Then she looked again.

Then she said, trying to keep her voice as cool as before: "Mack, this is a Heimdall drive."

Mackenzie, unsurprisingly, looked blank. "A what?"

"They're a Finnish company. Super secretive. They do, like, ridiculously high level encryption. All their stuff is custom made. It's supposed to be the best in the world."

"So. . . what does that mean?"

"People don't just have these lying around. Not even the Board. It means they went to the trouble of ordering one and paid a fortune for it."

He still wasn't getting it. "It means," Skyler said, trying to be patient, "that whatever's on here is a huge deal."

His face brightened. "So probably something I can sell?"

"Well, sure, if you could find out what was on it. Which you won't be able to."

He raised a hopeful eyebrow. "You know how to get into it?"

"You kidding? I've never even seen one of these before."

"You think anyone else round here could?"

She scoffed and unplugged the drive. "No. But I guess this explains why the Board are all over the place today. Looks like they're properly freaking out."

He stiffened. "What d'you mean?"

"What d'you think I mean? The Bullring's crawling with greycoats. You gonna be all right up here? How many people know where you live? Maybe you should think about –"

Mackenzie dived towards her, his face drained of colour. She wrapped her hand tight around the drive and stood up. "You all right, Mack?"

He took a very long, deep breath. "Can I have that back, please?"

He was like this sometimes. One minute he was pulling off a feat the city's most hardened criminals wouldn't have the nerve for, the next he was scared of his own shadow. She'd never been able to figure him out. It would be useful to have the daring version of him back about now, though. "C'mon, Mack," she said, coaxing. "Aren't you dying to know what's on it?"

"Uh, no. Not if I'm gonna end up as mincemeat in a warehouse somewhere when the greycoats get my name out of someone." He ran a hand through his hair, standing it on end. "Please, Sky – just give it back."

"What're you gonna do? Throw it away? Give it *back* to them? Have you got any idea how much of a waste that would be?"

But he was wringing his hands, dancing from foot to foot; he was too scared to listen. She tried a different tack. "And as if they're gonna stop looking for you now anyway. I'm pretty sure the damage is done."

"Come on, Skyler. This isn't your call."

He did have a point. The Board styled themselves as impenetrable, omnipotent. Sending the greycoats out so publicly was a virtual admission that they were panicking. Whatever was on the drive, then, must be important enough to risk embarrassing themselves to get it back. What they would do to the person who'd taken it, or the person who was found with it...

He was right to be afraid. But out of everyone she knew in the South, Mackenzie was by far the least frightening. And while it was kind of a shame to take advantage of that, this was too good an opportunity to pass up.

"Yeah," she said, edging towards the door. "Thing is, Mack, I think I'm gonna hang on to it."

"You can't!"

"Why not? It won't do anyone else any good. Let me take it. No one will know."

"They'll find out." He grabbed her arm, his hand clammy against her skin. "And then they'll cut both of us into little pieces."

"We're Northern, Mackenzie. If the Board catch up with us we're gonna end up on the other side of the Wall or hanging off it, memory stick or no memory stick."

"So do you really want to draw their attention to us? Jesus Christ!"

She tried to pull away from him, but he clung on like a limpet. "I'm not letting go of you till you give it to me," he said.

And he was trying to sound like he meant it, but he wasn't going to fight her. This was Mackenzie; there was no way he would try to hurt her. She made a show of trying to wriggle out of his grip and he just squeezed her arm, doing his puppy impression. It felt like desperation more than intimidation, it wasn't like Daniel grabbing hold of her.

"It's four o' clock," said the cheerful voice on the radio, and she went cold. She didn't have time to talk Mackenzie into trusting her. She couldn't afford to be late back again.

So what now?

One more chance. "Let go of me, Mack. I mean it."

He shook his head furiously. "Not till you give me that."

Well, no one could say she hadn't made the effort.

She twisted in his grip, breaking his hold. He flung up a defensive hand and she raised her arm and punched him, hard, in the side of the head.

She was almost too busy wondering whether she'd broken her hand to notice him collapse. When she looked down at him, half amazed it had actually worked, a pang of guilt cut through her.

But it was done now. And she had the Heimdall drive.

She started towards the door, then thought better of it, went back and arranged a prone Mackenzie in the recovery position. "Sorry, Mack," she whispered. Then she ran down the twenty-three flights of stairs.

4

THIN ICE

Fifteen frantic miles later, Skyler had never been more grateful to get back to the cellar. She sank onto her mattress, opened her laptop and turned the drive over in her fingers.

Mackenzie had broken into the Board headquarters. *Unbelievable.* She hadn't thought it was possible. The Board probably hadn't either. This wasn't like the old days when people could just walk into the Houses of Parliament. Those had burned down anyway, a few years into the Board's regime. It didn't matter, the Board had said; they were an outdated relic, a failed experiment, wasn't that so? And people had scrambled to agree, because dissent was unpatriotic. Which, according to the Board, was just about the worst thing you could be.

The new headquarters were not a tourist attraction. That was why they'd been moved up to a compound on the northern outskirts of Birmingham, behind a warren of checkpoints and a high mesh fence festooned with barbed wire. Armed guards stood at every entrance. Beyond the sprawl of buildings, the Wall and the watchtowers loomed.

Mackenzie had got in there, and more importantly out again, which pretty much made him a genius. And she'd stolen the product of all that hard work. He was going to be *really* mad at her.

But maybe it would be worth it.

The floorboards creaked above her head. She stiffened, slammed the laptop shut and shoved the drive back in her pocket.

Out in the wine cellar, the trapdoor dropped with a clunk. She sighed. Daniel sent his goons down here sometimes to poke through her stuff. Fortunately, he didn't hire his retinue for their imagination.

This time, though, it wasn't one of his apes.

She didn't see him that often. Daniel considered himself above mundane things and hanging out in a cellar, even if it was the cellar of his own mansion, was definitely mundane. Here he was now, though, brushing cobwebs off his jacket with a faint expression of distaste just visible in the candlelight. She faced him, ignoring the tightness in her chest.

But all he did was hold out a large paper bag to her. "Here," he said. "I brought you this. You don't look like you're eating enough."

She smelled fresh bread, good stuff, not the ballast-like substance they dished out on the ration lines. She was supposed to be grateful, like she didn't know there was a price attached. She wanted to refuse it, but that would be dangerous.

Her stomach betrayed her by growling. She took the bag and swallowed her disgust at herself. *Say thank you, for God's sake.*

"Thanks," she muttered.

He held out a hand. "I've got some work for you, too."

She took the memory stick from him. "What is it?"

"If it's what I've paid for," he said, "it's the details of

everyone on the Board's watchlist."

He didn't mind telling her stuff like this. She'd find out for herself soon enough, after all. She tried to make her eyes wide, innocent, awed. "What will you do with it?"

He gave her a conspiratorial smile. "There are people prepared to pay me a lot of money for that information."

She did her best to keep looking impressed. Did he really not realise she could work that out for herself? What else would he do with the information except sell it or use it to manipulate people? Still, the act was as important as it was irritating. The more he thought of her as brilliant but naïve, some kind of idiot savant who understood everything about computers and nothing about the way the world worked, the safer she would be.

He closed her fingers around the drive. His hand was cool and dry, and she stood perfectly still until he stopped touching her. "How long will it take you?" he asked.

She was desperate to get a proper look at the Heimdall drive. But Daniel would expect his information as soon as possible, and if he didn't think it was getting her undivided attention there would be trouble. She needed to keep him out of here for a few days.

She made her face doubtful.

"I don't know. If it's from the Board. . . A week? Maybe? It'll be complicated."

His jaw tightened.

"A week," she said, trying to sound conciliatory. "I'll have it done. Quicker if I can."

Just like that, he was genial again. "Good girl," he said. He did not, to her relief, try to touch her again. "I'll let you get on with it, then."

She knew better than to relax. He turned towards the door, and then paused as though something had just occurred to him.

"Oh," he said. "How's business, by the way?"

There was no right answer to this question. "It's... okay."

"Glad to hear it. I'm afraid you're due for a rent increase. As we discussed."

His apologetic tone was part of the game. They both knew there'd been no discussion, but if she called him out he'd say of course they'd talked about it, didn't she remember? If she protested that this was the third increase in as many months, he'd remind her that she could always find another landlord. On the other hand, if she took it in her stride, he might ask for even more money.

"Okay," she said. "Let me know how much."

He didn't move. She held her breath, shoulders aching, willing her face and body not to betray how much she wanted him to leave.

At last, he nodded. "I will."

She stood motionless, her fingers wrapped around the memory stick, until his footsteps disappeared above her head.

She still didn't know why he kept her down there. He didn't really want her money; no matter how many times he put her rent up, it was nothing compared to the income from his other enterprises. He could have found another hacker, even if they weren't quite as good as her. He didn't want her to be his protégée. Daniel didn't want to teach anyone his secrets.

And he didn't want sex, thank God. Whatever weird stuff he might take pleasure in, teenage girls didn't appear to be any part of it.

But he liked that she was afraid of him. She could see it, when he came down here; he watched her greedily, hungrily.

He liked that she knew she had nowhere else to go.

And it made her sick to admit it, but she needed him. She couldn't afford to fall off the radar. A hint of inconsistency in her work, and her reputation would disintegrate.

She put his memory stick down and pulled out the Heimdall drive. Perhaps, for once, she could make being stuck in this hole work for her. It was about time.

5

FAULT LINES

After the Board came to power the world changed the way a hunter stalks its prey: an inch at a time, all paranoia and imagined flickers of shadow, so that while you were being torn to pieces you were still wondering whether you were overreacting.

The first thing Skyler was really aware of was the general election being cancelled when she was nine. "It's a load of shit," she heard her mum's friend, Lauren, say one night. This was before the curfew, and Lauren often came round in the evenings for tea. Skyler liked her because she'd offered to dye Skyler's hair blue, like hers, when she was a bit older, and she always knew what to say when Skyler was sad because someone at school had made fun of her.

When Skyler and her brother Sam went to bed, their mum Ruby and Lauren would open another bottle of wine and, inevitably, start talking about politics. Tonight, as Skyler lay in bed listening, their conversation was more urgent, somehow, with less laughter.

"They've pushed the election back," Lauren said. "They reckon the country's not secure enough, an election would be destabilising. What does that even mean? How do we know they'll even do one next year?"

"Laur –"

"And have you seen the news? It's like they *approve*. Like it's all for our own good."

"Well, they're not gonna criticise the Board, are they?"

"Ru. Listen." Lauren's voice dropped as though someone might be listening, even in the flat. "There's a demo in Birmingham on Saturday. I'm going."

"*What*? You can't!"

"Come with me. You always used to. You used to organise them!"

"Yeah, and that was before –"

"Before what? Before there was really something to protest? Before this. . . *dictatorship* took over our country? Ruby, this is important."

"It's illegal now." Ruby sounded weary. "And the Board are brutal. Remember what they did in Cardiff. You can't go. It's not safe."

"That's the whole fucking point, isn't it? If we don't do something, who's going to?"

"We're not students anymore. I've got Skyler and Sam to think about. What happens to them if I get arrested or an enforcer throws me down a flight of stairs? What if *they* end up on a list somewhere, because of me?"

"Ru –"

"No. I'm not going." Skyler had never heard her mother use that tone with one of her friends. It was the tone she used with Skyler at the end of the month when the power ration was running low and Skyler didn't want to get off the computer. "And neither should you. And –" Lauren started to speak and Ruby cut across her, louder "– and you need to watch what you say. You don't know who's listening."

A silence. Then Lauren said, "It's late. I should get going."

The clink of a glass being set on a table, the rustle of a coat. The living room door opening.

Ruby. "Laur – please. Please don't go to the protest."

The front door opening and closing. Quiet.

The next time Skyler saw Lauren her face was mottled yellow and purple like the pansies in the hanging baskets on their balcony. "What happened to you?" Skyler asked, eyeing the bruises as they played Scrabble.

"I went to a protest and the greycoats arrested us," Lauren said.

Ruby gave her a piercing glance and started to say something, but Skyler interrupted her. "Why? Did you do something bad?"

"No," Lauren said. "Just being there was enough."

Sam looked upset. "So they hurt you?"

"Bed time," Ruby said, picking up the Scrabble board and tipping the tiles back into the bag. "Both of you," she added to Sam, even though he was fifteen and didn't have to go to bed till ten o' clock.

"We hadn't finished!" Skyler protested.

"Yeah," Sam said. "And why do I have to go to bed? It's not even eight o' clock. I haven't done anything wrong."

"Rooms. Now."

Skyler and Sam exchanged glances. Ruby so rarely asked them to do anything without explaining why that neither of them was quite sure how to handle the situation. After a moment, Sam stood up and held out a hand to Skyler. "C'mon, Sky. You can show me the code you've been writing."

"If that computer's not off in an hour I'm turning the power off at the mains," Ruby yelled after them, but she didn't mean it, not then. The power shortages wouldn't get really bad for another couple of years yet.

In Sam's room, he pressed a finger to his lips and propped the door open so they could hear Ruby and Lauren. "You're lucky you didn't get shot," Ruby was saying miserably. She sighed. "Are you gonna stop now, Laur?"

"How can I? What's gonna happen next?"

"You're gonna end up disappearing, that's what. And what about Cole?" That was Lauren's boyfriend. "Your sister? Your dad? D'you think they won't come after the people close to you?"

"They get it. They think this as important as I do."

Skyler hadn't heard it at the time, but years later, after the Wall went up and she ended up in the cellar and she had all the time in the world – too much time – to turn these memories over and over, she'd replayed those conversations and she'd heard the unspoken plea in her mother's words: *What about me?*

Lauren stopped coming round after that. She'd been Auntie Lauren Skyler's whole life, she'd been there at birthdays and school plays and come on holiday with them, and then Skyler never saw her again. Sam, who'd always had a soft spot for her – they'd teased him about it, endlessly – asked Ruby why she didn't come round anymore, but all Ruby said was, "She's busy," and then pressed down so hard with the knife she was using to chop carrots that it slipped and sliced into her thumb instead.

6

A CONFLICT OF INTEREST

Something prickled against Mackenzie's cheek, rough and scratchy. Carpet? Probably carpet. Why was there carpet on his face?

He opened his eyes, his head throbbing. His bedsit looked different to usual. It was, inexplicably, sideways. What was he *doing* there?

Skyler. Skyler had been here. She had –

He sat bolt upright.

The radio was still chattering away, the winter light only just fading. He checked his watch: just past four o'clock. He felt like he'd been on the floor for ages, but only a couple of minutes had passed. She couldn't have gone far.

He tried to stand and the room spun nauseatingly. He sank back onto the floor, cursing under his breath. Mackenzie usually tried to see the best in people unless they were actively trying to kill him. Right now, with Skyler, that seemed like a lot to ask.

He gritted his teeth and heaved himself upright. His head felt thick, fuzzy, and his thoughts bumped and crowded against each other: *What if she tells someone? What if she gets caught? What if –*

He halted abruptly, drawing a deep, shaky breath. This

was ridiculous. He needed to *stop*. He needed to take some painkillers and sit still for five minutes and make a plan to keep himself safe while he got that bloody memory stick back.

He checked the kitchen drawers: no painkillers. Brilliant. He'd have to go out and get some. He sighed, slipped on his trainers and opened the front door.

Outside, blocking out the fading light from the hall, were two men and a woman, all dressed in black, all wearing identical, humourless expressions.

Mackenzie tried to swing the door closed, but a heavy booted foot inserted itself into the gap and instead of slamming the door shut he discovered that he'd merely succeeded in slamming it onto the foot. He looked up into a face like a wall.

They weren't greycoats. They looked like enforcers, except that instead of the enforcers' navy uniforms they wore the universal outfit of the city's underworld: massive boots – all the better to kick the shit out of people with – and heavy leather jackets hiding inventively nasty tools. They could have been enforcers as well, of course. Some of the more ambitious ones moonlighted for the city's criminal element.

Behind the first wall-like countenance was one that he recognised. Rafe. Well, that couldn't be good news.

Mackenzie watched helplessly as the first man nudged the door open with his foot. Was it too much to hope they were here to offer him work? Of course it was.

Resigning himself, he let go of the door handle and stepped back. "I guess you might as well come in," he muttered.

The trio stepped over the threshold. "Sit down," the one who'd prised the door open rumbled.

"I'd really rather stand –" Mackenzie began, as Rafe picked up a plastic chair. Mackenzie, assuming he was about to get a chair to the face, flinched. But Rafe just plonked it down behind him and then gripped his shoulders, forcing him into it. The hands stayed on his shoulders like lead weights.

The one he was starting to think of as the head goon squatted in front of him. "Our boss," he said, "thinks you have something that belongs to him."

"Um," Mackenzie said. "Who's your boss?" That couldn't be right. He never held back anything he'd acquired for someone else. These people had no sense of humour at all about that kind of thing.

"You did a job for us last night," Rafe said, fingers digging painfully into his shoulders. "Remember?"

"I vaguely recall it," Mackenzie said, and then regretted it. Sarcasm was not going to get him out of this room with all his fingers still attached. "I mean – yes, I remember."

"Sure you're not holdin' onto anything of ours, then?"

What Mackenzie wanted to say was: how exactly are you defining 'stuff that belongs to you'? Because the thing I gave you this morning doesn't even technically belong to you, or your boss, and anything else I might have happened to help myself to along the way *definitely* doesn't belong to you.

Because he was not suicidal, what he actually said was: "Definitely not."

The woman started to crack her knuckles. He tried not to wince.

"I think," Rafe rumbled, "you'd best explain the situation to our friend here, Milo."

The squatting one – Milo, apparently – leaned towards him. "Here's the situation, kid. My boss is hearing where you might've picked up something valuable. Perhaps something you didn't know the value of? Perhaps something someone else asked you to get?"

Mackenzie squeezed his eyes shut and said nothing. He was desperately trying to figure out the least painful way out of this predicament. He kept coming up against dead ends.

"Well?" Rafe said. "Which is it?"

Mackenzie opened his eyes and discovered that Milo had produced a knife. He let out a gasp, which came out as a kind of squeak.

"Look," the man in front of him, the one with the massive fucking blade, said. "We *know* you took it. We know you were there, and it's not like anyone else round here could've done it, so stop dicking around. You don't even know what you've got. Hardly worth holding onto, is it?"

"*You* don't even know what I've got," Mackenzie said, before he could stop himself. He was rewarded with a blow that he could have sworn cracked his cheekbone. He wondered if his head was going to fall off.

"No need to get clever." Milo waved the knife at Mackenzie, who looked at him through blurred vision. "Don't make us think it'd be easier to just stick this in you and turn this place upside down."

"No, no, no," Mackenzie mumbled, through a mouthful of blood. "No need for that. All right. I did take it."

Milo looked satisfied. "So where is it?"

"Um," Mackenzie said, unable to tear his eyes from the knife. "I... haven't got it."

He had a feeling he knew what was coming next and unfortunately, he was right. The tip of the blade pricked his stomach. Something burned behind his eyes. *Jesus Christ, don't cry. Don't make this any worse.*

"Then who's got it?" Rafe said in his ear. "Who'd you sell it to?"

"I – I didn't sell it. I. . . someone took it from me."

Rafe chuckled, and Mackenzie hated him even more. "Someone *took* it from you?" Milo repeated incredulously. The blade stayed where it was, digging into Mackenzie's stomach, hard enough to hurt but not enough to draw blood. Yet.

"Yes." He closed his eyes again. Now he had a choice to make, and it was a really, really horrible one.

And he really, honestly had not intended to tell them the answer to the next question. He'd looked at the knife and thought about all the things you could do with a blade like that, and then into the face of the person holding it, which was the face of someone who'd definitely already done a lot of those things and probably felt all right about it, all things considered, and he'd thought: *I am not going to tell. I'm not.*

It was a rule. You took care of your own, and he and Skyler were, in some weird way, the same. Of course, it was also a rule that you didn't screw over your own by stealing from them, but hey. He could take the moral high ground.

"I. . . got mugged. On the way back from meeting Rafe. Some guy. Had a blade." He tried to gesture at the swelling bruise Skyler had bestowed on his temple. That was a good bit of improvisation.

"Unlucky," Rafe said. "Guess he took the cash too, then?"

"Oh, yeah," Mackenzie said. "All of it. Real bummer."

"What'd he look like?" Milo demanded.

"White guy. Tall. Not real heavy, but tall. Hat. Leather jacket. Nose ring."

"Well, well." Milo sat back on his heels. The pressure of the knife point retreated a little. "Bad luck for you, eh?"

"Yeah," Mackenzie said ruefully. He was now absolutely certain that the decision to take that memory stick was among the worst he'd ever made.

The woman, the knuckle-cracker, wandered back into view. She must have been off poking around his flat. And now she had something in her hand.

His heart sank.

The knuckle-cracker was holding an envelope. A very full envelope that looked an awful lot like the one Rafe had handed him by the side of the canal, and which Mackenzie had shoved into his kitchen drawer before he fell into bed that morning. "Look at that," she said. "It's a Christmas miracle."

Rafe's hands pressed even harder on his shoulders. Mackenzie strained automatically to get away, knowing it would do him no good whatsoever.

"Jen?" Milo said.

Jen put down the envelope and knelt in front of Mackenzie. Milo stood up and put the knife to Mackenzie's throat.

Mackenzie swallowed hard and then wished he hadn't because it made his Adam's apple press against the edge of the blade. He tried very, very hard not to move.

"Let's play a game," Milo said, and Mackenzie's fingers closed so tight his nails bit into his palms. "Hold out your hand. Fingers out."

He didn't see any other option except getting his throat cut, so he did as he was told.

"Game's called Statues," Rafe interjected. "Means you have to stay still. Could get messy otherwise."

Jen gripped his wrist in one hand and his index finger in the other.

Mackenzie closed his eyes and wished he could stop trembling.

With one abrupt, violent motion, Jen snapped his finger.

And that was how. He held on for three fingers before he blurted out Skyler's name and when he did he could see that they believed him at once, because of course she was one of the people most likely to have the damn thing.

Jen let go of his wrist and stood up. Rafe released his shoulders. Milo took the blade away from his throat, which was bleeding from shallow cuts because he had not, after all, managed to keep still.

As soon as the knife was gone Mackenzie doubled over with a moan, clutching at his hand. "See," Rafe said. "That weren't so hard, was it?"

He aimed a casual fist to the side of Mackenzie's face that sent him back into a painful, dizzy fog, and the three of them left the apartment. Mackenzie stayed where he was, very still, until the door shut behind them. Then he slid onto the floor and threw up on the carpet, coughing and cradling his broken fingers, tears streaming down his face.

7

SECRETS AND LIES

Mackenzie hurtled through Birmingham's dark streets, his fingers firing hot, sickly pulses through his body. The three that had been subject to Jen's tender ministrations were twice their normal size and an alarming shade of purple, but there was no time to worry about them. Skyler didn't deserve what was about to happen to her, and it was Mackenzie's fault. Well, all right, it was sort of hers as well, but he felt very guilty and also rather ashamed. He was pretty sure that if the roles had been reversed she would have held up better under torture than him. So he'd used a roll of sticky tape to hold his misshapen fingers together, biting his lip hard to keep from crying, shoved all his cash and his most important belongings into a backpack – he had a bad feeling about leaving anything behind, with the greycoats out – and then he'd run.

By the time he doubled up on AJ's doorstep he was on the verge of throwing up again. He made himself turn around and hammer on the door.

No answer. He swore and banged harder. When that didn't work he kicked the door out of sheer frustration. AJ *had* to be here. He leaned his forehead against the wood in desperation.

The door flew open. He fell forward and almost landed on top of AJ.

AJ, as expected, was not pleased to see him. "What the fuck do you think you're doing?"

He stumbled inside. AJ grabbed his collar. "Mackenzie, *what are you doing here*?"

Mackenzie turned his swollen face towards him. "Skyler's in trouble."

AJ dropped him. "What do you mean?"

"She's got some really bad people after her. I don't know how to warn her in time."

"Who's after her?"

"Someone's heavies. Their boss thinks she's got something he wants." He was not, under any circumstances, going to tell AJ the whole truth about this situation.

AJ's eyes narrowed. "Why do they think that?"

"I don't know. Look, can you get in touch with her or not?"

"Well, she doesn't have a phone. I might be able to reach her online."

Mackenzie followed him through into a small, cluttered living room, most of which was taken up with a half-assembled motorbike, and tried hard not to notice the smears of oil and half-empty plates scattered everywhere. He forced his attention back to AJ, who was leaning over a battered computer on a desk in the corner. It was a sign of how well he was doing that he had the thing at all, even though it was so ancient it was practically fossilised.

AJ glanced at him. "I don't really have enough power left to turn this on, you know."

"It's important, AJ. You know what she's like. If she winds them up, they'll kill her."

"Calm down," AJ said, jabbing at the keyboard. "They need to find her first."

With some relief, Mackenzie realised he was right. Skyler wasn't stupid; she hadn't kept her location so private for no reason. They would be able to get a message to her before the goons tracked her down.

He brightened a little. Perhaps he didn't need to feel quite so guilty, in that case. If she was going to be safe anyway, it had probably been worth not having all his other fingers broken.

But AJ was already shutting the computer down. "She's not online."

"Maybe she's out?" If she was out in the city somewhere, perhaps he could go and find her. He hovered, wondering if AJ was going to invite him to sit down. He hadn't been in this much pain since the time he'd fallen three floors down an elevator shaft. His fingers seemed to have a direct, uninvited line to every nerve in his body and his skull felt like someone was drilling straight through it.

AJ, though, was frowning thoughtfully into space. He either hadn't noticed the state Mackenzie was in or – just as likely – didn't care. Mackenzie waved a cautious hand at him. "AJ? You got any idea where Skyler might be now?"

"How would I know that?"

God, he could be hard work sometimes.

"I do know where she lives, though," AJ added speculatively.

You couldn't have bloody led with that, could you? "Really? I thought she wouldn't tell anyone that."

"She didn't tell me. She doesn't know that I know."

Mackenzie understood then. Skyler would be livid if she knew her secret was out. She didn't trust anyone – not even AJ, who actually liked her. AJ was debating whether it was necessary to give away his secret to let her know she was in danger, knowing it might cost him their friendship. If that was what you could call it. Mackenzie didn't think Skyler had anyone she herself would have described as a friend.

"How'd you find out?" he asked.

AJ stretched his arms over his head. "Accident. You heard of Daniel Redruth?"

"Has anyone *not* heard of Redruth?" AJ was talking about one of the South's most powerful – and unpleasant – career criminals. Mackenzie had never come face to face with him, but he suspected Redruth might have employed him on a number of occasions. Redruth didn't bother dealing with people at Mackenzie's level. He had other people for that, and Mackenzie was frankly grateful that was the case.

"Right," AJ said. "Well, I went to his house the other week. You should see that place, man." He shook his head, and Mackenzie wondered what it said about AJ that he'd manoeuvred his way far enough up the food chain to get himself invited to Daniel Redruth's actual house. He wasn't sure it was anything good. "I was hanging out in this big fancy living room overlooking his garden, waiting for him to show up, and I saw Skyler run across the lawn and down the side of the house with her hood up."

"You sure it was her? Not just, like, a gardener or something?"

AJ shook his head. "I'd know her anywhere."

"Well – what if she was visiting him? Like you?"

"You think Redruth just lets his visitors run in through the back door? No way."

"She might've been robbing him," Mackenzie said, but even as he said it he knew how unlikely that was. Skyler wasn't a thief by nature, despite recent evidence to the contrary, and not even he would have dared break into Daniel Redruth's mansion. It wasn't that he didn't think he could do it. He could definitely have done it. It was just the thought of what Redruth would do to him if he caught him.

"It makes sense, though," AJ said. "She's a hacker. How many places could she get enough power for that?"

"Fair point," Mackenzie said miserably. This meant they would have to go to Redruth's to warn her. That would not be fun. They could hardly ring the doorbell and ask if she could come out to play. "At least I guess she's sort of safe in there. I heard that place is like a fortress."

AJ nodded. "Who'd you say they were? The guys who were looking for her?"

"Well, I don't know who they work for. But there's a great big guy called Rafe, and a woman with a sort of squint called Jen, and a guy called Milo –" Mackenzie stopped, because AJ had frozen in his seat and was staring at him with his jaw clenched. "What?"

"What were those names?" AJ said.

He repeated them. "You know them?"

AJ stood up. Mackenzie took an automatic step backwards. He had a feeling he was about to get beaten up again.

"Yeah, I know them," AJ said, his voice low and dangerous. "They work for Daniel Redruth."

Mackenzie felt the blood drain from his face. "Are you *sure*?"

"Of course I'm fucking sure," AJ snarled.

Mackenzie covered his face with his hands and groaned. If AJ was right, they had got to Skyler already.

Perhaps if she doesn't lie to them, if she doesn't put up a fight, they won't kill her.

They would probably kill her.

AJ was pacing the room, his eyes wide and wild like an animal in a trap. Mackenzie didn't know whether he was going to cry or put his fist through the wall. "AJ –"

AJ turned on his heel and left the room. Mackenzie wondered whether he should just leave, but before he could make a decision, AJ was back. With a gun in each hand.

For one horrifying moment he thought AJ was going to shoot him. When he'd got enough of a hold on himself to realise this was unlikely – at least until AJ found out who'd set Rafe and his friends onto Skyler – he said carefully, "AJ – what are you doing?"

"You know what. You coming?"

Mackenzie backed away so fast he almost overbalanced. "Are you kidding? No, I'm not coming!"

AJ didn't say anything.

"I'm sorry, man," Mackenzie said. "But if you're right about this, it's too late for us to help her."

AJ cocked his head, lifted his right arm, and levelled the gun at Mackenzie's chest. "I said, are you coming?"

This was how Mackenzie found himself in a motor vehicle for almost the first time since the Wall went up, barrelling along a deserted road out of the city towards Redruth's estate. It turned out AJ was one of the five percent of the population with access to a car.

It was more like a truck really, painted in camouflage colours, and seemed to have been built out of lots of bits of different cars, but Mackenzie didn't ask for details. He was just relieved it hadn't been stolen from the enforcers, although if they'd been pulled over in this thing it would hardly have been much better. He could not believe AJ had a vehicle permit.

"Don't be stupid," AJ said, when Mackenzie asked him. He was driving far too fast, with no lights and one hand on the steering wheel. Mackenzie, who had in the last three years travelled no faster than he could pedal on a bicycle, was feeling ill again. The truck banged and juddered every time they tore over a pothole.

"How did you get petrol?" he persisted. There was a cold sickness in his stomach: *your fault, your fault, she's going to die and it's your fault.*

"I know a dealer," AJ said. "Hard to get hold of, like. I keep it for emergencies."

Mackenzie sighed and leaned against the cold glass of the passenger window, trying to ease the ache in his head. "Well, I guess this qualifies."

They went over another pothole and his head banged hard against the glass. He gave up. "AJ?"

"What?"

"What d'you think we're gonna do when we get there?" He couldn't think of a single scenario that wouldn't end up with all of them dead at best.

"You ever shot anyone, Mackenzie?"

"No!"

AJ swung the truck around a corner without braking. "Maybe just try not to piss yourself, then."

In the distance across the fields was a vast patch of darkness where towering treetops hid the bulk of the mansion. Mackenzie's stomach knotted. "You ever hear that story about Redruth putting bear traps in the grounds?"

AJ snorted. "That's not a story."

Mackenzie flattened himself against the seat. "It's *true?*"

AJ gave a terse nod.

"You're insane. You've actually lost your fucking mind. We're not even gonna get through the gates."

AJ spun the steering wheel and the truck plunged off the road into the field beyond. "We're not going through the gates."

"Okay?"

"That wall at the front's just for show. There's just trees and stuff at the back."

"Doesn't Redruth worry someone'll get in?"

AJ barked a laugh. "Look around. You can't get near the back without coming across these fields. Redruth has someone on watch all the time and his people are all over the grounds."

"So you're saying there's gonna be someone waiting for us."

"Yeah."

"Right. Fantastic. I can see you've really thought this through."

AJ jerked the wheel again, and now they were bouncing towards the mass of trees hiding the estate. The truck seemed to be accelerating.

Mackenzie shifted in his seat. "AJ," he said. "What are you doing?"

"Better hold onto something," AJ said. Mackenzie saw him grin unpleasantly for a moment, before he put his foot to the floor.

8

SHADOWS

Skyler knew it would have been sensible – it would have been safer – to get straight to work on Daniel's job when he left the cellar, but she couldn't resist a little look at the Heimdall drive first. Just five minutes.

Its encryption key was longer than anything she'd ever seen before. None of the programs she usually used for code-breaking would touch it. She would have to write a new one. Now *that* would be a challenge.

She lost track of time after that. Five minutes turned into an hour, and then two. This was what she craved: a task so complex, so all-consuming, that she could get lost in it. Something that would engulf the cold, the dark, the bruises on her throat, Daniel's presence upstairs. Just for a little while.

It all came back in the end, though. It always did. She rubbed her aching neck, registered that she was thirsty, that her eyes were dry. The unease that haunted her every footstep seeped back into her consciousness like water through the cracks in a dam.

Reluctantly, she tucked the Heimdall drive into her shirt pocket. It would take her days to make any real progress with it. In the meantime she had work to do, and it would be foolish not to do it. She plugged Daniel's memory stick into the laptop.

This drive was also from the Board, but the encryption on it wasn't anywhere near as complex. She'd seen these standard issue ones before. They'd been difficult to crack at first but she had the knack now.

What could possibly be on the Heimdall drive that needed protecting so badly?

Hopefully it would turn out to have been worth punching Mackenzie for, whatever it was. Perhaps that hadn't been such a great idea, in retrospect. He was one of the only genuinely good people she knew.

She shook herself. *Focus*. If Daniel got wind that she wasn't giving his job her full attention, she might never get the chance to crack the encryption.

If Daniel got wind of it. . .

Something nudged at the back of her mind. She pressed her fingers into her eyes. She hadn't been getting enough sleep. And she couldn't shake the nagging feeling that something was wrong.

She turned back to the computer, but this time she wasn't thinking about the drive.

She'd hacked into Daniel's emails so many times she could do it in seconds, but the hot fear that simmered inside her never went away. Alert for any creak or rustle overhead, she scanned the contents of his inbox.

Daniel had been busy today. He, like everyone else in Birmingham, had heard that the greycoats were out and about, oiling their thumbscrews. He'd been interested to hear that a second memory stick had been taken from the Board. He wondered what had become of it. He intended to make enquiries on the subject.

Jesus Christ. Skyler sat bolt upright.

Daniel had employed Mackenzie to break into the Board headquarters. Which meant he knew exactly where to start with his enquiries.

What happened next would depend on precisely how loyal Mackenzie was feeling towards her. In the circumstances, it seemed unlikely that he would be in a sentimental mood.

She sat back, twisting a strand of hair tight around her fingers, trying to piece together the thoughts ricocheting around her brain.

So Daniel would find out that she had the Heimdall drive, and then he would expect her to give it to him. He had no concept of other people's property, and if she didn't hand it over willingly, he would find a way to make her.

There was her choice, then. The drive, or her place in the cellar.

And she might never get another chance like this. And the next time he wanted something from her, the same thing would happen. He would keep demanding and she would keep giving in. And she would keep being afraid, all the time.

She stood up. If she wanted to keep the Heimdall drive, she'd have to get out of there. Fast.

She slid the laptop into her backpack and began a mental inventory. Clothes. Cash. The other things she'd hidden months ago, just in case.

Overhead, the floorboards groaned. She froze. She couldn't risk anyone seeing her leave.

She hovered, fists clenched, willing the person upstairs to go away. They didn't. In fact the footsteps seemed to be getting closer, and that was not likely to be good news. She pulled on her backpack and put out the candles, plunging the cellar into darkness.

When she sank into the corner of the room, her pulse fluttering so fast it snatched the air from her lungs, there was a new weight in her jacket. She still didn't know if she dared use it. She concentrated on what she held in each hand instead.

Whatever it takes. You can do this.

The trapdoor hinges creaked. They were trying to tread quietly, but Daniel's henchmen were all cut from the same extremely weighty cloth and were employed for their proficiency at breaking kneecaps, banging heads together and looking menacing. Stealth and delicacy were not their forte.

The cellar door opened to reveal a large silhouette in the dim light from the wine store. Too big to be Daniel. Milo, probably. The figure behind him would be Jen. They usually came as a pair.

"She in here?" Jen said.

"Dunno," Milo muttered. "Try the bed."

Skyler rolled her eyes and pressed herself deeper into the shadows. As if they actually thought anyone could sleep through that.

A thin torch beam passed over her conspicuously empty mattress. Jen turned towards the corner where she stood.

Skyler sprang forward, arm outstretched, and emptied half a can of CS spray into her face.

Jen yelled and threw her hands over her face, choking. The torch clattered to the floor, plunging them back into darkness.

Milo lunged at Skyler. "You little bitch –"

She dodged him, just. She aimed another jet of CS where she thought his face was but he knocked the can out of her hand with a jarring blow. She drew a deep breath which turned into a violent coughing fit, and Milo grabbed her wrist and hauled her towards him. "Get up those stairs," he snarled, "or I'll drag you by your hair."

He let go of her arm and she tried to run but then he grabbed her, as promised, by the hair.

She bit back a yelp of pain. *This is it. Now.*

She repositioned her other arm. As he dragged her closer, she thrust out.

Not hard enough. He was too solid, so that the thrust sort of bounced off, and by then he'd realised what was in her hand and she had only another fraction of a second to act.

She cut off his roar of fury with another stab, harder and more decisive, and this time the blade went all the way in and his roar changed from one of rage to one of pain and shock.

She wrenched it out, another movement that was sharper and needed more force than she'd expected, and Milo's roar trailed off into short, shuddering gasps.

He let go of her hair. As she backed towards the cellar door, there was a heavy, fleshy thud which must have been him hitting the floor. Somewhere nearby, Jen was still breathing in torturous, grating rasps.

She couldn't bring herself to be sorry.

She stuck the knife in her belt and scrambled up the ladder, ignoring her burning throat and streaming eyes.

Out in the hallway, Daniel was waiting for her.

9

FIGHT OR FLIGHT

He was leaning against the wall opposite the cupboard as Skyler burst out of it and she almost choked with terror. He looked relaxed, arms folded, expression mild. She was frozen to the spot in front of him and she hated herself for it.

"I must say," he said quietly, "I feel quite hurt, Skyler. It looks rather like you had this planned."

Her skin prickled when he said her name. With a huge effort, she kept her face expressionless. "I had to protect myself. I knew you'd do something like this one day."

"Do what? I just wanted to ask you a question. There was no need for all. . . this." His tone was reproachful: *I'm not the one being unreasonable here.* "What on earth did you do to Jen to cause all that noise?"

There was no point not telling him. "CS spray."

"CS spray," Daniel mused. "And a knife. Both of which she and Milo failed to find on the numerous occasions I sent them to search that cellar. Well, at least you've saved me the trouble of having to address that."

She shuddered.

"So now I have to wonder, Skyler – what else have you got stashed away that I don't know about?"

She prayed he couldn't sense the desperate thudding of her heart. "Nothing. Just the knife. I left the CS down there."

She was against the wall before she had time to react, her arm twisted behind her back, her face pressed against the cold smooth paintwork. The pain was immediate, searing. One more movement and he would break her arm. He would enjoy it. She bit her lip hard to stop a gasp escaping.

"Do you think I'm stupid?" he murmured in her ear. He let go of her and she suppressed a moan of relief, but then he pulled the backpack off her shoulders and yanked her back round to face him. He adopted a conversational tone: "Let's have a look, shall we?"

"You've probably seen it all already. I've got my laptop. Some clothes. I left your memory stick down there."

"How thoughtful. Are you going to give me the one in your pocket?"

"What if I do?"

"I think what you should probably be asking yourself, Skyler, is what if you *don't*? Let's see. I could call the greycoats, tell them you broke in here. I think they'd be delighted to meet you. And they would certainly find the memory stick. They have more imagination than Jen and Milo."

Well, that was probably true. But there was no way he was going to hand her over to the Board. If he was going to make her suffer, he'd want to do it up close and personal.

She tried to buy some time. "If I give it to you, will you let me go?"

He spread his hands. "Of course, if that's what you want. But where will you go?"

"I'll find somewhere."

"I doubt it, Skyler."

She still had time to change her mind. If she handed over the Heimdall drive now, he probably wouldn't hurt her that much. Bruises and broken bones would heal. He might even let her stay in the cellar.

Or she could try to keep it, and maybe he would kill her.

While she deliberated, he moved closer. His breath brushed her face. "One more question."

She stared at the polished floor, her head bent away from him.

"CS spray," he said. "A knife. I know you didn't think of that yourself. So who put you up to it?"

Oh, no.

When she made herself speak, the words came out in a whispered rush. "I'll give you the memory stick. Just let me go."

He raised his eyebrows: *well, go on then.*

She felt his greedy eyes on her hand as she shoved her fear down and reached into her jacket. Something coiled tight and sharp inside her, wire round her lungs.

Now.

She slammed her head forward. Her forehead met his nose with a sickening *crack.*

Fireworks exploded in her vision. Daniel reeled backwards, his glasses knocked sideways.

Skyler snatched her bag up and ran.

She hurled herself into the warmth of the gas-lit kitchen and threw herself at the back door, wrestling with the locks as his footsteps echoed in the hallway.

And then she stopped.

He would come after her if she ran, and sooner or later he would catch her up. And the longer it was before he caught her, the worse it would be when he did.

She took a deep breath, reached into her jacket and, with shaking hands, pulled out the final part of her insurance policy.

She aimed the gun uncertainly, because she'd never actually pointed it at a moving target before, and tried to force her hands to steady.

Daniel burst into the room. She'd expected him to at least be staggering, but he looked perfectly normal except for the blood smeared on his face.

Don't hesitate. Just do it.

She pulled the trigger.

The gunshot reverberated around the room with a deafening bang. Daniel jerked backwards and dropped to the floor.

She stared at him, at the dark pool seeping from beneath his body. He wasn't moving. Was he breathing? She couldn't tell.

The echo of the gunshot whined in her ears as she inched towards him. This wasn't real. He would get up, any second, and then he would kill her.

Eyes closed. White face. Blood on the wall, the cabinets, pooling at her feet.

I know you didn't think of that yourself.

Who put you up to it?

Her heart thumping so hard she thought it would burst out of her chest. A strange, metallic taste in her mouth.

She raised the gun again. The kitchen door burst open.

Skyler swung her arm towards the door and fired. Flecks of something warm and wet spattered across her face. The man in the doorway fell to his knees with a dull thud. The phone in his hand clattered to the floor.

She was out of time.

She flung herself out of the back door and sprinted across the lawn.

Over the ringing in her ears and the crunch of her footsteps on the frozen grass, a strange, unfamiliar rumbling came from the woodland. Her footsteps faltered. Had he managed to send something after her already?

Either way, she couldn't afford to stop running. She dragged her torch out of her bag and plunged into the shelter of the trees, tripping over roots, branches whipping at her face and arms, brambles snagging on her clothes. She wrestled herself free, stumbled, righted herself and dived under the wire fence at the edge of the woods.

When she looked up, an enormous truck was speeding directly towards her.

She threw herself out of the way and landed heavily on the frozen ground. The truck braked, sending lumps of earth flying into the air.

She squeezed her fingers around the gun and forced her legs to support her. She could do it again if she had to.

AJ stuck his head cautiously out of the window. "Skyler?"

Perhaps headbutting Daniel had given her a concussion. "AJ? What –?" Then her eyes fell on Mackenzie in the passenger seat. "What's *he* doing here?"

AJ looked extremely uncomfortable. "Just – get in, Sky, okay?"

This still didn't feel real. Maybe it wasn't. Maybe it was just an extreme case of wishful thinking.

She scrambled into the truck, dazed. AJ swung the vehicle around and began to drive at full speed across the fields while Skyler slid around in the back, fumbling for a seat belt and wondering if she was going to have escaped from Daniel only to end up being scraped off a tree instead. The truck bumped and lurched like it was about to take off. She gave up looking for a seat belt and clung on to the back of the passenger seat instead.

Thankfully, nobody spoke. Her head ached, her eyes burned, and her whole body was sore from grappling with Milo. She couldn't even begin to make sense of what she'd just done.

The silence continued until AJ had driven them all the way back onto the road. There, he glanced into the rear view mirror. "Sky," he said carefully. "Why have you got a gun?"

She looked down at the handgun as if she were in a dream. "I . . . shot Daniel."

AJ slammed on the brakes so hard she was catapulted into the back of the passenger seat. He and Mackenzie both jerked round. "*What?*" AJ yelled.

"AJ –" she began, and then stopped. She didn't know how to explain. Where would she even start?

"Skyler – you – *what?*" AJ ran a hand through his hair, shaking his head. "Since when do you carry a weapon? How do you even know how to shoot?"

"How did *you* know where I was living?" she retorted.

"I found out by accident. And you're welcome, by the way."

"AJ, don't pretend you don't know what he's like. You know why I had the gun."

"Skyler – shit. Why didn't you talk to me? I could've helped you –"

"No. You couldn't."

AJ might have been about to respond, but Mackenzie interrupted. "Did you kill him?"

"What?"

"Redruth. Is he dead?"

Was he? He certainly hadn't looked like he was going to be getting back up. "I don't know. I think so." *You should have put another bullet in him.*

"Well, you'd better hope so. Why didn't you make sure? What's the matter with you?"

"I didn't exactly have time to take his pulse, Mackenzie."

"You bloody idiot," Mackenzie said.

"Don't talk to her like that," AJ snapped.

"Whatever. You both know I'm right. You shot *Daniel Redruth*. You won't be safe anywhere in this city now. Even if you hadn't –"

The glare she gave him must have been ferocious enough to shut him up. AJ looked confused. "Even if she hadn't what?"

Skyler kept her face impassive.

"Even if you didn't owe loads of other people work you won't be able to do now," Mackenzie said quickly. "You're not gonna get on the internet again any time soon."

"I know that," Skyler muttered. So he hadn't told AJ about the drive, probably because he didn't want to explain the rest of the story. Well, that suited her all right. She didn't know exactly why, but it had suddenly become very important that AJ didn't find out about the Heimdall drive. She could almost hear Mackenzie wondering why she didn't want him to know about it. She could only hope he'd keep his mouth shut. He hadn't turned out to be very good at that.

She sighed. "You'd better get the truck back, AJ. Greycoats are out."

"And then what?" he said. "Redruth's lot will be all over too. You can't go to mine, they'll come looking there."

She gave him a sour look. "I bet they will." Her eyes fell on Mackenzie's hand. Something was definitely not right there and she seized on it, grateful for the distraction. "Mack. Why have you got sellotape on your hand?"

He yelped as she grabbed at him. "Ow! Get off!"

"What the hell happened to you?" AJ said, as if he was just now noticing Mackenzie for the first time.

He hesitated. "I. . . got my fingers trapped in a door."

Skyler glanced up at him. He looked away. "These are broken," she said, squinting at the purple, swollen digits in the light from her torch.

"Yeah," Mackenzie said. "I had noticed."

"Then we need to get you fixed, I guess." She looked at AJ. "Can you give us a lift?"

He nodded with weary resignation and started the engine again. "Sky?" he said, as the truck moved off. "What *happened* back there?"

Skyler stared out of the window into the darkness, mentally testing out and discarding each explanation as it occurred. At last, she said, "I guess I stood up to him."

10

SANCTUARY

AJ dropped them on the outskirts of the city, outside a parade of shops that had been derelict for years. Mackenzie recognised the decaying signs and rusting, graffiti-covered shutters with a twinge of relief.

"What're you gonna do now?" AJ asked Skyler.

"I'll go with Mack," she said. Mackenzie looked at her, considered arguing, and decided against it.

"You sure that's a good idea?" AJ said.

"Yes."

He looked nonplussed. "Well. If you're sure. . ."

"Yeah. What're you gonna do?"

The stiffness of AJ's jaw and the whiteness of his knuckles broadcasted his desire to get the hell out of there. "I'll go home. Someone's gonna come asking questions. I'll try and throw them off." He touched Skyler's arm and Mackenzie saw a flash of something different from the AJ he knew, who was kind of a dick. "I won't give you away. Go."

Skyler's expression didn't acknowledge any of this. "C'mon, Mackenzie." She jumped out of the truck and set off towards the shops. He scrambled after her.

One of the rusting shutters, with a bit of effort, could be prised open. Skyler forced it up and rang the bell underneath. It echoed, loud and shrill, into the dark shop beyond.

There was enough moonlight to see that her hands and clothes were covered in blood. She'd put the gun away, thank God, but there was a sharp, bloody knife stuck in her belt. Her hair was a tangled mass of dark blonde waves, her face blood-spattered and stony. Just then, she seemed terrifying.

The shop door opened to reveal a young woman bearing a torch, taller than both of them, with reddish hair cropped close to her head and pale, freckled skin. Her movements gave the impression of power like a coiled spring. She could have been anywhere between her late teens and early twenties. She held herself with a confidence and purpose that belied the youthfulness of her face.

She was called Angel. It was almost certainly not her real name. She was known amongst the underworld for two skills: healing, and putting people considerably beyond the help of a healer. Mackenzie had met her once after being bitten by a dog and again after he'd fallen down the elevator shaft. She was the only person he'd laid eyes on in the last twenty-four hours he'd actually been pleased to see.

Her eyes widened at Skyler's swollen, blotchy countenance and blood-soaked clothes. "Jesus," she said, stretching out a hand to her. "Are you all right?"

"I'm okay." Skyler jerked her head at Mackenzie. "He's the one feeling sorry for himself."

Mackenzie gave Angel a tired wave.

"Bloody hell," she said. "Look at you two. Come in."

This had once been a newsagents but now the shelves were empty, the floor dusty and littered with cardboard boxes. Angel led them behind the counter into a gloomy back room, through another door and down a flight of stairs into a vast cellar, lit with candles and much cleaner than the space upstairs. At the far end stood a huge metal cabinet and a folding bed propped against the wall, presumably for visitors who needed to stay for treatment. A screen obscured one corner, and a set of shelves was laden with medical equipment. The floor was bare concrete and the general effect was Spartan, but the walls were painted white and glowed in the candlelight. It was better than most cellars.

Angel motioned for them to sit at a battered table. "What happened?"

"Mackenzie got his fingers broken," Skyler said, as if highlighting a considerable character flaw.

Ruefully, Mackenzie held out his hand to demonstrate that this was indeed the case. Bemusement spread across Angel's face as she inspected his handiwork with the sellotape. "Why?" she asked.

"No time for anything else," he said wearily.

She produced a pair of scissors and started snipping at the tape. He stifled a moan as she pulled it away. "Fallen out with someone?" she said, as she concentrated.

"You could say that."

"Looks like the work of a professional." She gave him a knowing look. "What a mess."

For the first time, it occurred to him what lacking the use of those fingers might do to his career. His chest went tight. "Can you fix them?"

She nodded and walked over to the shelves. Skyler leaned across so her mouth was close to his ear and said, "You didn't tell AJ about the memory stick."

"No," he murmured. "Why don't you want him to know about it?"

She ignored this. "Why didn't you tell him?"

"I. . . thought it would be too complicated."

Her eyes narrowed. "You sold me out, Mackenzie. Didn't you?"

"I'm sorry!" he hissed. "I didn't mean to!" He waved his swollen, useless hand at her. "Redruth's crew can be pretty persuasive."

She said nothing. Mackenzie said, "If you knew what I did then why didn't you tell AJ?"

"Did you *want* me to tell him?" Her eyes flashed at him. "I figured you'd had a bad enough day already."

He didn't know whether to believe her. She was right – AJ would not have been sympathetic – and so presumably she must, on some level, have been in a forgiving mood. Or perhaps she just really didn't want AJ to know she had the memory stick.

Angel returned and dumped a handful of bandages and tape onto the table. "Skyler, could you bring that lantern closer? You might want to hold Mackenzie's good hand for this bit."

Skyler looked at her as though Angel had suggested she should give him a lap dance. "Why would I want to do that?"

A glimmer of amusement crossed Angel's face. "He might appreciate it." She took Mackenzie's wrist and he had a sudden flashback to his encounter with Jen. He flinched. Skyler rolled her eyes, edged closer and took his hand. He tried not to look at her.

"This is going to hurt," Angel warned.

She was right. Mackenzie immediately forgot about how weird it was to be holding Skyler's hand and clung on as if she were a lifebelt and he was drowning. He couldn't stop the tears springing to his eyes.

As soon as Angel had finished, Skyler dropped his hand and said, "Jesus. Were you trying to break my hand too?"

He scowled at her. Angel studied the bruising on his face. "Any headaches? Nausea?"

"Yes and yes," he said bitterly. Angel went back to rummage amongst the shelves.

"You know, you're right," Skyler said. "Jen and Milo *can* be pretty ruthless. Which I got the opportunity to find out, too."

"Bloody hell, I'm sorry!" Mackenzie groaned. "But how the hell was I supposed to know you were living in Daniel Redruth's goddamn cellar? What were you *thinking*, Skyler, didn't you know how dangerous he is?"

"I had noticed," she said, her voice flinty. "On account of not walking around with my eyes shut. It's not like I had a lot of choice, Mackenzie, is it?"

"I'm sorry," he said again, more quietly. She just glared at him.

He should have felt better – she was alive, his fear hadn't come true – but now there were so many new ones, flaring to life like someone had touched a match to all the terror he tried to keep suppressed, and they all felt so *real. Stop it, you have to do something to stop it.*

He started to tap his uninjured hand against his chair. Skyler gave him a puzzled look. He ignored her.

Angel reappeared and shone a small torch into his eyes. "You've got a bit of concussion. You should rest."

There was nothing in the world he wanted to do more, but also nothing at that moment that seemed more unlikely. Angel turned to Skyler. "Are you hurt?"

She shook her head. "The blood's not mine."

"Your eyes," Angel said.

"Oh. The CS spray. I think they'll be okay."

"We should rinse them. You need somewhere to stop for a bit?"

Skyler looked up at her with what might have been gratitude. "Is that okay?"

"Of course." She stood up. "Mackenzie, why don't you lie down? I'll keep an eye on you." She crossed the cellar and unfolded the camp bed. At that moment, it was just about the most inviting thing he'd ever seen.

Angel handed him a pile of blankets and went back to Skyler. As he pulled a blanket over himself, he heard her say, "So what happened?"

He strained his ears, but didn't hear Skyler's murmured reply.

11

ANGEL

Skyler remembered very little from the day, three years ago during her first winter in the South, when she'd first met Angel. She didn't remember AJ finding her under a railway bridge, delirious and running a 40 degree fever. She didn't remember him carrying her halfway across town either, but this was long before he'd been able to afford black market petrol, so he must have done.

What she remembered was his voice, urgent, even panicky. "She needs help. Something's wrong."

And a girl's voice, calmer. "I can see that. What's the matter with her?"

"I don't know. I found her like this."

"Do you know her name?"

"Skyler. She's called Skyler."

Movement, down, falling, dark, quiet. A smooth hand on her forehead. That cool voice again. "Skyler. Shh. It's okay." And then static, a feverish, fuzzy blur.

And sometime later – "Who is she?" The girl again, out of view. "Where'd you find her?"

AJ, guilty and uncomfortable. "You got anything against Northerners?"

"Do I look like a bigot to you, AJ? Is she Northern, then?"

"Yeah. She pitched up here a couple of months ago. She's been living on the streets."

"On her own? Where's her family?"

"Over the Wall."

"Poor kid." A pause. "And you've been looking after her, have you?" An edge of disapproval.

"Not like that. She's thirteen. Don't be disgusting. I just – she needed someone. Never lived on the streets, didn't have the first idea how to get food, how to defend herself. And the Board – you know what they'd do to her, as if the rest of it wasn't bad enough."

"She's lucky she met you, then." This time the girl sounded like she meant it.

"She gonna be okay?" AJ said.

"She'll be all right. Some antibiotics, fluids, that's all she needs. A few days' rest."

AJ, uncertain. "She hasn't got any money. She can't pay you."

"Now you tell me." But the girl didn't sound annoyed, only mildly amused.

"I'll pay for her. Send me the bill."

"You're all right. Keep your money, AJ. You're too soft, you know that?"

Another blank, another fizz of static. Something cold on her forehead, a careful, gentle pressure. Her throat felt shredded to pieces.

"Here. Drink this."

Skyler tried to lift herself onto her elbows. Her arms shook. A hand held a bottle of icy water to her lips and she gulped it gratefully.

The person holding the bottle came into focus. A girl, a bit older than her, sixteen, maybe. Red hair, cut very short; a solemn, thoughtful face. When Skyler met her eyes, she smiled. "Hello," she said. "Skyler."

Skyler flopped back down. She was on a camp bed, beneath a heavy, slightly scratchy blanket, a pillow under her head. Despite how ill she felt, it was the most comfortable place she'd been in months. It felt odd. Like being back at home, except –

Tears pricked her eyes. Her throat burned.

"I'm Angel," the girl said. "This is where I live. AJ brought you. You've got a good friend there, you know."

"Is it –?" Skyler tried to find the words, and gave up.

Angel smiled again. "It's safe," she said. "You're safe here."

She didn't talk to Angel much that first time. She wanted to, but she didn't know how. In the end she slipped out while Angel was asleep and didn't expect that she would ever see her again. When she next ran into AJ, though, she asked about her.

"Everyone knows Angel," AJ said.

"Because of the medicine, you mean?"

"Yeah, that... and the other stuff. You should see her fight. She takes commissions sometimes."

"What do you mean?"

He just looked at her. "What d'you think I mean? She's picky, though," he added. "I think she really wants to help people."

It was after she moved into Daniel's cellar that Skyler began to wonder if Angel could help her.

She put it off for a while. But then the days in the cellar dragged into weeks and months, and she began to understand that one day she would need to defend herself against Daniel for real. So she went back. She asked Angel to teach her self-defence, and Angel patiently taught her how to fight, how to use a knife, and kept watching her with worried eyes that said she knew Skyler wasn't telling her everything.

One day a few months later, Skyler went to meet her and found herself completely unable to concentrate. Angel had set her the task of getting out of her hold and taking a knife from her, but Skyler, usually so focused, couldn't stop shaking.

After she'd let Angel get several good hits in, Angel stopped. "What's wrong? This isn't like you."

Skyler tried to find the words, but they wouldn't come. "Sorry," she muttered. "I'm fine. Let's keep going."

"Yeah," Angel said. "I don't think so." She took Skyler's hand, led her over to the table and poured her a glass of water. "Sit down."

She sat. Angel pulled up a chair close to her. "What's happened?"

She looked away. "Nothing. I'm fine."

Angel frowned at her and lifted the candle on the table. Skyler shifted away, but Angel put out a hand to stop her. "You've got bruises on your neck," she said quietly.

Skyler said nothing. Angel reached out and brushed her fingers gently over the purplish marks.

Skyler couldn't remember the last time anybody had touched her in a way that was kind or tender and it froze her to her seat. Slowly, Angel took her hand away. "Tell me what happened," she said.

Skyler told her.

When she'd finished, Angel didn't say anything for a long time. She stared into space while Skyler, her heart beating faster and faster, tried and failed to figure out what she was thinking.

Eventually, she sighed. "Now I get why you didn't want to tell me everything. If it got back to him that you were coming here..."

Skyler looked up through her hair. "You ever met him?"

"I know what kind of man he is." Angel's voice was unexpectedly sharp. The lines of her face had gone cold and hard.

Skyler, stung, started to get to her feet. Angel took a deep breath and put a hand on her arm. "Wait."

Skyler fumbled for the words to explain herself, to show Angel, somehow, that she wasn't the same as Daniel. "He's a monster," she said. "I know that, and I hate myself for going to him. But. . ." She shrugged miserably.

"But there's nowhere else," Angel murmured.

She nodded. "I need to work, and hacking is the only thing I know how to do. If I don't have that, I don't have anything."

Angel's green eyes flickered towards her and the anger vanished from them as suddenly as it had appeared. "I understand." She gestured at Skyler's throat. "Does this happen often?"

"I. . . don't know. Sometimes. Sometimes a lot. Sometimes not for ages."

Angel's face was unreadable. "Does he do other stuff to you?"

"No," Skyler said. "Not. . . not that."

"And the guys that work for him? What about them?"

This time, it was a long time before Skyler could bring herself to answer.

"Not. . . anymore," she said, at last. She couldn't look at Angel. "At the beginning, there was. . . they would. . . Then Daniel and I worked out an *arrangement.*" The words felt bitter in her mouth, and hard to form. "I. . . pay him extra, and he. . . stops them. . . trying to do. . . that."

She ducked her head, squeezing her eyes shut.

"Look at me," Angel said softly.

Skyler shook her head.

Angel's fingers brushed hers, closed over her hand. "Try," she said.

Skyler stared at the table, feeling unbearably small and raw and exposed. Finally, she forced herself to lift her head a fraction.

Angel's cool, calm eyes watched her without blinking. Skyler searched her face for any hint of a change in the way Angel looked at her, but all that happened was that Angel gave her a slow, gentle smile and said, "Thank you. For trusting me."

Skyler didn't say anything.

"You're very brave."

She tried to laugh. "That's not true."

Angel squeezed her hand. "I know I can't talk you into leaving. But if you're ever in trouble – if you ever need somewhere to go – you come here. Understand? There'll always be help for you here."

Skyler nodded. Angel sat for a long time, chewing her lip, before she pushed back her chair and strode purposefully across the room.

When she returned, she was carrying a small handgun. Skyler stared at it. "What. . . uh, what's this for?"

Angel laid the gun on the table in front of her. "I think you're going to need it."

Skyler reached out to touch the weapon, then let her hand drop. She looked up at Angel uncertainly.

"One day you're going to need this," Angel repeated.

"I don't know how to –"

"I'll show you."

"I can't afford this –"

Angel sat down next to her. "It's yours."

"Why –?" Skyler sighed. "Why are you giving me this?"

Angel took hold of her hand again. "Because I know what he's like. When the day comes, he won't just come at you like those idiots who work for him do. He'll play with you. He'll let you try. He'll let you think you're going to get away, and then he'll make his move and you'll have no chance."

She looked suddenly much older and more tired where the candlelight caught the lines on her face. "You know him," she said. "You know I'm right. So when the time comes – don't hesitate. Just do it."

Skyler sat and looked at the gun for what felt like hours. At last, she reached out and touched the cold metal with a fingertip.

"Here." Angel picked it up and held it out to her. "It's not loaded. Take it."

It was heavy in her hand, and very different to holding a knife. She couldn't imagine daring to point it at Daniel and pull the trigger.

Angel moved her hands gently on the weapon. "You hold it like this. Here's the safety catch. Don't take that off yet." She stood up. "Come with me. You need to learn how to use that thing."

12

CROSSROADS

That conversation had taken place just over a year ago. Since then Skyler hadn't seen Mackenzie once, and she'd seen less and less of AJ too. And one by one, nearly all of Daniel's original retinue of large, violent men had disappeared and had to be replaced. Daniel had not been happy about this, but there didn't seem to be much he could do about it.

She'd mentioned the matter of the mysteriously disappearing heavies to Angel once. "Is that right?" Angel had said, her voice as expressionless as her face. And that had been the end of that discussion.

She hadn't seen Angel for months now either. It had been intentional. She'd told herself she didn't want to rely on anyone – and Angel, surely, had better things to do than hang out with her.

But it wasn't really that. At the back of her mind was a terrible fear that she couldn't shake: that if Daniel ever found out there was someone she cared about, he would take them away from her.

Skyler would never have admitted, even to herself, that there was anyone she missed, but the strength of her desire to see Angel today had startled her. And, finally, Mackenzie was asleep, and she could tell her the whole story.

Angel listened as Skyler talked and picked at the food Angel had put in front of her. "So there you have it," she finished, at last. "I'm a murderer."

"Are you sure Redruth's dead?"

She pulled a piece of bread apart. "I don't know. He. . . I don't know. I think he might be."

"If he's dead," Angel said quietly, "he deserves it."

"I know."

Angel seemed lost in thought. Eventually, she seemed to remember herself. She gave Skyler a searching look. "So what now?"

"I don't know."

"Are you going to give up the memory stick?"

That was the only thing she was sure of. "No."

"It's important enough to rearrange your whole life around?"

"Maybe." Skyler sighed. "Life was shit anyway, Angel. Maybe it's time to do something different."

"And you don't want AJ to know you've got it."

She tried to put words to the unease that had been dogging her. "It's just – he'll expect me to give it to him. Just like Daniel did."

"You don't know if you can trust him."

She nodded unhappily. "He's been working for Daniel. As in, joined his crew."

Angel's head snapped up. "He's *what*?"

"You didn't know?"

Her mouth tightened into a thin line. "No."

"Yeah. He doesn't seem to think it's a big deal." Skyler rubbed her still-raw eyes. "Anyway, the drive's no use to him without me. If it's not decrypted it's no use to anyone."

"You think you're the only one who can crack it?"

She shrugged. Angel grinned. "That's exactly what you think, isn't it?" She sat back. "Well. All right. You know you're not going to get a chance to look at that thing for a good while, Sky, don't you? You need to disappear. If Redruth's alive he'll come after you, and if he's dead his friends will. And the Board will be chasing you too eventually, if you're serious about holding onto that drive."

Skyler stared at the table. Angel laid a hand on her arm. "I'm not trying to scare you. I'm trying to prepare you."

"I know."

"Why do you want it so badly, anyway?"

But before Skyler could figure out how to explain herself, Angel lifted her head, face alert, and raised a finger to her lips.

From above, the sound of banging filtered down to them. Someone was hammering on the shutters at the front of the shop.

Skyler bolted off her chair. "Oh, no."

Angel got to her feet more slowly, her head on one side. "Not enforcers. They'd have blown the door off by now." She bit her lip. "Still, I think we should get out of here. Go wake Mackenzie."

"I'm sorry," Skyler whispered. "I didn't mean to –"

"I said I'd be here when you needed help. I meant it."

Angel crossed the room and shoved at the heavy metal cabinet against the wall, her face strained with the effort. As Skyler went to shake Mackenzie awake, she registered shouting mixed with the banging, faint but agitated. "Angel! *Angel!*"

She stiffened. "Angel? I think that's AJ up there."

Angel paused. "I think you're right." She glanced at Skyler. "He's been working with Redruth, you said?"

Skyler's heart sank. "He's not a bad person," she said,

hoping it was the truth. "He just... I don't know what he was thinking."

Angel was clearly not convinced. "You think we should let him in?"

"He came to get me last night. He didn't have to do that."

Angel tapped her hand fast against her thigh. "All right." She pulled her gun out of her waistband. "Get your stuff together, get Mackenzie." She disappeared out of the cellar.

Skyler bent over Mackenzie and prodded him in the shoulder. His eyes flew open. "What –?"

"We've gotta leave."

"Huh? How long have I been asleep?"

"Not that long. Come on. Get your stuff."

Resignedly, he swung himself off the camp bed. His face was bluish-purple and tender-looking, and she was pretty sure that was at least partly her fault. She surprised herself by feeling sorry for him. Poor Mackenzie, always so careful. If anything was going to teach him not to make impulsive decisions, this was it.

Angel burst back into the cellar, dragging AJ by the wrist. He was bleeding from his forehead and mouth. His right arm hung, limp, at his side.

Skyler's chest clenched. "AJ – what happened –?"

"Redruth's lot." His voice was ragged. "They know we know each other."

It was like seeing her brother frightened; the person who usually coaxed her into dangerous things and promised it'd be okay. A chill ran through her like ice water down her spine. "They wanted to know where I was."

"What'd you tell them?" Angel demanded.

"What the hell do you think? I lied my arse off. Told them I haven't seen her for months."

"They didn't buy it."

He shook his head.

There was a dangerous edge to Angel's voice. "Could they have followed you here?"

"I don't think so."

"You don't *think* so?"

He glared at her, holding a hand to his bloody mouth. "What's got into you, Angel? We've known each other years."

"You've been working for Redruth," Angel said. "It might be time to re-evaluate a few things."

"Oh, for –" He shot an exasperated look at Skyler. "You had to bloody tell her, didn't you?" Skyler scowled at him. "Look, Angel, I know you've got this thing about him, but you can't expect everyone to live by your rules. I'm still the same person. I'm still your friend."

Angel's eyes were on the wall behind AJ's head, her face blank, and Skyler suddenly wished she was shouting instead. Her fingers were white around her gun. For the first time in the years she'd known her, Skyler was afraid of what Angel might do next.

She reached out a tentative hand to her. "Angel. Please – don't."

A beat in which nobody moved, before Angel's eyes flickered towards Skyler and the hard blankness in them dissolved into something more recognisable. "One more time," she said to AJ. "Did you tell them where Skyler was?"

"For fuck's – No!"

"Can you be certain they won't follow you here?"

He ducked his head. "No."

Angel's fingers twitched on her gun. Skyler made an involuntary move towards her and then stopped herself.

"Right," Angel said. "We need to get out of here."

A stifling guilt settled on Skyler like a heavy blanket. "Your arm," she said to AJ. Her voice wobbled.

"It's dislocated," Angel said. "He'll live." She dragged a gigantic backpack from the depths of the cabinet, already half-full. *She's like me*, Skyler thought. *She's been ready to run the whole time.*

Angel handed her the bag, which was so heavy Skyler nearly dropped it on her feet. "Take a bit of everything you can find on those shelves. Quickly, now."

Skyler did as she was told. Angel put her shoulder back against the cabinet and inched it sideways, revealing a metal door set into the brickwork. When she unlocked it, it opened into blackness.

Skyler looked at AJ. "Are you okay?"

He shook his head. "Talk about opening a can of worms, Sky."

If he didn't understand by now, how was she supposed to make him? "He would've killed me," she said.

His face softened. "I know. I'm sorry. It's just – I'm usually on the right side of those guys. I didn't really realise how scary they were till they came and kicked my door down."

Well, maybe you should've thought of that a bit sooner. She didn't say it. It would hardly make things any better.

From above came a muffled, metallic banging. Skyler went rigid.

Angel just pulled her gun back out of her waistband and looked at AJ. "You carrying?"

He gave a terse nod. Skyler shook herself. "I can help."

AJ frowned. "I don't think –"

"You can shut your mouth," Angel said levelly. "Sky and Mackenzie, get in there." She nodded at the darkness. "AJ, I swear to God, the second you look like you're having trouble picking a side –"

Another metallic crash, followed by splintering wood and thundering footsteps above them. Mackenzie disappeared through the doorway into the darkness as quickly as a cat. Angel gave AJ another cold glance. "I mean it."

He just nodded miserably.

At the top of the stairs, the door crashed open and slammed off the wall. "Skyler," Angel hissed. "Go!"

She scrambled through the doorway, but she didn't follow Mackenzie down the tunnel. She needed to know what happened next.

"Oh, look." Rafe's gravelly voice rumbled from the top of the stairs, behind a powerful torch beam. "Fancy seeing you here, AJ."

"Turn around," Angel said. "Walk away."

He snorted. "She do all the talking for you, does she, boy? Look. We just want the girl. It don't have to be difficult."

Angel sucked in her breath. "Yeah. That *is* going to be kind of difficult, though."

"That little bitch is a murderer!" the woman behind Rafe snarled. Skyler recognised the voice as Frankie. Daniel didn't keep many women in his retinue, but the ones he did were just as unpleasant as the men.

"Oh," Angel said. "As opposed to the rest of us, you mean?"

"She's not worth protecting," Frankie said. "It's not worth what it's gonna cost you. Either of you."

Well, she probably had that right at least. Skyler stayed rooted to the spot, her legs shaking so hard she thought they might give way. If she tried to pull her gun out now she'd probably drop it.

"Fine," Rafe said. "You had to make it difficult."

Angel tipped her head back and let out a slow breath. "God," she said. "I was hoping you'd say that."

She shot him.

Frankie's answering bullet clanged off the metal cabinet as Rafe collapsed, but she only managed one before Angel fired again.

In the ringing silence, Angel turned to AJ with her gun still raised. "No more warnings. No more excuses. If you're not with us, AJ, you'd better walk away right now."

Skyler held her breath.

"I'm with you," AJ muttered.

"Right. Get in there, then."

Skyler fumbled for her torch as Angel slammed the metal door behind them. The beam illuminated brick walls glistening with moisture and slime, and a layer of something dark, sludgy and foul-smelling underfoot. A trickle of water cut through the middle of the sludge. Ahead of them, the tunnel swallowed the light of the torch.

"What is this?" she asked.

"Storm drain," Mackenzie said, picking his way through the sludge. "They run for miles under the city."

Angel nodded at him. "Do you know how to get to Edgbaston from here?"

He stopped, his mouth twisting thoughtfully. "Yeah. Uh... we're north of the city centre now, so..."

AJ shifted and cleared his throat. Angel shot him a sharp look. "Shut up, AJ."

"Yeah," Mackenzie said at last. "We follow this tunnel for a mile or so and then it'll branch in two... We take the left hand branch and then..." He nodded. "I can get us there."

"Good," Angel said, her voice slightly less dangerous. "Thanks."

AJ snorted. "What, just like that? How'd you know he knows what he's doing?"

"Not that I need to explain myself to you," Mackenzie said, "but I've probably spent actual weeks of my life in these tunnels. I know every inch of them." He gestured at the wall and they all peered at the tiny lines and symbols scratched into the brickwork. "Lot easier to outrun the enforcers down here. Long as you don't mind the smell, of course."

"Right," Angel said. "Are we all happy now, or shall we hang around to see whether any more of Redruth's people show up?" She strode away down the tunnel.

"Um," Mackenzie said, inching after her. "Why are we going to Edgbaston?"

There was no answer from Angel.

13

AFTER THE STORM

What followed were several hours of trudging through ankle-deep blackish mud in uncomfortable silence. By the time the tunnel came up into an empty canal basin, Skyler would have happily laid down and slept in it. She might as well have done. They were all covered in the stuff.

Angel gestured to an iron ladder set into the wall. "Up here. It's not far now."

Mackenzie immediately swung from listless to frantic. "Are you mental? Greycoats'll be all over the place. What're we –?"

"Mackenzie," Angel said. "Shut up."

He did as he was told.

"It's a risk. But it's either that or stay down here, which you're welcome to do if you'd prefer."

"I'm not sure I can do the ladder with this arm," AJ said.

Angel's expression was not sympathetic. "If Mackenzie can do it, so can you."

"Yeah," Mackenzie said. "About that."

"Or you can both stay down here. I really don't care."

She scaled the ladder with an ease and grace none of the rest of them possessed and peered out onto the towpath. "It's fine. There's no one around."

It was just as well the towpath was empty. Mackenzie's anxiety was entirely reasonable; between the blood, the bruising and the drain sludge, they looked like the cast of a bad horror film. When they got onto the streets, a woman with a small child turned the corner, saw them and swung in the opposite direction, dragging the child with her.

"Shit," Mackenzie said under his breath. "Someone's gonna call the enforcers."

Skyler tried to speed up, but Angel caught her arm. "No, don't run. Just walk like you've got no idea why anyone would look at you funny."

"She's right," Mackenzie said. "Running makes you look guilty, and looking guilty gets you shot." He looked down at himself and pulled a face. "Not that we could look a whole lot worse right now."

Angel ushered them down a street lined with trees and well-kept semi-detached houses. The electric streetlights would stay switched off when it got dark, of course, like they did everywhere, but here they'd been substituted with gas lamps. The people in Edgbaston weren't rich like Daniel was rich, but they were pretty comfortable. Skyler couldn't for the life of her work out what they were doing here.

Mackenzie and AJ had clearly both been here before. AJ looked uncomfortable, Mackenzie puzzled. "Hey," he said. "Are we going where I think we're going?"

Angel seemed to have decided she wasn't going to bother answering any more questions. She pushed open a gate, strode through a carefully tended front garden filled with colourful flowerpots to a house with a wide bay window and a shiny dark green door, and banged hard with the brass knocker.

The man who opened the door was so tall he dwarfed Angel, with broad, muscled shoulders, deep brown skin and a collection of scars and fresher wounds at varying stages of the healing process on his arms, neck and face. To his credit, he did not recoil at the sight of them.

"Angel," he said, rubbing a hand across his face. "Listen, kid, it's always a pleasure to see you, but right now might not be the best time. . ."

"I saved your life," Angel said, in the manner of someone playing a counter-move.

The huge man stared down at her. Then he grinned. "Callin' in a favour?" To her astonishment, Skyler detected a trace of a Yorkshire accent. "Fair enough. But there's a lot of upset just now. Lot of very unhappy people around."

"Way ahead of you, Joss," Angel said.

Skyler blinked. This she had not been expecting. Joss and his twin sister Lydia were two of the city's most notorious criminals. Skyler had never met either of them, but she'd done work for them and heard plenty of stories about them. They were famous adversaries of Daniel.

"Should've known you'd have something to do with it," Joss said cheerfully. "In you come, then. Your friends, too. Good to see you again, Mackenzie."

Skyler and Mackenzie shuffled over the threshold after Angel. "Nice to meet you," Joss said to Skyler. "I'd shake your hand, but you look like a bloody swamp monster." When AJ stepped forward, though, Joss barred his way with a muscular arm. "Not you. You've been working with Redruth." He raised an eyebrow at Angel. "What's he doing with you, kid?"

Angel's lips pursed. "AJ and I go back some," she said, after an uncomfortable pause. "And he's not exactly in with Redruth's lot right now. I'll vouch for him."

Joss' brows knitted together. "If you say so." He turned to AJ. "You can come in, but only 'cos she says it's okay.

No mucking about, or you'll be sorry. And don't get shit everywhere."

AJ trudged inside, an unreadable expression on his face. Joss ushered them into a wide, bright kitchen lit with gas lamps, a large pine table set in the centre. "Need anything?" he asked.

Angel started rummaging through her backpack. "Hot water, please. And if you can spare some food, that'd be amazing."

Skyler watched in fascination as Joss set the kettle on the hob. He caught her eye. "Which one are you, then?"

She wasn't sure how to answer that. While she hesitated, Angel spoke up.

His eyebrows almost disappeared into his hairline. "The hacker? You're shitting me."

"I assure you I'm not." Angel sat down, leaned her elbows on the table and rubbed her hands over her face.

Joss chuckled. The front door slammed. Joss carried on laughing. "Lyd!" he yelled. "Hey, Lyds, get in here!"

A marginally shorter, female version of Joss, with an equally impressive collection of scars, appeared in the doorway looking supremely unimpressed. "Joss," she said. "You've acquired a collection of waifs and strays. Waifs and strays covered in shite, no less."

"Yeah," Joss agreed amiably. He nodded at Skyler. "Remember the hacker? Skyler? We used her a couple of times, few months back."

"I remember," Lydia said, scrutinising her.

"Well," Joss said. "This is her."

A range of expressions flitted across Lydia's face, starting with disbelief and passing through amusement before settling on incredulity. "Is that right?" She sat down opposite Angel and drummed her fingers on the table.

"Huh. We thought you'd be older."

"Everyone always does," Skyler said.

"Well then, kid," Lydia said. "Half the city's looking for you. You must've done something pretty damn stupid to piss Redruth off this bad."

Skyler bit her lip.

"Well? His people aren't giving anything away, so go on. What'd you do?"

She took a deep breath. "I shot him."

For several long seconds, the twins did nothing except stare at her. Then, as one, they began to roar with laughter.

"Oh my God," Joss said, when he'd recovered enough to speak. "That's the most glorious bloody thing I've heard all year. What I'd have given to see the old bastard's face." He wiped his eyes, and then sobered abruptly. "Christ. You really are in trouble, then."

"Well, you can't stay here." Lydia folded her arms. "Sorry. I'd love to help you, but you're not safe in Birmingham now, no matter who you've got on your side."

"We realise that," Angel said. "We just need one night. Just to sort things out, patch this one up –" She nodded at AJ, who seemed to be trying to make himself invisible. "Can you give us that?"

The twins looked at each other. "Sure," Lydia said at last. "But you'd best get out of here first thing tomorrow. The further away the better, if you ask me."

"Can't say I disagree," Angel murmured.

Joss grunted. "House rules. No goin' outside. No telling anyone you're here. And" – he cast a stern glance at AJ – "no yelling when she does your arm, neither. Don't want to upset the neighbours. Understand?"

Mackenzie and Angel nodded. AJ looked at the floor. Skyler, though it was probably unwise, still couldn't take her eyes off the twins.

Joss raised his eyebrows at her. "Something we can help you with?"

To her intense irritation, Skyler felt her cheeks flush. She didn't know what to make of the two of them. She had long ago got used to the idea that large, powerful people equalled danger.

But Angel trusted them. That had to count for something. "Sorry," she mumbled. "It's just – your accents –"

"Oh, that," Joss said. "Yeah, Lyd and I grew up York way. Been down South maybe six years now."

"So – only three years before the Wall went up? I thought you had to have been in the South five years to apply for residency. And – well. How did you explain – you know – your line of work?"

Lydia pursed her lips but Joss, to her surprise, answered cheerfully. "We weren't always criminal masterminds, believe it or not. I used to be an immunologist. Worked at UCL. Lyd was an architect, weren't you, Lyd?"

"Yeah, right," Lydia said. "And that's ancient history now."

Joss looked at Skyler. "We knew the Board would never grant us residency, and we didn't fancy getting chucked back over the other side of the Wall. We saw which way the wind was blowing. So we got some new birth certificates, decided to... diversify."

Lydia glared at him. "Tell her our bloody life stories, Joss, why don't you?"

He waved a hand. "Relax. She's just like us."

She jabbed a thumb at AJ. "And him? When did you get so trusting?"

"I'm not gonna say anything," AJ muttered. He didn't have much choice. Lydia was eyeing him as though working out where she was going to bury him.

"Yeah," Joss said. "He's not stupid, is he?"

Lydia stood up. "Let's hope not. Listen up, you lot. Joss and I have to go out. There's a bathroom on the first floor. Please use it. You can come down here, and you can sleep in the attic. If we catch you in any of the other rooms. . . well. Make sure we *don't* catch you in any of the other rooms. All right?"

14

BURNING BRIDGES

As soon as the twins had left, AJ rounded on Angel. "I can't believe you brought us here."

She raised a sarcastic eyebrow. "What's the matter, AJ?"

"We can't trust them –"

Any patience Angel might have had left vanished from her face like quicksilver. "*I* can trust them. What've you been doing, while you've been getting cosy with Redruth?"

He glared at her, but had no reply. Angel slid off her seat, turned her back on them all and opened her giant bag again. "It's fine," she said. "The twins and I have an arrangement."

"Even so," AJ said, "you can't be sure –"

Angel stopped dead, the muscles of her back like stone under her shirt, and the whole room seemed to freeze with her.

The silence stretched out. Slowly, Angel turned on her heel.

"The only person I'm not sure we can trust here," she said, her eyes fixed on AJ, "is you. So why don't we all have a bit of quiet while I fix your arm?"

AJ threw himself into the nearest chair, looking mutinous. Angel, her brows drawn together in concentration, sat down next to him and took hold of his arm. He winced.

She smiled grimly. "You think that hurts. Wait till I –"

She yanked his arm, hard and sharp. AJ howled.

Angel let go of his arm and clapped a hand over his mouth. "All done. Don't be such a baby."

"I think I might be sick," he mumbled.

She rolled her eyes. "And I thought you were hard, AJ."

Danger crackled in the air, a spark creeping down a fuse to something inevitable and catastrophic. Skyler didn't dare take her eyes off the two of them. She was doing her best to ignore Mackenzie, whose expression said something along the lines of, *I told you taking the memory stick was a terrible fucking idea.* If he actually opened his mouth and said it, she was definitely going to punch him again.

It had been a long time since she'd had to consider anyone else's feelings, if you didn't count all the times she'd had to weigh up how likely it was that Daniel was about to hit her. But now, watching AJ's grey, sweat-sheened face, the guilt felt like it might crush her.

Angel sat back, her shoulders heaving in a silent sigh, and Skyler remembered, with another horrible wrench, that she wouldn't be going home any time soon either. "I'm sorry," she said. "AJ. And you too, Angel... I'm sorry."

Angel's face softened, but AJ's stayed fixed. "I wouldn't feel too bad for her if I were you, Sky," he said. "Let's not forget she had a part in all this."

Angel cocked her head, the warmth disappearing from her face. "You got something to say, AJ?"

"Yeah." He stood up, his chair scraping on the tiled floor, and stabbed a finger at her. "*You* gave her that gun. You put a gun in her hands and you taught her to use it. What did you think was going to happen when you did that?"

"Oh, I don't know." Angel was on her feet too, the dangerous edge back in her voice. "I had this bizarre idea that she'd be able to defend herself. And somehow you seem to have a problem with that."

"AJ." Skyler put a hand on his arm. "Angel was helping me look after myself. I'm not a kid."

"You're sixteen! I could've looked after you, if I'd known what was going on. If one of you had bothered to tell me. Instead *you*" – he gestured disgustedly at Angel – "you made her a murderer."

"I don't know if he's dead," Skyler muttered.

He shrugged. "Doesn't matter. Right, Angel? You know that. If you point a gun at someone you either want them dead or you don't care if they die."

Skyler jumped to her feet. "So it's all right for you but not for me? Oh, that's right. Did you think I don't know that you carry a gun now? And what would you even have done if I'd come to you? You knew where I was living, AJ, you knew all about Daniel, and you never said a word."

His mouth fell open. She didn't think she'd ever been angry with him before. She was almost always angry, of course. But angry *at* AJ? She couldn't remember that. "If it was to help you," he said, "I'd have done whatever needed to be done."

She turned away from him. "Yeah. Right."

"I always have, haven't I? Three years ago, when you said you wanted to go home – I put my neck on the line for you, or don't you remember?"

He was right. He'd put himself in danger for her more than once. She'd never doubted that he was a good person. Now she didn't know what to think.

"I came and got you today. I got you out of that mess you'd made." He shook his head at her. "You need to understand, Sky – guys like Redruth, they're okay as long as you keep them happy. Perhaps you should've just –"

"*What?*" Skyler spat. "I should have *done what he wanted*? Do you even know what you're saying? Should I have sold out everyone I worked for who wasn't on his side? Let Rafe and the rest of those idiots fuck me whenever they wanted? Is *that* the kind of thing you had in mind?"

"Of course not! Jesus Christ. Why are you *being* like this, Skyler?"

And the truth was she couldn't put it into words, why she was so angry. Why she couldn't just thank him and make things better. "Because you don't get it," she said. "You say you do, but you don't. You joined Daniel's crew! Why would you do that?"

AJ threw up his hands. "And you were living in his cellar! Are you telling me you never did any work for him? What about Mackenzie?" He jerked a thumb at Mackenzie, who pulled a *don't bring me into this* face. "How is that any different?"

"It is different," Skyler snapped. "People like Mackenzie and me – we don't always get to choose who we work for. Sometimes we have to do stuff just to survive. That wasn't about surviving, what you did. You had a choice, and you chose to tie yourself to Daniel. You help him get whatever he wants and it's all fine, isn't it, as long as he's on your side. Doesn't matter what he does to get it. Doesn't matter who he steals from or who he hurts."

She could tell he didn't recognise the person in front of him – and didn't like this new version of her, either. She'd never spoken to him like this before. "Of course I don't like the way things are," he said. "But this *is* the way things are. What am I meant to do – live in that shitty house forever, no money, no prospects, and feel good about being all moral?

Morals don't get people fed, Skyler, or hadn't you noticed?"

She laughed out of sheer exasperation. "You really don't get it."

"Is that what you think? You think you're the only person who's suffered because of the Board?"

"Oh, right. What'd they do to you – stop you getting hold of petrol whenever you want it? That's totally the same as obliterating half the fucking country, isn't it?"

"You don't know what the fuck you're talking about. My mum was a journalist, she used to speak up against the Board, and then she got fired and she still kept publishing stuff, even though my dad begged her to stop. And they came and kicked our door down in the middle of the night and took her away and we never saw her again."

"AJ –"

"And then my dad got cancer and we had to pay for his treatment somehow, and I was still trying to do things right and it didn't fucking get me anywhere, did it? So yeah. Perhaps I'm tired of trying to be the good guy and getting kicked for it. Being part of Redruth's crew makes life easier. So sometimes I have to do stuff I don't like. I didn't like seeing my mum get taken away or my dad die, either, and I still had to do that. Don't you fucking lecture me about the Board, Skyler. Don't you *dare*."

"I'm sorry," Skyler said. "I'm so sorry that happened to you, AJ. But – that doesn't make it any better! The North is a wasteland. Do you know how many people died up there? Millions of people went through exactly what you did, or worse. Why would you deserve to trample over all of them to get an easy ride now?"

"Fine. So I'm a selfish bastard. You tell me, then, if you're so much better than me – what was I supposed to do? What would you have done?"

You could still stop this. You could say sorry. You could make it better.

She turned away from him. "I'd try to do something my family would've been proud of."

The silence that descended was one that follows something that's been broken, and can't be repaired.

Angel's eyes followed AJ across the room. "AJ —"

The door slammed. Skyler flinched.

When she turned around, of course, AJ was gone.

She stared at the door. "Shit." Across the room, Mackenzie raised his eyebrows into his hair and she wanted to smack him. "Someone should go after him."

Mackenzie's eyebrows stayed raised. "Someone who's not you, you mean? Because it's so not going to be me."

She turned to Angel. "He's going to get himself killed."

"I doubt that," Angel said. "He can look after himself. Better he's out there sorting himself out than stomping around in here. And besides" – she gave Skyler a pointed look – "won't it be easier for you if he's not around anyway?"

"Oh yeah," Mackenzie said. "'Cos of the big secret and all. Yeah, it'll calm things right down when AJ finds out you didn't trust him enough to tell him about the memory stick. And after everything he's done for you." He shook his head mockingly.

Skyler gave him the most poisonous look she could muster. "Fuck off, Mackenzie."

"Sorry," he said. "Fight off lots of big angry men isn't really my thing. I'm sticking with you until this whole mess gets sorted out."

"You're not getting the memory stick back."

He opened the larder and peered into it. "It's not just about that any more, though, is it? God, these two must be doing well for themselves, I haven't seen this much food in one place in years. Anyway, thanks to *you*, I am now implicated in the murder of Daniel Redruth. So even if I got the Board off my case I'd still be a walking corpse. All of us are."

There was a lengthy silence. In it, Angel sighed.

"On that note," Mackenzie said, "anyone got any idea what we do next?"

"Yeah," Angel said. "How about everybody shuts up?"

15

THE GREATER GOOD

You weren't supposed to ask about the people who disappeared. You were supposed to understand that they'd brought it on themselves. Everything the Board did was for the security of the country, to put the Great back in Great Britain. If you didn't understand that – instinctually, unquestioningly – you were unpatriotic, and if you were unpatriotic you were dangerous.

At Skyler's school, there were a lot of lessons about how great things had been during the British Empire, and how liberal values and socialism and multiculturalism had brought the country to breaking point, and how the Board were rescuing people from all of this. Skyler wasn't sure how beating perfectly nice people to a pulp factored into that, and it seemed like lots of things were actually getting worse: there were a lot more homeless people on the streets, and her family hadn't been on holiday in several years even though Ruby picked up so many extra shifts she was hardly ever home anymore. Sometimes fights broke out in shops over the last bag of pasta or lentils on the shelf. The electricity often went off without warning. And it seemed odd that, somehow, the Board were always the good guys.

She couldn't say any of that to anyone, of course. If you heard anyone say bad things about the Board you were supposed to tell a teacher or call the hotline to report it.

On this particular day, though, she was more troubled than usual. Her classmate's sister had died of meningitis because her family hadn't been able to pay for her treatment. Skyler was worrying about what would happen if Sam or Ruby got sick. It didn't seem fair that the Board were happy just to let people die.

She voiced this, cautiously, to Sam as they walked home from school. She was eleven and he was seventeen by then, but he always walked with her instead of his friends and she'd never once had to ask him to.

"The Board aren't the good guys," Sam said. He had a way of making himself sound like a total authority on any subject; probably it was his unshakeable uncertainty that he was always right. Since Skyler held a similar belief about herself, their disagreements were usually extremely lengthy. "They just want to keep all their money and power, so they make out like poor people and immigrants are to blame for everyone's problems. And they hurt people who don't agree with them, so no one says what they really think. I've been reading. There's loads of stuff online if you know where to look."

Skyler hadn't heard anyone talk like this since Lauren stopped coming round. She wondered if she was supposed to report Sam. "I don't think you're supposed to say that stuff," she said experimentally.

Sam knelt in front of her and put his hands on her shoulders in a serious way that worried her. His brown eyes searched hers, earnest, intense. "This is important, Sky," he said. "Do you trust me?"

Who did she trust more, Sam or the Board? The answer to that, at least, was simple.

She nodded.

"Do you want to know the truth?"

That was easy, too. Sam knew a secret, and he wanted to share it with her. "Of course," she said.

That evening Skyler spent several illuminating hours learning how to bypass the Board firewalls which blocked websites, and then reading blog posts and watching videos. There were stories about major Board donors also owning huge news corporations, and about people who'd lost their jobs for criticising the Board. There were leaked memos authorising extreme force, photos of people who'd been tortured. There was a whole list of missing people with pleas for information.

It was like she'd been living in a dark room with the curtains drawn, trusting that what was in there with her was what she'd been told was there. Suddenly someone had come crashing through the windows and torn down the curtains, illuminating all the murky corners. It was frightening – but it was also exciting. She was special. She could see clearly in a way that others couldn't.

When she, Sam and Ruby had tea that night, Skyler said, "I can't believe people don't *know* all this. Tomorrow I'm going to tell Mr. Edwards about all the papers being owned by the Board's friends and how they make sure everyone's too scared to criticise them and – "

Ruby put her fork down too hard on the table. "Skyler? What're you talking about?"

"You must know, Mum," Skyler said. "You were already grown up when the Board got into power."

Ruby stared at Sam, her mouth in a grim line, while he concentrated on loading chips onto his fork. "What the hell have you been playing at?" she growled at him.

Skyler realised she might need to backtrack. Ruby was not as excited about this conversation as she'd expected. "It's not his fault," she said quickly. "I found it all by myself."

Ruby's hand shot across the table and grabbed her wrist. Skyler jumped. "Mum, what –?"

"You listen to me," Ruby said, gripping Skyler's arm so hard it hurt. "Both of you, you *listen to me*. I don't want another word from either of you about the Board. Not at Nan's house, not to your friends, not even in this flat. You never know who's listening and you never know who might report you – even if you think they're your friend. Even if you think they love you. So you don't talk about this stuff. Ever. And stay off those websites. They can track them."

"No they can't," Sam said, as though he was explaining something obvious to someone not as clever as him. A lot of conversations with him went like this. "I'm using Tor. That's an anonymous browser –"

"I know what bloody Tor is, Sam! Don't be so bloody stupid. Do you think they don't have spies on those forums?"

"But I haven't posted anything –"

"And you're not going to! Jesus Christ, what do I have to do to get you to understand? You can't beat the Board, not the way things are now. You just keep your head down and hope they don't notice you. That's all we can do."

Ruby's face was white and contorted as though she was about to cry. She sat back in her chair, pushed her plate away and put her hands over her face.

Skyler touched her hand uncertainly. "Sorry, Mum."

Ruby pulled her hands away and gave her a bright, brittle smile. "It's fine. Finish your dinner."

And later, when Skyler was supposed to be asleep but was actually lying in bed puzzling over the earlier conversation,

Ruby's voice in Sam's room next door: "What the *fuck* were you thinking?" She never used that word, at least not when she knew Sam and Skyler were listening.

"She asked." Sam sounded defensive. "She can see things aren't right. She deserves to know."

"You can't just give her all that information and turn her loose like that! What if she *had* gone and said all that to her teacher? D'you think the greycoats wouldn't have turned up to take her away?"

"She's only eleven –"

"And that doesn't matter to them! This is what I mean, Sam. You think you know it all, but you don't. So you bloody well keep your mouth shut, okay?"

Ruby's voice was cracked, wobbly. Was she crying? She never cried, either. But perhaps she was, because now Sam's voice was wobbly too. "Mum –"

"I just need you to understand how serious this is." Ruby's words were so choked they were barely audible. "I don't want to lose you, understand? Either of you."

16

SAFE HARBOUR

Mackenzie had expected to spend the evening hiding in the twins' attic, but they returned a few hours later unexpectedly cheerful and brightened even more when they discovered AJ was no longer there. Joss even offered to make them dinner – "You two don't look like you've had a proper meal in months. Least we can do after you put a bullet in Redruth." He pulled a bag of carrots and one of potatoes from the larder and handed them to Skyler and Mackenzie. "Get peeling, then."

"Stupid bugger," Lydia said, when Angel explained about AJ. "I don't know what he was playing at, going over to Redruth. He used to be one of the good ones. Reliable, like."

Angel sighed. "I guess he figured being one of the good guys doesn't get you paid."

Lydia sniffed. "No imagination, that's his problem. We never got in with Redruth and we're doin' all right."

This was something of an understatement. Mackenzie, though he'd been employed by the twins several times, had deliberately avoided learning much about anyone he met in the South, operating on the theory that the less he knew about pretty much anything the safer he would be.

The twins, though, had a knack for broadcasting their feelings about Redruth. What he didn't know was why they felt the way they did.

He had a feeling they wouldn't mind telling this story. He picked up a potato and a knife and said, "So what actually happened with you guys and Redruth?"

Opposite him, Angel grinned and rolled her eyes. "Here we go."

"Yeah, yeah," Joss said. "Just 'cos you've heard it all already." He started chopping onions. "What happened was, Lyd and I were living in London when the Wall went up. The day everything kicked off, enforcers showed up on all the Northerners' doorsteps to round us up. Lyd heard what was going on before either of us got home, so we managed to dodge 'em. Oh, they said there was an application process for residency and all that, but it was pretty obvious that were a load of shite. We thought about asking some mates for help, but even people who hated the Board wouldn't admit it, and to be honest, plenty of them seemed to think they had the right idea cutting the North's fuel and power rations."

"It all started getting a bit nasty, the last eighteen months or so," Lydia contributed unexpectedly. She was leaning against the kitchen counter watching her brother. "Digs about Northerners stealin' people's jobs. Graffiti on Joss' front door, that sort of thing. Someone on the tube started on me 'cos of my accent."

"Bet that ended well for them," Mackenzie said.

"Yeah, well, I had to be a bit careful. Only thing worse than being a Northerner in London by then was being a black Northerner in London. Couldn't risk giving the enforcers an excuse to start something. Anyway, the Wall went up and everything went to shit. Obviously weren't safe to stay in London – anyone who knew us could've shopped us to the Board. We'd have tried to get abroad but our accounts were frozen so all we had was enough cash to get up to Birmingham." She shrugged. "Seemed like as good a place as any."

"How'd you feel about being so close to the Wall?" Mackenzie asked, and then kicked himself. The twins weren't his friends just because they too were Northerners in exile, but there were so few people around whom he could speak freely, who might come anywhere close to understanding how he felt. Skyler was the only other one, and considering she'd spent most of the last few years ignoring him she hardly counted.

Perhaps the twins understood, though, because Joss only cocked an eyebrow at him and threw the onions into a pot on the stove, which sizzled. The smell made Mackenzie's mouth water.

"Not great," Joss said, stirring the pot. "As you might imagine. But it don't really matter how close it is, does it? It could be a thousand miles away. We'd still know it was there."

Across the table, Skyler gripped the knife in her hand like she was trying to stop herself throwing it. Angel watched her. Joss stirred the onions. Lydia's face was inscrutable.

"So, Redruth," Mackenzie said, slicing a potato in half. "You got to Birmingham and. . . then what?"

Lydia stretched. "Well, we had to make some money somehow. Go big or go home, that was what we agreed. But we didn't want to screw anyone over who couldn't afford it, so the first job we did was relieving some old fart of some of his art collection."

"I was shitting bricks the whole time," Joss said. "Chuck me those potatoes, will you? But it was worth it afterwards when we had a big pile of cash to play with. And then Redruth got to hear about it."

Skyler, across the table, still fiddling with the knife. Mackenzie wondered if he should take it from her. She'd probably stick it through his hand if he tried.

He decided to leave her to it. "Oh dear. What happened then?"

"Well, him and his boys turned up to explain to us that he runs this town, and since we'd done the job on his patch, we owed him a cut. Didn't like the sound of that, really, but there were about ten of them and we were still findin' our feet, so to speak, so what could we do? We handed over the money."

"And I was so pissed off I ran my mouth off to anyone who'd listen," Lydia said, sounding more upbeat than Mackenzie had ever heard her. "Joss kept tellin' me to shut up, but honestly, you should've heard that dickhead. Like, oh, I'm doing you such a massive favour. All you have to do is give me seventy percent of everything you make and you get my protection, lucky you." She wrinkled her nose. "Like it weren't obvious he were a total nutjob. Too much like the Board, thanks. So I didn't want to let it go, but most people were scared shitless of him. And then someone mentioned we might want to have a chat with Angel."

"We kept hearing the name," Joss said. "Heard she was some kind of badass who only cared about taking Redruth down. You had a pretty solid reputation by then, didn't you, kid?" He addressed Angel, who gave him a faint smile. "So when we set up a meeting, obviously we thought we were gonna meet – well, a grown up. Probably built like a tank and covered in scars. We're waiting in this bar and Angel shows up lookin' like she got lost on her way to preschool." He poured stock in with the vegetables on the stove and chuckled.

Angel laughed too. "You should've seen their faces," she said, and Skyler looked up for the first time. "I went up to them and said 'I think you're looking for me,' and they both stared at me with their mouths open. Joss goes" – she mimicked a Yorkshire accent – "'I don't think so, kid.' And I said, 'No, really. I'm Angel.' And Lydia just looked me up and down and went, 'Good fucking grief.'"

"I thought it was a piss take," Lydia said. "I nearly walked out there and then. But she had a hell of a reputation, and she was the only person up for going after Redruth, so. . ."

Skyler had stopped fiddling with the knife. "What happened?"

"Every dealer in Birmingham gets their supply through Redruth." Joss said. Then he grinned. "Well, I guess not anymore. Anyway, he'd get a big shipment in once a month and his boys'd go to this industrial estate and dish it out to all the little sods that run around for him. Towards the end of the night, when they'd shifted the stuff and got their cash together, Angel got up on a roof and started taking shots at them. Took out about five before most of the rest ran off looking for her."

Angel looked satisfied. "I ran them all over the city. Was a lot of fun, that night."

"The two that were left jumped in their truck with the cash and tried to make a break for it. And then we went to say hello."

"What'd you do?" Mackenzie asked.

Joss waved a hand. "Ah, nothing, really. We were a bit softer in those days. We just tied them up, took the money and left a note that said 'Tell Redruth we don't need his protection, thanks.'"

"I doubt they ever went back to him," Skyler said. "You killing them would've been the soft option."

"Maybe," Lydia agreed. "We had to get a bit tougher after that, anyway. We were all pleased with ourselves until Angel pointed out Redruth probably wasn't gonna leave it there. So we had to learn some more new skills."

"Yeah," Joss said. "Angel taught us both to shoot. So it turns out we owe her quite a lot. Get the bread out the larder, Mackenzie, will you?" He sighed. "Shame about AJ, though. He was a nice kid."

"He was a bloody moron," Lydia said.

"You're too harsh, Lyd. He was just young. Redruth would've promised him the world, given him a taste of the good life. It's easy to get sucked in by all that when you're used to having nothing. I know what I was like at that age. Thought I knew it all."

"You still do," Lydia said. She took the loaf of bread Mackenzie handed her and pulled a knife out of a drawer. "You lot better eat up. You're gonna need a full stomach for all the runnin' around you're gonna be doing after today."

17

LOST AT SEA

Mackenzie couldn't sleep.

The attic was comfortable enough. It was warmer than he was used to, and Lydia had shoved an armful of blankets and cushions at them – "Might as well get a decent night's sleep while you're here." Angel and Skyler were across the room, both apparently fast asleep. He envied them.

It wasn't that he wasn't tired. He was exhausted. His eyes burned, and the lingering effects of the concussion pounded away at the back of his skull. But he couldn't sleep, because he couldn't stop the pictures flashing through his mind.

They were horrifying, and they were relentless, as though someone had switched a projector on inside his brain and hidden the controls. And with them came overwhelming, dizzying terror, like he was choking on a lump of lead, like acid burning a hole in his stomach.

So he was tapping. Quietly, so as not to wake the others, but continually, his fingers counting out a constant rhythm on the floorboards. And he kept going, even though his fingers had gone numb and he was so, so tired, because if he didn't something terrible was going to happen.

A couple of times the terror subsided enough that he thought he might be able to stop. But every time he did, another image flashed into his head.

So he would screw his eyes closed and dig his fingernails into the palm of his uninjured hand to keep from sobbing out loud, and then start tapping again.

At some point his brain must have decided it'd had enough and just switched itself off. He woke in the grey light filtering in from the tiny skylight feeling like he might as well not have slept at all. His body was sore in places he hadn't realised it was possible to feel pain, and when he tried to rub the sleep out of his eyes he poked himself several times with his stiff, swollen fingers until he remembered why he couldn't bend them.

His brain felt quieter, though, thank God. That was going to be temporary, probably, so he needed to make the most of it. What was he going to do now?

Skyler and Angel were both still asleep. Ignoring his body's creaks and protests, he tiptoed over to them.

Could he get the drive out of Skyler's pocket and flush it down the toilet before she woke up and tried to kill him? At least then if the Board did track them down there wouldn't be anything to incriminate them. And once it was gone. . . well. There wasn't a whole lot she could do then, was there?

Well. She had stabbed someone yesterday.

And shot someone.

Even so, he'd take her over the Board any day.

He lifted his eyes to the rafters. *Come on, Mackenzie. Think.*

When he looked back down, Skyler's eyes were open and fixed accusingly on him. "I sincerely hope," she said, sitting up, "that you're not considering what I think you're considering."

And his chance was gone. Mackenzie cursed himself. "If you think I was gonna take the memory stick. . . yeah. I was thinking about it."

Her face hardened. "Did you want another concussion?"

He flung himself onto the floor and glowered at her. "Right. Apology accepted for the last one, by the way."

Beside Skyler, Angel sat up and yawned. "You woke Angel up," Skyler said to him reprovingly.

Angel stretched. "No bother. What'd I miss?"

"Just tell me *why*," Mackenzie said to Skyler. "Help me understand, for God's sake. Why do you want that bloody memory stick so badly?"

There was a stubborn set to her expression that he recognised as the sign of an argument he wasn't going to win. "Have you got any idea how much I can learn from a device like this? Some people don't even think the company that made this thing exists. I might never get a chance like this again. Don't you get that?"

"Can't *you* see how selfish you're being? So you're gonna go off and turn into some super ninja hacker or whatever and the rest of us'll – what? Stay here and clean up your mess? Fuck off."

Skyler swung to Angel. "Ugh. *Tell* him."

"Hmm," Angel said. "He kind of has a point, Sky."

To Mackenzie's astonishment, Skyler did not leap down her throat, but merely said, "What do you mean?"

"You know perfectly well what I mean. That drive wasn't yours to take from Mackenzie. And it's not just your life that's being turned upside down now."

Mackenzie could hardly hear what she was saying. Inside him, the panic was rising inexorably back to the surface like a great, toothed sea monster. To calm it, he started counting to seven inside his head over and over again.

"Well, what was *he* thinking?" Skyler demanded. "Why'd you take it, Mack, if you didn't want to know what was on it? What did you think you were gonna do with it?"

"I don't *know*!" Mackenzie cried, as frustrated with himself as with Skyler. "I don't know. I got paid so much for the other one that when I found it... it just seemed stupid to pass it up."

She looked scornful. "Come off it. You were stealing from the Board. Even if you'd only taken the one Daniel paid you for, they probably would've had the greycoats out after you anyway. You *know* that. You're not an idiot. So you took one more memory stick. What's the difference?"

"Apart from the fact that I'm pretty sure they're going to kill me as slowly and painfully as possible? And then probably hang me out on the Wall for everyone to have a good look at? Well, aside from that minor fucking detail, I can hardly sell it now, can I? Even if we knew what was on it, nobody'd bloody well touch it."

Skyler looked like she was gearing herself up for a shouting match, which he was fairly certain would give the twins more than enough incentive to kick them all out onto the street. Fortunately, Angel interrupted. "Think about this, Sky," she said gently. "I know you want this. But just – think for a minute. Is it really worth it?"

Skyler's shoulders slumped. She looked, for an instant, like a lost, scared, unhappy teenager. Mackenzie wondered if she was going to cry.

Then the flicker of vulnerability was gone.

"I am being selfish," she said to him. "In case you hadn't noticed, that's pretty much what it takes to stay alive round here. And I shouldn't have stolen the drive from you. I get that. You don't have to care about me, Mack – but care about this. Whatever's on that drive, the Board went out of their way to hide it in the digital equivalent of a fortress."

"And?" Angel prompted. "What's that to you?"

Skyler's mouth was a hard line. "I hate the Board. So do you." She locked eyes with him, every word a challenge. "You were there, after the Wall went up. You know what they did."

"And it's done now," he said helplessly, trying to squash the tiny inner voice that hissed that he was being a coward. "There's no way to fix it."

"Who said I wanted to fix it?"

"Then *what*?"

She catapulted herself upright. "You know what I want?" she spat. "I want every single person on the Board to *suffer* for what they did to us." She wrenched the drive from her pocket and thrust it at him. "They're hiding something on this thing, and they haven't cared very much about hiding all the other shit they've done, so I can only assume this is something that'll absolutely ruin them if it gets out. And when I find out what it is, I'm gonna make sure the rest of the world knows about it too."

"Do you *want* to die, Skyler? You did all that to get away from Redruth just so you could goad the Board into coming after you instead, is that right? You think once you've shown the world whatever's on that drive you're gonna live happily ever after?"

"Like that's ever gonna happen anyway. What've I got to look forward to, fifty more years in some psychopath's cellar? What've *you* got to look forward to?"

"Don't make this about me," Mackenzie snapped. "I *like* my life, thanks."

She just looked at him.

"I like bits of it! I especially like the bit where I have all my arms and legs!"

"Then walk away. Set them onto me." The words *Like you did with Redruth* hovered in the air between them, unspoken.

He winced. "You know I'm not gonna do that."

"Don't forget, Mackenzie. You were the one who started this."

"Like I'm ever bloody well going to forget that," Mackenzie muttered. He looked at Angel. "Well, what do we do now?"

"Why are you asking me?" she retorted.

A fresh wave of panic. "You're not staying with us?"

There was a bang on the attic door. Lydia opened it and towered over them, her face grim.

Angel got to her feet. "Everything okay?"

"Eh, not really. Greycoats are outside."

Mackenzie let out an inadvertent moan. Skyler went white.

"What do you want us to do?" Angel said.

She snorted. "Teach my brother not to be so bloody soft, maybe. Your best bet's the bathroom window. I'm sure me and Joss can entertain 'em for a bit."

Angel opened her mouth as if to argue and then seemed to realise they didn't have time. "Looks like I owe you again, Lyd."

"Aye," Lydia said. "Don't go too far. We'll be comin' to you next time one of us needs patching up." She jerked her head towards the staircase. "Get moving."

18

DOWNWARD MOBILITY

Two minutes later Mackenzie was hanging halfway out of the bathroom window, considering their options. Downstairs, a murmur of conversation between the twins and the greycoats was just audible.

As escape routes went, he'd seen worse. There was a drainpipe three feet to the left of the window. From there it was one storey down to a paved yard. There was nowhere soft to land, but that was all right – if he needed that, it would just be embarrassing. It was broad daylight, too. Being able to see where he was putting his hands and feet was a luxury he didn't usually have.

This is fine. You've done this loads of times. You got out of the Board headquarters just the other day. Although, admittedly, that had been with two working hands.

He was pretty sure Angel wouldn't be too fazed by the drainpipe either. Skyler, on the other hand, seemed to have turned a little pale.

"You okay?" he asked her.

She grimaced. "I thought there'd be, like... a ladder or something." She had the grace to sound embarrassed. "Do we actually have to climb down that?"

"You got a better idea?"

Her scowl deepened.

"It'll be okay, Sky," Angel said. "It's easier than it looks."

Skyler did not look convinced. Mackenzie decided not to comment on the fact that Angel's last statement had been a lie. "How are we gonna do this?" he asked her.

"I'll go first. If they come into the yard I can deal with it from there."

"Are you sure –?" he began, but Angel had already swung herself out of the window. Skyler peered out to watch her descent. Her knuckles, gripping the window ledge, were white.

He gave a disbelieving laugh. "You're scared of heights."

"And? What's it to you?"

"Nothing, I just never expected –"

"Look, one of the best things about hacking is that you never have to dangle yourself out of any windows. I think you lot are mental."

Angel had reached the ground quicker than he'd expected, had her gun out and was gesturing furiously at him. He turned to Skyler. "Your turn."

He was afraid she was going to argue, but then she clambered onto the windowsill. He reached out a hand to her. "Here. Give me your bag."

She didn't move. He suppressed the urge to shake her. The conversation between the twins and the greycoats rumbled on downstairs and every word felt like sand slipping through an hourglass. "Look, it'll be easier if I take it. I won't let anything happen to your computer."

She thrust the bag at him. "Fine. You better not." She looked at the drainpipe and swallowed. She'd gone from pale to actually looking ill. "Uh. . . how do I do this?"

"You'll have to sort of swing yourself across," he said, trying to sound encouraging and not yell at her to just get on with it before they all got shot. "You'll be fine. It's not far."

"Looks far enough to me." She took a deep breath, stretched out an arm and lunged clumsily out of the window.

Mackenzie waited until the lack of a thud reassured him she hadn't just thrown herself onto the concrete and then peeked outside. Skyler was clinging to the drainpipe and giving him an unfriendly look.

"The quicker you move," he said, "the quicker you'll be on the ground."

"Is that supposed to be helpful?"

He glanced at his bandaged fingers. It wasn't going to be easy to get down the drainpipe one-handed. "Sky, please can you just move?"

She gave him one last glare, conveying that she held him single-handedly responsible for her predicament, and began to inch towards the ground.

She took a *long* time to get down. Mackenzie started to feel like he might throw up. At least down in the yard there was Angel and her gun. Up here he had nothing except Skyler's backpack, which admittedly was probably heavy enough to deliver an incapacitating blow if he swung it the right way. He had no faith whatsoever in his ability to do this.

A backpack and three broken fingers. Yep. Brilliant.

He tried to focus on the one thing he knew he could actually do. But when Skyler was still only halfway down the drainpipe, the voices downstairs grew louder. Lydia's voice echoed up the stairs: "Of course you can look around, officers."

Oh, *hell*.

Without stopping to think, he swung himself onto the drainpipe.

When he looked down, Skyler was staring up at him with something approaching a look of terror on her face. He scrambled towards the ground, but then realised if he kept up that pace he would end up landing on her head. He slowed down, which turned out to be a mistake.

Mackenzie always worked alone, figuring that other people could only be trusted to screw things up and take half your earnings. So he'd never climbed a drainpipe that was also occupied by a second person, and had failed to consider that a structure capable of supporting one skinny teenager might struggle to cope with the added weight of a second one.

The cracking noise from just above his head was not, therefore, something he had expected to hear.

Below him, Skyler hissed: "What was *that*?"

He opened his mouth and then realised that the drainpipe had answered the question for him by detaching itself from the wall.

Skyler yelped, let go of the pipe and hit the concrete with a thud and a flurry of breathless expletives. Mackenzie, on the other hand, was still several metres from the ground and as he peeled away from the safety of the wall he cast an uncertain glance downwards. *All right. This is nothing to worry about. You've definitely had worse falls than this.* This was true, but those falls had been, as he recalled, rather painful ones. *Maybe if you hang on the pipe'll just bend backwards and you can drop off when you're closer to the –*

The drainpipe snapped. Mackenzie found himself airborne for a brief, unwelcome moment, before he hit the concrete on his back. "Ow," he wheezed.

Skyler appeared in his field of vision, looking, if possible, even angrier than she had done at the top of the pipe. Mackenzie moved some limbs experimentally and discovered that he was considerably more mobile than he'd expected. "Hey," he said, pulling himself to his feet. "That actually didn't hurt too much."

Skyler did not look like this was news worthy of celebration. "That's because my laptop broke your fall, you stupid arse." She grabbed his wrist and dragged him towards the gate at the end of the yard. "*Move.* They'll be out here any minute."

"Right." He stumbled after her. "Uh, let's get out of here?"

"I think that would be a wonderful idea," Angel said, studying the gate. She turned to him. "It's locked. You're up."

All the greycoats had to do was look out of the kitchen window and that would be the end of them.

Okay, that's not helpful.

He squatted down next to the lock and squinted at it. "Any time you're ready," Skyler said, and he shot an incredulous glance at her.

Inside the house, a woman's voice bellowed: "GET DOWN ON THE FLOOR. DOWN ON THE FLOOR AND PUT YOUR HANDS ON YOUR HEAD."

The air in Mackenzie's lungs solidified. *The twins.*

From inside the house came a cacophony of smashing furniture and yelling. He whipped around, but the kitchen was empty. "Mackenzie," Angel hissed. "Get it done!"

He forced his attention back to the gate and fumbled in his pocket for his tools. *Okay. Two lever mortice lock. A very old one.*

More shouting and crashing inside. He selected a tool and slid it into the lock. *Focus. You've got this.* He couldn't remember ever having picked a lock one-handed before, but there was nothing like a challenge to distract you when you were probably about to get shot in the back of the head.

As the lock sprang open and they tumbled out of the yard into the alleyway, the noise inside the house died away. At least there hadn't been any gunshots.

After that, Mackenzie had to work so hard to keep up with Angel that he forgot to worry anymore. They ran and slid and scrambled down alleyways, across the deserted cricket pitch and through allotments until they were into the countryside south of the city and finally, thank God, Angel said, "I think we can probably slow down a bit."

They were surrounded by nothing but empty fields and a cold grey sky. Skyler, her face bright pink and her chest heaving, threw herself onto the ground. Mackenzie followed suit, so glad to be off his feet that he hardly even noticed the freezing earth. "What now?" he wheezed.

"I need... electricity," Skyler managed between gasps. "And thanks to *you*" – she gave him a filthy look – "I probably need a computer as well."

"Is that... really the priority... right now?"

"No," Angel said, studying the horizon with her hands on her hips. She seemed barely out of breath. "You can't crack any encryption if you're dead, Skyler. We need to get out of town."

Skyler looked up. Mackenzie wondered if she'd noticed the same thing he had. "We?" he said. "You mean you're staying with us?"

"We need to get as far from Birmingham as possible," Angel said, as if he hadn't spoken. "And I don't know about you two, but I don't fancy walking the whole way."

That had been the start of the first argument. Stealing a car was out of the question. A brief conference revealed that none of them knew how to drive well enough to be inconspicuous, and car ownership was so unusual that spot checks from the enforcers were common. Mackenzie offered to steal a horse and cart – there were just as many on the roads as cars these days – but Angel vetoed the idea. "It'll get reported stolen. Besides, do you have any idea how to look after a horse?"

He had to admit that he didn't. Angel suggested the train, but there were often enforcers on public transport. "We'll just be sitting there waiting to get caught," he protested. "We might as well draw targets on ourselves."

She made an impatient noise. "Are you telling me you can't do an impression of a normal member of society for a few hours? How are you still alive?"

"It's all right for you two. At least you got to bring a change of clothes on this little adventure." He'd been trying not to think about the fact that he was still wearing the same clothes he'd walked through a storm drain in the day before, because every time he did his brain started clanging like a fire bell.

Angel glared at him. "Yeah, this whole thing's really been very convenient for me."

He decided not to get into this. "Well, we can't go to New Street. There'll be enforcers everywhere."

"New Street would be best," Angel said. "It's so busy nobody'd look twice at us. But we can't go back to Birmingham, not with Redruth's lot on the prowl."

In the end they walked to Coventry, which took nearly five hours. There, they bought Mackenzie some clean clothes and made their way to the train station, still debating where they were supposed to go next.

"As far away as possible," was Skyler's less than helpful contribution, delivered with such sulky indifference that Mackenzie was almost convinced she really believed their predicament was anyone's fault but hers. But when he looked closer her lips were bitten raw and her eyes flitted constantly, scanning the people around them, and he suspected that she understood only too well what she'd done.

He hated train stations. There were posters everywhere: *Protect the South's Resources. Does the Person Next to You Belong Here? If You See Something, Say Something.* They reminded him of not just how unsafe he was here, but how unwelcome; that most of the people surrounding him would happily watch him get shot if they knew where he'd grown up. It was paralysing. He couldn't help Angel make a decision. Eventually, throwing up her hands in exasperation, she bought three tickets for the final stop of the next train leaving. They were going to Bournemouth.

"Where's that?" Mackenzie asked.

"As far away as possible," Angel said dryly. "It's on the south coast." Before they reached the platform, she pulled him towards her and said in an undertone, "If you could do something about that accent, Mackenzie, I assume you would have by now. So keep your mouth shut on the train, okay?"

It was a sore point. Skyler's accent had flattened over the years, perhaps because she hardly ever actually spoke to anyone anymore. Mackenzie, on the other hand, had always had a broad accent and his attempts to neutralise it had generally been unsuccessful to the point of being embarrassing.

Maybe he should have tried harder. The problem was that he didn't *want* to lose the accent. It was his last link with home. And that was a dangerously sentimental thought, but there it was. He didn't know if he would ever be ready to let it go.

They boarded the train separately and it gathered speed, putting reassuring miles between them and all the people who wanted them dead. Skyler stared at her knees. Angel's eyes passed over him without interest. And Mackenzie began to worry again.

Nobody on the train *looked* like a greycoat or an enforcer. There were no uniforms in the carriage. But any of the passengers could have been Board in plain clothes, and even the ticket inspectors were allowed to demand ID. And as soon as anyone wanted to speak to him. . .

He started tapping the table in front of him. The woman opposite lowered her book and gave him a sharp look.

You can't stop, it's not safe –

For God's sake, don't draw any more attention to yourself.

He made himself put his hands back in his lap. *It's going to be fine. It's going to be fine. Just don't think about the enforcers. Don't think about –*

"Tickets from Coventry, please."

Mackenzie nearly choked on his tongue. He looked up at the conductor, a woman who resembled his old science teacher. She held out her hand. "Ticket?"

He fumbled in his pocket and tried to contort his face into something approaching polite neutrality. Across the aisle, Skyler was twisting a strand of hair into painful-looking knots. *Don't look at her. Don't.*

"Thanks," the conductor said. Mackenzie nodded shakily and sank down in his seat.

Skyler handed her ticket over wordlessly, with an expression surly enough to discourage small talk. The conductor moved onto Angel.

But something was wrong. Angel was staring at the conductor too intently, jiggling her leg in a way he'd never seen her do before. As the conductor handed the ticket back to her, she chewed a fingernail, her leg jiggling faster and faster. What was she *doing*?

A rustle behind him. He looked over his shoulder to see a middle-aged woman in a dark suit and a neat bun walking purposefully towards them.

Oh God. Oh no.

She might just be a normal passenger. Probably she was just going to the loo.

She passed him, and then Skyler. And stopped in front of Angel.

Mackenzie couldn't feel his legs.

"Excuse me," the woman said to Angel. "I'm going to need you to step outside the carriage."

Shit shit shit.

Angel's eyes widened. "I haven't done anything." The words came out in a babble. "I swear I haven't –"

"Come with me, please."

What little colour there was in Skyler's face vanished. The other passengers cast surreptitious glances at Angel as she followed the greycoat. This was dangerous – when the Board were going about their business, you were supposed to look straight ahead and pretend not to notice. But it was like passing the scene of a horrible accident. It was hard not to stare.

Mackenzie stared after Angel, fighting to keep breathing as the carriage doors closed behind her. *This is your fault, you did this, you weren't careful enough.*

The train sped onwards. Skyler chewed her lip until it looked bloody. Mackenzie kept his hands in his lap and started to tap again.

Ten minutes passed.

Fifteen minutes.

The carriage doors hissed open. Mackenzie just stopped himself jerking his head up, but it was all right; plenty of other passengers had turned to look.

Angel stumbled back to her seat, white-faced. A couple of passengers looked sympathetic, but most of them looked at her like she was contagious.

Skyler's terrified eyes flickered towards Mackenzie and he gave a tiny fraction of a nod. It was all he dared do.

Angel covered her face with her hands. The train rocked onwards.

It was dark when they arrived in Bournemouth. By the time Mackenzie had shuffled off the train, Angel had already disappeared into the crowds on the platform. He followed the back of Skyler's head past racks of hire bikes and a small collection of horse-drawn carts waiting for fares. She strode ahead, ignoring him, until they'd left the crowds behind them.

Alone on a dark, empty street, she glanced back at him and he hurried to catch her up. "D'you think we're all right?" he murmured.

"I think so," she said. "But Angel –"

"Here," a voice by Mackenzie's ear said, and he almost threw himself into the nearest hedge.

Skyler moved towards her. "What happened? Are you okay?"

"Yeah," Mackenzie said. "Why'd you look so nervous? That greycoat went straight for you."

"Don't talk to me about looking nervous, Mackenzie. You might as well have been wearing a t-shirt saying 'Ask me about my citizenship status.' I had to distract her somehow. And since I'm the only one here who actually has an ID. . ."

He swallowed. "Christ. I'm sorry." *I told you. It was your fault. You weren't careful enough. You could've got her killed.*

"What'd she do?" Skyler asked. "Are you okay?"

"I'm fine. She ran my ID, it came back clear. Searched me. Lucky I took all my weapons off me before we got on the train, or there'd have been no explaining that."

"You put on a good act," Mackenzie said. "The whole scared shitless thing was pretty convincing."

"Yeah, well, it was only half an act." Angel wriggled her shoulders as if to loosen them. "Anyway, we'd better move. It'll be curfew soon."

She set off at a march. Skyler hurried after her, but Mackenzie couldn't shake the creeping dread that they were going to be stopped or followed, and the urge to do something to prevent a catastrophe was impossible to ignore. Over and over came the need to touch something, to step a certain way, to go back and repeat his movements.

He tried to do those things surreptitiously, but it was slowing him down. "What are you *doing*?" Angel snapped when he doubled back, trying to cross a manhole cover in the right number of steps to stop his brain screaming at him. "Stop pissing around."

Mackenzie's face burned. He forced himself to catch them up and swallow the terrible wrongness of it all.

"We need to find somewhere to spend the night," Angel said. "Any ideas?"

He tried to think. The town was run-down, dilapidated. Lots of shops that seemed permanently closed. That meant plenty of abandoned buildings.

"Let's find somewhere empty and I'll break in," he said, resolving to at least try to be helpful. "There won't be any power, but it'll get us off the streets."

"Good idea," Angel said, her voice slightly warmer. "Let's do that."

In the end they found a whole row of boarded-up houses on a dark, silent street. Inside the one they chose, their feet scuffing on the bare floorboards sent dust billowing into the air. Wallpaper peeled in ragged strips, cobwebs hung in thick swathes from the ceiling, and –

"Jesus," Mackenzie said. "Look at the size of those spiders."

To his horror, Angel scooped one up in her bare hand and offered it to him with a wicked grin. "Want to hold it?"

He backed away. "No I bloody well don't."

She released the spider, which scuttled off into a corner, and sighed. "Well, it's somewhere to hide, at least. I can't imagine anyone's going to come looking for us here."

19

SURFACING

It's just a door.

Just a door.

You just put your hand on the handle and turn it and step outside.

This was what Mackenzie had been telling himself for the past three days. He still hadn't made it out of the house. His brain kept getting in the way.

First, to get down the stairs, you have to put your feet exactly in the middle of each step. Don't make a sound. Don't touch the bannister. Don't touch the wall. One wobble, one creaking step, and you start all over again.

Then say you make it to the bottom of the stairs. From there all you have to do is get to the front door in exactly eleven steps. Then you turn round and go back to the foot of the stairs and do it again until it feels right. Which could be three times, or it could be twelve, or it could be thirty.

If you make a single wrong move. If Skyler or Angel interrupt. If you think about Redruth or the Board, or Mum or Dad or Bex. About getting sick, or getting hurt, or Skyler or Angel getting hurt.

If you do any of those things, you'll have to go back and

start again to make sure nothing bad happens.

If something bad does happen, it'll be your fault.

At first it had seemed like it was going to be easier to stay in the house. None of this was new to Mackenzie, but it had never been *this* bad before. He'd never wanted to bang his head against the wall hard enough to make everything just *stop*.

And when this had happened before, he'd always been alone. He'd been able to deal with it in his own time, in his own way. But now, on top of the maddening, sickening buzz of his thoughts, there was the scalding humiliation of knowing that Angel and Skyler could see how oddly he was behaving, and that if they asked him what he was doing he wouldn't be able to explain.

So at first it had been easier to just stay still. The others didn't seem to want to talk anyway. Skyler was still sulking about her laptop, and Angel. . . well, it was impossible to know what she was thinking.

And then, a couple of days in, a clear thought started clamouring for attention amongst the treacherous hissing of the anxiety. *You don't have to just let this happen to you. You can decide what happens next.*

You have a choice.

That choice had, it turned out, involved taking three days to get out of the house. The first few times Angel had seen him on the stairs she'd asked if he was all right. "Do you need anything?" she'd said, and then, later, "Mackenzie, are you *sure* you're all right?" He couldn't tell her about all the wrongness in his brain. He'd said he was fine, he just needed to be on his own, and although Angel had given him a look that said, approximately, *you're full of shit*, she'd given him a bottle of water and left him to it.

It had been so tempting to give up. At midnight on the first day, when he still hadn't made it down the stairs, he'd sat down on the step he was stuck on and cried until his face was raw. *What if this is it, now? Am I always going to be like this?*

And then: *Tomorrow. You'll try again tomorrow.*

And now he was, finally, in front of the door. Just a piece of wood between him and the rest of the world, and then God knew how many hoops his brain would create for him to jump through once he actually got out there.

He stared at the door handle.

It's not clean. You'll get sick, you'll pass it on to Skyler, to Angel, and then – and then –

No. No. No. Not that. Don't think about that.

He reached out, and his heart pounded so hard he thought it might give out altogether. His hand hovered over the door handle.

He snatched it away.

This is ridiculous. It doesn't make any sense.

You know how bad it could be. What if it happens here? Because of you?

He'd thought if he just did what his brain was telling him to do, if he could only get it right, the fear would go away. But instead it just got worse and worse.

Think about the last three days. All the stuff you've done to try and keep everyone safe, and it never feels like enough. It's never going to feel like enough.

This isn't about germs. This isn't about it being your job to keep everyone safe. This is about fear.

You have a choice.

Mackenzie squeezed his eyes shut, took a deep breath, and – fast, so he didn't have time to change his mind – opened the door.

The gnawing dread didn't go away once he was outside, but having a purpose – and knowing that he needed to be back before curfew – made it easier to suppress.

It took him most of the day to get everything he wanted. When he returned to the house Skyler was at the top of the stairs, halfway to her feet. She looked down at him and her expression changed from trepidation to surprise. "Oh. It's you. Where've you been?"

Mackenzie, both arms laden down with bags, beckoned to her. "Come with me."

She scowled. "What for?"

"Oh, I'm sorry. Am I interrupting your busy schedule of sitting on your arse sulking? Come with me."

Her scowl intensified. But then, to his amazement, she came downstairs.

The kitchen door opened. Angel peered out and cocked her head at him. "Hey. You've been out." Her tone said she hadn't thought he was capable of leaving the house.

"Yep." He ducked past her into the kitchen and dumped the bags on the scratched, stained counter.

Angel sniffed. Her face brightened. "Did you buy food?"

"Yep. It's about time we all had a proper meal. And a proper conversation about what we're gonna do now we're stuck out here."

She peered into one of the bags. "A chicken," she said, and the pleasure in her voice gave him a tiny glow of pride. "It's cooked and everything. Still warm. Where'd you get this, Mackenzie?"

He was pleased that she was impressed. Meat was difficult to get hold of now that it wasn't freely imported, and even if he'd been able to buy a chicken in a shop it would have been no good raw. It had taken a good few hours of surreptitiously following interesting-looking people, sniffing the air, and a couple of careful, risky questions to get hold of this one. And even then, if he was really honest, he probably wouldn't have managed it if he hadn't spotted one of the chickens making a break for freedom under a garden fence. He'd mumbled his way through an awkward conversation with the owner with his hood pulled over his face – pet ownership did not equal Northern sympathies – and the woman had looked ready to slam the door in his face until Mackenzie had shown her a big wodge of cash. That had loosened up the conversation enough that she'd agreed to cook the chicken for him and thrown in a bag of apples too. Then she'd mentioned that she knew a couple of other people with produce he might be interested in, and so he'd gone to investigate while the chicken was cooking. He had paid a frankly ludicrous price for the bird, but it was only partly about the food, and partly about hoping that she would remember him fondly if the Board turned up.

Skyler slunk into the room behind them and he grinned. Even she couldn't keep up her usual degree of sullen indifference in the face of a hot meal. "What's with all this?" she asked, moving forward to help him unpack the apples, a loaf of bread and a lump of cheese.

"I figured it's time we sat down and made a plan. And if we could not end up murdering each other, that'd be good too."

She held up a large glass bottle. "And what's this?"

"Not sure exactly, but I'm assured it's alcoholic."

"What's it for?"

"Well, I don't know about you, but I could really do with a drink."

She opened the last package and snorted. "Plates. You bought crockery."

"What, you want to eat off the floor?" He started trying to carve the chicken with a table knife. Out of nowhere, Angel produced a much sharper knife with a long thin blade and offered it to him.

He gave it a dubious look. "You stabbed anybody with that?"

"Not recently," Angel said cheerfully.

"I'll stick with this one," he muttered.

When they were settled on the floor, balancing their plates on their knees, there were a few minutes of satisfied silence before he said, "So we still need to talk."

Angel nodded. "We might be okay here for a bit, but as soon as we advertise our presence – if any of us does any work, for example – there's a chance it'll get back to Redruth's people. He's got. . . extensive contacts. Plus, at some point the Board will probably get one or both of your names out of someone."

Mackenzie tried to focus on his food and not on the crashing panic that threatened to overwhelm him at her words. "One thing at a time. Skyler shot Redruth. He might be dead."

"I wouldn't bank on it," Angel said flatly. "Not without proof."

"Well – Skyler, you could find out, right, if you could get on the internet?"

Skyler had been attacking her food as though she was afraid it was going to walk off her plate. Now she looked up, frowning. "Yeah, I could. If I had my laptop." She gave him a reproachful look, which he chose to ignore.

"Right," he said. "So that's that. The Board. . . I don't know what we do about them."

"Me either." Angel put down her fork and sighed. "Is it time for the alcohol yet?"

"I thought you'd never ask," Mackenzie said. He handed her the bottle. "So basically, we sit here until the bad guys start crashing around and then...what? We go on the run again?"

"You got a better idea?"

"Well, for one thing, you realise none of this is your problem? You didn't kill Redruth and you didn't have anything at all to do with the memory stick. You could walk away from all this if you wanted."

She looked amused. "Are you saying that's what you want me to do?"

"Well, no. No thanks. I'm just saying. You could."

Angel looked from him to Skyler. She said, as if he hadn't spoken, "Hey, I have a question."

Skyler lifted her head. "Hmm?"

"What AJ said about helping you get home after the Wall went up. What'd he mean?"

Mackenzie raised his eyebrows. He couldn't imagine Skyler would be willing to talk about this.

For a long moment, Skyler didn't say anything. Then she grabbed the mystery bottle and gave it an appraising look. She took a swig and choked, clapping a hand to her mouth. "Ugh," she spluttered. "What *is* that?"

He laughed. "It gets better."

She screwed her face up. "I don't believe you." She took another gulp and glanced at Angel. "It was true, what AJ said. After the Wall went up, I was down here and my family were in the North. I didn't really understand what was happening. I told him I wanted to go home."

Angel's brow wrinkled. "I thought no one got over the Wall."

"Well, it turns out you can get into the North if you know the right people. He introduced me to Daniel."

Mackenzie had never heard this part of the story before. Angel's mouth fell open. "He did *what*?"

Skyler shrugged. "I guess he figured Daniel could make it happen. He was right. The Board do reconnaissance trips over the Wall sometimes. He bribed a greycoat to take me with him."

"Bloody hell," Angel said. "You were thirteen. What was he thinking?"

Skyler pushed her food around her plate. "He was trying to help. He didn't know. . . what it was like over there. And I don't think he understood how bad an idea it was to owe Daniel a favour."

"Moron," Mackenzie muttered.

She glanced at him. "Did you ever meet Daniel?"

He shook his head. "I didn't even know it was him I was working for."

"Well, count yourself lucky. I heard so many people who'd just met him for the first time say they couldn't believe all the horrible stories, he was so *nice*." She pulled a disgusted face. "And that was the thing – he did act really nice, until suddenly he wasn't anymore. And you never knew when it was coming."

"Why do you think he was. . . like he was?" Mackenzie said. "I mean, some of the stories about him, they were like. . . next level stuff. It wasn't just that he had a temper. Normal people don't do stuff like that."

"I've no idea how he turned out that way," Skyler said. "And I don't care. But you're right – it wasn't about having a temper. I mean, he did, but it was more than that – he *thought* about how to hurt people. He enjoyed it. I think he built up that whole criminal empire because it gave him an excuse to make people scared of him." She wrapped her arms around herself as though trying to protect herself.

Angel reached for the bottle and took a long drink, then another one. Mackenzie stared at Skyler. "That must've been –"

"Yeah. It was." She sighed. "And I know, I know, I worked for him. And I was being selfish, because it was that or live on the streets. And I guess that makes me as bad as him."

"That's not true. You're nothing like him."

"Well." She looked away from him. "I tried, anyway. When he got me to find information for him, I'd take out important bits, stuff I thought might get someone hurt. I did my best. I don't know if that makes any difference."

"Sounds pretty dangerous."

"It was the least I could do."

He frowned. "You were just trying to survive, Sky. We all are. We're all just doing the best we can."

Angel, he realised suddenly, had gone very still. She hadn't touched her food while they'd been talking about Redruth.

"Hey," Skyler said to her. "You okay?"

She nodded and took another gulp from the bottle.

"You sure?"

"Yeah. So – you actually went back to the North?"

"Uh. That's right."

"But then how did you get back here?"

Skyler's face closed down even more than usual. Mackenzie didn't think she was going to say anything at all. Then, unexpectedly, her eyes flitted towards him.

He did his best to keep his expression neutral.

She reached for the bottle again. "Sorry," she said, giving Angel a small, apologetic smile. "I'm nowhere near drunk enough to tell you that story."

Mackenzie let out a quiet, grateful sigh.

"What was it like?" Angel asked. "In the North, after the

Wall went up? I still don't really understand what happened up there."

He blinked. He'd spent so much time trying to forget everything that had happened that it somehow hadn't occurred to him that other people might not even know.

He opened his mouth to answer and realised he couldn't. Trying to put it all into words felt like a kind of curse.

Skyler knew, though. She understood. And, to his gratitude, she answered so he didn't have to.

"They cut everything off," she said. "No electricity. No fuel. No clean water. No one allowed in or out. It was. . . You can't even imagine. It was like a nightmare."

"I'm sorry," Angel said quietly. "I didn't know."

Mackenzie reached for the alcohol, which tasted faintly of apples and strongly of paint stripper. He should probably slow down – but God, it was such a relief. The alcohol was doing something no amount of cleaning or retracing his steps could: it was slowing his thoughts, adding a layer of protective padding between him and all the horrors that lay like traps beneath the surface of his mind.

"So." Angel took the bottle from him, and he relinquished it a little reluctantly. "We're out in the arse end of nowhere. Bad guys are after us and they're not going to give up any time soon. And we've got the memory stick. What do you both want to do with that?"

He waited for Skyler to say "Decrypt it, obviously." Instead, to his amazement, she looked at him again. "It's yours, I guess," she said. She sounded extremely grudging, but he had never heard her concede anything to anyone before and it struck him that it must have been costing her a great deal to do so now. "It's up to you."

"You think there's something important on there. Something the Board don't want to get out."

She nodded.

He tried *so hard* not to think about the North. About his life before the Wall went up, and afterwards. He buried it, all the time, and he hated himself for doing that because it was a betrayal of his parents, his sister Bex, his friends.

But he had to because if he let himself think about any of it he would break apart.

"What would you need to try and crack it?" he said. "Another laptop, or your own one fixed?"

"I don't think I could get a good enough replacement. There are programs on it that I wrote myself. I need it fixed."

"Right." He could hardly believe what he was about to say. "That answers that, then."

"It does?"

"Two birds with one stone, right? If we fix your laptop, you can crack the encryption and find out what happened to Redruth."

Skyler's eyes were so bright with enthusiasm she was almost unrecognisable. She looked alive.

Since they'd first met, when both of them had been fighting too hard to survive to be enthusiastic about anything much, she'd always been pretty much the same during Mackenzie's rare encounters with her: intensely focused, monosyllabic, and almost entirely lacking in a sense of humour. Now it occurred to him that if he'd been living in Redruth's cellar all that time he probably wouldn't have had much of a sense of humour either.

"You mean it?" she said. "We're really gonna do this?"

He shrugged. "Guess so."

"Why?"

He grabbed the now rather empty bottle from Angel and upended it. "Screw it. The Board are gonna come after us anyway. We might as well use the damn thing."

20

BOSCOMBE

Skyler woke early the next morning to a throbbing ache in her skull and a stomach insisting that it needed to eject its contents. She just made it to the bathroom before the previous night's meal made a reappearance.

She hunched over the toilet bowl, her stomach heaving. What had she been thinking? Alcohol had never even been in her frame of reference before. It could only have made her more vulnerable than she already was.

Perhaps last night was the first time she'd ever felt safe enough to think about getting drunk.

A fresh wave of nausea sent her doubling back over the bowl. All things considered, it had probably not been worth it.

A floorboard creaked behind her. As she looked round, Mackenzie folded himself up just outside the bathroom and slid a bottle of water towards her. He, too, looked a little fragile.

"All right?" he croaked.

Skyler wiped her streaming eyes and gulped some water. "You fucking poisoned me."

He laughed. "You never had a hangover before?"

She screwed her eyes up against the light. Their voices

were making her head pound. "What do you think?"

"Right," he said. "Sorry. Listen. You up for finding someone to fix your laptop?"

"Today?"

He nodded. "I might've found somewhere you could get an introduction."

"You did?"

He looked modest. "I think so. You'll have to wait till tonight. And you'll probably want to take Angel with you."

She drank some more water and leaned against the bathroom wall. "What's got into you, Mack? A few days ago you were ready to fight me for that drive."

"I'll take that as a thank you." He shrugged. "Well, you weren't going to give the bloody thing up, were you? And – well." He swallowed. "You were right. About the Board. If you can find a way to hurt them, Sky, I'm gonna help you do it."

He stood up. "You gonna be all right?"

She nodded. As he tiptoed away, she said, "Hey. Mack. Thank you."

That evening, when darkness had fallen and the worst of Skyler's hangover had subsided, she and Angel set out into Bournemouth.

The address Mackenzie had given them was a couple of miles away in a place called Boscombe. It meant a long walk during curfew hours – something she would have avoided at all costs back in Birmingham, where she'd conducted her business virtually whenever possible – but here, somehow, Angel's presence gave her courage.

The enforcers were much less visible than they were in Birmingham; it was well past curfew but they'd only had to duck into a side alley once to avoid a Board vehicle.

Following Mackenzie's directions, they cut through a deserted, overgrown park to the sea front and turned left past a row of shabby beach huts. Beside the wide, sandy beach sat a large white building which the lettering on its twin domes proclaimed to be the Oceanarium. A pier stretched out to sea, dark, motionless fairground rides silhouetted in the moonlight. Skyler had been on holiday somewhere similar once when she was very small. She remembered the squeal of the arcade games, the music, the gaudy lights glowing against the evening sky. The electricity to run something like that must have cost a fortune.

When they reached the smaller pier at Boscombe they turned away from the sea front into another, much darker park, crowded with trees which blocked out the moonlight. A more familiar unease crept back up on Skyler. She stuck a little closer to Angel, who put a brief, reassuring hand on the small of her back.

Out of the park, they reached a row of apartment buildings with wide windows and, further along the road, houses with bay windows and small balconies. Like everywhere else, there were few signs of activity. Lights glowed behind curtains in a few apartment windows, but the houses were all in darkness. Skyler wondered if they'd come to the right place.

Then, ahead of them, two men stumbled out of a shadowy doorway and staggered off into the night. Angel put out a hand to her. "I think we've found it."

No bouncers stood guard outside. Skyler expected the door to be locked, but when Angel tried it, it swung open. They stepped through into velvety blackness. The floor vibrated with a faint, thudding bass.

Angel touched her arm. "This way."

Skyler couldn't see a thing, so she took Angel's word for

it. "Stairs," Angel murmured, a guiding hand still on her arm, and they began a careful descent. Skyler thought that in her old life she could never have imagined how much of another world was hidden underground. And that one day she'd be happy never to set foot in another cellar, if there ever came a time when all of this was over.

They were halfway down the stairs when a sudden light flared in the blackness at the bottom. She gasped.

The lantern illuminated a heavy-set woman with slicked back hair and a leather jacket. Her stony face became less friendly still as she peered at them. "I think you might be in the wrong place, ladies."

Angel met her stare head on. "Looks about right to me."

The bouncer adjusted her stance. "Yeah? Not local, you two, are you?"

"No," Angel said. "We're visiting."

"Visiting." The woman was sceptical.

"We're looking to do some business. No trouble."

"Oh, good." The bouncer's mouth twitched. "Wouldn't want any of that, would we?"

"I should think not." Angel stepped forward. "Look, my friend and I are busy. The sooner you let us in, the sooner we'll be out again."

The bouncer didn't move. "What brings you down here, then? Hardly a holiday destination, is it?"

"Look," Angel said. "We could go through a whole pantomime where I make up a nice convincing story and you pretend to believe me. Or you could just let us in."

The bouncer scrutinised them, considering. At last, she stepped to one side and motioned grudgingly at the door behind her. As Angel went to pass her, though, the woman caught her by the arm.

Angel gave her hand a long stare, but said nothing.

"No trouble," the bouncer said. "I mean it."

"Not from us," Angel agreed. She removed her arm from the woman's grip with a deliberate movement and walked on past.

The door opened into a long, low-ceilinged room. Inside, small groups clustered around battered, mismatched tables, their faces lit by lumpy candles jammed into bottles and flickering in brackets on the walls. A buzz of chatter hummed below the beat from an ancient, battery-powered radio.

When Angel and Skyler entered, the bar's occupants looked up as a collective. Skyler made out muscles tensing, hands reaching towards belts and under jackets. A lot of eyes looking them up and down, sizing them up. In more ways than one.

Angel strolled over to the bar and leaned her elbows on the counter as though she hadn't noticed any of this. "Hiya," she said to the barman, who managed to imbue his nod of acknowledgement with an impressive lack of enthusiasm.

"I'll have an apple juice, please," she said. "And the same for my friend."

He gave her an incredulous look, but poured the drinks and set them on the counter.

"Bathroom?" Angel asked.

He pointed to the far end of the room, into the shadows. Angel glanced at Skyler. "You okay here a minute?"

She really didn't want Angel to leave her on her own, but it would have been too humiliating to admit that. She nodded.

"I'll only be a second."

You're fine. You're fine. Skyler stood at the bar, motionless, trying to block out the watching eyes, the pinprick stabs of danger on her skin. *You're fine.*

The barman's eyes flicked up over her shoulder. Before

she could look round, a bulky, solid weight pressed up against her.

She shifted, trying to get away, but the man moved with her. His hands rested against the bar either side of her, pinning her in place. Her heart hammered against her ribcage.

Stamp on his foot. Elbow him in the stomach. Scream. Do something.

She couldn't move.

His breath brushed the back of her neck and a sick lump rose in her throat. She still couldn't move.

The pressure against her body vanished. Angel's voice, cool and measured, said, "Get the fuck off her."

The conversations around them stopped abruptly. Skyler turned, her legs shaking treacherously, to see Angel behind a bald man with a shaved head and a neatly trimmed beard, holding one of his arms twisted behind his back.

Every pair of eyes in the room was fixed on them. Angel, apparently oblivious to the audience, shoved the bald man up against the bar. "The bouncer explained very politely that she didn't want any trouble," she said, loud enough for her words to carry to the corners of the room. She adjusted her grip and the man stifled a yelp. "So you get one warning. If you even look at my friend again, I'll make you wish all I'd done was break your fucking arm. Understand?"

When he said nothing, she jerked his arm again. He groaned. "*Do you understand?*"

He mumbled something that could possibly have been interpreted as a "yes." Angel let go of him and he swung towards her, shoulders squared, fists clenched. She didn't take her eyes off him. Her face was blank and cold and hard.

Skyler's chest was so tight it hurt.

There was a long moment in which no one moved, before the bald man slunk towards the exit.

Angel watched the door close behind him. Then, still ignoring the rest of the room, she pulled up a stool and took a sip of her drink.

Skyler perched uncertainly next to her. Angel touched her hand. "You all right?"

She nodded, not sure whether she was telling the truth.

"I'm sorry," Angel said. "I shouldn't have left you."

Skyler shook her head. "It's fine."

"We can go if you want."

"No." Skyler made her voice as firm as she could. "It's okay. I'm okay."

Across the room, somebody murmured something. Someone else sniggered.

The hum of chatter resumed. At length, a young man came and pulled up a stool a couple of feet from Angel.

"Well," she said, studying her glass. "You're not close enough to try to grope me, so I assume you must be wanting a sensible conversation."

"We could give it a go," the man agreed. He was of Asian descent, with bright brown eyes and a bounce to his demeanour that put Skyler in mind of an overgrown schoolboy. "Think I met a friend of yours last night."

"Is that right?" Angel said.

The man sipped his beer. "Smart kid. Said you're looking for someone who knows computers."

"He might have been right."

"You're not from around here, are you?"

She shook her head. He regarded her thoughtfully. "North?"

The word triggered a violent pulse through Skyler's veins, but Angel didn't even blink. "Would that be a problem?"

"Not with me. Enforcers. . . they're the same everywhere."

"Right," Angel said. "I'm not really looking to meet any enforcers."

"So what do you need?"

Angel took another sip of her juice and nodded at Skyler, who found her voice. "Someone who knows hardware and has access to decent parts. I need them to work quickly and not ask questions."

The man nodded slowly. "That's not gonna be cheap."

"I can pay."

He carried on nodding. "I think I know just the person. I'm Rob, by the way."

"Nice to meet you, Rob." Angel shook his outstretched hand and Skyler reluctantly did the same. "So, can you sort us an introduction?"

"Yeah, why not?" He waved at the sullen barman. "Hey mate, you got a bit of paper?"

The barman shoved a scrap of cardboard and a pencil across the bar. Rob scribbled an address and, after a moment's thought, added a figure too. "Basic fee," he said, handing it to Skyler. "Parts are extra, obviously."

"Look reasonable?" Angel asked her.

She shrugged. "Sure."

"Looks like you've got yourself a job," Angel told Rob.

"I'll meet you there tomorrow night at eight," he said. "Whatever needs fixing, bring it with you. Bring the cash, too."

Angel tucked the card away inside her jacket. "Thanks."

Rob glanced around the room and lowered his voice. "You look like you can handle yourself. But just watch yourself, yeah?" He gestured towards the door. "That Brendan, he's a bit. . . tantrum-prone. Doesn't like being shown up."

Angel grinned. "Thanks for the warning."

"You planning on sticking around long?"

"Probably not."

"Shame," Rob said. "Between you and me, I proper enjoyed that."

21

RESCUE ME

As they walked back towards the sea front, Skyler had a strange urge to fill the quiet between her and Angel. This time together, private and peaceful, felt like an unexpected treat. But Angel was silent, and Skyler didn't know what to say.

They reached the park and entered the darkness of the barren trees. Skyler finally found the courage to speak. "Angel? I wanted to ask –"

Angel laid a hand on her arm. "Shh. Not now."

Skyler recoiled. She'd never expected Angel to silence her. Angel wasn't even looking at her; her eyes were fixed on the shadows ahead of them.

Footsteps echoed behind them. Skyler glanced over her shoulder to see a shadowy figure hurrying towards them. She swung back to Angel, and another dark shape detached itself from the shadows ahead of them. All at once, she understood where Angel's attention had been.

The two figures closed in on them. She tried to keep her eyes on them both, but it was impossible.

A freezing wave of terror crashed over her, scouring her raw, rolling her over and over until she didn't know where she was or what was happening. She was choking, inky water in her mouth, in her nose, and all she could think of was Daniel's hands around her throat, Milo grabbing her by her hair.

Angel's voice cut through the roaring in her ears, pulling her back to the present: "Don't move. Trust me."

When Skyler fought her way back to the surface, Angel was no longer by her side, but was darting forward to meet the figure in front of them. In the shadows, Skyler saw blurred movement, heard damp thuds, fists and feet connecting with tissue. A grunt and a quickly-stifled male groan. No sound at all from Angel. Skyler stood frozen, the winter air crystallising in her lungs, as the second man strode past her, the moonlight bouncing off his shaved head. Brendan.

She was lost in the storm again, blinded, suffocating.

The first man did something to Angel that made her gasp and double over and Skyler slammed back into her body with a white-hot bolt. She lurched towards them, fumbling for the knife in her belt.

And then Angel fought back.

Closer now, Skyler saw that her movements were lithe, graceful, like a dancer. She spun and kicked out at the first man. Her foot connected with a *snap* and he buckled, howling. Angel kicked him again, hard, and the howling stopped.

Something cold and sharp pressed against Skyler's neck, and all her muscles locked together.

Everything went very still. Angel stood a few feet away, her face in shadow. Skyler wanted to tell her she was sorry, but she didn't dare move.

"Let go of her," Angel said, for the second time that evening.

Brendan laughed. "Or what? I'm a lot closer than you are, love."

Angel didn't move. Skyler wondered if she could still reach her knife. She twitched her fingers experimentally and Brendan's fingers dug into her arm.

Maybe not, then.

I know this type. He's not going to cut my throat. Not before he's got what he wants from me.

Probably, anyway.

She grabbed the hand wrapped around her arm and yanked Brendan's little finger back as hard as she could.

It didn't *quite* work. Brendan roared and the pressure of the blade disappeared from her throat, but then he turned and slapped her across the face so hard she tasted blood. Skyler stumbled. He lunged at her –

A resounding *crack* echoed off the trees surrounding them. Brendan screamed, staggered backwards and hit the ground.

While Skyler was still trying to figure out what had just happened, Angel lowered her gun and stepped towards her. "You all right?"

Skyler tried to catch her breath. "Yeah. Are you?"

"Don't you worry about me."

"We should go," Skyler said.

Angel looked at Brendan, moaning on the ground behind them, and tipped her head to one side as though considering something. She raised the gun again.

"Angel," Skyler said softly.

A heartbeat, and another one. Angel turned back to her. "Let's go."

They walked back to the sea front in silence. Skyler tried, unsuccessfully, to stop herself shaking.

"You should've let me handle it," Angel said as they

reached Boscombe Pier. "I didn't realise –"

"I'm sorry," Skyler said. "I didn't mean to get in the way – I just – couldn't just watch them hurt you."

Gently, Angel pulled Skyler round to face her. "You're shaking."

"I'm all right."

"You're bleeding, too."

Skyler touched her throbbing lip. Her fingers came away wet. "It's nothing."

Angel's eyes were still on her, dark in the moonlight. Skyler swallowed and looked down at her boots.

Fingers brushed across her chin. She lifted her head in surprise.

"I'm sorry." Angel's voice was a strange mixture of concern and amusement. Her hand lingered on Skyler's cheek. "I didn't mean for you to get hurt." She gave a small laugh. "I didn't expect you to try to take him on yourself."

Skyler raised her eyebrows. "Well, maybe next time I'll just wait for you to rescue me."

Angel's lips twitched in a smile. Skyler took a deep, shaky breath.

"You stopped coming to see me," Angel said. "I hadn't seen you for months before this week."

"I know. I – I didn't think you'd notice."

"I noticed."

"I wanted to see you. But. . . I knew how busy you were. And – I. . ."

"You were scared."

She nodded. "I thought if he found out what I was doing – that I was seeing you – he might –"

Something in Angel's face shut down. She dropped her hand, and Skyler felt its absence like an ache.

"We'd better get on," Angel said.

Courage. "Angel? Do we. . . have to go straight back?"

"What did you have in mind?"

Skyler's cheeks flushed hot. "I don't know. Sorry. Stupid of me."

Angel looked from her to the pier in front of them. Then she reached out and took Skyler's hand. "C'mon."

Skyler had almost forgotten what it was like to feel warm: properly warm, the languid, enveloping heat of summer sunshine that soaked into your muscles and flowed, syrupy, through your veins. But inexplicably, as she followed Angel onto the pier, that was the memory that stirred, somewhere in a part of her mind she thought she'd walled up long ago. As they reached the end of the pier and stood side by side, looking out to sea, she glanced up at Angel and the words came out unbidden: "I missed you."

"I missed you too."

"Can I ask you something?"

"Sure. Anything."

"Where'd you learn all that? Who taught you?"

Angel took a long breath. "That's a good question. I. . . taught myself."

"How?"

She shrugged. "You know what it's like. People see a teenage girl and they think they can do what they like. You either get pushed around, or. . ."

"Or you push back."

Angel gave her a small smile. "Half of it's about reputation. The best thing I ever did was make people think I was crazy. The first time I went into a bar and some guy groped me I ran away. The second time, I pulled a knife."

Skyler half laughed. "That doesn't sound like the safest strategy."

"Well," Angel said. "I didn't really have anything to lose."

They leaned against the metal railings, not quite touching. The waning moon left a shimmering path in the satiny water. Angel gave a small, contented sigh. Skyler stayed quiet, not wanting to disturb her tranquillity.

In the end, it was Angel who broke the silence. "It happened by accident, you know," she said. "What I am. What I do, I mean."

She seemed to want something from Skyler. "How did it happen?" Skyler asked.

"Well. You have to play to your strengths, don't you? It turned out I'm good at fighting. I got a bit of a reputation and then one day someone came to me and said look, there's this guy over on Ladywood terrorising half the estate. Enforcers weren't interested – he *was* an enforcer. They didn't know what to do, so they came to me and I agreed to. . . help. And I guess it just went from there."

"Weren't you scared? I would've been."

"A bit. Scared of screwing up, mostly. These people had put their trust in me and if I cocked it up, they'd have been in even more trouble than before."

"But the job itself – that didn't scare you?"

"It's hard to explain, but. . . no. And it was weird, because afterwards I thought I'd feel guilty but I didn't. I was glad he couldn't hurt anyone else. I felt like I'd done something good."

"I don't feel bad," Skyler said, startling herself. "About Jen and Milo, or Daniel. I think maybe I should, but I don't."

"How do you feel?"

She probed inside herself for an answer. "I don't really feel anything," she said at last. "Except that they had it coming."

Angel nodded.

"Mackenzie would feel bad. He'd be torturing himself over it." Skyler pressed herself against the railing and stared into the black water below. "D'you think there's something wrong with me, because I'm not?"

"Mackenzie didn't have to live through what you did," Angel said. "I don't think there's anything wrong with you." She was quiet for a moment. "I don't want you to think – I don't feel guilty about taking out people who deserve it, but I don't enjoy it. I'm not like *him*."

Skyler looked up, brushing her hair out of her eyes. "I'd never think that. Besides, it's pretty obvious you're not. I mean, I can't see any of that lot running a healing business on the side, can you?"

A noise that was almost a laugh. "Perhaps not."

"How'd you end up doing that, anyway?"

"Oh." This time Angel did laugh. "I haven't got any medical training. Again, I just taught myself. But healthcare's expensive, you know? And you can't go to a hospital without ID – well, you know that. I suppose I feel like it evens things out a little bit." She snorted. "I guess that sounds pretty stupid."

Skyler shrugged. "I lived in a cellar for two and a half years. Who am I to tell you what's smart?"

Angel glanced at her. "You did what you had to do, didn't you?"

"Yeah. I guess I did."

"And what about you? All the computer stuff? You must've learned it before the Wall went up. How does a thirteen-year-old know all that?"

Skyler blinked. No one had ever asked her about this before. "It was my older brother, really," she said. "I was always messing around on his computer, so he started teaching me programming. We started sort of competing with each other

– we'd try and hack into each other's computers, change the passwords, stuff like that." She giggled, to her own surprise, at the memory that came into her head. "I used to mess around on the school networks, trying to bypass the firewalls. I must've been about – eleven? That got me suspended from school, and I spent the whole time at home on the internet learning new things. How to break passwords, find flaws in code... It's addictive. Way better than being in school. There's always something new to learn."

"I can just picture you wreaking havoc and then looking innocent while everything went haywire around you." Angel sounded amused.

"Ha. Yeah. After that I used to sneak home during the day to get online. Up till the last year before the Wall, anyway. It got a lot harder then."

"The power rationing."

"Yeah." Skyler bit her lip. "The electricity got so expensive I wasn't allowed to use the computer at home, but I was stupid – and an asshole... I kept sneaking on anyway, and I ran up some massive bills. My mum was so angry – And then they just started cutting the power off altogether."

She fell silent, watching the tiny pinpoint lights of a ship at the horizon. She'd never been able to exorcise the sickly spectre of the guilt that clung to her when she thought about how much she'd failed to understand back then.

"Tell me about your brother," Angel said suddenly. "What was he called?"

Her throat ached. "My – uh, my brother?"

Angel touched her arm. "Only if you want to."

The touch gave her strength, somehow. She realised that she did want to talk about him.

"He was called Sam," she said. "He was six years older than me and I basically hero-worshipped him. I must've driven him nuts, but he never showed it. I never knew my dad, my mum split up with him before I was born. Sam's dad lived in Southampton and he only saw him a couple of times a year – so it was just the three of us, and we were really close. He made me feel... like we were on the same team."

"He was smart? Like you?"

"Yeah. One of our teachers said to Mum once it was a good thing there was such a big age gap between us because the school would've never coped with both of us for more than a year. He was... better with people than me, though. He was funny, so he had lots of friends. Most people thought I was a bit weird, to be honest. But he didn't." She shook her head and laughed. "Our mum was a really outdoorsy sort of person. She loved hiking and camping and all that. Somehow she ended up with two kids who would've lived in front of a computer if she'd let us."

"It's good," Angel murmured. "You had someone who got you."

"I missed him like crazy when he went to uni. He went to Oxford and I knew I was supposed to be excited for him, but I hated it."

"Oxford? So he was in the South?"

Skyler closed her eyes. "Yeah. I know what you're thinking, but he was home for the Christmas break when the Wall went up. And anyway – he was a Northern citizen, he'd lived in Leeds all his life. The Board would've never let him stay in the South..."

She'd worked hard to keep each word measured, steady. Still she hadn't been able to stop her voice from wobbling. Now, when she tried to keep talking, the words dissolved into salt water instead.

Angel's hand tightened on her arm. Skyler wiped her eyes and tried to force the tears away. "I'm sorry," she whispered.

"No," Angel said, and her voice, too, was ragged, uneven. "I understand. It hurts. All the time. I know. I'm sorry."

Skyler took a deep breath. "What about you? Have you got brothers or sisters?"

No answer. When Skyler turned to Angel, her shoulders were shaking. Her hand was still on Skyler's arm, but she'd turned her face away.

The salty wind blowing in from the ocean stung Skyler's wet cheeks. She let it. She kept breathing. There was nothing else she could do.

"Sky?" Angel said at last, sounding more like her normal self. "How'd you end up in the South?"

"What?" The question came out sharper than she'd meant it.

To her surprise, Angel sounded awkward. "I didn't mean to upset you – I just wondered –" She shook her head. "You were so young to end up here by yourself."

Skyler said nothing. Angel said, "You don't have to –"

"It's okay," Skyler said. "It's just I don't normally – well. You know." She squeezed her hands around the railing in front of her. "I... was an idiot, basically. A few days before the Wall went up, I broke into the school computer labs and hacked a Board website."

"Seriously?" Angel sounded almost impressed.

She nodded. "Our power got shut off at home because I'd gone over our ration and my mum couldn't pay the fine. I managed to get into the database and change their records. Mum was so upset – I thought I was helping." She swallowed. She hadn't counted on how much it would hurt, putting all this into words. "But then the greycoats turned up at the school."

"Oh, no."

"Yeah. I panicked. I thought they'd put me in prison, maybe Mum too. I ran away."

Angel waited.

"I got on the first bus I found and ended up in Birmingham scared out of my mind. Spent a couple of days sleeping in doorways before I convinced myself I was overreacting and decided I'd just go home and deal with it."

"And then the Wall went up," Angel said quietly.

"Then the Wall went up." Skyler sighed. "So... here I am."

22

HELPING HANDS

The next evening, Angel came to find Skyler at about five in the evening. "But we're not supposed to be there till eight," Skyler reminded her.

Angel gave her a slow, enigmatic smile. "I know. We're going to get there early, just in case they've got any funny ideas."

She frowned. "D'you think they're planning something?"

"Not really. But we're new here and we don't know these people. It doesn't hurt to be safe."

"That happened to you before?"

Angel pulled on her jacket. "Once. I learned from it."

The address Rob had given them was for an apartment in a high rise on the outskirts of town, with no lights in the hallways and a lingering sharp, unpleasant smell in the lobby. Skyler wrinkled her nose. "Gross."

"I know," Angel murmured.

The flat was on the fifth floor. When Angel banged on the door, a snatch of muffled conversation came from inside before a boy in his late teens wrenched it open. Behind a long fringe of shiny blue-black hair was a pair of bright blue eyes, and a scowl. "You're early," he snapped.

"Yeah," Angel agreed. "Are you going to let us in?"

He held the door open as if doing them a considerable favour. "I suppose you might as well."

They stepped through into a small living room with dark, peeling wallpaper and a stained and threadbare carpet. It was lit only by candlelight, but Skyler spotted a couple of lamps, a small, dusty television and a table covered with an assortment of wires and circuitry. Rob, the man from the bar, was sprawled in a battered armchair with his feet up on a coffee table. He caught her eye and winked.

Angel stood beside her, close enough that their arms brushed against each other. The boy looked at the bag across her back. "That it?"

"Yes," Skyler said reluctantly. She hadn't let anyone else lay a hand on her laptop since the day she got it and she was less than thrilled at the prospect of handing it over to a stranger with a silly haircut. She unhooked the bag, but held it protectively to her.

The boy's lips twisted, sceptical. "You must be a hacker."

She raised her eyebrows. "I must?"

"You don't look rich enough to own a laptop just for the sake of it, and you're not old enough to have one for work. And if you did you wouldn't be bringing it to me anyway. Where'd you learn how to use it, preschool?"

"I'm not sure how that'd be any of your business," Skyler said. "The only thing you need to know is that I'm paying you to fix it."

Rob stood up, laughing, and slung an arm around the boy's shoulders. "This is Fox," he said. "He doesn't really know how to talk to people. He makes up for it by being a freaking magician with technology, though."

"Let's hope so," Angel said mildly.

Fox looked at her. "If she's the hacker, who're you? Her babysitter?"

"She's the one I told you about," Rob said.

Fox's expression changed. "More like her bodyguard then, by the sound of it."

"How about we just get on with this?" Skyler said. The guy was irritating her already and he hadn't even touched her laptop yet. She slid it out of the bag and handed it to him.

He held it up to the nearest candle, wearing an expression of admiration mixed with envy. "What the hell you been doing with this? You know how expensive these are? Especially one like this... Where'd you *get* this?"

"Someone fell on it," Skyler said, failing to keep the resentment out of her voice. "And I'm well aware of how expensive it was. Please try not to destroy it."

Fox used his arm to sweep everything on the table into a pile and set the laptop down. He plugged the cable into the wall socket and then looked up at her. "You realise I'm gonna be charging you for the power as well?"

"I'm not an idiot. Turn it on."

"Just making sure we're clear." He pressed the power button and the computer whirred quietly into life. After a couple of seconds, it beeped loudly. The cracked screen lit the room with a blue glow.

Fox lifted the machine and pulled a face. "I'm gonna need some proper light for this. That'll be extra."

She waved a hand. "Fine. How long's it going to take?"

He considered. "A day?"

"You sure?"

"Barring unforeseen complications. I assume you want the hard drive intact?"

"If it's not, I won't be paying you *anything*."

Rob coughed out a laugh. "I see the two of you went to the same school of social communication. I bet you'd get on like a house on fire."

"I doubt it," Fox said.

Skyler had been about to offer the same opinion. She glared at Fox. "Just don't break it."

"You mean, any more than it's already broken? Don't worry, I actually know how to look after an expensive piece of kit. Besides, I wouldn't mind a look at what you've got on here."

She snorted. "Yeah, right."

"Oh, you don't think I could get into it?"

"I *know* you won't be able to. And if you want to keep the use of both your hands I'd suggest you don't try."

He put the laptop back down. "Big talk, small stuff. I guess whoever taught you how to use a machine like this didn't also teach you to talk nicely to the person who's gonna fix it for you."

"Do you want me to pretend you're smarter than me, or do you want me to pay you?"

Angel cleared her throat and stepped forward. "How about we draw the pissing contest to a close? Fox, you said you need a day, so we'll be back tomorrow night. You get half the money now and half when Skyler gets her machine back in working order and without any tampering. I'm not going to ask you if we've got a deal. That *is* the deal. If she thinks you've been dicking around with it, you get nothing. Trust me when I say I'll find a way to get the money back."

Fox ignored her. He was back to inspecting the laptop. Rob grinned. "Guess I'd better ask you for the money, then."

Skyler handed him an envelope. He peered inside and nodded in satisfaction. "I think that'll be all, then. See you tomorrow, ladies."

When they got back to the house Mackenzie was sitting cross-legged on the kitchen floor, squinting at a paperback book by candlelight. Only he would have been out stealing books at a time like this.

"What?" he said, at Skyler's raised eyebrow. "I had to pass the time somehow." He peered at her. "You okay? You look grumpy. More than usual, I mean."

She scowled at him. "You're funny."

Angel sat down next to him and examined the cover of his book. "She's worried about leaving her laptop with a stranger."

Skyler blinked. She hadn't said a word to Angel about how she was feeling. It seemed churlish, considering the effort Angel had gone to to help her.

"Ah," Mackenzie said. "You worried he's going to get into it?"

"No." Skyler joined them on the floor. "He won't be able to. And I'll know if he tries."

"Wouldn't like to be him then," Mackenzie said, and Angel grinned.

It might have been the first time she'd seen him sitting still. He was always pacing around the place like he'd lost something important, and he seemed to spend half his time scrubbing relentlessly at the walls or the floor, the same spot over and over. And then there were the times he got outside the front door or even partway down the street, and then turned round and went back into the house as if he'd decided to start the whole endeavour again from the beginning. Often this went on for a long time. She pretended not to notice.

In the daylight, you could see that the skin of his hands was red and cracked and painful-looking. She pretended not to notice that, too. He tried so hard to hide it and he always looked so stricken when she found him cleaning that she thought he'd be embarrassed if she asked about it. And besides, she had no idea what she would say.

He was talking to her. She snapped her attention back to him. "Did I ever tell you," he said, "that you remind me of my sister?"

This was dangerously personal territory. His sister was called Bex, possibly, but she'd only ever heard him talk about her way back when they first met, when all their wounds were still raw and open. The only thing she could think to say was, "I guess your sister must have been a massive pain in the arse, then."

Angel raised her eyebrows and Skyler immediately regretted her words. "Sorry. That wasn't –"

But Mackenzie laughed. "Yeah. Actually, she kind of was."

"What was she like?" Angel asked.

He put the book down on the floor. "Well, she was two years older than me and she thought I was the world's biggest dork. She was always cooler than me. Braver than me, too. She'd bunk off school and climb out of her bedroom window to go to parties, and I was just this kid who did athletics for fun and cried when I got a detention. I used to worry about her all the time – that she'd get in trouble, you know. I worried about it more than she did."

Skyler laughed. "You can't be serious."

"What?" Mackenzie said.

"Sorry. It's just so – well. Here you are, working for gangs, breaking into the *Board's offices*, and you were worried about your sister going to parties? I don't understand you."

He gave her a lopsided smile. "I don't understand me either, all the time."

"Anyway." She leaned against the wall and stretched her legs out in front of her. "So far she doesn't sound much like me. She would've thought I was as big a dork as you."

"Maybe," Mackenzie agreed. "But she never cared what anyone thought of her. Just like you. And she used to give me this look. . ."

"Like what?"

"Like I was a fucking idiot. Again, just like you do."

Angel giggled. "Hey," Skyler protested. "I don't –"

"You kind of do," Angel said. "Sorry."

Was it true, what Mackenzie was saying? Didn't she care what anyone thought of her? She hadn't, back at home. It would have been too painful to care what her classmates thought, because most of them thought she was really weird. If she'd allowed it to matter she'd have been miserable.

She'd cared about what Sam thought, though. That was why she'd pushed herself all the time. She'd wanted to impress him. And she'd wanted to be better than him, too, one day.

In the South, then? Well, how many people did she know whose opinions were worth caring about?

Angel. Perhaps not at first, but somehow, gradually, over time. She'd started to wonder how she appeared, through Angel's eyes; whether Angel approved of what she saw.

"I don't think you're an idiot," she said to Mackenzie.

He looked nonplussed. "Really? Thanks."

"Mack? D'you think about Bex a lot?"

He nodded, slowly, like it hurt. "Yeah."

"I think about Sam a lot, too."

Mackenzie stared at the candle flame as though he'd gone somewhere far away inside his head. She wondered if she should say something else, or poke him, maybe. But then he looked up and said, "D'you want to see a picture of her?"

"You've got photos?" Angel sounded surprised.

He nodded. "After – when I left home, I took a few with me. I don't get them out much. But –"

Angel smiled at him. "I'd love to see them."

"Yeah," Skyler said, and found, unexpectedly, that she meant it. "Me too."

Mackenzie scrambled up and disappeared out of the room. Angel glanced at Skyler. Their hands rested close to one another's on the floor and Skyler thought: *I could move, just a centimetre or two, I could touch her hand.*

And what would she do? Would she be pleased? Would she move away? Would she wonder what the hell I was doing?

Does she think this much about touching me?

Mackenzie clattered back into the room. "Here," he said, holding the photos out. "This is her. This is Bex."

Skyler took the photo by the edges. It showed a girl of about sixteen: long-limbed, dark-haired, with the same thin face as Mackenzie. She was leaning back on a sun lounger, dressed in shorts and a vest top, hand shading her eyes, laughing.

Angel peered over her shoulder. "She's pretty."

Mackenzie held out the second picture. There was Bex, a little younger, with longer hair and her arm around an awkward, gangly Mackenzie. They were standing on top of a wide, flat rock, obviously high up, a hazy greenish-purple expanse of moorland dropping away behind them. Beside them stood a woman with short dark hair and glasses, and a round, olive-skinned bald man. All four of them were grinning broadly at the camera.

"You look happy," Skyler said, studying the photo. She didn't dare look at Mackenzie. She didn't know what she'd do if he cried. "Hey – this is Brimham Rocks, isn't it?"

"That's right. You ever go there?"

"At least twice a year. It was one of my mum's favourite

places." Seeing Angel's puzzled expression, she explained: "It's out in the countryside between Leeds and Harrogate. These massive rock formations, loads of them. Like twice as tall as a house, some of them, and you could just go and climb on them, do whatever you wanted." She grinned at Mackenzie. "I bet you were brilliant at it."

He blushed. "I was pretty good, yeah."

"I was never that good. Or that brave."

She'd thought it would be dangerous to talk like this, to open up all these feelings, like exercising a torn muscle. But Mackenzie seemed to be okay, despite the sadness round his eyes. He was even smiling as he explained to Angel that Brimham Rocks was where he'd got his love of climbing from.

Skyler wished she had something, anything; some tangible memory of Sam and her mum, instead of the ghosts in her head that drifted into fragments when she concentrated too hard, dissolving at the edges when she tried to get a grip on them so she was always left wondering, *was that how it really happened?* But she hadn't known, the day she walked out of her flat for the last time, that that was it. That the greycoats would turn up, that she'd make that split-second decision to run, that by the time she wanted to change her mind, it would be too late.

Mackenzie took the photo from her. "Hey, I've been thinking. You're gonna need an electricity supply, aren't you?"

"Yeah," she said, a little relieved. They were edging back onto safer ground.

"Well, I think I found you one." He sounded rather proud.

She blinked. "What? How? Does Bournemouth have an equivalent of Daniel, by any chance?" Even saying his name felt dangerous, an invitation to fate.

"I have no idea, and do you really think I'd be that stupid? No – you know the power companies shut off the supply as soon as they know a house is empty? But they don't if the owner's only away for a bit. I had a walk up the fancy end of town, found a house with a load of post piling up in the porch. Maybe they're in hospital or something. Can't be anyone going in to collect stuff 'cos they'd have sorted that out by now. It's like they want to be burgled. Anyway, it wasn't hard to get in. The power's still on, and there's a router, too, so I guess they're rich enough for internet. You'd have to be careful, of course. Still. . . might your best shot."

"You might be right," Skyler said. "Uh – could you help me get in, do you think?"

"What, you think I was gonna let you do it by yourself? I'd rather you didn't get caught."

"Ha. Thanks, Mack."

She went to sleep that night astonished. She had not been kind to Mackenzie, on reflection. She had no idea, really, why he'd want to help her now, but for some reason he'd chosen it above his other option of getting as far away from her as possible. Although he did owe her one considerable debt, it seemed like they were going to be more than even by the time this was through.

She sort of wished she didn't find it so difficult to spend time with him because, really, he was all right. If she had friends, if she could remember what that was like, perhaps Mackenzie would be a person she'd like to be friends with. But every time she looked at him she had to work so hard not to slip back into another time and place, and although she knew – of course she knew – that it wasn't his fault, she still found it so very hard to forgive him for it.

23

NORTH

Skyler was walking down a deserted motorway in the middle of the night. It was four months since the Wall had gone up and the Board vehicle that had brought her back over the border from the South had disappeared hours ago, its driver satisfied that he'd done what Daniel had paid him to do. She was alone.

It was early April and there was frost on the ground, the trees still almost bare. The wind cut all the way through her clothes. If she tried to sleep out here she'd freeze, so she kept walking. There was nothing else she could do.

The motorway stretched out in front of her, vast and still. Her only company was the cars abandoned on the hard shoulder, her own footsteps on the crumbling tarmac, and the occasional rustle in the tangle of bushes at the side of the road.

She was tiny in the midst of all this, a piece of driftwood on an empty ocean under a dark and silent sky. This was a place meant for humans, thousands of them, and they were all gone. The world seemed much bigger with only her in it.

Something was terribly wrong. Of course there'd been hardly any petrol in the North even before the Wall went up, so she'd expected the roads to be empty, but she hadn't seen any signs of life at all and that didn't make sense. Millions of people didn't just disappear. They had to be *somewhere*.

As dawn broke, she reached the sign for Mansfield. She recognised the junction from her trips to visit Sam at university. There would be shelter. People. Perhaps someone who could explain this strange new world to her.

She made it up the slip road off the motorway before the breeze wafted a lungful of something dreadful towards her that hit her like a wave.

She doubled over, retching. Some primitive instinct recognised the scent of decay, sickly and heavy, thick on her tongue, and now the terror sprang to life and spiked inside her. Where did a smell like that come from? What did it mean? Surely no one could be living in that town, with that deadly stench.

She turned back to the motorway and ran until her eyes stung with sweat and tears and the stitch stabbing at her ribs forced her to stop.

She needed to get home. It couldn't be that difficult. All she had to do was stay on the motorway and before too long, surely, she would get back to Leeds.

But in the end daylight came and went again before she reached the outskirts of her home city. She'd run out of food and water hours ago and was cursing herself for having been so thoughtless. Her lips were cracked with cold and dehydration, her feet blistered and bloody. She kept her hands shoved deep in her pockets, but they were still reddened and numb.

And she was home. This was what she'd wanted.

She couldn't get the smell from Mansfield out of her mouth and nose. The thought of venturing into Leeds and finding the same thing there made her want to scream.

But she was here now. She'd made her choice.

It was so *quiet*. The Leeds of her memory had never been quiet or dark. Even in the depths of the night there'd always been a background rumble of traffic like the sea on a shore; the gaudy orange streetlights had lit the night when she looked out from their flat on the eleventh floor. Up until the last few months, anyway. She'd been frightened when they first turned the streetlights off and all she could see was a vast expanse of blackness, like being lost in space. It was only temporary, Ruby had assured her; things would be back to normal soon.

The blackness now was oppressive, stifling. There was no moon. Skyler stumbled between abandoned vehicles along the once-familiar path of the motorway into the city, hoping this was how she would finally reach safe ground. But there were still no people, no lights, no sound, and the sense of wrongness grew by the second, a hungry parasite, swelling and grotesque, that she couldn't shake.

By the time she reached the ring road, the sky was lightening and her legs shook with every step. Something buzzed in her ears as she trudged past the signs for Wortley and Armley, past dark houses with boards nailed across the doors, shops with shattered windows and overturned shelves inside. The stillness was overwhelming, like being trapped a museum after closing time. Or a crypt.

And she was aware, through the weariness in her bones and the fuzziness in her head, that she was no longer alone. Someone was nearby, between the out of control weeds and the rusting cars, tracking her.

What was she going to do with this new predator? She could run or she could fight. Except she probably couldn't do either of those things, because she was about to collapse.

A shadow moved on the pavement and her heartbeat quickened. She ducked, grabbed a chunk of tarmac from a pothole, and hurled it.

She was rewarded with a yell. "Argh! What the fuck –?!"

A boy's voice, with a broad Leeds accent. A lump hardened in her throat. She was home. Except this wasn't home anymore.

She should have run then, but before she could make her legs work the owner of the voice erupted onto the road in front of her, clutching his head. "What the bloody hell d'you do that for?" he said. "Jesus!"

She crouched, defensive. "Don't come any closer."

"Don't worry, I wasn't going to! You might hit me with another fucking rock!"

"Why were you following me?"

He was a little taller than her and even skinnier than she was, his clothes grimy and ragged, dark hair falling into his eyes. He moved lightly, one hand over the cut on his forehead that was pouring blood. "You could've killed me," he said reproachfully.

She didn't move. "I still might. What do you want? Food? I haven't got any."

"I can see that. You look dead on your feet."

"Then what? You gonna try and rape me?"

"*What*? No!"

"Money? I haven't got any of that either."

He barked a laugh. "Why would I want money?"

She said nothing. He squinted at her. "Where did you come from, anyway? Reckon I know everyone left around here now. I don't know you."

She lifted her chin. "This is where I'm from."

"Well, you haven't been around for a while, have you? Don't you know there's nothing left?"

"What do you mean?"

He looked at his bloody hand. "Why should I talk to you? You just nearly brained me. Mind you," he added grudgingly, "it was a good shot."

"Please," Skyler said. She was so, so tired. This boy, despite the head injury, had so much energy. Maybe it was just nerves, but whatever it was, she needed some of it. "I'm sorry about your head. I thought you wanted to hurt me. Please. . . I've just got back and – I don't know where anyone is – I need to find my family."

"Just got back from *where*? You make it sound like you just popped out for a pint of milk!"

That was the point at which Skyler's legs gave up and she found herself in a heap on the tarmac. The boy moved towards her, anxious, then wary. She looked up at him wearily. "I'm not gonna hit you again."

He grinned. "As if you could. Look at the state of you."

She bit back her retort. He squatted beside her. "Want to sit for a minute?"

She screwed up her eyes. "All right."

"So. You want to tell me what's going on?"

She told him the important parts. When she'd finished, he stared at her for a long time. "You're serious," he said at last. "You're telling the truth about all this?"

"Do I look like I'm making it up?"

He shook his head. "I – uh. Okay. I hate to tell you this, but. . . you're kind of in for a shock."

"I already got that. How bad is it? Where *is* everyone?"

The pity on his face was worse than any other look he could have given her. He took a deep breath. "Mostly," he said, "they're dead."

It was as if, having allowed his words in through her ears, her brain had somehow rejected them. The more she replayed what she thought she'd heard, the more she thought she must have imagined it.

"I'm sorry," the boy said. His voice was flat, resigned.

She forced herself to speak. "What – what do you mean?"

He took another long breath. "Everything just... stopped. Right in the middle of winter. No electricity, no food, no way to grow anything. No clean water. No medicine. Nothing." His voice cracked for the first time. "That's what I mean. Anyone with any sense took off for the countryside ages ago."

Skyler still wasn't sure she wasn't hallucinating. Her voice came out surprisingly calm. "So what're you still doing here?"

"Ah... I sort of ran into some trouble on my way up to the moors." He rubbed a hand over his face, smearing blood everywhere. "Shit," he said absentmindedly. "I had a disagreement with some... unfriendly types. I figured they wouldn't bother chasing me all the way back down here." He shrugged. "I was right."

"Are you from round here? Before all this, I mean?"

He nodded. "Morley. You?"

They'd grown up only a few miles from one another. "Seacroft."

A silence. "What're you gonna do now?" he asked.

"I need to find my family. My mum and my brother." That was the only thing that mattered.

"How're you gonna do that?"

She didn't want to say 'I don't know,' again, so she didn't say anything. Eventually, she sighed. "I guess I'll go home. Even if they're not there, maybe there'll be something." *Maybe they left a message, in case I came back.*

The boy kept his mouth shut, but she could almost hear his thoughts. "What else can I do?" she said helplessly.

"You sure you want to do this?"

Four months since anyone had put their arms around her, told her she was going to be okay. She hadn't known the yearning for such a simple thing could burn such a hole in her. And now it could be within arm's reach.

She was going home.

"Yes," she said. "I'm sure."

The boy sighed. "At least let me come with you, then. It's... not very nice down there. There's the odd crazy wandering around."

She looked at him. *And you're going to protect me, are you?*

He laughed. "I know what you're thinking. Better than nothing, though, eh? Besides, this is gonna be... hard to take. Best you're not on your own."

She still wasn't sure this wasn't some elaborate set up to trick her into trusting him. But really – he could see she was exhausted. If he was going to attack her, it was hardly worth waiting.

He could obviously see her sizing him up. His face softened. "I'm not gonna hurt you. I swear." He grinned suddenly. "You can even bring your rock if you want."

She dragged herself to her feet and tried not to stagger. "Let's go, then."

"I'm Mackenzie," he said conversationally, as he fell into step beside her.

He seemed to be expecting something in return. "Skyler. What kind of a name is Mackenzie? First or last name?"

He shrugged. "Just Mackenzie. It's not like it matters any more, is it?"

They lapsed into silence. Skyler tried not to notice that the rancid, cloying smell was getting worse. Instead she concentrated on putting one foot in front of the other and wondered whether Mackenzie had any food or water. She couldn't really ask him. It would be pretty rude, considering she'd introduced herself by hitting him with a rock.

Seacroft lay on the outskirts of Leeds and it took them a long time to reach it. Skyler told herself the burning of her raw, blistered feet didn't matter. Nothing mattered except that soon she would be home. She tried to take small breaths, tried to filter out the sickly scent of decay that soaked, heavy, into the dread in her stomach. *This isn't real. It's not. It can't be.*

They cut through a deserted shopping precinct where signs hung askew and broken glass crunched underfoot. "Looters," Mackenzie said, by way of explanation. He hung back, twisting his hands together. She turned to him impatiently. If she stopped moving, she didn't think she'd be able to start again.

"Skyler," he said. "You do... you do understand what I was saying earlier, don't you? There really aren't many people left here. Almost everyone's gone."

"I got that."

She focused on the glass shards crunching under her feet, but she couldn't block out the misery in his voice. "And by gone, I mean..."

"I know. You said. Lots of people died. But not everyone. My mum, my brother – they were healthy, there's no reason –"

"Skyler –"

She wished he'd stop saying her name like he knew her. "Can we just get on, please?"

In the city centre, cold sunlight glinted off the jagged edges of shattered windows. An entire shopping centre was burnt out, charred beams protruding into the sky like a whale's ribcage. When they reached the Parkinson Building with its white stone tower rising into the sky, the steps were stained rusty, blackened. Litter blew across them. The clock on the tower had stopped.

This area had always been filled with students scurrying around like ants on an anthill. People sat on the steps in the summer, eating their lunch and chatting. There was no one here now. And Mackenzie was watching her, waiting for a reaction, and if she tried to speak, if she let herself acknowledge that any of this was real, she would disintegrate. She wouldn't be able to stop herself. So she just kept walking.

And then, when they were less than a mile from her old home, Mackenzie stopped again.

"Seacroft," he whispered. "Oh. No."

"What? What is it *now*?"

"Where in Seacroft did your family live?"

"The estate. The high rises. Why?"

He rubbed his hands over his face. She wanted to shake him. "For God's sake, what is it?"

"Remember what I told you. No hospitals. No emergency services."

"I remember! Just *tell* me!"

He swallowed. "It happened real early on. Like probably only a few days after everything went crazy. People realised the water was going to run out and they started fighting for it. There were riots. Gangs trying to break in places. The people in the tower blocks barricaded themselves in."

Skyler's mouth went dry. "And?"

"Oh, God. Uh... the mob – they threw firebombs through the windows. There were no fire engines, Skyler. No help. The people in there were trapped."

She stared at him, and then she turned and ran. She didn't know whether he was following her and she didn't care. She no longer had to think about where she was going.

Her feet, remembering a thousand childhood journeys, led her home.

The building she'd grown up in, which had once seemed tall enough to reach the clouds, was a blackened, crumbling mess. The patches of grass outside, where Sam had taught her to ride a bike, obliterated. Nothing left but bare earth, melted tarmac, lamp posts warped into strange, alien shapes.

She was standing in the middle of a tomb.

Her knees buckled. If there'd been anything in her stomach she would have been sick. Instead, she curled up on the ground, arms wrapped around her legs, fighting for air between the choking sobs that engulfed her and threatened to sweep her away.

Running footsteps brought her back to the freezing ruin that had once been home, and for a violent moment she hated their owner. She raised her head to hiss at Mackenzie to get away, to leave her alone, and then the words died in her mouth.

He didn't try to touch her. He sat down in the road a couple of feet away and waited while she fought for breath. When at last she lifted her head, he said, quietly, "I'm really sorry."

She wiped her eyes on her jacket. The roughness of the wool stung her cheeks. "You did try to warn me."

"Yeah, well. I'd have done the same thing if I were you."

Perhaps they weren't in there. Perhaps they left before the fire.

Except they hadn't known where she was, or if she was coming back. And they would have waited for her. They would never have left without her.

The sobs rose up again, drowning her. It didn't matter. Nothing mattered anymore.

At some point, a hand on her shoulder. "Skyler. C'mon. You can't stay here."

She couldn't move. Mackenzie gripped her shoulder. "Come on. Come away."

She wiped her hands across her face. It felt raw. "Where am I meant to go? What do I *do*?"

"I know somewhere. It's a bit of a way. But it's safe enough, and there's, you know, a roof and stuff, and food."

Food. She started to cry again.

"Don't get too excited," he said. "We're talking tins of beans, mainly. Still, it's better than nothing."

24

A WOLF AT THE DOOR

And that was why it was difficult with Mackenzie. It was why, for nearly three years, Skyler had done her best to avoid him. Every time she looked at him, all she could think about was that day.

She kept waiting for it to get easier, but it never did.

Twenty-four hours after she and Angel had delivered her laptop to Fox, they were heading back to collect it. They were almost there, halfway down a street where yellow light spilled onto the pavement from the houses either side, when Angel laid a hand on Skyler's arm.

She started. "What is it?"

Angel nodded towards the shadows. "We're being watched." To Skyler's horror, she raised her voice. "I know you're there. Come out."

A figure emerged from behind a dustbin, half-crouched. A girl, about eleven, with a puffy jacket and a high ponytail. She kept her hands raised and her wary eyes on Angel.

Angel didn't relax, but she didn't go for a weapon either. "What do you want?" she asked.

The girl stood firm. Perhaps she'd seen scarier things than the two of them. "Rob sent me."

"Did he, now?"

"Yeah. Said you're not to go to the flat, it's not safe. You gotta meet him here." She thrust a piece of paper towards Angel, who edged closer as though approaching a hungry wolf.

A chilly trickle of dread in Skyler's bloodstream. *My laptop.* She opened her mouth to ask the girl a question, but Angel got there first. "Did he say anything else?"

"Said you owe me now."

Angel pulled a small wad of cash from her jacket and held it out to the girl, who snatched it and shot backwards. "Thanks for the message," she said. "Are you all right out here on your own?"

The girl wrinkled her nose as though this was by far the strangest part of the conversation. "Yeah," she said at length. "I'm good. You better go see Rob. He'll be in a hurry." She darted away into the shadows.

Angel peered at the scrap of paper. "And he's given us a code word. That's not good." She sighed. "Well, we'd better get over there." As they picked up their pace, she nudged Skyler gently. "If anything kicks off this time, you let me take care of it, okay?"

The new address was a disused launderette in a small parade of shops, all in darkness. When they tried the door, it opened.

Inside, everything was still. Angel stood with her hand at her waistband and said into the gloom, "The fox is a crepuscular animal, and by God you'd better not have brought us here to waste our time."

Behind the row of big drying machines, a torch flicked on. Skyler tensed and then relaxed as Rob shuffled out, moving stiffly.

One eye was dark purple, swollen shut. His cheek was grazed. Skyler's laptop bag was slung across his back.

"What happened?" Angel asked.

He lowered himself onto a bench in front of a row of washing machines, wincing. "Sorry. Everything hurts."

"Have you had medical attention?"

He shook his head. "Not that bad."

"What happened?" Angel said again.

"Board came asking questions."

Skyler heard herself say, "Oh, shit," at the same time Angel said, "Fox?"

"He's not in good shape." There was a tremor in Rob's voice.

"Is he going to live?"

Skyler just managed to stop herself asking, "Did he fix the laptop?"

"I think so," Rob said.

"Can he go to a hospital?"

He shrugged. "He's a Southern citizen so they'd let him in, but it's not cheap, is it? That's why I had to get this bloody thing back to you." He nudged the laptop bag with a twisted smile. "We're gonna need the money."

Skyler's shoulders sagged.

"Tell me," Angel said gently.

"Greycoats turned up about three. Fox'd finished with the laptop – he was up all night working on it, couldn't wait to get his hands on the damn thing." Rob's lip wobbled. "Anyway, we heard all this noise outside and he shoved the laptop under the floorboards where he keeps all his illegal shit. And then the greycoats came in, wrecking stuff, asking questions. . ."

"What questions?"

"Wanted to know about some memory stick." Rob screwed up his face in disgust. "Or if he'd seen anything unusual. Like, I don't know, some Northern kid turning up with the highest spec laptop you've ever seen, wanting no questions asked."

"And what did you tell them?" Angel's voice was level, but Skyler had heard that tone before and underneath the calm there was a grenade waiting to go off.

"The fuck do you think? If we'd given you up he wouldn't be in the state he's in now, would he?"

"I had to ask."

"Trust me, if we were gonna hand you over to the Board we'd have just let you come to the flat. They'll have eyes on it now. Everyone round here knows what Fox does. He loves to show off."

"Why didn't you just give me up?" Skyler asked.

"Good question," he muttered. "Look. You're either with the Board or you're not. They might've acted all nice if we gave them what they wanted today but tomorrow they'd have been back to arrest us for something else. If you're not with them, you've gotta stick together. My enemy's enemy is friend, or some bollocks like that. Otherwise there's no resistance, there's just them." He gave Skyler a knowing glance. "Besides, Fox said he hopes if you do have that damn memory stick you're gonna bloody well do something good with it."

He held the bag out to her and she took it with a stomach-churning lurch of relief and guilt. "I don't know how to thank you," she said. "Or him."

He sniffed. "Well, you can bloody well pay up so I can get him a doctor, for starters."

Angel stood up. "I can do better than that. Where is he?"

"Back at the flat."

"Can he wait an hour?"

Rob looked her up and down. "What're you gonna do,

beat him better?"

"Hidden depths, Rob. How bad is he?"

His face dropped. "Bad. But it's gonna take me ages to get him to a hospital. I can't afford an ambulance. No good taking him to hospital if there's no money left to pay for treatment." His lip wobbled again.

Angel sat down next to him and put her hand on his. "I'll be as fast as I can and I'll do everything I can, okay? No charge. I need to collect some things and I'll come straight there. Go to him now. I'll meet you there."

"If they're watching –"

"I won't be seen. Go."

"Be quick," Rob said. "Please."

He hurried out of the launderette. Angel turned to Skyler. "Can you get yourself home?"

"Of course. What're you gonna do?"

"Steal a bike. Get there as quick as possible." At the door, she hesitated. "Get home safe, okay? Be careful."

"Yeah," Skyler said. "You too."

She followed Angel outside, but Angel had already vanished. Skyler set off into the night, hugging the laptop to her, the guilt like a rock on her chest.

Perhaps getting caught was nothing more than she deserved. She'd kept on dragging people into this, not thinking about anything except what she wanted, what she thought she needed. And now somebody had got hurt.

But then she thought about Angel returning to the house, looking for her, asking Mackenzie where she was, Mackenzie getting even more anxious than usual. The two of them searching for her, out in the dark. Being arrested or shot by the enforcers.

She pulled her gun out and kept it down by her side, and stuck to the darkest shadows, the streets where nothing moved, and whenever she heard a car engine growl she ducked behind the nearest wall or bin or hedge until it faded away into the night.

When she got back to the house it was nearly midnight. She put her gun away and switched her torch on. "Angel? Mack?"

Nothing. She moved from room to room, but no one was there. Her throat tightened.

A couple of hours ago she'd wanted nothing more than to get her laptop back and start figuring out how to break the encryption – and check that Fox hadn't done anything horrendous to it. Now she didn't know what to do with herself. She sat on the floor in the empty living room, lit a candle and opened the laptop.

It worked perfectly, and there was even enough power in the battery to get a couple of hours' work out of it, but her heart wasn't in it. She couldn't stop thinking about Fox, wondering when Angel was going to come back. In the end she closed the laptop and leaned against the wall, cold plaster against her back, the darkness pressing down on her like it would bury her alive.

25

BREAKING POINT

When the front door opened a few hours later, Skyler grabbed the candle and shot out into the hallway.

The dark figure at the door froze. Something bright and metallic flashed in the candlelight before Angel relaxed. "Hi," she said quietly.

"Hi." Skyler bit her lip, full of questions she was afraid to ask. "How – how's Fox?"

Angel's eyes were dark in the candlelight, rimmed with red. She shook her head.

Skyler stared at her. "How bad is it?"

Angel moved towards her, took her hand. "Sky. Fox is – he – he died. He's dead."

Skyler's throat closed up. She tried to speak and no words came out. She tried again. "He's – dead? But – Rob said he was gonna be okay –"

Angel tightened her hold on her hand. "Here. Come and sit down."

Numb, Skyler let Angel lead her into the living room. They sat against the wall in the little puddle of candlelight with the dark closing in around them, and Skyler stared at the flame until her eyes watered and tried to make sense of Angel's words.

"What happened?" she said at last.

Angel picked at the skin around her nails, her head down. "I stole a bike. Maybe took me half an hour to get back here to get my stuff and then out to the flat. Rob was right – greycoats had the place under surveillance. I don't know how he lost them earlier. I don't know how he had space to even think about it." She swallowed. "Fox was unconscious when I got there. Rob said it'd only just happened. They'd really. . . they were vicious, what they did to him."

"Oh," Skyler said softly. She was cold all over.

"I did everything I know how to do. Rob was crying, begging me to help him. . ." She took an uneven breath. "I tried. I drilled a hole in his skull, for God's sake."

"You did *what*?"

"To relieve the pressure on his brain. I've done it before but it scares the shit out of me every time. If I got it wrong. . . And Rob was right there, and he kept saying 'Please don't let him die, please don't let him die. . .'" Angel drew her knees up to her chest and put her head in her hands. "And I couldn't save him."

Skyler didn't know what she was supposed to do, whether she should touch Angel, how she could possibly comfort her. She put a tentative hand on her shoulder. "I'm so sorry." Her voice broke.

She didn't cry anymore. All those years of being scared, all the time, and she never let herself cry, because what good would it have done?

But this heavy darkness seeping from her heart into her limbs, like a lead blanket wrapping around her – this wasn't fear. This was something else, and it was almost unbearable.

Angel glanced up at her. "Are you all right?"

She shook her head.

"It's not your fault, Sky."

Skyler laughed, though nothing was funny. "We both know that's not true."

"He doesn't blame you, you know. Rob, I mean."

"He should." Skyler pulled her own knees up tight as though she could somehow squeeze the darkness out of herself. "I never even thought about what might happen to them. I was just thinking about myself."

"And that's not your fault. Thinking about yourself first is what you had to do to survive in the world the Board created."

Skyler's eyes were hot and stinging and she knew that if she looked at Angel she would cry. Instead she focused hard on the way the candle flame crept down the wick, curling and blackening it as it went. "I didn't have to do this. I did it because I wanted to. And I got Fox killed."

Angel made a sudden movement, as though she was going to touch Skyler and then thought better of it. Skyler found herself wishing Angel hadn't stopped herself, wanting to reach out to her, not knowing how to.

"I sat with Rob afterwards," Angel said. "He talked a bit. He said Fox believed in responsibility where it's due. The Board killed him, not you. He said Fox knew the risk he was taking doing the work he did. He was a Southern citizen – he could've gone legit. He could've worked for the Board, even. He chose a different path because he believed that was the right thing to do."

"I wish I was that noble," Skyler muttered.

"Do you think any of us are, really? Don't you think we're all just thinking about ourselves, one way or another?"

"Not you," Skyler said. "I don't think you are."

Angel shot a small, sad smile at her. "I'm not so different to anyone else."

Skyler thought about Angel holding her hand all those months ago, all the hours patiently teaching her how to fight, the gentle smile she rewarded her with when she'd finally mastered something, the way Angel had listened to her talk out on the pier.

And now Angel was there beside her and she smelled of antiseptic and fresh air and something sweet and salty, and her shoulder pressed, warm, against Skyler's, and Skyler wanted. . . something, but she didn't know what.

Angel glanced towards her, and she was suddenly shy and embarrassed. She looked away, pressing her lips hard together. There was an ache in her chest, a solid, relentless pressure. It was so heavy it would drown her if she let it.

"Oh, Skyler," Angel murmured, and this time when she reached out their hands met with an unexpected warmth that lifted Skyler's head back up above the dark water.

She almost didn't dare breathe. But somehow, when Angel didn't move away either, she found that their fingers had intertwined.

The ache in Skyler's chest tangled with her thoughts until she didn't know what she was thinking or what to say. The only thing she knew was that she didn't want to let go of Angel's hand.

"Are you feeling okay?" Angel said eventually. "About tomorrow?"

Skyler blinked. "Tomorrow's the easy bit. No matter how hard the encryption is. . . that's always the easy bit. It's everything else that's difficult."

"I wish," Angel said slowly. "I wish I could've got you out of that cellar."

"It was my job to do that. No one else's." Skyler was startled to realise that, for once, it was Angel who didn't seem able to meet her eyes. "Angel," she said. "It wasn't your responsibility."

"But I knew. I knew what it was like for you down there."

Skyler took a deep breath. "Those guys who worked for. . . him." She couldn't bring herself to say Daniel's name. "The ones I told you about, ages ago."

Angel nodded, her eyes fixed on the candle flame.

"They all disappeared," Skyler said carefully.

Angel stiffened. Skyler gripped her hand. "Did you. . . Did you make that happen?"

Angel's eyes, luminous in the candlelight. Her lips parted like she didn't know how to get the words out. Their hands twined together, a fragile spell that might break at any moment.

Then – "Yes." Her gaze flickered towards Skyler, uncertain. "You must think I'm a monster."

Skyler would have laughed, but Angel's face was serious, unhappy. "Angel – never. What you did. . . I can't believe you did that for me."

"I should have done more. I should've helped you more."

Skyler reached out with her free hand and touched Angel's knee. "You did help me."

Angel looked at her hand. Skyler drew back. "I'm sorry. I didn't mean to –"

Angel shook her head. There was a trace of a smile on her face, but it was full of sorrow. "Don't apologise."

Skyler opened her mouth to say – what? Something. Anything. Anything to spin the spell out for another few seconds, another minute, to keep them here in the candlelight with the warmth of Angel's body next to hers, the touch of skin on skin.

But then Angel sighed. "Come on," she said lightly. "You should get some sleep. You've got state secrets to uncover tomorrow."

She squeezed Skyler's hand, and then she let go. Something in Skyler's chest tore. She got to her feet.

For the briefest moment, when their eyes met, the ghost of Angel's smile blossomed into something alive. "Good night, Skyler," she said.

Upstairs, Skyler wrapped herself in her sleeping bag on the floor. It was so cold she could see her breath in the candlelight, and her hand, where she had held Angel's, was the only part of her body that felt warm.

Skyler lay in the darkness and wondered how she was ever supposed to get to sleep now.

26

INTO THE DARK

Mackenzie woke Skyler at four in the morning. "Enforcers hand over shifts at six," he explained. "There'll be less on the streets."

She'd expected him to be a nervous wreck, but it had actually only taken him three or four attempts to get out of the house. Of course, he was in familiar territory now. Breaking into a house on a residential street was child's play for him.

Skyler's legs, on the other hand, were wobbly. It had cost so much to get to this point. For the first time, she was worrying about Mackenzie; about what he was putting at stake because of her.

They passed through the town centre onto a long road lined with gas lamps and detached houses with expansive front gardens. All of this equalled people with a decent electricity ration. He'd chosen well.

"Thanks," he said dryly, when she voiced this, but she could tell he was pleased. "I do know what I'm doing sometimes." He gestured at the houses. "What kind of people do you think live here?"

She snorted. "Definitely not our sort of people."

He chuckled in acknowledgement, but then he sobered.

"I keep thinking, you know. About what Angel said – how she didn't even know what happened in the North. Do you think these people know what the Board did so they could keep living like this?"

"Doubt it. Most people only hear what the Board want them to hear." But then, plenty of Southerners had seen the Wall go up, had watched the enforcers shooting at the crowds on the other side. Even if they didn't understand exactly what had happened in the North, surely they must know that it was nothing good.

"D'you think any of them would care?"

She shifted the weight of the laptop on her back. "I don't know. It's like Joss and Lydia said, there was all that anger before the Wall went up. All that talk about how the North was a drain on the country's resources. There was always stuff on TV about it. Do you remember?"

He nodded. "My parents made me stop watching the news after a while because I got so anxious, but. . . yeah. I remember the way people talked."

"Maybe some of them would feel bad," Skyler said. "But in the way you do about something that's not really anything to do with you. Like, oh, that's terrible, and then forget about it. Like it's not really real."

He grabbed her arm and she jumped. "Jesus! What's the matter?"

"Car coming."

He was right. Somewhere nearby was the purr of an engine.

"Over here. Quick." She scrambled over the nearest privet hedge into a manicured front garden. Mackenzie tumbled over after her and nearly landed on top of her. "Watch it!" she hissed, before she could stop herself. "If you jump on my laptop again now, Mackenzie, I swear to God –"

"Oh my God, Sky, shut up."

Well, she probably deserved that.

On the other side of the hedge, headlights lit the road. Mackenzie started whispering to himself. Skyler prayed that the people who lived in the house behind them were not early risers. Nobody who lived in a house like that was going to appreciate the sudden appearance of two scruffy teenagers behind their hedge.

"Can I open my eyes yet?" Mackenzie muttered, between whispers.

"Not yet."

The car rumbled on, out of sight. She exhaled. "I think we're okay."

As they set off again, she made a decision. "How're you feeling?"

"Huh?"

God, Mackenzie, don't make this any more awkward. "Just – you know. How're you feeling? About – all this?"

"Um. All right, I think. Better than – you know. A few days ago."

This had been a mistake. What was she supposed to say now? "Okay. Good."

They walked on.

"Are you scared?" he asked, out of nowhere. "Of getting caught?"

Could she admit it, to him, even to herself?

"Always," she said. "All the time."

He gave a breathy laugh. "Glad it's not just me."

"I don't know how you cope, Mack. I mean, like it's not bad enough worrying about getting caught, you have to worry about falling and breaking your neck, or getting eaten by guard dogs, or –" She stopped. His expression suggested she was not being helpful. "I just don't know how you do it. Especially when –"

She didn't know how to finish that sentence. *When you have to do most things twenty times over for no apparent reason.*

"When I can hardly even walk through a door some days?" He sounded amused. "It's not always like that. It's not always this bad."

She waited.

"I'm not always like that," he said slowly. "It sounds stupid, but it's actually worse when I'm not working. When I'm in the middle of a job, I know what I have to do to survive. My brain still wants me to do stupid shit, but it's a lot easier to ignore it when I know that stopping to wash my hands five times is gonna get me killed." He hesitated. "It's afterwards. All these questions go round and round in my head – did someone see me on the way out, did an enforcer follow me, did I get someone hurt? That's the worst one, thinking I've got someone else hurt. That's partly why it's been hard since I've been with you guys, I think."

He gave a sort-of chuckle, though Skyler couldn't see what was funny. "That's how it goes. When it's quiet, and I should be able to relax – that's when I can't get that stuff out of my head."

"So it's not always as bad as it has been recently?"

He shook his head. "I mean, I've had some pretty rough times, but I think this is the worst it's ever been."

"Thank God. You lived on like the twenty-third floor in Birmingham. Climbing those stairs thirty times a day probably would've killed you."

He let out a startled laugh. "Do you actually just say everything that comes into your head?"

"Not usually," she admitted. "Sorry. I wasn't making fun of you, I promise. I can see how awful it is."

He grinned at her. "Do you know how long it's been since I had anyone to joke around with?"

Oh, no. More feelings. She tried to think of something to fill the silence. "So why'd you do the whole thieving thing, if you just worry afterwards? Why keep putting yourself through that?"

He snorted. "Oh, yeah. Maybe I'll just go work in an office. Maybe I'll train as a plumber, what do you reckon?"

"All right. You know what I mean. There's much easier things to do than break into the Board headquarters. Why make life harder than it has to be?"

"I don't think you'll get it."

"Try me." When he didn't say anything, she said, "I promise not to do the 'you're a fucking idiot' face."

He laughed. "All right. Well, to be honest. . . I like it. It's kind of fun – you know, when you're not shitting yourself. And the money's good, and the more useful you are, the safer you are." Skyler nodded. This was all true. "But most of all. . . the counting and the cleaning and the worrying. . . That's not *me*. It's this pain in the arse thing that lives in my head, that's all. I need to believe that, so I can't let it be in charge. As soon as I start turning down jobs because of it, it wins. I don't want to be that person. I can't be that person."

"You'd rather be scared all the time?"

"D'you think we'll ever not be scared all the time?"

Skyler had got so used to the constant background hum that ran through her like an electrical current, that she found she couldn't imagine life without it. "I don't know."

"Besides," he added. "I haven't got it so bad. Not when – well. Not when you see what other people have to deal with."

She'd thought she'd got over the whole wanting to punch him thing, but if he started feeling sorry for her it was definitely going to make a reappearance. "You made your choice," she said. "I made mine. It could've been worse."

"I don't know if I believe you."

She shrugged.

"You still beat yourself up, don't you? About working for him?"

"Oh my God, Mack –"

He caught at her arm. She frowned at him. "What's the matter with you?"

"I had the luxury," he said. "I kept my head down and my eyes shut and I made sure I didn't know any details. I told myself I was keeping myself safe, and I was, but really. . ." He sighed. "I worked for people who did bad things, and I helped them do those things. And I made sure I didn't know who I was working for or why they wanted me to do those jobs, because then I didn't have to choose between getting paid and doing the right thing. I was the same as you, Sky. Just more of a coward."

"I hate it," she said. "I gave AJ all that shit and I'm no better than him, really, am I? We're all supporting the system that fucked us over."

Mackenzie gave her one of his lopsided smiles. "Well. Not anymore."

He stopped in front of a garden more overgrown than the others. "This is it." He led her towards the front door, pulled a pouch of tools from his pocket and knelt down.

"Don't you need more light for that?" Skyler asked.

He grinned and slid a slim piece of metal into the lock. "Nah. I could do this with my eyes shut."

It took him less than twenty seconds to get the door open. Skyler followed him inside with a giddy rush of relief and flipped the nearest light switch.

The hallway light came on. She let out a sigh. "Well done, Mack."

"It's not exactly the Ritz," he said.

The house was crammed with dark, heavy furniture. There was a strong emphasis on floral patterns, a slightly stale smell, and a thin layer of dust over everything. There was also a stair lift.

She pursed her lips. "This is an old person's house."

"Yeah. Like I said, probably in hospital, so they could come back any time. And if they die the power'll get shut off, so the quicker you're done here, the better."

"Hmm."

"Something wrong?"

"Just not sure how I feel about stealing electricity from a sick old person."

"What, suddenly you're Robin Hood?" He pulled a face at her. "They live in a place like this, they can afford it. Better than we can, anyway."

"Yeah." Her mind was back on the Heimdall drive. "I guess you're right."

He was talking again. "Stay upstairs, okay? That way if anyone does come in you'll be able to hide. Figure out your escape route before you do anything else. Don't turn any lights on. And don't forget to eat, will you?"

She smiled in spite of herself. "Don't worry. I'll be fine." She took a step towards the stairs. "I'll see you soon."

"Be careful, Sky."

"Thanks, Mack. You too."

He nodded, and then he was gone.

27

REVELATIONS

Skyler had been working on the Heimdall drive for a week, but it didn't feel like it. She'd lost track of time; despite Mackenzie's parting reminder, she kept forgetting to eat. She'd been entangled with the encryption, which had come to feel like a sentient opponent, and had barely moved from the bedroom she was camped in. She only slept when she actually fell asleep in front of the laptop. Her time here was too precious to waste on something as trivial as rest.

She'd had to work harder in the last week than she ever had in her life, but she didn't care. She'd learned so much. And it was blissful, to be doing something so complicated it took every scrap of energy, leaving her no room to think about anything else. In some ways, she never wanted it to end.

There was no quick way into the drive. She couldn't break the encryption by brute force – the key was too long, it would take years for any program to work through every possible combination. Instead, she'd reverse-engineered the encryption technique to figure out how it worked, and then she'd written a program to search for a flaw that she could exploit.

It was the morning of her eighth day in the house and her brain was so full of code it felt like it might start coming out of her ears. She'd finally finished the program and she set it running with more than a touch of regret, because now she had to think about the other task she'd come here to do.

She'd been putting it off because she was scared. She'd kept telling herself the drive was more important, but now she was out of excuses. She had to find out whether Daniel was still alive.

She pulled the laptop towards her and her stomach gave a sickly lurch, like the mere thought of him could conjure him up. Swiftly, before she could change her mind, she picked the old, familiar path into his emails.

There were hundreds of unread messages in the account. Frowning, she double-checked she had the right account. She checked the date of the last login, the last sent email.

She began to let herself hope.

Phone records next. His phone hadn't been used either.

Finally, she did an internet search.

The first result was from a Birmingham newspaper. It was titled "Tributes Paid to Local Businessman."

Daniel Redruth, well-known businessman and community leader, passed away unexpectedly at his home...

Skyler stared at the screen. She didn't know if she trusted her own brain.

She clicked through more articles. Rubbed her eyes. Checked the emails and the phone records again.

He's dead.

He's really dead.

She buried her face in her hands, let out a long, shaky breath.

Maybe it was time she had a break, after all that. She'd

done all she could with the encryption. The program would keep running until it found a flaw. It would be all right just to rest for a bit.

She curled up on the floor and kept her eyes on the laptop until she couldn't keep them open any more.

She returned to consciousness with a start and shot upright, her heart pounding. It was still light outside. She checked her watch. Three in the afternoon.

Her eyes were sticky; her thoughts moved sluggishly. The laptop screen was dark. She reached for the bottle of water next to her and tapped the keyboard, urging it back to life.

Then she stopped. The laptop had gone to sleep. Which meant the program had stopped running.

Which meant either it had stopped working – or –

When she touched the keyboard again, her whole body shook.

It was over.

She massaged her temples, trying to dislodge the odd rustling at the edges of her hearing. The few hours of sleep seemed to have made things worse, not better. She was hearing things: a faint clinking that sounded like it was coming from downstairs. She shook her head hard.

A rattle, and a murmur of voices.

She wasn't hallucinating. Someone was outside the house. And – *shit* – that was a key in the lock.

It wouldn't be Mackenzie or Angel, not in the middle of the afternoon.

Fuck.

As she shoved her things into her bag and swung it onto her back, a male voice downstairs said, "There you go, darlin'. Get a cup of tea on. Someone'll be over this evening to see you."

And an older woman's voice, quavery: "Thank you very much."

Skyler clenched her fists. *Think.* There had to be a way out.

She should have listened to Mackenzie, but his advice had seemed like a tedious triviality. She made a mental note not to admit to him that he'd been right. And unfortunately, the only ideas that sprang to mind now involved drainpipes, something she'd hoped she'd never have to contemplate again.

From downstairs came the sounds of someone home from a long absence: doors opening and closing, water running, a kettle being set on the hob. She crept into the back bedroom and opened the window.

It was pouring with rain. Well, that would make this whole thing a lot easier. At least the drainpipe was within reach, if not easy reach. Below her was a glass conservatory, a patio covered with flowerpots, and a long stretch of lawn. So if she fell she'd land on something hard, make a lot of noise, and she'd be extremely visible on her escape across the garden. Excellent.

Somehow this was worse than trying to get away from the enforcers or Daniel. She wasn't going to hurt an old woman to escape, and that didn't leave her with many options.

She wished Angel and Mackenzie were there. She screwed up her courage, climbed onto the windowsill as quietly as she could – perhaps the old woman was deaf? God, she hoped so – and leaned out.

She had to stretch her arms as far as they would go to reach the drainpipe. Her fingers grasped for it, found it slippery with the rain – and let go.

She looked down at the ground and wished she hadn't. It was a very long way away.

You got out of Daniel's house. You survived three years in that bloody cellar and now you're going to get caught because you can't escape from a pensioner? That's pathetic.

This time, when she reached out, her fingers found a more secure hold. She took a shaky breath, slid off the windowsill and let the weight of her body swing her across to hug the drainpipe.

Okay. Good. Fine. Now all she had to do was get down.

When, a million years later, her feet finally found solid ground, she wiped the sweat from her forehead and opened her eyes.

She was right next to the conservatory. In which stood a white-haired woman with her back to Skyler, talking on the phone.

There was nothing but glass between them. If she turned round –

She turned round.

Her shriek was audible even through the glass. Skyler put her head down and sprinted across the lawn.

At the end of the garden a compost bin stood against a fence two feet taller than she was. She hauled herself up into the bin, her feet squelching into rotting cabbage leaves and potato peelings, threw herself over the fence, getting her hands full of splinters, and landed heavily in a puddle.

She dodged down alleys and side streets, rain soaking her hair and clothes. Her legs were weak, unsteady. She wished she'd bothered to eat a bit more over the last week.

Somewhere out of view, a siren started to howl. Mackenzie's words echoed in her mind: *Running makes you look guilty, and looking guilty gets you shot.*

She forced her footsteps to slow, pulled her hood down, straightened her shoulders.

When she turned a corner and saw two navy-clad enforcers heading towards her, though, it was all she could do not to turn and bolt.

Just walk. It's okay to walk fast, it's raining. They wouldn't expect anything else. They wouldn't expect eye contact, either. She'd risk seeming cocky if she acknowledged them. *One foot in front of the other. Keep going. Keep going.*

She felt their eyes on her as she drew nearer. She didn't dare look up from her boots.

One of their radios crackled. Their footsteps slowed.

Don't look up. Don't look up. You're so close, don't fuck this up now.

One of the enforcers murmured something to the other and lifted his radio. She was only feet from them, they could reach out and grab her if they wanted to –

The enforcers swung round and headed back in the direction they'd come from, their footsteps thudding on the pavement in time with the urgent beat of Skyler's heart. She watched, every muscle taut, as they retreated into the distance.

The urge to run was impossible to resist this time. All she wanted was to be back with the others.

When, at long last, she reached the boarded-up house, drenched through, her feet throbbing, she had to blink away tears. Before she reached the door, it flew open. She stumbled over the threshold, a lump in her throat, and the next thing she knew there were arms around her, a warm cheek against hers. She closed her eyes and fell into Angel's embrace.

When she pulled back, Angel was smiling. Behind her, Mackenzie hovered. "We were getting worried," he said. "You've been ages."

She slid the bag off her back, wriggling her shoulders. "It was hard. And I got seen," she added guiltily.

"You okay? Did anyone follow you here?"

"Don't think so."

"Did you crack it?" Angel asked, as Mackenzie said, "Did you find out about Redruth?"

She nodded. "Yes. Both."

Angel stiffened. "And?"

"He's. . . dead. He's gone."

Angel stood motionless. "You're sure."

"The internet seemed pretty certain."

Angel closed her eyes. "Oh," she whispered.

"Thank God for that," Mackenzie said brightly. "And the memory stick?"

"I found a flaw in the encryption. I think I can open the drive."

"Well, what're we waiting for? Aren't you dying to know what's on it?"

She hesitated. She really was. But now there was nothing in the way, the weight of what she'd put them all through for this was suddenly suffocating. What if, after everything, the drive contained nothing more than a new income tax proposal?

She sat on the living room floor and opened her laptop. The battery was fully charged. She had time to see what the program had given her.

Angel disappeared and returned with a bottle of water and a towel, and she drank gratefully. She hadn't realised how thirsty she was.

The rush of adrenaline swept away her exhaustion. She held her breath as she navigated the code, made strangely self-conscious by the others hovering in the doorway. Maybe this was how Mackenzie felt when he had to pick a lock in front of someone.

She was so absorbed in the process that she almost

missed the moment when the drive opened and its contents appeared on the screen in front of her.

The first document was titled "The final report of the Northern Containment Committee."

She forced herself to breathe, and began to read.

Sentences stood out. *Approximately sixty thousand survivors colonised in rural areas, of which around fifty percent remain after three years... The Wall has proved an effective deterrent... The main population centres are now uninhabitable.*

Recent concerns about international interest... Aid workers may have entered colonised areas by air... Recent UN motion demanded an explanation of the Wall's function. Foreign journalists have requested access...

Northerners may provoke sympathy from the international community. Surveillance indicates discussion of a rebellion... Risk that sympathetic governments may consider arming the rebels...

Military response not viable. Deaths of trespassing foreign aid workers and journalists likely to be perceived as an act of war, risking retaliation...

... Most viable solution is the release of a biological agent.

Skyler realised that the choked noise that reached her ears had come from her.

"What?" Mackenzie said. "What is it?"

She turned back to the screen.

Agent DX17, the next page read. *Synthetic agent... adapted smallpox virus. Waterborne... highly contagious from both living and deceased carriers... symptoms within 24 hours. Death within 72 hours. Mortality rate 98%. Vaccine development will take at least five years...*

This Committee considers that releasing this agent is the most effective possible solution to the current issues and will act as a deterrent to international trespassers.

Skyler pushed the laptop away and stumbled from the room. Out in the hallway, she doubled over.

Her stomach was empty but she couldn't stop it from heaving. Angel was behind her, a hand on her back. "It's okay. It's okay."

She wiped her streaming eyes. "It's not okay," she gasped. "Angel, it's not okay."

Angel's voice was soothing. "Then we'll figure out how to fix it." She wrapped her arm around Skyler. "Come on."

In front of the laptop, Mackenzie was scrolling frantically, his mouth contorted in horror. "Oh my God," he whispered.

Skyler slumped down next to him. "I know."

They sat huddled in miserable silence as Angel pulled the laptop towards her and started to read. Mackenzie stared into space. Skyler couldn't stop shaking.

Finally, Angel looked up. "This is barbaric," she said. "They can't do this."

"It's the Board," Mackenzie said dully. "They put the Wall up and nobody stopped them. I think they reckon they can do what they like."

Skyler picked up the laptop again. Something new caught her attention, grabbed her by the throat. "They've got a date."

"Huh?" Mackenzie said.

"A date to release this thing. February tenth."

"That's three weeks away," Angel said.

Nobody spoke. Skyler didn't even know if she could. The horror had spread all the way through her, numbing her.

"What are we going to do?" Angel said at last.

Mackenzie gave a hopeless, spluttering laugh. "Do? What makes you think we can *do* anything about this?"

"Well, can't we?"

"What do you think we are, some kind of vigilante initiative?"

"We could be. Or we could be the people who had this information and did nothing while the Board committed genocide. Which one would you rather be?"

He scowled. "I'd quite like to be a person who made it to my eighteenth birthday."

"Right," Angel said. "And I get that. But this is bigger than all of us." She turned to Skyler. "God knows you fought hard enough to find out what was on that drive. You wanted to hurt the Board, didn't you? Well, there's got to be something we can do with this."

Skyler stared at her. Her brain felt like it had been through a food processor. Nothing made sense.

But this did.

She stood up and headed for the kitchen. "Hey!" Mackenzie protested. "Where're you going?"

"To eat something. I'm starving. Then I'm gonna figure out what to do next."

He just looked at her like she was mad, but Angel's eyes were gleaming. Skyler thought she knew how Angel felt. Through the pain and shock and the rage stirring underneath it all, one thing was suddenly very simple. The Board were planning something horrific, and they had to be stopped. And if the three of them were the only people who could do it – well, then they were going to have to do it.

28

OUTSIDE THERE'S A CURSE

It was two in the morning and Mackenzie had been cleaning the kitchen by candlelight for the last four hours. There wasn't even much to clean – a scratched counter, a few cupboards, tiles that were barely sticking to the walls. But he couldn't stop. He'd been stuck on the same tile for at least an hour.

Skyler had long since gone to sleep and Angel had disappeared out somewhere into the night. He was alone with his thoughts, and ever since he'd read the Board document, his thoughts wouldn't shut up. Cleaning was the only thing that muffled them.

It wasn't helping enough.

At some point, he became aware that he was no longer alone. Angel leaned against the doorframe, arms folded, wearing an expression he almost didn't recognise because he hadn't seen it in so long. It might have been sympathy.

He gripped the rag in his hand tighter and kept scrubbing.

"Mackenzie," she said quietly.

He ignored her.

She crouched beside him. "Mackenzie. Your hands are bleeding."

He closed his eyes and turned his head away from her. "Please just leave me alone."

Gently, but extremely firmly, she tugged the bottle of bleach and the rag out of his hands. He tried to resist, but it turned out she was a lot stronger than he was. "You need to stop," she said.

He took a breath. To his horror, it turned into a sob. "I can't stop. I've tried. I can't."

"Yes, you can. Come on. I'll sort your hands out. The last thing you need is them getting infected."

He got to his feet. The dark voice in his head rose from a hiss to a clamour: *you can't stop, you can't, they'll all die, it'll be your fault –*

A jagged knot pulled tight in his chest. He reached for the bleach, but Angel held it out of his reach.

"Angel – please – you don't understand –"

"It's okay. Nothing bad's going to happen if you stop."

He tried to laugh through his sobs. "Easy for you to say."

"Not really." She took his arm and he found himself being led out of the kitchen.

He tried to pull away. "Please, Angel. Please don't."

"It won't help," she said.

If it had been anyone else he would have screamed at them. The only thing that stopped him was that even through the agony he was still a bit too scared of her for that.

She led him into the living room and disappeared. He curled up onto the floor and buried his face in his burning hands, a sharp ache stabbing at his chest. He didn't know if he hated Angel or wanted to thank her.

She returned with a handful of bandages and a lamp. "I can't do this," Mackenzie whispered into his hands. "You don't get it, something really bad's going to happen –"

She laid a hand on his shoulder. "It'll pass, I promise. If you don't give into it, it'll get easier."

"Did one of your medical books tell you that?"

"No. I had to learn that for myself."

He tried to swallow the lump in his throat. "You really think it'll get easier?"

"I'll stay with you until it does." She rolled up her sleeves and poured antiseptic onto a cotton pad. Then she said, "Has it always been like this, Mack?"

He looked away. He was exposed and ashamed and he hated it. But Angel wasn't rolling her eyes or telling him he was stupid.

"Not always," he said at last. "I mean, I was always a worrier, even when I was a kid. But it's only been like this since. . . since the Wall."

She took his hand and started dabbing antiseptic onto it. "You were in the North when it went up, weren't you?"

He tried to choke back the tears long enough to speak. "Yeah."

She started to bandage his hand.

"I watched them all die." The words came out in a rush, from the darkest, loneliest part of him, the place he tried never to go near. "My mum, my dad, my grandparents, Bex – they all got sick, one after the other, and I tried *so hard* to look after them, but I couldn't – it didn't help. And every time I thought we were through the worst of it – every time I thought we were going to be okay – someone else got sick. And then one day there was only me left."

He ducked his head. "I would've done *anything*. Anything at all, if it would've kept them safe. And I couldn't, and it kills me – I think about it every day, all the things I should've done differently, all the ways I should've been more careful. That if I'd tried harder, maybe they'd still be here."

Angel's face clouded. "Oh, Mack. I know. I know."

"And now. . . I think about all the bad things that could happen. They're in my head, all the time. They never stop. I feel like if I don't do something – I could never forgive myself. If you or Skyler got hurt, and I could've done something to stop it –" He stared at his bandaged hand, at the thin line of blood seeping through the gauze. "I know it doesn't make sense. I do get that. I'm not mental. But I just. . . can't make it stop."

"Do you know why it's so bad tonight?"

"Honestly? It feels like it's my fault, all that stuff on the memory stick." He held up a hand as she started to protest. "I know, I know. And. . . well. You guys are talking about a full on battle with the Board. . . "

"And you think we've lost our minds."

"You could put it like that." He looked up at her. "You know if we do this, we're going to die?"

"Maybe," Angel said. "Which, don't get me wrong, I'm not super excited about either – but if we don't do anything, everyone in the North will die, and no one will ever know what the Board did. To you, and your family, and the rest of us."

"You're not from the North, are you?"

A muscle flickered in her face. This was a risk. There were plenty of rumours about Angel but very few verified facts and there had to be a reason for that, the most likely one being that she did not tolerate questions well. For a moment she looked as though she was considering not tolerating this one.

Then – "No. I've lived in the South my whole life."

"Then why –?"

"Does it matter? Do I have to be Northern to care about this? People are people, Mack, and the Board are evil. If I knew all this and did nothing, I'd be complicit."

"I *want* to help. When I read that stuff, that there might be a rebellion, I actually got excited. I mean, imagine if we could overthrow the Board. Imagine if there could be something different. But. . . I just don't see how it's possible. And yeah, I'm scared. I don't want to die. But more than that – what about *this*?" He waved his bandaged hand at her. "What if I can't get this under control? What if I just end up making life harder for you two?"

Angel drummed her fingers on the floorboards in the way she did when she was thinking. "That's the fear talking," she said. "Look what we've achieved already. It's taken all of us to get this far, hasn't it? We need you, Mack, and you know it."

He let out a breathy laugh. "I'm not sure Skyler would agree."

"Skyler knows it too, even if she doesn't know how to say it." Angel smiled. "So. What do you think? Will you stay with us?"

He thought about it, but he didn't need to think for long. He was as scared as he'd ever been, the grief for his family raw and aching, the compulsions a burning itch in his brain. And none of it mattered as much as this did.

He managed a grin at her. "Of course I'm staying."

29

LIGHTS

Naturally, when they gathered the next morning to make a plan, they immediately began to run into dead ends.

"We need to leak the information to someone who cares," Mackenzie said. He didn't seem to be doing well today. He kept pacing back and forth across the kitchen, and his hands had acquired a new array of bandages. "We're not gonna pull this off alone. We need someone powerful to care."

Skyler nodded. She'd gone out to get them some bread for breakfast, figuring that if they were going to do this, they might as well do it on a full stomach, but as soon as they'd sat down her appetite had disappeared. "There's no point sending it to the Southern media," she said. "It'd never see the light of day."

Angel folded a piece of bread in half. "What about the UN? NATO?"

"Well, the Board pulled the UK out of NATO what, ten years ago? And there are fuel crises over half of Europe. The UN have their hands full with countries that actually *want* their help. They've been happy enough to leave us to our own devices so far."

"What the Board are planning is genocide," Angel said.

"Somebody will step in."

"Well, getting anyone's attention is gonna need an internet connection," Mackenzie said, still pacing. "How are we gonna get that?"

Skyler wound a strand of hair round her fingers and tugged it tight enough to hurt.

"But would that even be enough?" Angel said. "Would other countries be able to stop it in time?"

Skyler shook her head. "With this timescale, it's not gonna matter who knows. As soon as the Board get wind the information's out, they'll just release the virus and make excuses later."

"So what do we do, then?" Mackenzie said. "Destroy the virus?"

"Yeah," Skyler said. "I think that's exactly what we've got to do."

He spun to face her, his eyes wide and horrified. "I was being sarcastic!"

"I know. Sorry."

Angel shrugged and cut another piece of bread. "I think you might be right, Sky. It could be our only option."

"Uh," Mackenzie said. "Are we sure it *is* an option?"

"Good question. I know we've got the best thief in the city with us" – Mackenzie looked like he didn't know whether to feel flattered or suspicious – "but I think you're right, Mack. This is going to take more than the three of us."

He sat down and bounced straight back up. "What're you saying?"

Angel stretched her head back and studied the ceiling. "I think we need to get more people involved."

He pulled a face. "Sounds like a recipe to get shot to me."

"Not necessarily. I know pretty much every criminal in Birmingham, and it's amazing what people will tell a healer. What they do, where they come from, how they feel about the Board. This is going to be hard. The more skilled people we get on board the better."

"And what're we gonna do, this collective of skilled people?"

"Exactly what we said we would. We're going to expose the Board and stop them releasing the virus. And you both need to eat something."

"We're gonna get ourselves killed," Mackenzie muttered.

Skyler had had enough. She didn't need him to voice everything that was already on a loop in her own head. "We get it, Mack. Mortal peril, impending doom, blah blah blah. Either get over it or pull out now. Anything except the brooding and complaining."

"That's rich," he retorted. "You're the moodiest person I've ever met. When your laptop broke all you did for days was sulk and whinge."

The fact that he had a valid point was incredibly annoying. She sighed. "So we're going back to Birmingham."

"I think we have to," Angel said. "That's where the lab is, and if anyone can help us, that's where they'll be too."

Skyler twisted her hair tighter round her finger until it went numb. For once, watching Mackenzie tapping the walls and counting under his breath, she thought she knew how he felt. She could feel the past waiting to swallow her like a wolf at her heels. "I know. It's just –"

Angel reached out and gently unwound the strand of hair from her finger. Skyler's breath caught. "It's okay," Angel said, as Skyler looked up at her. "He's gone. And if his people cause problems, I'll take care of them."

Skyler took a deep breath. *This is bigger than you. This matters more.*

"How are we gonna do this, then?" she said. "It'll be hard work convincing anyone this is a good idea."

Mackenzie paused his pacing to say, "I think Angel's gonna have to do the talking."

"I might," she said. "If it seems best."

"Well, Skyler can't do it."

Skyler scowled. "What's that supposed to mean?"

"Well, let's face it, your reputation's for two things: being a genius, and acting like you hate everyone. I can't see you sweet talking anyone into a suicide mission."

Unexpectedly, Angel giggled. In spite of everything, somehow, that rare gift made the day seem lighter.

Skyler tore her eyes from Angel's face. "Maybe you should do it then, Mack," she said, deadpan. "Everyone likes you."

He went pink. "Well –"

"I'm screwing with you, before you start hyperventilating. It has to be you, Angel."

"So that's the plan?" she said. "We're looking for people with the skills and resources to help us leak the information abroad and destroy a virus in a secure lab, and who don't mind getting killed in the process."

"Sounds about right," Skyler said.

"Well, then," Mackenzie said. "That doesn't sound difficult at all."

There were many things that were difficult about living in Birmingham but getting a roof over your head wasn't one of them, as long as you weren't fussy. The empty apartments in the high rises had no gas or electricity and were a convenient venue for various nefarious affairs, so there was always the chance of accidentally witnessing a murder, but Mackenzie had lived inconspicuously in a place like this for years before Skyler had shown up and ruined things for him.

Almost as soon as they arrived, Angel prepared to leave again.

"Do you know where you'll go?" Skyler asked as she hovered, watching Angel check her weapons.

Angel slid a knife into a sheath on her calf and straightened up. "I've got some ideas. I might be a day or two."

"You sure you're gonna be okay?"

She grinned. "People have been trying to kill me for years. I'll be fine."

When Skyler didn't smile back, Angel tilted her head to one side, an odd expression on her face. Skyler felt stupid. "Sorry. I know you don't need anyone to look after you."

Angel shook her head. "Don't apologise. It's just – it's been a long time since anyone worried about me."

She took a step towards Skyler, and her smile was suddenly softer, sadder, more real. Skyler found herself smiling back. It felt odd, alien. Since the Wall went up, smiling was for being polite and for keeping the peace; for keeping herself safe. This was different. This was the hopeful bubble, the warmth and longing that rose inside her when she looked at Angel, demanding release.

Every time Angel came near her recently she found herself shy and awkward, unable to meet her eyes and equally unable to look away. And now Angel was standing in front of her, studying her with that inscrutable look on her face, and she would have given anything to know what she was thinking, to find out whether Angel's thoughts and hopes and feelings mirrored her own.

She was close enough to touch. Skyler's heart was racing, but for once it wasn't because she was scared.

Angel reached out and tucked a stray strand of hair behind her ear. Her hand lingered against Skyler's face, and

Skyler looked up and saw the same mixture of excitement and uncertainty and hope in Angel's eyes that she knew was in her own. And she was never sure which of them was the first to move closer, but suddenly there was no more space between them.

Angel's lips brushed hers, once, and then again. In the darkness of Skyler's heart, an unexpected, unfamiliar spark flared into life. Something she hadn't been able to make sense of fell into place in a bright moment of clarity: *this, this is what I want.*

The kiss took on a life of its own. Angel's hands were on her, at her waist, in her hair, and she responded without thinking, her arms around Angel, Angel's body pressed against hers, soft and muscular at the same time. Her hands found Angel's hips, brushed across the sliver of exposed skin between her shirt and her jeans. Angel let out a quick, soft gasp and smiled into the kiss; Skyler's pulse quickened in response.

And then the living room door opened and reality returned with a crash. Skyler drew back, her head spinning.

Mackenzie was already backing out of the room, looking mortified. "Sorry," he mumbled.

Angel shot him a small smile and reached for Skyler's hand. "I'll be back soon. Be safe."

She didn't want to let go of Angel's hand. She wanted to rewind the last few minutes and replay them, to find a way of keeping hold of what had just happened. "You too," she whispered, instead.

Angel slipped out of the door and was gone. Skyler's throat ached. She didn't know whether to laugh or cry.

Across the room, Mackenzie was very obviously bursting to ask a lot of questions. "Not now," she said, before he could speak. For now she wanted to keep it to herself: something private and magical in a world where she had long ago given up believing in magic.

30

THE COLLECTIVE

"Do you think she'll actually be able to do it? Do you think anyone'll care enough to help us?"

Skyler and Mackenzie had been alone in the flat for twenty-four hours, waiting for Angel and annoying one another. Mackenzie's attempts at conversation had not been a resounding success. He was determined to keep trying, though, if only to take his mind off his impending death.

For once, Skyler actually gave him more than a one word answer. "Well, I wouldn't have the first idea where to start. But I guess that's why Angel's doing it and not us. I trust her."

He blinked. This was the most she'd said in one go since Angel had left. Maybe she was finally feeling talkative. It was worth a try, anyway. "Look," he said, "just so you know... you don't have to be embarrassed about the thing with Angel. It's not like I'm going to think any differently of either of you."

She looked blank. "Why would I be embarrassed? I don't care what you think of me."

"Right. Well. Good." He sat down on the floor next to her. "So what exactly's going on there?"

She shrugged. "I'm not sure."

"Well – do you know how you feel about her? Or how she feels about you?"

Skyler's expression suggested she had very little idea what he was talking about and even less idea why he would want to ask her about it. Mackenzie sighed. Trying to talk about feelings with her had clearly been an error. Fortunately, he was saved from trying to salvage the conversation by a knock at the door.

Skyler got to her feet and stood on tiptoe to peer through the peephole. After a second, the tension left her stance. "It's Angel," she said. "And she's got people with her."

Mackenzie was both surprised and impressed that the first people to follow Angel into the flat were Joss and Lydia. Their presence dominated the space so much that it took him a moment to notice there was one more person, a muscular young man with a shaved head and a humourless expression.

"Guys," Angel said, "you know the twins. And this" – she nodded at the stranger – "is Col. Col, meet Skyler and Mackenzie."

Mackenzie thought he might have heard stories about Col. Possibly he'd been in the army before the Wall went up. Not altogether to his surprise, Col did a double take at Skyler. "You," he said. "You know Redruth's boys are after you, right?"

"I'd heard, yes," Skyler said wearily. "So if you could, like, not advertise my presence here, that'd be great."

Col sniffed. "What'd you do?"

Angel gave an almost imperceptible nod, and Skyler seemed to relax. She told Col, whose mouth fell open. "That was *you*?"

She nodded curtly.

"Smart of you to get out of town. His boys turned the city upside down lookin' for you." He gave her a sarcastic grin. "As if it was a kid who took him out. He thought he was untouchable."

"Well, he wasn't," Angel said. She had shadows under her eyes, Mackenzie realised.

"Well," Col said. "Congratulations, I guess. You did this town a favour." He held out a hand to Skyler, who took it, looking faintly suspicious.

Lydia shifted her weight and made an impatient noise. "Yeah, yeah. Well done, kid. Let's talk business."

"How much do they already know?" Skyler asked Angel.

"Angel tells us you have news about the North," Lydia said. "That you're goin' up against the Board to save the world or something." She arched a sarcastic eyebrow. "Can't say we're a hundred percent sold on this idea, but we figured it was worth hearing you out."

"Right," Joss agreed. "Plus, Angel tells us the reason we had to get ourselves arrested so you lot could destroy our drainpipe was 'cos you'd got hold of this news. So we'd like to know what's going on."

"Yeah," Mackenzie said. "Thanks for that, by the way."

Joss gave him a sharp look. "Don't flatter yourself, kid. Just that when someone's saved your life as many times as Angel has. . . .eh, well, that feels a bit like owing a debt."

"Bloody big fine we had to pay," Lydia added. "Reckon that debt's quite a bit smaller now." She nodded at Skyler. "Go on then. Impress us."

Skyler's face pinched with irritation, which Mackenzie suspected might have been a way of camouflaging her discomfort at being elected spokesperson. She hoisted herself onto the windowsill and perched like a bird surveying its terrain. Then she pulled the drive out of her pocket and held it up.

Col squinted at it. "What's that?"

"Mackenzie stole this from the Board headquarters," Skyler said.

Every head in the room snapped towards him. His face went hot. *Thanks, Skyler.* "He asked me to find out what was on it." *Ha.* "This is the best technology the Board can get their hands on. I cracked it." There was a note of pride in her voice.

"And?" Joss said. "What's on it? Stuff about the North?"

Skyler took a deep breath. "When the Wall went up, the Board cut the North off. No power. No fuel. No supplies. It was the middle of winter. The water got shut off." Her voice was flat, as though she'd rehearsed the speech in her head. She kept her eyes on the wall behind them all. "Lots of people died. I mean *lots* of people. The Board think there's about thirty thousand left up there now. The survivors left the cities and formed new communities."

The twins watched Skyler with their arms folded, stiff and expressionless. It was impossible to know what they were thinking. Col shifted on his feet, his mouth set in a hard line. Angel, her eyes on him, got to her feet quietly.

Skyler held up the drive again. "The Board found out that the survivors are talking about a rebellion. On here is the plan they made to deal with that. They modified a smallpox virus and they're going to release it into the North in less than three weeks."

"So." Joss gave her a hard look. "Good story and all, but you still haven't explained why Angel dragged us all up here."

"We're going to stop the Board releasing the virus. You're here because we think you can help."

He raised his eyebrows. "You reckon, do you?"

"Look at it this way. We're all here illegally. None of us have any chance of a decent future unless something changes."

"Speak for yourself," Lydia said. "We're doin' all right, ta."

"Yeah," Skyler said. "In a house the Board could take away whenever they feel like it. Wondering every time an enforcer asks for your ID whether this'll be the time they realise it's a fake. No idea what happened to your friends and family up in York. Brilliant, right?"

Lydia's lips tightened. "You got a better alternative?"

"Not really. That's kind of the point. I mean, maybe we could try and get abroad, claim asylum somewhere, but what're the odds of that? And if we don't do something about this, no one else will. No one else even knows this is happening. How many of you were in the North when the Wall went up?" She looked between them. Each of them shook their head.

"Obviously not," Lydia said, "or we wouldn't be here now, would we?"

"Yeah, well. Mackenzie and I could tell you what it's like. What they've done. What's happened to your families, your friends." She kept her voice steady somehow.

Discomfort rippled through the room. Skyler was breaking an unwritten code: if you met another Northerner, you didn't talk about the Wall. You didn't speculate about what was happening on the other side of that vast stretch of concrete. What was the point of reopening all those wounds when there was nothing that could be done anyway?

Except now maybe they needed those wounds opened. Maybe the sting could force them into action.

"So what do you want to do?" Lydia said. "Tell the world? Destroy the virus?"

"More than that. I want to take down the Board.

The whole system's twisted, it's wrong. There has to be something different."

"You're talking about war," Joss said.

"I guess I am."

"Well, shit." He met his sister's eyes, and some unspoken communication passed between them.

"Right," Col said. "And how d'you think you're gonna make that happen?"

"I'm going to leak the document to the international media," Skyler said. "Along with everything else I can get my hands on about what the Board have done. Once people outside know what's happening, they'll help."

He snorted. "Yeah? Didn't see anyone stepping in the first time around."

"Perhaps they didn't know everything. If even people in the South don't know what the Board did, how would anyone else? But if we can get this information to the right places, there's no way they can suppress it."

Col didn't look any less sceptical. The twins didn't look convinced either. "That's all well and good," Lydia said, "and I'm sure little miss prodigy here's good enough to do as she says, but what about the virus?"

"Yeah," Mackenzie said. "We're still working on that."

"And what about us?" Joss asked. "What're we supposed to do after we've unleashed all this chaos?"

A silence. "We think," Angel said carefully, "it would probably be best for us to go North after that."

A longer silence.

"Well, I guess that makes sense," Lydia said at last. "Not that it sounds like a whole lot of fun, mind you."

"People up there will need to know what's happening," Skyler said. "And we'll need to be well out of the Board's way."

The twins looked at one another.

"We've got a life here," Lydia said.

"We've got family there," Joss said.

"We *had* family. Maybe not anymore."

"Yeah," Joss said. "'Cos of the Board. Haven't done us any favours, Lyds, have they? They'd kill us or throw us in prison as soon as look at us."

Lydia scratched her chin. "When you put it like that. . ."

Joss' mouth twisted thoughtfully. "Gonna be hard, though. We're pretty comfortable here."

"Well," Lydia said. "We do love a challenge, don't we?"

Mackenzie held his breath. Most of what was passing between the two of them was not being spoken. This was important. The twins were smart. The group needed them if this was going to go anywhere.

"I dunno if I could live with myself," Joss said abruptly. "All those people. Not right, is it? Not just for the sake of being comfortable."

Nobody moved.

Lydia looked up. "We'll do it."

Skyler let out a very quiet sigh.

"Good," Angel said. "I knew you'd want to do the right thing."

"Yeah, yeah," Lydia said. "I've got a fucking heart of gold, haven't I? Let's get on with it, then. How are we gonna get over the Wall and keep the Board off our tail?"

"I could take down their communications," Skyler said. They all looked at her. She grinned. "I reckon I could make us time for a getaway."

"We haven't got long to do any of it," Angel said. "They're going to release the virus in seventeen days. Skyler needs a power supply if she's going to do anything."

"Well, we've got power," Joss said. "Guess we won't be using it for much else if we're going to move a hacker in, but hell. What does it matter?"

"The rest of us need to figure out how to destroy that virus," Angel said.

"Well, that's easy." Col cracked his knuckles. "You said it's in a lab here in the city?"

"Right."

"So you blow it up." He made it sound like the simplest thing in the world. "Can't do nowt with a pile of rubble, can they?"

Skyler's face broke into an incredulous smile. "And you'd know how to do that, would you?"

He sniffed. "I used to be an explosives expert, didn't I? Course I could bloody do it. Course," he added, "I'm not saying I'm gonna help. You talk a good talk and all, but how do we know you're tellin' the truth?"

"I can show you the documents."

"Aye. And maybe you really are as good a hacker as you say. But you and the thief" – he shot an unfriendly glance at Mackenzie, who did his best to look as cool as Skyler did – "you're full of it, you two. You reckon you got over the Wall? Sounds like bullshit to me."

Skyler didn't even blink. "What do you want from us?"

"I want the truth. I want to know how you did it."

It was clear both that Skyler didn't like being challenged and that she didn't want to talk about how they'd got over the Wall. It wasn't something Mackenzie particularly wanted to think about either, come to that.

And, to his astonishment, she was looking to him. "This is your story too. You want to tell it?"

He didn't, really. He and Skyler had gone through this together, and it was a story they'd kept between the two of them until now. Mackenzie wasn't sure he appreciated having it dragged out of them by this surly stranger. Or what it would be like having Col as part of this operation.

On the other hand, Col's expertise with explosives would definitely come in handy if they could convince him to stay.

He met Skyler's eyes and nodded.

31

HOMETOWN

In the aftermath of the Wall going up, Mackenzie had set up home in a warehouse on the outskirts of Leeds. He'd made it as comfortable as it was possible to be, which was not very. It was just a vast, empty corrugated iron shell and the wind howled through the gaps in the metal sheets at all hours of the day and night.

Skyler couldn't do anything at all for the first couple of days. If she'd been able to she would have slept the whole time and not thought about Ruby and Sam and the huge, ridiculous mistake she'd made in returning to the North, but her treacherous brain wouldn't let her. Mackenzie put food in front of her, let her sleep when she could, and kept his distance.

She stayed with him mostly because she didn't know what else to do. She was exhausted, and if she was honest, she was afraid she wouldn't survive on her own. Mackenzie, despite his permanent expression of wide-eyed confusion, must have been doing something right to keep himself alive all this time.

She didn't ask him where his own family were. There wasn't much to be certain of just then, but she was pretty sure he wouldn't thank her for asking that question.

One morning, after she'd been in the warehouse about a week, he came over and handed her a tin can and a spoon. It was some sort of stew, a dubious shade of brown and stone cold. She wouldn't have even considered eating it before she ran away, but it turned out pretty much everything looked appetising if you were hungry enough. She dug the spoon into it.

At this point Mackenzie would usually retreat across the warehouse and they would eat in silence. This time, he pulled a crate across the floor towards her, raised his eyebrows and took a mouthful of whatever was in his own tin.

"So," he said. "You got any idea what you're gonna do next?"

"What do you mean?"

"Like, with the rest of your life."

It seemed a ridiculous question, in the circumstances. Where could she go? And what would be the point anyway?

"I don't know," she said at last, when the silence started to get awkward.

"Yeah," he said, with a valiant attempt at what was presumably meant to be cheerfulness. "Me either."

"You must've had some kind of plan. I mean, how did you end up here?"

He screwed up his face like it hurt to think about it. "How long ago did the Wall go up?"

"Four, five months?"

"Right. Well, people started getting sick pretty fast, what with the water and that, and there wasn't really anywhere to put the bodies. . ." He squeezed his eyes shut. "Uh, people started heading out of town after the first couple of weeks. The smart ones."

"Was that when you left?"

"No."

"Why not, then?"

It wasn't very tactful of her and for a moment he stared at her with his mouth half open. It was the first time she'd seen anything approaching anger on his face.

Then his shoulders sagged in defeat. "It was the young, healthy people who left. Families, with little kids or old folk, it was harder for them. Long way to go on foot, right? So people stayed and tried to make the best of it. It was a pretty big gamble either way. It's not like out on the roads everyone's all pally and helping each other out. People are desperate for food and blankets and stuff. It's pretty brutal."

"So you stayed behind. With your family."

He sighed. "Yeah. My mum's parents – they were old, frail. They wouldn't have managed the journey on foot. They said we should go anyway, but none of us wanted to leave them. By the time we realised we really needed to get out of there... well. It was too late by then."

He balled his hands into fists and swallowed. "Everyone got sick. One at a time. And what were we gonna do, leave them behind? To die on their own?"

Her eyes were suddenly hot and prickly. "You did a good thing."

"I tried to be careful," he said quietly. "With the water and everything. I tried and tried. But –"

She knew she should reach out to him, comfort him somehow, but she felt like she was made of ice. He shook himself. "So, anyway. When I was... on my own, I went north. Must have been... three months ago? But like I said, I ran into some trouble."

"What happened?"

He winced. "There were a few others on the road you'd run into from time to time. This one group...

They were a bunch of arseholes, basically, intimidating people to get food and water and stuff." He pulled a disgusted face. "They tried it on me. I *hate* bullies. People who think being stronger and more of a dick means they can treat other people like shit."

For the first time, Skyler saw a glimpse of something different from the awkward, hesitant boy who'd been hovering around her all week. She began to pay closer attention.

"Anyway, they took what I had and luckily I ran into a few kind people who kept me alive. I kept heading north. Couple of weeks later, those dickheads popped up again."

"What happened then?"

"Well, I kind of wanted to teach them a lesson."

"Figures."

"They'd set up camp in, like, a service station. Had loads of supplies 'cos of all the folk they'd robbed, and they'd rigged up this booby trap system. Quite a few people gunning for them by then, as you might imagine. It took me a few days but I figured out their system. I broke in one night and took everything I could carry."

He looked as though he still couldn't quite believe what he'd done.

"What'd you do then?" she asked. "With all the stuff?"

"I gave it back to the people they took it from," he said, as if it were obvious.

"That was brave."

He laughed. "Didn't feel so brave when they found out it was me. Anyway, I knew they wouldn't chase me back down here. No one in their right mind would, eh? I figured I'd lie low for a bit. Give them time to forget about me."

"And how long have you been lying low for now?"

She didn't know why she was asking. She'd stopped caring about anyone else somewhere along the dark, horrible journey of the last few months. But now she found that focusing on Mackenzie made her own pain somehow less unbearable.

"Couple of months, I guess. It's been a while since I've had a conversation, let's put that way." He gave her an unbearably sad grin. "I was actually glad when you hit me with that bloody rock."

She gave up on the cold stew. She stuck the spoon into the remnants and set it down on the floor. "So what're you gonna do now?"

He looked as blank as she'd felt when he'd asked her the same question. "Uh. I'm. . . not really sure."

"I am."

"Huh? Just like that? Half an hour ago I asked you and you looked at me like I was nuts."

"Yeah, well. You made me think."

He gestured at her to continue. When she didn't, he said patiently, "This would be the point where you talk some more. What're you thinking? You heading north?"

"No. I'm going back across the Wall."

Mackenzie's mouth opened and closed a couple of times. "Well, at least you've still got a sense of humour."

"Do I look like I'm joking?"

He stared at her. "No," he said at last. "You don't. In which case I can only assume you're actually mental."

"I got over here, didn't I?"

"Yeah, and you realise it's gonna be about ten times harder to get back the other way, right?"

She jumped to her feet. She only knew one thing: she could not stay here. She couldn't stay in this town where her family had died waiting for her. She couldn't drag herself further north and endure the conditions Mackenzie had described, more men who would demand things from her and force her to keep running or fighting or hiding or just to give up.

She'd learned how to survive in the South. She knew how to do that now. She didn't think she could start all over again and learn how to do it here.

"You telling me I've got something to lose?" she said.

"I'm telling you you're gonna get yourself shot." When she didn't say anything, he sighed. "I'm sorry," he said, and he sounded like he meant it. He was kind, Mackenzie. He didn't want anything from her, not a thing. He might have been the first person she'd met in all these months who didn't.

"I'm setting off tomorrow," she said.

He stood up too. "Then I'm coming with you."

She blinked. "What?"

"I can't stay here on my own. I can't. I'm so sick of not having anyone to talk to. I –" His voice cracked.

She raised her eyebrows. "You're gonna risk getting shot so you can have someone to talk to?"

He half laughed. "It sounds pretty pathetic when you put it like that."

"You're not wrong."

"Seriously, though. I can't stay here forever. I'm gonna run out of food sometime. And if those bastards ever catch up with me they're gonna break my neck. So..." He shrugged.

Well, she could hardly say no. He was going to tag along if he wanted to. And really, it might not be the worst thing in the world to have some company.

"All right, then," she said.

He lifted his head. He actually looked pleased. "Really?"

"Don't look so excited," she reminded him. "We're probably both getting shot, remember?"

They spent the rest of the day trying to figure out a plan.

"We could tunnel over," Mackenzie suggested. "Maybe someone's already dug one, even. There must be at least a couple of people who've made it across."

"If there are, I never met any of them," Skyler said. She brightened. "We could get to the coast and find a boat."

He snorted. She glared at him. "Like a rowing boat, I mean."

"Sounds like a great idea, except I expect the Board have thought of it. They'll have patrols out on the water. Besides," he added, "I'm pretty sure we'd drown."

She kicked a piece of wood across the floor. "Then what are we gonna do? We can't climb the bloody thing."

"I don't know. D'you want something to eat?"

She didn't really, but they had a long journey ahead of them; she would need the energy. She'd always been a little on the heavy side before. *Puppy fat*, her mum had called it. She'd never really cared – she couldn't think of many things less interesting than what size jeans she fit into – but people had always been at pains to reassure her that it was just a phase she was going through. "It'll fall off when you get a bit older," her nan had said, almost every time Skyler had seen her, and her nan had been right, in a funny sort of way, although it didn't seem very funny now.

She accepted a tin of beans from Mackenzie and they sat side by side, chewing speculatively. Her mind was a frustrated whirlwind that kept banging up against dead ends.

"Tell me again how you got over here," he said.

"There are gates in the Wall. The Board send people over here sometimes, I don't really know why. This guy my friend knows paid a greycoat to bring me over – but I don't know how that's any use to us. What would we do, bribe them with tins of beans?"

"How do the gates work?" he persisted. "Did you see how they open?"

"They're electronic. Where I came through, there was a key pad either side of the Wall, near the gate. The greycoat used a code to open it."

"You think we could get hold of the code somehow?" Then he shook his head. "Wouldn't work, would it? It's not like we could just walk up to the gate."

An idea occurred to Skyler. "Actually. . . there might be a way."

Mackenzie put down his beans, his eyes bright and hopeful. "Really?"

She hesitated. "I think it depends," she said, "on how you feel about the idea that we might have to hurt someone."

32

THE WALL

They set off the following day, laden down with as many bottles of water and tins of mystery food as they could carry, which didn't look like nearly enough. As they trudged up onto the flyover that led South, Mackenzie stopped and turned back towards Leeds, where the tall buildings that had once been homes and offices and shops stood dark and still, crumbling in the watery sunlight.

Skyler looked at him, at the hollows under his eyes and the lines around his mouth that didn't belong on the face of a fourteen-year-old. "You all right?" she said. *What a stupid bloody question.*

He stared at the dead city. "I just... kind of used to think I'd live here forever."

She didn't know what to say to that and part of her wished she hadn't asked. She patted him awkwardly on the shoulder and shifted the leaden weight on her back. "C'mon. The sooner we get out of here the better."

They stuck to the motorway, the same path she'd taken to Leeds. She still couldn't shake the feeling that she was trespassing, that an enforcer was going to appear and ask them what the hell they were playing at walking down the middle of a motorway – but the motorways didn't smell of rotting flesh and there were fewer signs, out here, of the desperation and violence that had swallowed the North. Abandoned cars were easier to take than houses that had become mausoleums.

They set up camp at the side of the motorway a few miles from the Wall. Mackenzie, who was brighter than he looked, set up a rudimentary rainwater filtration system so they at least had some clean water, but they were in serious danger of running out of food. They took turns to keep watch, which meant they weren't speaking much to one another, but by then they were both freezing and hungry and exhausted and there wasn't a lot to say.

Mackenzie was on lookout when it happened. The first Skyler knew was him shaking her shoulder in the rosy dawn, his voice low and urgent: "Sky. Wake up. It's time."

She wrestled her way out of her sleeping bag. "How far away?"

"Pretty close. You ready?"

She nodded.

They crouched in the bushes at the side of the road and watched as the black shape on the horizon sped towards them. Mackenzie was trembling. It took Skyler a moment to realise that she was, too.

The car shot past them, juddering as it ran over the boards stuck through with nails they'd laid in the road. It screeched, swerved wildly across the lanes, and stopped about twenty-five metres from them. Skyler tried to remember to breathe.

The car door opened and a man emerged: young, with glasses and curly hair and light brown skin. In spite of his long grey coat and leather boots, he reminded her of Sam's friends, the lively, laughing group who'd piled into his room to watch films and listen to music and who sometimes let her sit with them. She'd never said very much. She'd been happy just to be in their presence, listening to their conversations and absorbing their confidence, the ease with which they inhabited the space around them.

Her throat constricted. The other greycoat had been older, cold, frightening. She hadn't expected this one to look like a friend.

Mackenzie's hand was like a vice on her arm. "He's getting out! What do we do now?"

"Stay calm," she said under her breath. "This is the best thing that could've happened."

"But it's not in the plan –"

She couldn't reassure him. She was too busy trying to block out the insistent inner voice: *I don't think I can do this.* The greycoat knelt beside his car and inspected the nearest tyre with a small but powerful torch, a worried crease in his forehead. Was he scared?

He stood up, reaching to his belt.

A gun. He's got a gun.

The realisation jolted through her like she'd ridden too fast over a pothole. This wasn't one of Sam's friends. This was an enemy.

And then she was on her feet too, and he turned towards her, hand still at his hip.

Her only advantage was that her weapon was already in her hand. As he pulled his gun from its holster, her stone left its slingshot.

His gun clattered to the ground. Skyler swore and fumbled for another stone. Beside her, Mackenzie stared. "Good shot," he muttered.

"I was aiming for his head," she said, from between gritted teeth.

The greycoat ducked to retrieve his weapon. She fitted another stone into the slingshot and let it fly. This one hit him on the temple and he crumpled.

She'd never really hurt anyone before. She'd *wanted* to, lots of times over the last few months, but she was small and under-nourished and it had always been patently obvious that picking a fight wouldn't work out well for her. Seeing the greycoat on the ground was strangely exhilarating. She felt powerful. And she had a savage urge to hurt him more, just because she could.

She shook herself. She was wasting time. He wouldn't be down for long.

The greycoat was sprawled in the road, blood pouring from a gaping cut on his forehead and a purple bruise blossoming around it. They stood over him and Mackenzie wrung his hands together, hopping from foot to foot. "What now?"

"Get the coat off him. He'll have a radio."

She hadn't reckoned on how difficult it would be to get a coat off an unconscious man a foot taller and considerably heavier than her, and by the time she'd taped his hands and feet together he was already stirring. She sort of wished he hadn't woken up, even though they needed him to. She didn't know what she would do if he sounded like a normal human being when he spoke. She thought about taping his mouth too, like she'd seen people do in films, but that was stupid. They needed him to talk, and who would he possibly call to for help anyway?

The greycoat was definitely awake now, shaking, his bloody face contorted. She squatted down next to him.

"What are you *doing*?" he said, before she could speak. "Why are you doing this?"

He sounded confused. Scared. Hurt, even. *What did I ever do to you?*

"Look," he said, as she faltered. "This is silly. I – I understand things are tough up here. But my colleagues will know something's wrong if I don't come back. And if they find out what you've done... It's a serious offence, assaulting a Board official."

She tried to speak, but no words came out.

"Listen. We can sort something out if you untie me. No one needs to know there was a problem."

He sounded so *reasonable*. She shook her head, trying to dislodge his words. "Your code," she said. "We want your code."

His forehead wrinkled. "My what?"

"The code you use to get through the Wall."

"This is crazy. You're just kids. I really don't want to have to turn you over to the Board."

She inched towards him. "Just tell me."

"Look, I don't know where you're getting this from, but I really have no idea what you're talking about –"

Had she got it wrong? She'd been tired and scared the first time she crossed the Wall. Perhaps she'd reinvented it in her mind.

"Come on, kid. Enough of this."

Her eyes landed on his gun, on the tarmac near her feet. *He looks like a normal person but he's not. He helped do this. Mum, Sam, Mackenzie's family –*

Mackenzie nudged her. "He's stalling us. They'll come looking for him eventually."

"What? That's not what I'm –"

She choked down bile.

"Come on. Just untie me, and we can –"

She picked up the gun and pointed it at him, trying not

to look like she'd never held one before. "Shut up. Tell me the code."

"I really think you're going to regret this —"

A flash of something hot and sharp, razors in her blood. "And you're looking out for us, are you? Jesus Christ. Look *around* you. You did this — you and the rest of the Board. You did this to us! Stop acting like you're on our side!"

He was shaking. "We're not all like that. Not all of us agreed with what happened up here —"

"But you didn't stop it, did you? You didn't help! You just let it happen!" She waved the gun at him. "Tell me the code, *now,* or I swear to God I'll —"

"All right! All right! I don't know how you know about it, but clearly you do. So — what if I tell you? You'll let me go?"

"We'll leave you somewhere the Board'll find you easy. If not, we'll make sure someone else gets to you first."

He took a deep breath. "Okay. I can see you're not going to give up. Just... put the gun down, okay, and I'll tell you the code."

He was trembling even more violently now. She'd never seen someone shake like that.

No. Not shaking. He was moving his hands behind his back.

She swung to Mackenzie as the greycoat brought his arms round and slashed at the tape binding his feet. "He's got a fucking *knife*, Mackenzie —"

Mackenzie dragged her backwards, his mouth open in horror, as the greycoat wrestled free of the tape and staggered to his feet. Skyler looked at him, looked at Mackenzie, and suddenly everything seemed to be happening very far away.

She pulled the trigger before she'd even thought about what she was doing.

She didn't hit him, of course. But he kept coming towards her, so she kept firing. And at some point he was on the ground again.

There was a lot of blood, so much that she wasn't sure at first where he was bleeding from. He was still alive, though, judging by all the swearing and yelling. When she gathered the courage to move closer, he was clutching his shin.

She'd had enough now, enough of being scared and being talked down to, and this was going to end, right now, one way or another.

She held the gun with more conviction and stood over him. "Now you have a choice. The Board can find you injured and you can get back over the Wall in nearly one piece, or the folk left round here can find you like this. I don't fancy your chances if you can't even run away, do you?"

The greycoat's breath was fast, raspy. He might have been crying. She took another step towards him. "The code."

"Where. . . are you going. . . to leave me?"

She hesitated. She hadn't thought this bit through. But unexpectedly, Mackenzie stepped forward. "Here," he said, and she was taken aback by the vitriol in his voice. "Out of sight of the watchtowers. If we get over the Wall safely, we'll do an anonymous tip off. If we don't, I expect someone here's gonna find you first."

The greycoat really was shaking now, his face grey and sheened with sweat, his breath hissing between his teeth. Mackenzie prodded him with his foot. "What's it gonna be, then? The code – the *right* code – or shall we leave you here to find out how sympathetic the locals are?"

The greycoat curled in on himself. They waited.

Eventually, he looked up at them. "How. . . do I know. . . I can trust you?"

"You don't," Mackenzie said. "But you're better off at

least giving us an incentive to be trustworthy."

More silence, filled with the greycoat's agonised breathing.

"Well?" Mackenzie said.

The greycoat mumbled a string of numbers so quickly they had to make him repeat it. When he did, he kept his face averted like he couldn't stand to look at them.

It was difficult to move him. Skyler had to keep telling herself: *He wouldn't think twice about doing the same to you. If it was the other way round you'd have a bullet in your head by now.*

It didn't make it any easier.

The car was upholstered in leather and highly polished wood. She had to pull the drivers' seat all the way forward to reach the pedals. Her hands shook when she turned the key in the ignition.

"You sure you can do this?" Mackenzie said.

"Shut up." She tried to put the car into gear and the gearbox responded with a horrible grinding whirr. She let go of the gearstick.

"Clutch," he muttered.

She gritted her teeth. "I know."

"You sure? Because –"

She took a deep, deliberate breath and pressed her left foot on the clutch. Put the car into gear. Pressed her right foot down on the accelerator.

The engine roared. She eased her foot off the clutch. *Slowly. Careful.*

The car lurched and stalled with a bang. Sweat pricked at her forehead. "Don't say *anything*," she growled.

Wisely, Mackenzie did as he was told.

She got the car to move on the third try. Mackenzie slumped back in the passenger seat and Skyler focused on letting the car creep along the road. Every so often, her foot slipped on the accelerator and she had to wrestle for control while the car bounded forward and skidded around on its flat tyres. Once she got it above twenty miles an hour, the rhythmic slapping of deflated rubber on tarmac became audible.

Mackenzie began to whisper to himself. It sounded like he was counting. She had no idea why.

The watchtowers were dotted at intervals along the length of the Wall: tall, square concrete blocks topped with a glass-panelled control room. A no man's land stretched a mile on either side, the boundary marked with a crude barbed-wire fence from which strips of red material fluttered.

The wire wasn't really to keep people out. It was to let the guards know when people came close enough to shoot. South of the Wall, the fence encompassed a reasonable swathe of northern Birmingham, and was adorned with bright yellow signs: NO ENTRY. TRESPASSERS WILL BE SHOT WITHOUT WARNING. On the North side, the guards just opened fire.

The gates in the Wall were big, rolling steel things. The one she'd come through was right beside a watchtower, which made sense but was inconvenient; she had no idea what they would do if they were stopped. Shooting the greycoat had been nothing more than blind luck. She and Mackenzie would be riddled with bullets before they pulled off anything like that again.

The Wall loomed before them, twice as tall as a house, topped with an ugly snarl of barbed wire. Mackenzie whimpered. "It's really real," he whispered.

"Of course it's bloody real."

He shook his head. "I know. It's just – I haven't seen it before. I didn't realise –"

She found herself pitying him. She had actually seen

the Wall go up, or part of it, anyway. The barbed wire had been rolled out first, grey-clad guards standing to attention in front of it, their machine guns not exactly aimed at the gathering crowds but not exactly not aimed at them either.

"What's going on?" a young woman behind her asked the nearest guard.

He stared straight ahead, stony-faced, and didn't answer. Behind him, cranes were hoisting the great slabs of concrete into place.

"I heard it's to keep the Northerners out," a young man in a suit said to a grey-haired man with him.

"Good," the older guy said. "About time we let 'em fend for themselves. See how they get on without us bailing them out all the time."

"Better than that," a woman in a red beret and a smart black coat said, with the kind of poorly contained glee you sometimes heard in people's voices when they were sharing a piece of really bad news that didn't affect them personally. "They're rounding them up. Gonna put them all back over there."

The crowd murmured their approval. The grey-haired man sniffed. "Long past time. I hope they shoot the ones that resist."

Up until that point, Skyler had been wondering if she should ask one of the adults in the crowd for help. That was the moment she'd understood that she had better keep her mouth shut and turn around and walk away from the barbed wire as quietly as possible.

Now, beside her, Mackenzie's face crumpled. "How could they hate us so much they built *that* to keep us out? What did we ever do to them?"

She glanced at him. Then she reached out, keeping one careful hand on the steering wheel, and, just as carefully, punched his arm as hard as she could.

He yelped, and for a moment she thought she'd just succeeded in making him cry, but then he glared at her. "Ow! What the fuck was that for?"

"Don't get upset. Get fucking angry. Crying isn't gonna keep you alive." She stabbed a finger at the Wall. "*Fuck* those guys. They want to keep us out – well, we're gonna be smarter than them, you hear me? We're gonna get over that stupid wall and there's nothing they can do about it."

He stared at her, holding his arm, and then he nodded.

She looked at the greycoat's code, scrawled on the back of her hand. Doubt stabbed at her stomach. What if he'd given them the wrong one?

No point worrying about that. Nothing you could do about it now.

If it was the wrong code, the best case scenario was that they'd be stuck in the North forever. Fleetingly, she considered sharing her fears with Mackenzie. Would it help? Probably not. He seemed to be barely holding himself together as it was.

They'd nearly reached the gate in the Wall. The keypad stood on a metal post within arm's reach of the road. On it, a red light winked at her.

Terror fizzed in her limbs. Her hands slipped, sweaty, on the steering wheel. She couldn't do this. Could she? She could. She couldn't.

You don't have a choice.

She pressed the brakes carefully, her arms rigid as she tried to keep the car straight. She stabbed unfamiliar buttons with clumsy fingers, trying to roll the window down, and squinted at her hand. Mackenzie's nonsensical whispering became frantic.

Skyler squeezed her hand into a fist, willing it to stop

shaking. When it didn't, she reached out of the window and pressed the code into the keypad, murmuring each digit to herself as she did so.

She entered the last digit. The light stayed red.

She fought down a scream.

"Press the 'enter' button," Mackenzie muttered.

She really might have screamed. She pressed the button.

The little red light went green.

Ahead of them, the steel gate rolled open with a quiet, metallic rattle. Her breath came out in a sob.

Mackenzie touched her arm and she jerked round, hands raised, flattening herself against the seat. She must have looked wild, ridiculous.

"C'mon," he said quietly, as though he understood exactly why she'd reacted that way. "We've gotta go."

A lump of rock in her throat. *Don't stall. Don't stall.*

You could be dead any second now.

She put the car into gear and pressed the accelerator.

She got a brief, blurred impression of the base of the watchtower, dark buildings, shadow, as the car shot through the gateway. She jammed her foot harder on the accelerator. The greycoats and the enforcers all drove like nutters anyway. They would hardly look out of place. "What now?" Mackenzie asked, as she wrestled the car away from the watchtower.

"We get outside the wire. Ditch the car."

But the car was no longer in her control. One moment they were rolling forward, the next they were skidding across the road while she slammed on the brakes and wrenched the wheel, which somehow managed to make things worse, and then there was a jarring bump and a bang as the car mounted the pavement, and *then* an even bigger bang as the front of the car embraced a lamp post.

Skyler was flung forward and then back against her seat. And then everything was still.

She closed her eyes. "Mackenzie?"

His voice came out small and timid. "Yeah?"

"You all right?"

"Think so. You?"

"Yeah."

"What do we do now?"

She glanced at the watchtower in the rear view mirror. "I think we run."

"Together?" he said, as they scrambled out of the car.

No time for this. "Split up. Better one of us gets away than neither of us."

"How will we find each other again?"

"I don't know. *Run,* Mackenzie."

She didn't look back to see whether he'd followed her instructions. And she didn't see him again for months.

33

BEST LAID PLANS

Col eventually conceded that their story sounded believable enough. This, he seemed to feel, was reason to join them. Mackenzie wasn't at all sure how much of a good thing this was, but there was no denying that his skills would come in useful.

The group had migrated from the high rise back to the twins' house. Now they were seated around the kitchen table while Joss heated up soup on the stove and Lydia glared at them as though she was conducting an interrogation. "It's all very well, all these big ideas, but have any of you actually thought about how it's gonna work?" She nodded at Col. "You were on about blowing up the lab. Where're you gonna get explosives?"

He scratched his chin. "Take it we've ruled out nicking from the army?"

"Unless you've got a cast iron contact, I think that would be a spectacularly bad idea," Angel said.

Mackenzie coughed. "Um. I might have a contact."

Skyler raised her eyebrows. "You know people who deal explosives?"

"Well, I've never used them myself. I've heard stuff from people who go for the really heavy duty break-ins, though.

I mean, I think the people they go to are, like, arms dealers. They're not very. . . nice. But they'd probably sell us a load of C4 and not ask any questions."

Lydia wrinkled her nose. "You say you don't know them personally?"

"Nope. I mean, can you really see me using that stuff?"

"Fair enough. You could give us a name, though?"

"Yeah."

"Right."

"Um." Mackenzie picked at his bandaged hand. "I don't – I'm not actually gonna have to go and buy this stuff, am I?"

"Nah," Lydia said. "We actually want them to take us seriously."

"Bit unfair," Joss said mildly. "The kid's got quite a reputation."

"He's twelve years old. They'd laugh at him. No" – she addressed Mackenzie – "you give us the names and we'll sort it."

He tried to be offended by her comment, but really he was just relieved. "Fine."

Joss passed around a collection of mugs. Mackenzie peered into his. *Is it safe?*

Don't be ridiculous. Of course it is.

Is the cup clean enough, though?

He could almost see the bacteria clinging to the sides of the mug. *It's just your imagination.*

You don't know that.

From across the table, Angel watched him. His face went hot. *Stop being stupid.*

But he couldn't bring himself to eat the soup.

He was missing things. He forced himself to pay attention to Joss: "How do we know we're not just gonna release this virus into the air and kill the whole city, including us? 'Cos I don't really fancy getting smallpox, thanks."

"The virus is waterborne, not airborne," Skyler said. "So unless we blow open a mains water pipe, it's not going to hurt anyone."

Col sniffed. "That's not such a bad idea."

"Uh," Mackenzie said. The conversation was sending his pulse racing. *Stop it. Just stop it.*

Joss frowned. "The whole point's to make sure no one uses that virus. We need to make a big enough fireball to denature it."

"Will the explosive on its own do that?" Angel asked.

"Maybe not. We'll need petrol as well. Lots of it."

"Christ," Lydia said. "That's gonna be nearly as hard to get as a pile of C4."

"At least we know a dealer for that," Joss said. "Won't be cheap, though." He looked at Skyler. "What do you need for your bit?"

"Internet access. Pretty much constantly."

"Well, we've got a decent power ration. We'll be fined if we go over – but I suppose that doesn't really matter." His shoulders slumped.

"It's not like we're gonna be here much longer," Lydia said quietly.

Joss fiddled with his cup. "And then we go North."

Angel nodded.

"And this is the best idea we've got, is it?"

"Unless you can think of a better one."

He inspected his mug. "We do need to get over there, don't we?" he said at last. "All right, then. How're we getting into the lab and across the Wall?"

"There'll be information in the Board records," Skyler said. "Once I've got that we can figure it out."

Col squinted at her. "And you're gonna build this computer virus as well, are you? Sure you can manage all that?"

Her eyes narrowed. "Unless you think you can help, take my word for it that I can get it done."

"Right," Lydia said. "We're gonna need to know the layout of that lab down to the last detail, inside and out. Mackenzie, you must be used to this kind of thing. Can you go and scout the place out?"

If I can get out of the house.

He picked at his bandages. *You're going to have to. You don't have a choice.* "Yeah," he said, to Lydia's dubious expression. "I can do that."

*

It was a relief when the talking stopped and Skyler was left alone to get on with breaking into the Board's files. She'd installed herself in the kitchen – it was warm and bright, as different from Daniel's cellar as she could get, and if it meant she got interrupted every time someone was hungry or thirsty, she was prepared to put up with that. In truth she hardly registered anyone else's presence once she was immersed in unravelling the Board's firewalls. Angel and Mackenzie understood that she needed to be left alone.

Lydia, however, did not seem to get this. She'd come into the kitchen to make a drink and Skyler was doing her best to ignore the woman's eyes on her, but Lydia wasn't taking the hint.

When it became clear that she wasn't going to go away, Skyler lifted her head. "What?"

"How's it goin'?" Lydia asked.

It'd be going a lot better if I didn't have to make small talk with you. "Fine."

"And you're sure you know what you're doing, are you?"

"You've seen my work." Skyler turned back to the laptop. "You know what I can do."

"I'm not talking about that. I'm talking about this whole blow up a government building thing. It's a lot for a kid your age."

Skyler considered pointing out that this was none of her business, but if she pissed Lydia off enough she might decide that the contents of the drive were none of her business either. "Not really," she said instead, reluctantly. "Mack and I know what we're getting into. We're fine. Why? You getting cold feet? You've got a pretty nice life here, after all."

Lydia snorted. "You reckon, do you?"

"Compared to the North, or Redruth's cellar, yeah. You guys have done well for yourselves, and you're about to throw it all away."

"You talkin' me out of it now?"

"No. Just curious." *Just wondering what happens if you have a change of heart.*

Lydia leaned against the counter and folded her arms. "Joss and I have it easy compared to the rest of you, it's true. When everything went to hell – when I couldn't tell anyone what I thought about the Board, when I was worried I was gonna lose my job for having a Yorkshire accent – we always had each other. But this is it, isn't it? We've got a decent life, by your standards, but they're pretty messed up standards. We've got no other family. Can't have relationships 'cos we can't trust anyone. I used to think me and Joss'd live in London forever, meet people, get married, have kids. Joss had a fiancé when the Wall went up. Nice lad, but he could never go back to him, not even to say goodbye. Even if he'd had the stones to stick with him, Joss wasn't gonna let him get taken away by the greycoats for trying to help him.

This" – she gestured at the kitchen – "this is a lot compared to some people, you're right. But this is all it's ever gonna be. And it's not right. It's not fair."

She gave Skyler a sarcastic grin. "So fuck the Board. If a bunch of kids have the guts to stand up to them, I'm not gonna say I'm too scared. If we're gonna die, at least we'll die honest."

"Right," Skyler said.

Lydia raised her eyebrows. "Did I pass, then?"

"Just glad we're on the same page." She turned back to the laptop, but Lydia didn't move. Skyler sighed. "Did you want something else?"

Lydia's lips twisted thoughtfully. "Just interested, that's all."

"In what?"

"Well. You and Angel, for starters."

Skyler was too startled to remind her that this was definitely none of her business. "What? How'd you know about that?"

Lydia headed for the sink and filled the kettle with water. "We've known Angel a long time," she said over her shoulder. "Never saw that coming."

"What, me and Angel?"

Lydia took a tin out of the cupboard next to the sink. "Want some tea?"

This seemed to be an attempt at friendliness. Tea was expensive, and often only available on the black market. "Sure," Skyler said. "Thanks."

Lydia set the kettle on the hob. "Not just you and Angel. I mean Angel and anyone. She's always been very... self-contained. Never told me or Joss the first bloody thing about herself. Oh, don't get me wrong – she talks about what she's been up to, and she's dead helpful when you're bleeding to death, but she's, what, nineteen? And the way she talks, all posh like that, she didn't grow up in that bloody cellar, did she? I don't have a clue who she was before she turned into Birmingham's answer to Batman. And I don't reckon anyone else does either."

Skyler had been about to say, *I know Angel.* But now she thought about it, what did she know? Angel listened a lot more than she spoke. "What're you getting at?"

"I'm sayin' the girl's got history. And whatever it is, you can be damn sure it ain't pretty."

Skyler found her voice sharpening. "Are you saying me and her shouldn't –? Because –"

Lydia waved a hand. "Nah, settle down. You've obviously got something special, otherwise she wouldn't bother with you. Don't see it myself," she added speculatively. "But you've got yourself one of the good ones somehow, and all I'm sayin' is, that's a big deal. This is a big deal for Angel."

The kettle whistled. Skyler looked Lydia in the eye. "I thought you didn't know her very well."

Lydia poured steaming water into the mugs and set one in front of Skyler. "Let that brew for a bit. That's not what I said. I said she don't talk much. I know enough about her. Can't fight alongside someone that many times without learning a few things."

"And what've you learned?"

"Well, for a start, I've seen her do some bloody stupid stuff for someone as smart as she is. I've seen her take on people bigger'n her, stronger, better armed. Watched her climb a six storey building with the smallest handholds I've ever seen in the pouring rain, take jumps across rooftops I didn't think she had a hope in hell of making. Honestly, I've lost count of the number of times I thought she was about to die, and she never even blinks. She's not scared of anything. And I mean *anything*."

"Well – isn't that a good thing?"

Lydia wrinkled her nose. "I dunno, to be honest. I'm pretty tough, but sometimes things go so far and this little bit in your brain goes, eh, maybe you better sit this one out. Angel doesn't seem to have that. I wondered sometimes if she was a bloody robot till I saw the way she looks at you. I've never really seen her act like she felt anything. Except maybe pissed off sometimes."

Skyler wondered how she could make Lydia get to the point. "What're you saying?"

"I'm saying – yeah, she's great when you're doin' dangerous stuff. And she'll throw herself into harm's way to help someone on her team without even thinking about it. But you might need to keep that in mind, when it comes to gettin' over the Wall. You might need to prepare yourself."

"Prepare myself for – what? She'll be all right. She's not going to do anything stupid." *She wouldn't. Would she?*

"Maybe," Lydia said. "Maybe you know her better than I do. I'm just saying – it's not normal, the way she is. Nobody's that calm, not when they think they're about to die."

"Well, she is," Skyler said. "She's all right. There's nothing wrong with her."

Lydia waved an irritable hand, as though she'd had enough of the conversation. Skyler had too. She gestured at the laptop. "I should get on with this."

Lydia took her tea and headed for the kitchen door. Before she opened it, though, she paused. "Think about it," she said. "It's not a good thing, Skyler, being fearless. Fear's there for a reason. The only way someone could turn out the way Angel is, I reckon, is if they really believed they didn't have anything left to lose."

34

CLOSER

They'd been at the twins' house for three days. Skyler didn't want to sleep, there wasn't enough time. But her body demanded it, so when the screen blurred in front of her and her fingers slipped on the keyboard, she took herself off to the attic. Joss had tried to repair an air mattress with duct tape but it still deflated every night and she ended up on the floorboards. It was okay, though. Better a hard floor in the twins' attic than a mattress in Daniel's cellar.

She thought back to her conversation with Mackenzie: *do you think we'll ever not be scared all the time?* Would there always be another new fear, assuming they could all stay alive long enough for there to be another one?

And Lydia's comments about Angel, which had sounded like a warning. Had she been right? Skyler couldn't believe it, and she couldn't think about it. She certainly couldn't bring herself to raise the subject with Angel. Too much. It was all too much.

She lay on the air mattress, staring into space. Her eyes burned dry but her brain wouldn't switch off. In the dark, it was harder to remember where she was, that every rustle and creaking floorboard didn't signal danger.

The attic door opened. As she shot upright, Angel

stepped into the room, holding a candle. "Hey. It's just me."

Skyler relaxed. "Hi."

"Can I sit down?"

Skyler smiled at her. "You don't have to ask."

Angel set the candle on the floor and settled herself on the mattress beside Skyler. Skyler offered her the blanket and Angel pulled it over her legs.

They sat, side by side, not quite touching. "Did I wake you?" Angel asked.

Skyler shook her head. Angel touched her arm. "You need to sleep, Sky."

When Skyler said nothing, her expression softened. "You can't sleep."

"No."

Angel looked at her with her head on one side. "What do you need?"

What did she need? She didn't know. It had been so long since she could afford to have needs.

"Talk to me," she said, at last. "Tell me something that's not sad or scary. Tell me something about you."

Angel considered her for a long moment. Then she smiled. "All right," she said. "Lie down, and I'll tell you a story. I'll tell you about the best thing that happened to me in the last five years."

Skyler lay on her side and Angel lay too, pulling the blanket up over them both. She laced her fingers through Skyler's and Skyler searched her face in the golden light: dark liquid eyes, the scar by her bottom lip that Skyler wanted to kiss every time she noticed it.

They both shifted at once, closer now, their bodies touching, and some of the tension Skyler had been carrying for as long as she could remember drained away. "Tell me," she said.

"Three years ago," Angel said. "I was sixteen. I'd been living under the shop about six months. People came to me when they needed protection, or when they were sick. I knew some basic first aid, and when I started living... the way I do now, I set up a deal with a couple of people at the city hospitals – paid them to divert meds, equipment, textbooks, that sort of thing."

"You taught yourself medicine from books?"

"How else? Anyway, I guess I managed not to kill enough people that they wanted to come back. I got to know this guy called AJ. And one day he brought me someone who needed help."

"Really," Skyler said.

"Uh huh. This girl. She had a fever, she was really sick. But tough. She stayed for two days and then she left in the middle of the night, even though she was hardly strong enough to walk. And I didn't see her again for – must have been nine or ten months, I reckon."

"Are you talking about –?"

"Shh. I'm telling a story. Anyway, I looked for her, but it was like she'd vanished. A few months later she turned up at my door again, told me she needed to learn to fight. So I agreed to teach her."

"What happened then?"

"Well." Angel smiled. "I taught her to fight, which wasn't the easiest job. She wasn't what you'd call a natural." Skyler laughed. "The first time I gave her a knife she kept dropping it. She nearly put it through my foot. I remember thinking, oh my God, what am I doing? But – she was determined. Fierce. She'd practice over and over until she had something right, and she was always a little bit better the next time.

"And... I started to look forward to her coming. I didn't look forward to anything, but one day I thought, *she's coming today*, and that was. . . a good thought. She was the most sarcastic person I've ever met. She made me laugh, and I thought I'd forgotten how. But she was still in danger. I worried about her. And after a while, she stopped coming to see me."

"That was pretty dumb of her," Skyler said.

"I figured she had her reasons."

"Well, maybe they were stupid reasons."

"Hey, who's telling the story here? Anyway, I was afraid something had happened to her, but I asked around and it seemed like she was okay, so I left it alone. I figured – I hoped – she'd come back, when the time was right. And she did. She turned up one night out of nowhere, covered in blood, and I – well. There was all this scary stuff happening, but I was just. . . happy to see her. And when I had to make a decision about what to do next, the only thing I knew – the only thing that made sense to me – was that I wanted to be where she was. I didn't expect anything to happen between us. I just knew that out of everyone in the whole world, she was the one I thought about when I was away from her.

"And then I got to know her better. And I started to wonder if maybe she was looking at me the way I was looking at her."

Skyler watched the reflection of the candle flame in Angel's forest-green eyes. "Did you figure it out?"

"I took a risk. The scariest thing I've done in years."

"Did it pay off?"

Angel traced a fingertip down Skyler's face. "I think so."

Skyler wriggled nearer and Angel pulled her in close, ran a hand down her back. Skyler tilted her head to meet her eyes. "In case you were wondering," she said, "your mystery girl looks at you the same way you look at her."

"And how's that?"

Skyler took a deep breath. "Like... for the first time in years, something's happening that I don't want to block out. Like I was sleepwalking, and then I woke up."

Angel's smile made her feel like she was glowing from the inside. "Yes. That's exactly how I feel."

Skyler reached up to touch her cheek, the warmth of Angel's body against hers making her blood sing in a different way: not the buzz of the electric fence humming *danger, danger*, but something new. Something she wanted to move towards, not away from.

Angel's hands on her, their hips pressed together, Angel's leg draped over hers. Closer. Closer.

Angel's breath on her cheek, on her lips. "What do you need now?"

Closer still.

"Kiss me," Skyler said. And then: "Keep kissing me."

35

OLD WOUNDS

Mackenzie had hoped things would be different once they were back in Birmingham, but they weren't. His thoughts never stopped racing. The twins' kitchen was clean enough to do surgery in. Angel understood and didn't comment even though she could see he was getting worse. Skyler just pretended she hadn't seen anything. But the twins had noticed now, too.

It wasn't that he didn't care about the looks they gave him, about Lydia muttering under her breath. It was just that he couldn't do anything about it.

On the day he went to scope out the lab it took him the best part of the morning to get outside. He'd dressed as a binman, because even dictators needed their bins emptied and he quite enjoyed the fact that dressing in a fluorescent orange vest was one of the most effective ways to become invisible. He'd done this plenty of times before, but just then his brain was a constant tug of war between logic and the relentless, hissing fear, and he felt like he might as well have just gone up to the nearest enforcer and let them take him away.

The lab was to the east of the city, within a sprawl of warehouses and empty offices with cracked windows, subtly concealed behind a twenty foot wall topped with razor wire. There were – unusually these days, and most unhelpfully – cameras perched atop the wall. Mackenzie shied away when he saw them. He wouldn't be able to look at the whole building now. What possible reason would he give for needing to walk all the way around it?

He strode past the front of the lab, trying to look as though he had urgent bin-related business to attend to. There was one entrance, a metal gate big enough to get a lorry through, with a small hut beside it manned by a guard. The guard looked bored, but raised his head as Mackenzie passed. Mackenzie gave him a brief nod. The most important thing was to act as though he had every right to be here.

The guard nodded back and he walked on, ignoring the splinters of dread in his veins. At least he'd established something, even if it was only that getting in would be bloody hard work. Still, they'd work something out. Probably Col would be only too happy to shoot someone.

He left the industrial estate and turned for home. As he navigated the city markets he calculated the distance back to the twins' house, counting down the metres to safety. He couldn't shake the thought that the guard at the lab had sensed something amiss, would call in his sighting. The Board knew someone had the Heimdall drive, although they were probably counting on the idea that no one would be able to decrypt it. If they got wind that anyone knew what was in that lab, they would up the security or move the virus. Perhaps they'd even release it early and all of this would be for nothing.

Your fault. You were careless, it's all going to go wrong, it's your fault.

It'll be okay if I can get from here to the fruit stall in less than twenty steps.

It'll be okay if I can get out of the market without seeing any more enforcers.

It'll be okay if I can get home without thinking about anything bad.

Don't think about it. Don't think about it.

A hand on his shoulder.

He spun, flailing, and punched out blindly. By the time his voice of reason had piped up to point out that this was a really stupid idea, the punch had landed.

"Mackenzie!" The voice wasn't friendly but it wasn't especially menacing either. "Cut it out."

With an effort, he focused. The person holding him was AJ.

"Christ," he said. "You couldn't just say hello like a fucking normal person, could you?"

AJ frowned at him. "You're back in town."

"Obviously."

"Where've you been? Where's Skyler?"

Telling him seemed like a bad idea. Mackenzie could imagine exactly how she would react if he presented AJ to her without any warning.

AJ's hand tightened on his shoulder. "Where is she, Mackenzie?"

He did his best. "Look, man, I'd better check with her first. You guys didn't exactly part on the best of terms –"

The hand got tighter still. "Tell me where she is," AJ said, "or I'm going to follow you around until you do. Could get inconvenient."

Mackenzie gave him a baleful look. "You're a right dick sometimes, you know."

"Just walk," AJ said.

Mackenzie couldn't remember ever having had a conversation with AJ that consisted of more than a few sentences, but for once AJ seemed to be feeling talkative. "Bit stupid to be wandering around here, isn't it? What're you doing back?"

"Skyler can tell you that," Mackenzie said. When AJ's expression suggested he was going to argue, he glared at him. "What're you gonna do, beat it out of me? Never had you down as *that* sort of person, AJ. Maybe you spent a bit too much time hanging out with Redruth."

That shut him up. Mackenzie decided to leave the rest of the conversation to Skyler.

Predictably, she did not thank him for this. He'd intended to make AJ wait outside the house while he explained the situation, but as soon as he got the front door open AJ pushed past him. "Skyler! Sky!"

Skyler burst into the hallway, poised to run or fight. When she saw AJ her stance lost some of its edge, but her scowl deepened. "What the hell are you doing here?" She turned the scowl on Mackenzie. "What is this?"

"Not my idea," Mackenzie retorted. "He followed me here."

"I just want to talk to you," AJ said. He sounded completely different addressing Skyler: softer, apologetic. "It was shit, how we left things."

Mackenzie rolled his eyes. "I'll be upstairs," he said, and trudged off.

*

Skyler jerked her head towards the kitchen. "Come in then, I guess."

AJ was clearly trying to figure out what she was doing back in the twins' house. Fortunately, they were out. Skyler had heard more than one disparaging comment about him in the last few days, and she didn't think they would be pleased to find him there uninvited.

She closed the laptop and sat down at the table. "What do you want?"

AJ pulled out a chair next to her. "Bloody hell, Sky. We've been friends all this time and then everything just blew up out of nowhere, and then you vanished. I just wanted to talk to you. See how you are."

"I'm fine."

"It was silly," he said. "That fight – we both said things we shouldn't have."

Speak for yourself. She suspected he wanted an apology, which she didn't feel like giving. Still – was she really ready to burn this bridge once and for all?

"I guess," she said at last.

AJ looked like he was wondering if this was the best he was going to get. But what else could she say? If anything, her error had been in letting herself off the hook too easily, not in being too hard on him.

"What are you doing back in Birmingham?" he said. "You know it's not safe."

She kept her expression blank. "Isn't it?"

Oh for God's sake, stop trying to antagonise him. His forehead creased, half puzzled, half frustrated. "Skyler –"

She took pity on him, sort of. "Redruth's lot."

"Yes, Redruth's lot! What's the matter with you? Why would you even *think* about coming back?"

Warm brown eyes. Callused hands. A person who'd been kind to her, over and over. What was she doing?

She swallowed. "Can I trust you, AJ?"

"You know you can –"

"I mean *really* trust you. Even if you're mad at me, even if I'm doing something you don't agree with. Can you promise you wouldn't sell me out?"

He was still scanning the room, his forehead wrinkled. "What are you doing in the twins' house?"

"Why does it matter?"

"I didn't know you were so tight with them."

She wanted to shake him. "AJ, if I can't trust you, you might as well leave now."

Finally, he was paying attention. He put his hand on hers. "Sky. Whatever it is, you can tell me. I swear."

This was *AJ*. He'd fed her when she was starving, taken her to Angel when she was sick. He'd put the word out that anyone who hurt her would have to answer to him. He'd found a way to get her home, because that was what she'd wanted, and he had wanted to make her happy.

And things were different now. They had a job to do – *she* had a job to do – and it was too big a risk to hope that he would understand.

She pulled her hand from his. "You need to leave."

"What?"

"I mean it. You need to go."

His face tightened. "You're unbelievable. You're just throwing me out?"

Just because you want to trust him doesn't mean you can. She swallowed. "Yes."

She thought he was angry, but when he spoke his voice was quiet, hurt. "I thought we were friends."

She closed her eyes. "We were."

He scraped his chair back and stood up. She couldn't look at him. She desperately didn't want him to go. And he had to, because there was no way to close the distance between them now.

"You *killed* people, Sky," he said. "Doesn't that bother you at all?"

There was a knot in her chest, hot and dark. "Well, if we're talking about being a total fucking hypocrite, AJ, let's talk about you working for Redruth, shall we? Let's talk about all the people *he* killed. And how about you? What's your tally now?"

"He had a family," AJ said. "A wife. A daughter. People depended on him."

His words ran through her like ice into her veins. She bit her lip hard, and forced her voice to be harder still. "Am I supposed to be sorry? Do you think he gave me a choice?"

Once she would have known what he was thinking. She didn't have any idea now. "You've changed," he said.

"Good. Because the old me was going to end up dead. Better him than me."

"Is Angel still with you?"

"What does *that* have to do with anything?"

"She put you up to all this. What'd she do, convince you Redruth was some sort of monster?"

"Do you think I couldn't see that for myself, AJ?"

"I dunno." His voice had a bitter, sarcastic edge that didn't sound like him at all. "I guess she's pretty good at manipulating you." When Skyler stared at him, speechless with irritation, he said, "Why do you think she gave you that gun, Sky?"

"AJ, I have no idea what you're talking about."

"Ask her." He wrenched the kitchen door open, and then looked back at her. "His crew are still after you, you know. You need to be careful."

"And you're okay, are you? How did *that* happen? What did you do to convince them you had nothing to do with it?"

He looked at the floor. She sighed. "Maybe I don't want

to know."

His face crumpled. "No," he said. "Maybe you don't."

She listened to the front door slam behind him. She leaned her elbows on the table and put her head in her hands.

Quiet footsteps pattered towards her. She looked up into Mackenzie's tired, pale face.

"You okay?" he said. "I'm sorry... he insisted. I thought you might feel weird about it."

She rubbed her eyes. They stung. "Yeah. It wasn't great. He wanted to know what we were doing."

His eyes widened in alarm. "Did you tell him?"

"Don't be stupid."

He sat down next to her. "Sky – d'you think we're doing the right thing here?"

She took a deep breath. "I do. I really do. But – it's all more complicated than I thought it would be."

He said nothing.

"I wanted to get even," she said. "I wanted to make them pay for what they did."

"I think saving some lives is a better ambition," Mackenzie said gently. "Don't you?"

She let out a long sigh, straightened her back. "AJ said something kind of weird."

"Why does that not surprise me?"

"About Angel."

"Oh. Well, I guess he's known her a while. What'd he say?"

Skyler chewed her lip. She didn't want to admit how much AJ's words had got to her. "Something like, she manipulated me when she gave me the gun."

Mackenzie rolled his eyes. "He doesn't let go of things in a hurry, does he?"

"I don't know. I don't know what he meant."

"Well, I guess it doesn't really matter. I mean, Angel got you out of that cellar alive. You could ask her what he meant, though. I'm sure she'd tell you."

She didn't answer him. After a minute he got up, gave her another awkward pat on the shoulder, and went back upstairs.

She ran a hand through her hair. Damn AJ. He'd broken her train of thought. Now her head was crowded with all this other stuff and she was exhausted. She was so aware of the hours slipping past, of the need for everything to be perfect, kept checking and rechecking her work. She was getting as bad as Mackenzie.

There was an ache in her chest when she thought about AJ. She didn't think she'd ever see him again.

36

A CLEAN SLATE

In a resigned sort of way, Skyler had been okay with going back to the streets after she crossed the Wall and returned to the South. She had a much better idea how to look after herself now and anyway it wasn't any more awful than the last few weeks had been. At least it was easier to get food and clean water here.

Her most pressing thought had been that she needed to find AJ. She needed to explain why she'd come back, and work out how she was going to repay him the money he'd given Daniel. She hoped he'd be pleased to see her.

But when she got to his bedsit, the door was boarded up.

She made some enquiries of the other people who lived on the city's streets, but nobody had seen AJ for some time and they clearly hadn't been expecting to see her again either. They were suspicious, and she had to press for information.

"Where is AJ?" she asked, for the hundredth time. "Is he okay?"

The man she was talking to was called Crazy Rick. He was approximately ninety years old with no teeth, and wore an oversized red bobble hat that stood out like a signal flare and a strange string necklace. Rumour had it the decorations on it were human teeth. She'd always tried not to look too closely.

Despite his disturbing fashion sense and even more disturbing smell, Crazy Rick was good for one thing: he knew *everything*. Skyler had no idea how he even kept himself alive but he was always there, shuffling down the streets in his bobble hat and a pair of slippers held together with duct tape, and he always knew exactly what was going on.

Right now, though, he was cackling. She'd forgotten that on a bad day you would have to endure a series of nursery rhymes and cryptic clues to get the information you wanted.

After about five minutes, the cackling stopped. "Enforcers got him," Rick said, at length. "Out on licence, wasn't he? Broke his conditions."

Skyler swore. "Is he all right?"

He began to sing "Humpty Dumpty". She waited for him to finish, but when he started adding in extra verses she gave up. "Rick! Is AJ okay? Where is he?"

"Back in prison," Rick said, slipping seamlessly out of the song. "Got four months left on his licence. Not having a great time in there."

"What do you mean? He's been in prison before. He can take care of himself."

Rick mumbled something unintelligible. Skyler, afraid this was the beginning of another nursery rhyme, waved a hand in front of his face. "Rick. What's the problem with AJ?"

"Stupid sod owes that prick Redruth money, doesn't he? Can't pay him back if he's banged up."

Her stomach lurched.

"Yeah," he said. "Redruth's boys've been giving him a bit of a hard time."

She swallowed. "Is he okay?"

"Oh, don't worry. Your lad's still got all his bits at the moment. His face ain't looking too pretty just now, though, I hear."

He gave a heavy, phlegm-laden laugh that turned into a coughing fit. Skyler waited to see if there was going to be anything more, but Rick had lost interest in her. She turned away.

AJ owed Redruth money because he'd taken on her debt. She had to fix this. She knew where she had to go next.

But when she reached the bar where AJ had first introduced her to Redruth, she faltered. She hadn't had a proper wash in months. Her hair was knotted, her clothes torn and mud-stained; she couldn't imagine she would be allowed over the threshold of this gleaming establishment. And sure enough, the doorman was eyeballing her, signalling that she had better move on before she brought the tone of the place down by her mere proximity to the front door.

She held her head high and marched up the marble steps towards him. "I want to talk to Daniel Redruth," she said, before he could speak.

He burst out laughing. "Get out of here, you little rat."

"I'm serious. Is he in there?"

"Does it matter? He's not gonna have anything to say to you."

"Either let me in, or go and tell him there's someone who wants to speak to him."

"Fuck. Off," the doorman said. "Seriously. He's not the type to take a joke, love."

"I'm not joking," she snapped. "I don't care what he does, okay? At least give him the message."

He eyed her with extreme scepticism. "He's got a nasty temper."

She straightened her back. "Tell him I want to settle a debt."

She'd clearly found the magic words, because with that the doorman turned on his heel and marched into the building. She forced herself to stand her ground. She would speak to Redruth. She owed it to AJ.

A reflection moved in the polished steps before her. She looked up.

Daniel Redruth stood before her, wearing an expression of great distaste. When he recognised her, though, his sneer of disgust turned to open-mouthed shock. It took him a moment to recover.

"Well." He took a step towards her. "I wasn't expecting to see *you* again."

She said nothing.

"My friend the doorman tells me you want to settle a debt. I certainly hope so. I wouldn't like to think you'd brought me out here to waste my time."

"I –" He voice accidentally came out very small. She tried again. "I'm not here to waste your time. I'm here to talk about AJ's debt."

He yawned theatrically. "If you're going to beg for leniency on his behalf you're wasting both our time. AJ is a businessman, like me. He understands how these things work."

Don't. Move. "I – I understand that," she mumbled, through dry lips. "But it's not AJ's debt, it's mine. It's me you should be after."

He grinned. "Oh, that's cute, offering to take a beating for your friend. But I don't think you understand. What I want here, young lady, is my money back. I doubt you can give me that. AJ, on the other hand, can pay me back easily enough if he fulfils a few simple requests." He considered her, head on one side. "Although he does seem to need an incentive to do as he's asked. Perhaps you could help with that."

She cursed herself. She was an idiot. This man would hurt her if he thought it would make AJ do what he wanted.

Every instinct that sparked to life flashed dangerously: *Run. Get out of here.* But running wouldn't help AJ. And now Redruth knew she was back he'd probably track her down, chop bits off her and post them off to AJ in prison until he'd done whatever Redruth wanted him to do.

If this went wrong, she and AJ were both going to get hurt.

She made herself meet Redruth's eyes. "It's my debt," she repeated. "And I can pay it."

He raised his eyebrows. "Then you really must have some remarkable talents. I certainly hope so. If I wanted somebody to whore out I think I could do better than you."

Jesus. She was going to be sick. She spoke the next words very carefully. "Not that. I – I can do better than that."

"If that's true I'd love to hear it." He rubbed his chin. "I suppose you did make it back over the Wall. Maybe you're smarter than you look."

"I am." She gritted her teeth. "Find me a computer with an internet connection and somewhere to use it. Give me two days. I'll get you the money back, plus the interest, and I'll double it."

And there it was: the hard lines of his face softened. He took a step towards her and smiled at her in a way that made her want to throw up.

He took another step towards her and put a hand on her shoulder. "Well, then," he said. "Let's see what we can do for you."

She'd told herself it was just to clear the debt. Then, after that, it was just till she'd got a bit of money behind her, till she found another place to make a living as a hacker. But really she'd known, right from the second she'd set foot in that cellar, that he was never going to let her leave.

37

FRESH CUTS

Skyler couldn't concentrate after AJ slammed his way out of the house. She kept coming back to his parting shot about Angel. She didn't know whether to be relieved or not when Angel walked in a couple of hours later, sat down next to her at the kitchen table and said, "How're you doing?"

Skyler couldn't look at her. "A bit rattled. AJ was here."

"*What*?"

"He saw Mack and followed him here." Skyler slumped in her seat, exhausted and miserable. "It didn't go well."

Angel took her hand. "What happened?"

"Nothing, really. I made him leave. I didn't tell him anything."

"That must've been hard."

"I wanted to tell him," Skyler admitted. "I know it's stupid, but I wanted to. But he wouldn't have understood."

"No. I don't think he would."

She chewed her lip. "He said Redruth's lot are still after us. You need to be careful."

Angel raised her eyebrows. "And AJ's fine, is he? How'd he manage that?"

"I don't know. He said I didn't want to know. I don't even know what that means."

"Nothing good," Angel murmured. She sighed. "I'm sorry. He was your friend."

Skyler kept biting the skin from her lip. "I just assumed we saw the world the same way, and I don't think that's actually true. I mean... he didn't *have* to join Daniel's crew, did he? I don't get it. He was always so kind... How could he be okay with working for Daniel?"

"It's complicated," Angel said. "When I first met AJ, all he was interested in was mechanics. He was soft-hearted, too. I can understand how he ended up resenting that doing the right thing got him nowhere. I think Redruth exploited that."

"Still," Skyler said. "He made a choice."

Angel touched her cheek lightly. "He cared about you. I imagine he still does. But as soon as you set yourself against Redruth, he was going to have to pick a side."

"He – uh." Skyler swallowed. "He said something weird. About you."

"Oh?"

She wasn't sure she wanted to bring this up at all. She wanted to focus on Angel's hand on hers, not the petty rubbish AJ had spouted out of anger. But his words were stuck in her head, and she needed Angel to tell her they didn't mean anything.

Angel gave a small chuckle. "You don't have to be so nervous, Sky, it's okay."

Just get it out. Then you can forget about it. "He said – you had a reason for giving me the gun," Skyler mumbled, her eyes fixed on the table. "He said you manipulated me."

She'd expected Angel to laugh, but she didn't. She didn't say anything at all. Her hand tensed on Skyler's, and Skyler immediately wanted to take her words back. "I'm sorry," she said. "I didn't mean to upset you – I know it's ridiculous, I just – didn't understand what he meant."

Angel stared into space. An uneasy current stirred deep in Skyler's stomach. "Angel?" she said. "Was he – right?"

Angel let go of her hand and pulled away from her. "That sort of depends," she said, "on your point of view."

Now the seed of doubt AJ had planted blossomed into a terrible, enveloping fear. All her years in the South, Skyler had fought for agency, to be under nobody's control but her own. If Angel had had her own reason for wanting Daniel dead – if she'd pretended she was helping Skyler in order to get a gun into his house. . .

"What does that mean?" she said.

"I gave you the gun because I knew what Redruth was capable of," Angel said slowly. "I wanted to protect you. Never doubt that. But if you're asking if I'd ever met him before – then yes. I had. And I. . . wanted him dead. You can't possibly know how glad I am that he's gone. But I didn't want you to be the one who had to do it."

Her voice was flat and controlled, but Skyler recognised the pain below the surface fighting for release. She wanted to comfort Angel, but she also sort of wanted to throw something at her.

"What did he do to you?" she said at last.

Angel seemed to have folded in on herself. She shook her head. "I can't tell you."

"Well, I think you should bloody well try," Skyler snapped. "If you were so hell bent on getting him out of the way that you got me to settle your score for you without even bothering to let me in on it – I think I deserve a bit of an explanation, don't you?"

Every muscle in Angel's colourless face was tight. "If you really believe that's what happened," she said, "then you have no idea who I am. I didn't put you in that cellar,

Skyler. You did that, and you came to me because you knew he would end up killing you."

She met Skyler's eyes. "Have you ever seen someone he wanted to hurt? I mean *really* hurt? Afterwards?"

"I – no." They were teetering on the edge of a deadly void, and it was already too late to stop them from falling.

"I have." Angel shoved her chair back and stood up, turning away from her.

"Whatever it was he did, you should've told me –"

Angel swung back around. "I should, should I? I should relive the worst moments of my life so you can feel like I've shared *appropriately*?"

Skyler said nothing.

"He took everything away from me," Angel said quietly.

Skyler took a deep breath. "Well, then maybe you should have killed him yourself."

Angel stared at her. Then she turned on her heel and walked out of the kitchen, slamming the door behind her.

*

Over the next few days, the atmosphere between Skyler and Angel permeated everything and set everyone else on edge. Mackenzie had learned long ago that Skyler didn't bother with even her usual cursory level of social nicety when she was angry or upset, and Angel was just downright terrifying. It was impossible to have a proper conversation with either of them.

Skyler wouldn't tell him what had happened. He supposed that whatever AJ had been hinting at had turned out both to be true and to be particularly troublesome for her, which he'd probably known all along would be the case. Typical bloody AJ, seeing an opportunity to shit stir and grasping it with both hands.

Under any other circumstances Mackenzie would have happily stayed well out of the situation, but they really needed to talk to each other. They only had a week until the Board planned to release the virus, and there were some fairly serious differences of opinion about how much blowing up of things they should be doing.

"Why just do the lab?" Col said. The six of them were gathered around Joss and Lydia's kitchen table. Well, five of them were. Skyler was cross-legged on the counter beside the stove, laptop on her knees, ignoring them all. "We could do the headquarters as well."

"You mean kill everyone," Mackenzie said.

"Everyone on the Board, yeah. Why not? Get rid of 'em all in one go."

"I'm not sure," Mackenzie said slowly, because he didn't think 'you're nuts' would go down well. "I thought we were trying to save lives, not kill people."

"They've all got blood on their hands," Lydia pointed out.

"Well, yeah, but don't you think blowing dozens of people into pieces might be kind of crossing a line?"

Col cracked his knuckles. "Murderers, Mackenzie. An eye for an eye."

"And what's the rest of the world gonna think if we do that?"

"Does it matter? They're not fucking doing anything for us now, are they?"

Throughout the conversation, Angel had been absorbed in sharpening a long knife on Joss' whetstone. Now she gave Col an irritated look. "Enough of this. We'd never get all of them, you know that. How much C4 would we need to take down the whole headquarters, even if we could get it in there?"

"She's right," Joss said. "Besides, they'd just get the

army in. We're not gonna take them on."

Angel started running the knife along the whetstone again with careful, deliberate strokes.

"The point is," Mackenzie said, "I really think we should be trying to limit the bloodshed as much as possible. I don't want to kill anyone unless I have to."

Col leaned across the table. Mackenzie met his eyes unwillingly. He'd always tried to put as much distance as possible between himself and people like Col; you never knew whether they were going to shake your hand or smash your face in.

"Dream on, kid," Col said, staring him down. "What d'you think's gonna happen? They'll just roll over and say oh, okay, we'll take the Wall down, come on back over and don't worry about all the terrorism? There's gonna be blood, no matter what. You're gonna have to find a way of being okay with that."

There was a long, uncomfortable silence.

"It's not going to happen," Angel said, her blade scraping along the whetstone. "Even if we wanted to, there aren't enough of us, there aren't enough explosives and there's not enough time. Getting rid of the virus is the important thing."

Lydia pulled a face. "Maybe you're right."

Col snorted. "What, so Angel makes all the decisions now?"

Angel's head snapped up. "I do if this is the sort of stupid fucking decision you're going to make."

Skyler looked up for the first time, eyes wide, as Col shoved his chair back. "Don't start with me, Angel."

Angel was on her feet too, the knife still in her hand. "Then don't give me a reason to."

Joss slammed his hand on the table, glaring at them.

"Bloody sit down, both of you. What's got into you?"

Nobody moved.

"I mean it," Joss said. "Just in case you'd forgotten whose house you're in. Col, sit. Angel, put that bloody knife down."

Col sat, sulkily. Angel lowered herself back into her seat and laid the knife on the table with exaggerated care.

"All right," Lydia said. "Regroup. Col, you reckon we've got enough explosives?"

He nodded.

"So what do we still need?" Joss said. "Skyler, you thought about how we're gonna get over the Wall?"

She didn't look up from her laptop. "There's a gate about fifteen miles west of here. You either need a key code or you have to do a manual override from the nearest watchtower. I could change the code remotely but I can't guarantee someone won't have changed it back by the time we get there."

"So we're gonna need to get into the tower," Lydia said. Skyler nodded.

"Right. Get some information on the layout and go over it with Angel. Angel, you can work out what we'll need to get in there."

Silence from Angel. Lydia's face pinched. "That gonna be a problem?"

More silence. Mackenzie hardly dared breathe.

Col glowered. Skyler stared at her computer. Angel was a statue and Mackenzie, sitting beside her, was the only one who could see that her knuckles where white in her lap.

"All right," Joss said at last. "I think that's enough for today."

"Thank fuck for that." Lydia stood up and stretched. "I don't know what the matter with you two is," she added to Angel and Skyler, "but whatever it is, you bloody well sort it out. We don't have time for this kind of shite."

"I wouldn't bother telling her that," Skyler said, without looking up. "She'll probably just get someone else to do it for her."

Lydia threw her hands up and shook her head. Angel stood very still for a moment, and then turned and walked out of the room.

Lydia followed, still shaking her head. The rest of the group dispersed.

Mackenzie was the last to leave and he hurried to follow the others out. Skyler was impossible in this mood and he didn't feel like setting himself up as her punching bag. But as he opened the door, he saw her lift her sleeve-covered hand and hastily wipe her eyes.

He hadn't seen her cry since the first day they'd met. He closed the door again quietly.

She gave him the briefest of glances. "You can't clean in here now, Mackenzie. I'm busy."

Well, she wouldn't be Skyler if she made this easy for him. He walked over to her and took the laptop in both hands. She grabbed it, glaring at him like he'd put a hammer through the screen.

He didn't let go. "Either fight me for it and risk losing all your work," he said, "or put the damn thing down for five minutes and talk to me."

"I could bloody strangle you, Mackenzie."

"No, you couldn't," he said amiably. "So just save your work and tell me what's going on."

"It's none of your business. Leave me alone."

"Normally, I'd be delighted to agree with you, but that's not true right now. We're all in this together, or at least we were until you and Angel decided you hated each other. We *need* to be in this together, Sky."

Skyler's glare intensified, and then burned out. "Let me save this first," she muttered.

She pressed a few buttons, set the laptop aside, and buried her head in her hands. Mackenzie hoisted himself up onto the counter next to her. "You and Angel," he prompted. "What happened?"

"I asked her about what AJ said," she said, her voice muffled. "I just wanted to – I thought she'd tell me he was making it up."

"And? What did she say?"

She lifted her face out of her hands. "I think Daniel did something to her. Or someone she knew. Something really bad."

Well, that would make sense. Everyone else in Birmingham's underworld had history, if you asked the right people. Not Angel. According to rumour, she had more or less come from nowhere. "And this turned into you two having a massive falling out – how?"

"Because she didn't *tell* me! She wanted him dead and she got me to do it for her and she made it seem like she was doing it to help me!" Skyler's voice was sharp, but under the familiar current of anger there was, unexpectedly, something raw and vulnerable. "Don't you *get* it? Nearly everyone I've met in this bloody city has tried to make me do stuff – tried to bully or threaten or manipulate me because they thought I couldn't fight back. Do you know how *exhausting* that is? How scared I was, all the time?"

The words tumbled out as though she was trying to get through them all before she choked. She dropped her head. "I thought Angel was different," she said quietly. "I never thought she'd use me like that."

He felt a sudden wave of compassion for her. She looked

heartbroken. "Sky – d'you really think that's what she was doing?"

"She must have been. Otherwise why didn't she tell me what he did so I could make up my own mind?"

"Some things hurt too much to talk about. We both know that." He put a cautious hand on her shoulder. "Angel cares about you. Like, a lot. And if she's seen first-hand what Redruth was capable of, maybe that just means she was even more worried about you."

She said nothing.

"Why do you think she's even here?" Mackenzie said patiently.

She frowned. "What're you on about?"

Apparently she was going to need it spelled out for her. "She didn't have to stay with us after we rocked up at her place, did she? If all she wanted was Redruth gone, she'd got that by then. She could've just kicked us out, but she chose to go on the run with us. Because of you."

She looked puzzled. "Do you really think that's true?"

He rolled his eyes. Skyler stared at the floor. "Shit. She must really hate me."

"She's pretty mad, yeah. But I don't think she hates you. It's easier to be angry than hurt, that's all."

She groaned and hit the counter with her fist. "Fuck! Why am I so stupid? What do I *do*, Mack?"

"Well – how do you feel about her?"

For the first time in days, the abject misery on Skyler's face lightened. "I feel... When I'm with her, I feel like there's this whole new amazing thing in the world that I didn't even know existed. Like... nothing could be so terrible if she was there too."

"Then you need to *talk* to her. You know, with words and feelings and stuff. Tell her what you told me. Say you're sorry."

"She's not gonna want to hear it."

"In a couple of days," Mackenzie said, "everything's gonna be different. And some of us might be...well. Maybe not all of us will still be here. If you don't say it now, you might never get the chance."

38

GHOSTS

Skyler had never imagined taking advice from Mackenzie about anything that didn't involve picking locks or climbing drainpipes, but she had to admit what he was saying made sense. Not that it made the prospect of doing as he suggested any less terrifying.

Angel was avoiding her, too. But early the next morning, when Skyler had been working all night and was ready to fall asleep at the table, she came into the kitchen with her jacket on.

She walked past straight Skyler, opened a cupboard, stuffed something into her bag and turned to leave.

Skyler took a deep breath. *Now or never.* "Angel."

Angel glanced back at her. Her face could have been carved out of stone.

"Can we – can we talk?"

A flicker in her expression, a softening in the line of her mouth, gone so quickly Skyler might have imagined it. "Not now."

Skyler stood up. "Please. Five minutes."

"I have to go out."

"Angel –"

Angel opened the door. Skyler sat back down, misery

coiling tight inside her.

But then Angel hesitated and looked back at her. "Later," she said. "We'll talk later."

And then she was gone.

Skyler worked until she started to make mistakes and then she rested her head on her arms on the table and closed her eyes.

When she opened them again, the house was still and quiet. Knocking echoed from the front door. It must have been what had woken her.

She'd intended just to wait for the knocker to go away, but the banging grew more insistent. Perhaps Mackenzie or Angel had locked themselves out. She closed the laptop, went to the door and peered through the peephole, ready to back away fast.

But it was fine. Well, sort of fine. AJ was outside.

She took a quiet step back. What was he doing here? He never bloody listened, that was his problem. He always thought he knew best. She should just walk away, leave him out there. He'd get the message eventually.

But... they'd been friends for a long time. Perhaps he had a good reason for coming back.

She stood, deliberating, for a long minute. Then she opened the door.

Something was wrong. AJ looked ill, with shadows like bruises under his eyes. She reached out a hand to him. "Are you all right?"

He shook his head.

In the street behind him was a large, shiny four by four with blacked out windows. Skyler went cold. "AJ," she whispered. "What did you do?"

Something moved behind him. She grabbed his arm and tried to pull him inside, but she didn't move fast enough. Because in the next second the hand and the knife came out of nowhere from behind him and sliced across his throat.

As she stood, stunned, a fountain of AJ's blood, hot and dark and far, far too much of it, spurted across her face.

His eyes went wide. His mouth opened, but no sound came out.

Skyler couldn't move, couldn't speak, couldn't breathe.

AJ swayed and collapsed in the doorway.

From behind him, Daniel gave her a wide, bright smile. "Hello, Skyler."

Just move, just fucking move, why aren't you running away? Her brain was screaming at her but she was as rigid as iron, trying to work out how to get AJ into the house and stop the bleeding and slam the door on Daniel all at once. And while she was still figuring it out, Daniel stepped over AJ's body – it was a body now, there was too much blood on the floor and the door and all over Skyler for it to be any other way – and finally, too late, she turned and ran.

Her gun was up in the attic. Stupid, *stupid*. Unspeakably naïve, to believe that she was safe. Of course Daniel was capable of playing dead to get her to let her guard down. She should have known he'd never let something as petty as a bullet to the chest get between him and his revenge.

She slammed through the kitchen, up against the back door and of *course* the key wasn't in the lock. She hammered on the glass in the door, trying to shatter it.

And then he was there, knife in one hand, a fistful of her hair in the other, and he slammed the side of her face against the glass.

Pain exploded through her skull. The glass cracked. He jerked her head back, shooting white hot sparks down her neck, and slammed it back against the glass.

And he was going to make damn sure the visit was worth his while, of course. So when he let go of her hair and wrapped his hand around her throat, she knew better than to think this was the end of it.

She tried not to struggle, not to give him the satisfaction, but it *hurt*. And his eyes, pale blue and amused, bored into hers. He was enjoying this.

The knowledge sparked a fury that swallowed her terror. She kicked out, caught his kneecap. He let go of her and she staggered away from him, but she only managed a couple of steps before his right hand shot out and grabbed her wrist. His expression was no longer unassuming, but blank and nasty.

He hit her so hard it knocked her halfway across the room.

When she looked up from the floor he was standing over her, shaking his head. "Oh, Skyler. Did you really think you could get away from me?"

Her head throbbed. Something warm trickled down the side of her face. He seemed not to be using his left hand, the one that held the knife. Perhaps he was still injured from the gunshot wound. Perhaps –

He kicked her in the stomach. In a painful flash, all the air was gone from her lungs. "So that little bitch you run around with gave you a gun."

Another kick. She curled in on herself, clamping her mouth shut. He was not going to hear her scream. He was not going to hear her beg.

She tried to drag herself away from him. He moved closer. "Is she here?"

She didn't answer.

This time the kick landed on her ribs and she let out a groan. "I said *is she here?*"

"No," Skyler gasped. She wrapped her arms around her torso. Her whole body shook.

"Where is she?"

"I – I don't know." *The twins will be back at some point. They can take him easily. You just have to stall him long enough.*

Daniel shrugged. "It doesn't matter. She'll be back soon enough. Her and the boy."

"She's going to kill you," Skyler croaked.

He chuckled. "Is that what you think? Do you think when she walks in here and sees you I won't have the chance to cut her open first?"

Terror crystallised into icicles on her skin. "Your problem's with me," she whispered. "They didn't do anything. You leave them alone."

His grin widened. Immediately, she knew the magnitude of her mistake. "Oh," he said, delighted. "I *see*. You actually care about them, don't you? And here I thought you only cared about yourself."

He crouched and gripped her chin, tilting her face so she had no choice but to look at him. "Well, here's what we're going to do. I'm going to keep you alive until they get back, so you can see what I do to them. And then, Skyler, *you* can decide when they die. How does that sound?"

Shut up. Don't say a word. She'd made enough mistakes. She needed to block Daniel out, she needed a weapon. This was a kitchen, for God's sake, there had to be *something*. But her head was thick and fuzzy, and there was nothing she could reach from the floor.

"Get up," he said.

She might as well have already had concrete blocks tied to her legs, ready for him to throw her in the river, for all she could move. She dragged herself into a sitting position against the kitchen cabinets. Not fast enough for Daniel.

His face hardened. "If I have to say it again, you'll be sorry."

He was toying with her, taunting her, and she couldn't find a way to stop it happening. She seized the nearest drawer handle and pulled herself upright, her muscles screaming with every movement.

The next thing she knew he had her up against the counter, her arm twisted so tight behind her it was going to break if he moved another centimetre. She couldn't help it. She let out a sob.

His breath brushed her ear. "You're on your own," he murmured. "I'm reliably informed that the idiot twins are miles away. No one's coming to help you."

Breathe. Keep breathing. You're not dead yet.

He gave a swift, sharp jerk.

Skyler's arm snapped.

39

REVENANT

Mackenzie's brain had been telling him something was wrong the whole time he was out of the house. It never shut up these days, so he tried to ignore it. *Your brain's playing tricks on you, like always. It's fine. Nothing's wrong.*

Then he rounded the corner onto the twins' street and saw the car: big and flashy, with tinted windows, way too expensive for this neighbourhood. The nagging wrongness that haunted his footsteps began to whine more insistently.

When he got close enough to see the house, the front door was ajar.

The nagging whine solidified into a cold and terrible certainty. No one staying in that house would have been stupid enough to leave the door open. He pulled his hood up, crossed to the other side of the road and approached the vehicle from behind, trying to look as though he was on his way somewhere that was definitely not the twins' house. *What now?*

From inside the house, Skyler screamed.

The sound ran through him like a spear. He lurched towards the front door.

And what are you gonna do, exactly?

If he was lucky, he might get to see Skyler roll her eyes very hard at him before they both died a horrible death. No. They needed Angel.

He set off at a sprint. No rituals now. Only Skyler's scream in his head, over and over, a thousand terrible images, a desperate, repeating prayer: *Please be okay, Skyler. Please.*

Angel had gone to get medical supplies, since it was a fair bet somebody was going to need them at some point during all the blowing up of things. She was meeting a contact at Queen Elizabeth hospital, she'd told him.

His lungs burned. His feet skidded on the icy pavement. He cannoned into someone, mumbled an apology and accelerated away. He'd reached the road the hospital was on and his chest felt like it was being crushed. If Angel wasn't there –

Somebody else smacked into him and nearly knocked him over. Hands seized his shoulders. He jerked his head up.

"What the hell are you doing?" Angel hissed. "Do you *want* to get arrested?"

He gulped air, fighting to get the words out. She shook him. "Mackenzie!"

"Skyler," he gasped. "Angel – you've got to –"

She was already running.

*

Skyler had never broken a bone before and she was completely unprepared for the way the pain shot, burning, from her arm through her entire body. She couldn't have stopped the scream if she'd wanted to.

Daniel was pressed up against her, laughing in her ear. She choked down the rest of the scream.

He spun her back round to face him and a fresh bolt

of pain seared through her. Her legs shook and almost gave way.

She summoned the last shreds of her energy and swung the fist of her good arm around.

It connected with his jaw with a *crack* that under any other circumstances would have been far more satisfying. She lunged for the knife in his hand.

But he'd recovered his balance. He shoved her, hard. She crashed onto the tiled floor, onto her limp, useless arm.

She must have lost consciousness. When she opened her eyes, she was propped on a kitchen chair, her hands tied behind her back. She tried to adjust her position, but the agony in her arm ratcheted up several notches and she was suddenly on the verge of blacking out again.

When the black spots had cleared from her vision, she lifted her head. Daniel sat in front of her, his legs crossed. On the table next to him was a blowtorch and a length of wire. He was using a tea towel to polish the knife he'd used to cut AJ's throat.

When he saw that she was awake, his face lit up as though he were greeting an old friend. He folded the tea towel and held the knife as casually as if he'd been doing the washing up.

"You have no idea," he said, "how much pleasure it gives me to see you like this."

Skyler looked at the knife in his hand and the things on the table and tried to work out whether she could do anything to reduce the amount of pain she was going to be in before she died. It seemed unlikely. "About much as it gave me to see you lying on that kitchen floor, I expect." Her voice came out thick and raspy.

His grin didn't flicker. He leaned forward and tapped her leg with the knife. "You know, I was almost impressed. I genuinely didn't think you had it in you. If I'd had any idea what you were up to I'd have done this a long time ago." He spread his hands. "But never mind. We're here now."

"Yeah. You're beating the shit out of a teenager. If that makes you feel better about yourself or something."

He folded his arms and sat back. "You know, I really feel all right about it. It's no good playing the age card when you're grown up enough to point a gun at someone and shoot them, Skyler. If you're old enough to do that, you're old enough to pay the price."

"And AJ? What was he paying for?"

"Oh, he was paying off your debt. Just like he has been for years."

She should have expected that, but it was still like a punch to the stomach. "He had nothing to do with it. He would've tried to talk me out of it."

Daniel's face hardened. He pointed the knife at her accusingly. "He helped you get away. He was always going to pay for that."

She looked away from him, as much as she was able to.

"Of course," he added, "he tried to make it up to me, after you two had your little falling out. He thought if he made me a good enough offer I'd forgive and forget." He tutted. "He had a lot to learn, that boy."

She wondered if she could go somewhere else in her mind so she wouldn't have to hear Daniel's next words, so she wouldn't have to die with them ringing in her ears. But her mind was right here, stuck in this broken, useless body, and apparently it was going nowhere. "You're lying," she whispered. "He thought you were dead. He told me you were dead."

Daniel snorted. "He knew I wasn't dead. He lied to you. It was his idea, even. He offered to give you back to me if I let him carry on working for me."

Skyler closed her eyes. When she'd forced the bile in her throat back down, she opened them again.

"Oh, that's right," Daniel said. "He sold you out. Came straight back after he'd run into you and that other gutter rat you hang around with, and told me exactly where you were."

She wanted to scream at him, call him every name she could think of. He would just have kept laughing at her.

"Apparently he couldn't make his mind up, though." His voice took on a flinty edge. "He snuck out here today to warn you."

She jerked her head up and was rewarded with a jarring sensation all the way down her spine. Through the buzzing in her ears, she heard him say, "Like I said. He died paying off your debt." He shrugged. "He brought this forward by a few days, that's all."

She hung her head. She had no way to fight Daniel anymore. Nothing she could say or do would hurt him. He was going to kill her, he was going to enjoy it, and the only option she had left was to spoil his fun by dying as quickly and quietly as possible.

He got to his feet. "Anyway. I think we're done talking. I can't imagine you've got anything interesting to say." He looked her up and down. "You know, really the only problem I've got now is deciding where I'm going to start."

Oh, the hell with it. She lifted her head and looked him in the eyes. "Maybe you could hurry up already. This is getting kind of boring."

He grabbed her hair, yanked her head back. She choked back a yelp. "Is that right, you miserable little bitch? Let's see, then." He touched the knife to the skin just below her eyelid. "I think we'll start. . . here."

She felt the cut open along the bottom of her eye socket before the sting caught up. Daniel stood back and studied her as blood welled and spilled from the wound. He smiled. "Don't cry, sweetheart."

And then the kitchen window exploded and he was, inexplicably, no longer standing over her, but was sprawled on the floor. At Skyler's feet lay his knife, and a brick.

She stared at the brick, the knife and the broken glass glittering over everything like deadly snow, and kicked out as hard as she could.

The knife shot across the kitchen. Daniel climbed to his feet, fists clenched, mouth open in an ugly snarl – but that was the moment someone crashed through the remnants of the window in a tornado of red hair and blurred limbs and shards of glass.

Angel sprang over the sink, hit the floor and bounced upright. And Daniel hesitated; he didn't know what to do.

Angel flew across the room, knife in hand, and knocked him to the floor with a thump. She was on top, but they were struggling together, flailing limbs everywhere, and Daniel was wrenching his way out from under her and all Skyler could think was: *he's bigger than her, God, he's going to kill her.*

Angel was wild, her onslaught relentless, her face etched with fury. Daniel's fist connected with her cheekbone with a sickening thud but she didn't even flinch. She threw him off her and kicked him in the stomach. He staggered backwards and they circled one another: two predators fighting over their prey.

Bloody slashes streaked Daniel's arms and torso, but he didn't seem to have noticed. He was studying Angel like she was some kind of rare, fascinating specimen. "You," he said. "I did wonder, but honestly – I never really believed it." He looked, suddenly, like he'd just got the punchline to a joke. "Dear me. All this time, you've been thinking about me... And you still haven't learned to keep out of my way."

Angel was crouched, ready to leap. "Evidently."

"I would've thought you'd have had enough of seeing the people you care about get butchered in front of you."

She didn't move a muscle.

Daniel wiped his mouth and looked at the bloody smear on his hand with distaste. "Well, what do I care? I haven't thought about you once, you know, in all this time. But I bet you picture my face every day, don't you?"

Angel hurled herself at him. She slammed him against the doorframe and thrust her knife outward, but he twisted and it lodged in the door. She punched him in the stomach, her movements fluid, elegant, each blow landing with a fleshy thud. Rage made Angel explosive. It only worked for Daniel while he was the one in control, and he wasn't in control now.

He lunged for her throat. She twisted his hand away, and Skyler saw the effort it cost him not to cry out. He grabbed her wrist instead and when she broke his hold he shoved her backwards and advanced. Angel righted herself, but not before Daniel had hit her again, hard.

She absorbed the first blow and dodged the second, but in dodging the third her foot tangled in a broken chair behind her and she tripped. As Skyler waited for her to bounce upright again, her head clipped the edge of the table with a reverberating *crack*.

And then she was on the floor, and she didn't get back up.

A hoarse, terrified scream erupted from Skyler's throat. "Angel –!"

Nothing.

Behind her, Daniel started to laugh.

He stepped back into her field of vision and looked down at Angel. His lips twitched. "Oh, my. You know, if anything could've made today better than it was already, it was this."

He kicked Angel. Skyler willed her to open her eyes, to say something, to do *anything*.

But she didn't.

"No," she whispered.

Daniel strolled across the kitchen and picked up his knife. "Oh, I'm afraid so, darling. So where were we?"

She sat, numb, as he stood over her, between the chair she was propped on and Angel in a heap on the floor. What was wrong with her? Surely one knock couldn't do that much damage?

She wanted to scream at Angel to get up but she bit her tongue. This was already bad enough.

She closed her eyes against Daniel's grin. "I'm not afraid of you."

He chuckled. "If you say so."

His blade was icy cold. It trailed over her cheek like a caress.

The knife jerked. Daniel gave a ragged gasp.

Skyler's eyes flew open.

He was rigid, his mouth opening and closing like a fish drowning on air. Angel was on her feet behind him. His gaze travelled downwards, incredulous, towards the spreading crimson stain on the front of his shirt.

His eyes met Skyler's. He was still holding the knife to her face.

She threw her chair to the side and crashed onto the floor. Above her, Angel jerked the knife out of Daniel's back.

He fell to his knees and toppled sideways. Skyler, stuck

on her side with her arms behind her, saw his chest heaving, his eyes bulging, heard the jagged breath that turned from gasping to gurgling and then, finally, to nothing at all.

In the silence, she and Angel stared at one another. Then Angel's knife clattered to the floor. She dropped to her knees and fumbled with the cords that held Skyler, disentangling her as gently as she could.

Every tiny movement made Skyler gasp. Angel helped her sit up and held her close, rocking her back and forth while she shook with all the fear and agony she'd been trying so hard to suppress. "It's okay," Angel whispered, "it's okay, it's okay. He's gone. You're going to be okay."

40

THE DANCER

Mackenzie crashed into the kitchen a couple of minutes later. He sagged against the doorframe, wheezing, and when he looked at Skyler his lip trembled. When he saw Daniel's body on the floor he stared, open-mouthed, before his whole frame slumped with relief.

He and Angel hauled the body into the hallway because nobody could stand to look at it a second longer than they had to, and then Angel collected her medical supplies. Mackenzie slipped off somewhere else at that point. He probably couldn't stand to be around this much blood and broken glass without trying to clean it up. Skyler didn't mind that he'd gone. She was aware, fuzzily, that he had been the one to get help, and she would thank him later. Right now she didn't want anyone to see her like this.

Angel eased Skyler's shirt off while Skyler whimpered and tried not to cry. "It's a bad break," she said, her frown deepening as she inspected Skyler's arm. "And I think some of your ribs are broken too."

Skyler glanced at her arm, which did not seem to be quite the shape it should be. The mottled reddish-purple of her ribcage made her queasy. "Can you do anything about it?"

Angel pulled a face and then nodded. "I'll try. It's going to hurt a lot, and it'll take a long time to heal. I'm sorry."

"Why are you sorry? You just saved my life."

Angel didn't reply. "You want me to get Mackenzie?" she asked, glancing up just before she set to work.

"I'd really rather you didn't."

Angel put an empty bowl in front of her. "I'm just going to do it as fast as possible, okay?"

Skyler started to nod, and then Angel moved her arm and she screamed instead.

Her vision blurred and fizzed. Angel kept hold of her arm as she doubled over and retched into the bowl. "It's all right," she said, over Skyler's moans. "It's all right. I'm nearly done. You're doing great."

Skyler gasped for air and retched again. "We're nearly done," Angel said. "Just let me bandage it." She began to wrap the arm. "I'm sorry. I'm going as fast as I can. Just hold on."

When she'd finished, she held a glass of water to Skyler's lips and smoothed her hair back from her forehead. "You okay?"

Skyler nodded and blinked away tears. While Angel poured a bowl of hot water and started to clean the blood from her face, she tried to find the right words.

At last, she said, "I'm sorry, Angel."

Angel hesitated, the cloth halfway to her face. Then she lowered it again. "You don't have anything to be sorry for. I get why you were angry. You were right. I should have killed him myself."

"I thought I'd killed him."

"I know."

"I wish I had."

"I know."

"AJ. . . told me he was dead. I never thought he'd do something like that."

"No," Angel said. "Neither did I."

Skyler took a deep breath that turned into a shuddering gasp. The shock of AJ's betrayal reverberated through her.

Angel laid a hand on her shoulder. "Shh. Don't think about it now."

Skyler looked up at her, at the purple bruise blossoming on her cheekbone, her slim, pale hands wringing out the bloodstained cloth. "Angel?"

Angel dabbed at her face. "Yes?"

"He did something awful to you, didn't he?"

Angel let out a long sigh and dropped her gaze. She opened her mouth, closed it again.

Skyler put out a hand to her. "You don't have to –"

"I was fifteen." The words came out in a rush. Skyler fell silent.

"I was still at school. I had parents who cared about me. A little brother and sister. We weren't perfect, but we loved each other. We were happy."

Skyler nodded.

"I got a dance scholarship to a really fancy school. I was an amazing dancer." Angel's lips twisted in a smile full of grief. "My parents were so proud. They'd tell anyone who'd listen that I was going to be a professional. But I was just. . . an ordinary kid. I thought I was a bit of a rebel. I didn't really know anything about the world."

She took a deep breath. When she spoke next, her voice was flat and distant. "I figured out I was gay when I was pretty young, but I was fifteen when I fell in love for the first time. With a girl called Erin Redruth."

Skyler stared at her. "Related to –?"

"His daughter."

Skyler understood enough about Daniel to guess what was coming next. She held her breath.

"I had no idea who he was, what he was capable of," Angel said. "I'm not sure Erin did either. I knew she was scared of him but... I didn't *get* it."

Her hands shook. Skyler covered them with her own. "She took me to her house one weekend." Angel's voice had a brittle edge, like it might crack at any moment. "We were all excited, giddy, but she warned me we had to be careful, her dad would go mad if he knew she was with someone. I didn't really take it seriously. He was there when we arrived, he made us lunch – he was friendly – charming, even."

She closed her eyes. "I was an idiot. I should have known."

"You couldn't have," Skyler said gently. "He was like that, when he wanted to be. Even after I knew what he was really like, he had me questioning myself sometimes."

"It was my fault," Angel said. "My fault. I thought Erin was just nervous about coming out. He seemed so *nice*. I thought it would be good for her, even, if he did know. He'll understand, I thought, and she'll feel better, once she doesn't have to pretend anymore. So I... was careless. Arrogant. And he saw something, I guess. Anyway, he knew. He didn't do anything straight away. But then later on we were in her room and he just walked in and grabbed her."

Her face was fixed, every word clipped, deliberate. "He pinned her against the wall, but he didn't even look at her. He didn't say anything. He just looked at me, like, *what are you going to do about it*? I tried to get him off her, and he just laughed at me. And Erin said, 'Dad, don't, please don't.' I thought at the time she was asking him not to hurt her, but now I know... now I know she was asking him not to hurt me.

"After a couple of minutes he let go of her and walked out. He didn't take his eyes off me the whole time. When he was gone, Erin lost it. She was crying, she kept saying, you have to go, you have to go. I said I wasn't leaving her. She said no, you don't understand, you have to get out of here *right now*. In the end I did. I was scared of what he'd do to her if he came back and I was still there, so – I went home. I mean – that's what you do, right? When something goes that badly wrong – you go to your parents, and they help you fix it."

She swallowed, and for the first time, her eyes were glassy, over-bright. "But when I got home, he was there too. He'd waited for me."

"Oh," Skyler said softly.

Angel's voice cracked. "I can't. . . tell you. What he did to them. But he made me watch."

Skyler gripped her hand tighter.

"It was me he wanted to break, you see."

"I –" Skyler's voice broke too. "Angel, I'm so sorry."

Angel gave her a brief, brittle smile. "So I understand Mackenzie, you see. Why he's like he is. He feels like it's all his fault. And I get that."

"It's not your fault, Angel. It's not. How could you have known –?"

"I don't know. But I should have done. I just had no idea people like him really existed until that day, you know? I spent so much time trying to figure out what could possibly have been going through his head. I still don't understand."

Skyler took a painful breath. "I understand," she said, and Angel glanced at her. "Daniel doesn't. . . he didn't. . . He never saw people. He just saw stuff that belonged to him. I guess his own daughter would've been like. . . the ultimate possession. And you showed her there could be something else. She didn't have to be his."

She stopped, because she didn't think Angel could take another word. She lifted a careful hand and, very gently, brushed away the tears spilling onto Angel's cheeks. "I don't know how you kept going," she said. "How you survived."

Angel gave a sort of barking laugh. "Me either. At first it was just a blur. I just kept reliving it. I was alone, I didn't dare go to anyone I knew in case he came after them too. Then – I don't know when or how, but at some point I started thinking maybe I could stop him, one day. So. . . I tried. I learned how to fight and I learned how to help people. I kept putting one foot in front of the other."

Skyler managed half a smile. It hurt. "And here we are."

"Here we are."

"How did AJ know – you know, what he told me? Did he know the whole story?"

Angel's lips pursed thoughtfully. "He didn't know. He can't have, because I've never told anyone this before. He just had a guess based on what everyone knows about me. And you heard *him* earlier – he never realised who I was until today. When I. . . after what happened, I had to be a different person. I've lived in this city my whole life but the way people talk about me, I might as well have arrived in a spaceship. Ask about me in any bar in Birmingham and you'll hear ten different stories, and every person you talk to will swear theirs is the truth."

"How come Daniel never came after you? He must've known someone was trying to get to him."

"He did," Angel said. "And he tried. But I suppose after a while enough people liked having me around that they wanted to help me. And once I knew what he was capable of. . . I could be better prepared."

She picked up the cloth again to sponge the blood from Skyler's forehead. "When you came to me, I was so scared for you. You were in his house. . . you were so vulnerable. And at the same time, you can be such a cocky shit." She grinned suddenly, the first time in days Skyler had seen anything approaching genuine humour in her face. "Please believe me – I wanted to help you. That was the only thing I was thinking about. I was afraid if I didn't give you the gun you'd have no chance. So I sent you away with it and kept trying to get to him, but I couldn't get close enough. And then before I knew it, you showed up on my doorstep again."

"I'm glad you gave me the gun." Skyler winced as Angel touched the side of her head. "And I'm even more glad you were here today. I'm sorry you got hurt."

Angel gave her a crooked smile. "It was worth it."

Their eyes met. And all at once, Skyler's dizzy, disorientated feeling, the beating of her heart, had nothing to do with Daniel anymore.

"Angel?" she said.

"Yes?"

"Lydia told me you don't care what happens to you. She said you take crazy risks because you've got nothing to lose."

Angel raised her eyebrows. "Is that right?"

"Yeah. And – I know this is selfish of me, and I'm sorry, but – I'm scared. When we do this thing, I'm scared you're not going to be careful, and you're going to get hurt. I don't want to lose you. I can't lose you."

Angel held her gaze. "You know," she said, "for the longest time, I would've said Lydia was right. I thought I had nothing to lose. I thought there was nothing in the whole world that could ever make me feel happy again. And now I think that I was wrong."

Skyler laid a hand against her cheek, careful to avoid the bruising. "What's going to happen to us?"

"I don't know," Angel said. "We've got a job to do, and we've got to get it done." She took Skyler's hand. "All I know is – whatever happens next, wherever we end up – I'll be there with you, Sky. I promise."

41

LIVE THROUGH THIS

Mackenzie covered the bodies with sheets because they made him want to throw up, and because he knew it would upset Skyler to have to see AJ like that. The sheets made things slightly less horrible. It still meant, however, that when Lydia and Joss returned an hour later it was to a hallway strewn with bodies and a house decorated with blood, broken glass and smashed furniture.

Mackenzie heard the front door open and braced himself.

"*What the fuck –?*"

Joss' roar echoed through the entire house and probably most of the surrounding ones too. Mackenzie winced.

The yelling continued along similar lines. Reluctantly, he went downstairs.

Lydia was standing over the bodies with a knife in her hand and a face like thunder. Mackenzie put his hands in the air and tried to back away up the stairs.

The dual beam of the twins' stares bored into him. "Mackenzie," Joss said, sounding slightly calmer but no less terrifying. "Kindly explain who the bloody hell is under those sheets."

It would have been quite nice if Angel had come out to help him explain this, but she was nowhere to be seen.

"Um. Well, one of them is, uh, Daniel Redruth."

Lydia looked like she was working up to adding to the body count. "Tell me you're fucking joking. I thought he was already dead, for fuck's sake."

"Uh, yeah. We all did."

"This is the last thing we need," Joss snarled.

"Can I just point out," Mackenzie said, "that none of this was my idea?"

This didn't seem to count for a lot. "Keep explaining," Lydia said.

He did his best.

She assessed the bodies with her hands on her hips. "Well, we need to get rid of these. Won't take long for his people to start sniffing around, and if there's one thing we don't need right now it's spectators." She stepped over the bodies and headed for the kitchen.

"Canal?" Mackenzie said to Joss.

"Nah. No one'll believe he's just gone missing. He needs to show up somewhere." He scratched his chin. "Reckon we stick him in the car, leave it somewhere obvious and make it look like AJ did it."

"Yeah, that works," Lydia said, emerging from the ruins of the kitchen with a handful of bin liners. She and Joss knelt over the bodies with the pragmatic air of people for whom this was all in a day's work. "Plus, this means we can take AJ's truck. It's bigger than the one we had lined up."

Mackenzie hovered. This was awkward; it would be polite to help them, but he really did not want to touch the bodies. "You reckon?" he said.

"Sure. We can make it look like an army truck easy enough. I'll go and sort it after this. Silver linings and all that."

"So what are they gonna think happened to AJ?"

"He can go in the canal," Joss said. "Hopefully they'll think he killed Redruth and did a runner. Redruth's boys are none too bright. Lots of muscle and no brains, that's what he liked having around." He finished wrapping duct tape around AJ's body and looked up. "You gonna help me lift this or what?"

The whole enterprise made Mackenzie feel as though he would have to take about a thousand showers just to feel anything approaching human again. He wasn't bothered about Redruth, but getting rid of AJ's body had been awful.

He hadn't expected it to be quite so hard. AJ had generally seemed to view him with nothing but contempt. Mackenzie had seen the way he looked at Skyler and had surmised that AJ was jealous of him. Which was ridiculous, since Skyler could barely stand to be in the same room as him, but then AJ always had been kind of an idiot. Besides, his last-minute change of heart didn't change the fact that he'd sold Skyler out to save his own sorry skin. Mackenzie couldn't have that much sympathy for him. But still... he didn't deserve to be dumped like this, just thrown in a canal and forgotten about.

He didn't sleep much that night. When he woke, about six in the morning, the house, for once, was quiet and still.

He went downstairs thinking he might get a drink and, to his surprise, found Skyler sitting at the kitchen table in the dark. Her laptop was open in front of her, but she didn't seem to be working.

"I thought you'd still be asleep," he said, lighting a candle. Lydia had nailed a board over the window, grumbling as she did so, but it was freezing in there. He put the kettle on the hob and got a couple of cups out. The twins probably wouldn't mind him drinking their tea. It wasn't like they were going to have much use for it soon.

"I meant to say," she said abruptly. "I know you went to get Angel. Thank you."

He kept hunting for the tea. Skyler would hate it if he made a big deal out of this. "I'm just glad I found her in time. I'd have tried to help myself, but. . . you know. Didn't think I'd be much use."

Through the gloom, she gave him a tired smile. "I realised something today, you know."

"Oh yeah? What's that?"

"I don't want to die."

He laughed. "Glad to hear it."

"I mean, I didn't think it mattered before. That's why I took the drive from you in the first place. I knew I was probably gonna end up dead one way or another and. . . I didn't care. It would still have been better than staying in that cellar any longer."

He stared at her. She pulled a face at him. "Sorry. This is awkward."

"No," he said quietly. "No. I just never realised."

She inspected the cast on her arm. "But today – I didn't know you guys were coming. I thought he was going to kill me, and you know what, Mack, I was *really* scared. I don't want to die."

He sat down next to her and passed her a mug. "You having second thoughts?"

She shook her head. "No. It just made me realise I do actually care whether I live through this or not."

He would have liked to give her a hug, but he was pretty sure she wouldn't appreciate it. "Good call," he said instead. "Then you and me are on exactly the same page. I don't want to die either." He raised his mug in a mocking toast. "Here's to staying alive."

A day and a half later, Col arrived at the house. It was almost time.

As usual, Col was as tactful as a bulldozer. "Jesus," he said, when he saw Skyler. "Look at the state of you."

Skyler just straightened her back in a dignified sort of way, which was quite impressive given the circumstances. "I'm fine, thanks for asking."

Mackenzie marvelled at her composure. Forty-eight hours ago, she'd been a bloody mess on the kitchen floor. Now – well, she was still a mess, but he had no doubt she was as capable as ever as she stared Col down. He passed no further comment.

As for Mackenzie, he was alight with the kind of excitement that only came with the anticipation of pulling off a really spectacular job. This was going to be his last break-in for a very long time, and for once it wasn't to steal something, but to leave something behind. He hoped the Board would enjoy it.

He hadn't been able to eat all day, but he felt *alive*. He couldn't control the chaos they were about to unleash, and it felt oddly liberating. They would change the world or they would all get shot, and it didn't matter how long he spent cleaning, how many times he replayed his thoughts. It would make no difference.

As soon as dusk fell and he and Col got into the truck formerly owned by AJ, though, his excitement dissolved into dull, heavy dread. They might as well have been driving around with a big flashing sign saying TERRORIST ACTIVITY HERE, and when a massive black four by four passed them, he nearly choked. He clutched his radio, screwed his eyes shut and started counting to seven in his head over and over so he didn't scream with the wrongness of everything.

"What the hell d'you think you're doing?" Col said out of nowhere.

Five six seven one two –

"Mackenzie!"

I can't, I can't, I can't –

He forced himself to open his eyes. "Nothing," he said, trying to sound as though Col was the one acting strange. "I'm fine."

"Lydia said you had some weird thing going on where you have to clean and count everything."

Thanks a lot, Lydia. "I'm fine," Mackenzie repeated.

"You look like you're gonna shit yourself."

"All right, so I'm scared! Aren't you? This is kind of a big deal, if you hadn't noticed."

Col scoffed. "The only thing I'm worried about is having to babysit you."

"Yeah, well, thanks for your concern, but I don't need a babysitter."

Col gave him a hard stare. "You don't know how long I've been waiting to fuck up the Board. If you and your weird shit screw this up –"

"Right. I wouldn't know anything about how that feels, would I? And excuse me, but maybe you've forgotten the whole reason we're doing this is because *I* broke into the Board HQ and stole that drive. I'm not gonna fuck this up."

"Good. We're not the Three Musketeers. If you start lookin' like dead weight, I'm cutting you loose."

"Oh, stop. You're making me feel all warm and fuzzy."

Col pulled the truck in abruptly behind a factory with all the windows shattered. "Are you taking this seriously?"

"No. You got me. I'm actually doing this for a dare."

Mackenzie shook his head. "Are you done? 'Cos I don't think we really have time for this, do you?"

Col's brows had merged into one. "I'm telling you, Mackenzie –"

"*What*? What do you think you could possibly say to make me take this any more seriously? Honestly, Col, can you try to remember we're on the same side here?"

Col opened his mouth to say something that was almost certainly going to make them both feel a lot better, and Mackenzie's radio bleeped in his hand.

"Well?" Col said. "Answer the bloody thing."

Mackenzie lifted the receiver. "Send over."

Skyler's voice, reassuringly normal, crackled out of it. "Hello Charlie Four from Echo One. I'm done here. You're good to go, over." Her first job of the night had been to put the feed from the lab's security cameras on a loop.

Mackenzie's hands shook a little. "Received with thanks. Charlie Four out." He looked at Col. "Cameras are down."

Col sniffed and restarted the engine. "I just hope that girl knows what she's doing. She talks a good talk, but that's not enough right now."

"Now you're gonna start with Skyler? For God's sake, don't you trust any of us?"

"Since we're gettin' touchy-feely," Col said, navigating the industrial estate, "no. I don't. I was in the army when you and her were still eating crayons. So the two of you pulled off a few smartarse moves. That don't make us partners and it don't make us equals. I'd do this on my own if I could."

Oh, fuck off. "What a shame for all of us that you can't, then."

Col gave him a look so filthy even Skyler wouldn't have

been able to match it. Mackenzie forced himself not to start counting again. *Ignore Col. Concentrate on not swallowing your tongue.*

When they reached the laboratory gate, it was occupied by a lone guard reading a newspaper and eating a sandwich. Behind him was a wall of video screens.

The guard was middle-aged, rotund, and too absorbed in either the Sudoku or the woman in her underwear on the opposite page to be paying attention to the cameras. He looked up as the vehicle approached, but then relaxed. Col was wearing his old army uniform and looked almost bored as he held up his now defunct ID and wound down the truck window.

The guard strolled out of his booth. "Evening, sirs. Wasn't expecting anyone."

Mackenzie held his breath. Col might look the part, but he was another one whose accent was too broad for comfort. But Col just held his ID up a little out of the guard's reach. When the guard stepped forward to take it, he picked up the gun across his knees, stuck it out of the window butt first and smashed him between the eyes.

Mackenzie flinched. Col got out of the truck, knelt beside the crumpled guard to retrieve the keys from his belt, and took the man's head in both hands.

Surely he's not going to –

Col snapped the guard's neck with a nauseating crunch that Mackenzie felt in his bones. He watched, blank with disbelief, as Col dropped the body to the tarmac and got back into the truck.

He swallowed the bile threatening to make an appearance and mumbled, "I thought you were just gonna knock him out."

"Well, you wanted him to wake up and raise the alarm?

Board would've killed him anyway. At least I did it quick." He drove them through the gate, stopped and jerked his thumb back towards the body. "Better get that out of the road."

Mackenzie wondered if Col was going to help him, but Col didn't move. Too numb to argue, he got out of the truck. Perhaps it was a good thing he hadn't eaten today after all. He'd moved more bodies in the last twenty-four hours than he'd ever intended or wished to and he could only hope this was going to be the last of it.

The guard was heavy, like a sack of wet cement. *Like a bag of meat.* The eyes stared sightlessly. Mackenzie tried not to notice the unnatural, flopping angle of the dead man's head as he dragged the body inside the fence, wiped his eyes on his sleeve, and closed the gate behind them.

They pulled up at a service entrance at the back of the lab and began to load the steel cans of petrol and boxes of explosive onto a trolley. Partly to prove to himself that he wasn't too much of a coward to touch them, Mackenzie had peeked into the boxes at the twins' house and had discovered to his surprise that the lumps of C4 reminded him more than anything of plasticine.

The guard's keys got them through the service door. Even the Board couldn't afford electronic locking systems these days; instead the inside of the lab was similar to a prison, with a heavy iron gate every few metres. On paper, this had seemed like a good thing. Once they were inside, however, the problems started.

The first problem was that there was too much petrol and plastic explosive to fit onto the trolley. The second was that the guard's keys didn't open all of the gates inside the lab.

Mackenzie tried every key, trying to tune out an irritated Col behind him, but it was no good.

"Now what're we supposed to bloody do?" Col said.

This was the one thing Mackenzie actually felt all right about. He put his box of C4 down and reached into his jacket. His fingers curled around his tool set with a small, happy beat of relief. He was home.

This was the only thing that ever seemed to quiet his mind. The locks *spoke* to him; all those tiny clicks and vibrations and barely discernible movements. He closed his eyes and probed gently. Everything else faded away.

Any second now, he'd be through the gate.

Yep. Any. . . second. . . now.

"What's the hold up?" Col demanded.

Go away, Col. "Just give me a moment."

"We don't have a moment —"

Just occasionally, Mackenzie wished he was the sort of person who solved problems by smacking people in the face. "Col. Does this seem helpful?"

Col sniffed and stepped back. Mackenzie heard him pacing. *Come on. You know how to do this.*

Something clicked inside the lock. The gate swung open. Mackenzie lifted his eyes to the ceiling and breathed out.

"You better go on ahead and get those gates open," Col said. "We'll come back for the stuff."

Mackenzie did as he was told. Skyler had found a blueprint for the lab tucked away in an obscure Board file and from it he'd memorised the path into the heart of the lab, which led them through shadowy corridors into a series of basement rooms. Everything was white and clinical: shiny plastic floor and echoing halls. Mackenzie marvelled at how modern it was. In here, you'd never realise that outside people were using candles to light their rooms and horses and carts to get around.

It wasn't long before he stopped marvelling and started

wondering how the hell he'd got lumbered with this bit of the operation. It turned out the amount of plastic explosive and petrol needed to destroy an entire building and create a hot enough fireball to denature a virus was, well, a lot. It took three trips to get it all down to the basement, and because Col needed one arm free for his gun – just in case he felt like killing anyone else – Mackenzie ended up doing most of the carrying.

It wasn't that he was weak. All those nights spent leaping across rooftops and dangling from window ledges high above the ground had given him the kind of strength you only develop when your life depends on it. But he was never going to be built for lugging heavy objects around, and the seconds slipping past seemed to increase the weight in his arms, dragging him down and slowing his movements. His palms slipped against the handles of the petrol cans. Blood roared in his ears like a rising storm.

He'd never wanted anything to be over so badly in his life. Even crossing the Wall hadn't been this bad. If he screwed this up, if anyone was in the building, if someone found the dead guard. . . So many terrible things could happen in the next precious, horrible minutes, and if any one of them did it would be not only his life but the lives of everyone left in the North that would pay for it.

And the gates – Christ, the gates. They had to leave them open, of course. To Mackenzie, who would return to a door a dozen times to make sure it really was locked, this was almost unbearable; it was an itch that writhed and burned in his stomach, a buzz in his head that rose to a scream. He swallowed the metallic taste on his tongue and tried to remember that returning to the gates was far more likely to get them killed. It was hard work.

By the time he'd deposited the last armful of explosive

in the basement storeroom and they'd opened the petrol cans, his limbs were like jelly. He thought he might actually fall apart; literally dissolve into a puddle on the floor. Had anyone ever spontaneously disintegrated from terror before? Perhaps he would be the first. What a dubious honour.

Col fished a messy arrangement of wires and batteries wrapped around a cardboard tube from his pocket. This was the charge that would detonate the initial explosion.

"You make that?" Mackenzie's mouth was so dry he could hardly speak.

Col nodded.

"Looks like a firework." He knew it was stupid. He just wanted to keep talking, because the only alternatives were screaming or crying or something equally useless.

Col fiddled with the device. "It is a firework." He set it on the floor, pointing at the explosives.

"What if it goes wrong?" Mackenzie said, unable to help himself.

He was rewarded with a poisonous look. "You really think that's helpful?" Col pointed at the light flashing on the change. "That's five minutes to go, that is. Shall we talk a bit more about our feelings?"

Mackenzie forgot to worry about anything else except getting the hell out of the lab.

When he heard a Southern accent behind him, he thought his heart stopped beating.

42

PARTING GIFTS

Skyler wished she could have been there to see the lab explode – and to make sure Mackenzie didn't completely lose his mind – but she still had work to do. Back at the kitchen table, she checked the package she'd put together for the international media over for the hundredth time. The evidence against the Board was solid. The world, surely, would not be able to ignore it.

There was only one thing left to add. She really hadn't been keen on this idea, but the others had thought it was necessary.

"It needs a human face," Mackenzie had said. "This is all just documents and graphs and chemical formulas."

"Yeah," Skyler said. "Of genocide. Isn't that enough?"

But Angel, annoyingly, had agreed with Mackenzie. "People will understand intellectually," she'd said, "but they won't *feel* how terrible it is until they can associate it with a real person."

They were all looking at her in a way that was frankly off-putting. "Oh, no," she'd said. "I don't think so."

But here she was. She'd put it off until the last possible minute because she didn't know what to say. And now it was the last possible minute. Hell.

She hadn't realised how worried she'd be about Mackenzie. She hadn't heard from him since she'd radioed to tell him the power was out.

And she couldn't think about that now. Reluctantly, she turned the laptop's camera on.

The girl on the screen was a stranger. There'd been no mirrors in Daniel's cellar, and every time she'd caught a glimpse of her reflection over the last few years she'd been caught unawares, startled by how pale she was, how thin, how much older she'd grown without noticing.

Today the bruises spread over half her face, dark fingerprints smudged on her throat. The cut under her eye was stitched closed. Her lip was split open.

Everything hurt. She was ignoring it – because what other option did she have? – but her arm throbbed and her ribcage protested with every breath. Angel had given her painkillers, but they'd only taken the edge off.

It hardly mattered now.

She cleared her throat and pressed the record button. "Uh." Amazingly, her pulse sped up. This was ridiculous. Yesterday she'd faced down a ruthless sadist. Today she had to talk into a camera. *And convince the international community not to let thousands of people die.*

For God's sake. She started again. "So we just blew up a laboratory." *Well, I hope we did.* "Um, and I guess people are gonna say a lot of stuff about why we did that. The Board will say we're criminals, and that's true. Not many other ways of surviving in the South, not when you come from north of the Wall and the Board don't even treat you like you're a person anymore. But we never wanted to hurt anyone."

She leaned forward. "Look. I don't want to be doing this. All I want to do is go home, but the Board took that away from me. They made people hate us and then they built the Wall and nearly everyone in the North died, and apparently that wasn't good enough for them because then they made a biological weapon to kill everyone who's left up there. So. . . we blew it up."

She shook her head. "The people in the North – they're just normal people. *We're* just normal people. We didn't do anything wrong except live on the wrong side of some arbitrary line the Board invented. We didn't deserve what the Board did to us. Those people up there don't deserve to die just because a bunch of sociopaths decided it was convenient.

"So, yeah. They made a weapon and we destroyed it. And they'll call us terrorists and murderers, and they'll lie to you about what was in that lab and what they did in the North. But the evidence is all there. All you have to do is open your eyes and look at it.

"Me and the others, we've done everything we can. We've bought the North some time, maybe, that's all. But if those people are gonna survive – if this isn't all going to be for nothing – We need your help, now. We're just people, we're just like you, and we need your help. Please. If you're listening. . . Don't let them do this to us."

Was that enough? It didn't seem like enough. But she didn't know what else to say, and she was out of time.

She added the video to the package and checked it over one last time.

All this work. All that fear. All that pain and loss. All for this moment.

She set it free.

A dizzy rush of adrenaline swept through her. She let out a long sigh, closed her eyes.

But she wasn't done yet. The virus she'd engineered would shut down the mobile networks, render the Board's email systems useless, jam the radio channels with static. It was a masterpiece. And all she could think about was how much she wished she could show Sam what she'd made. About what he'd say if he could see what she was doing and why.

I hope you'd be proud of me, Sam.

The virus should give her and the others time for what would otherwise be an impossible getaway. Except that the internet had stopped working.

The screen came up with an error message. The connection had failed. Skyler's heart thudded more urgently as she refreshed the screen. "Not now. Come on, not *now.*"

The screen tried and failed to load again. She bit back a yell of frustration, took a deep breath and tried one more time.

This time it sprang to life, but she'd been kicked out of the Board's internal network. She would have to hack her way back in.

Every wasted second inched them closer to disaster. Forcing herself not to rush, to execute every movement precisely, Skyler wrestled her way back into the system and fed the virus into it.

A laugh of sheer relief bubbled up in her throat as the system disintegrated in front of her. It *worked.*

She lifted her radio to share the good news with Mackenzie, but all that came over the airwaves was the crackle of static. That was unexpected. And worrying, but better too many radios out than not enough. She wondered what was happening out in the rest of the world, what the agencies who'd received her package would make of it. She couldn't resist a quick look. She couldn't go anywhere until Mackenzie and Col got back anyway. Assuming they came back.

But the internet was down again and this time it wasn't coming back. The laptop was no longer running off the mains.

The kitchen door opened. She looked up.

Angel came in and sat down beside her. "All okay?"

She rubbed her forehead. "I'm not sure. I think the Board have cut the power. I should've known they would. A blackout's the easiest way to stop news spreading."

"Did you manage to get everything done?"

"Yeah, but –"

Angel took her hand, and Skyler's breath caught in her throat. "Then it's okay."

"I haven't heard from Mackenzie. I don't know if they made it out."

"It's okay. He'll be okay."

"You think so?"

"Have to." Her eyes searched Skyler's face. "What about you? How's the pain?"

"It's all right."

Angel stroked a strand of hair from her cheek. "You're lying," she murmured. "I know it hurts. I just... need you to block it out, okay, Sky? I need you to get over the Wall."

This isn't fair. It's not fair. We're just kids. Why do we have to do this? Why can't we just find somewhere safe to hide?

"Please be careful, Angel," she whispered. "Please don't get hurt."

Angel brushed her lips across Skyler's, as soft as a whisper. "I won't. Don't you worry."

Joss stuck his head through the doorway. "Ready? They should be back any minute."

They followed him into the back yard, which was piled with crates of water, food, all the medical supplies Angel had been able to scramble together, and several large cans of petrol. Col would return the truck to the alley behind the yard, where they would be less likely to be seen loading it than in the street at the front.

They didn't know how long it would take to reach the Northern settlements. They might get a couple of hours over the border before the Board came after them, but sooner or later there would be helicopters in the air, scanning the ground for the only moving vehicle for hundreds of miles, and then they would have to find somewhere to hide before they could move on again.

Lydia joined them. "All done?"

"Yeah," Skyler said. "But the Board have shut off the power. And I haven't heard from the others."

"You think they've shut off the power to the watchtowers too? Could be trouble for us."

"I don't know."

Lydia slotted a gun into its holster. "Guess we'll see."

43

BLOOD SACRIFICES

The voice was a woman's, echoing from somewhere down the corridor behind them. "Hey, Pete, you still up here? You left the gate open!" The tone was familiar, teasing. "What's the boss gonna say, eh?"

Mackenzie froze. "What the fuck are you doing?" Col growled.

"There's people here! I thought they'd all have gone home!"

"So? Come *on*."

The woman's voice again, closer. "Oh – *shit* –"

Mackenzie couldn't help himself. He swung round.

She was dark-haired, wide-eyed, wearing a white lab coat. Maybe not much older than Bex would have been now. As they stared at each other, her face crumpled.

Mackenzie wanted to tell her to run. She looked so normal, standing there in front of him, as terrified as he was himself, that he couldn't make himself think of her as the enemy. He just couldn't.

Col snarled and raised his arm. "For fuck's sake –"

Mackenzie went to grab him and was rewarded with a rough shove that sent him crashing into the wall. The woman stumbled backwards, tugging frantically at her belt. An alarm wailed through the corridor.

Col's gun fired. The woman collapsed.

Mackenzie stared, dazed. Col shook his arm. "Fucking *move*."

The menace in Col's voice jerked him back to reality. He turned his back on the dead woman and sprinted down the sterile corridors, banging through the open gates and praying, even though he didn't believe in anything that could possibly help him now, that they weren't too late.

He burst out of the exit into the shock of the winter night and threw himself into the truck. How long had it been? What if it hadn't worked? He didn't think he could face going back in there.

But any minute now it would be swarming with the Board anyway. They'd only had the one chance.

Col, his jaw stiff, leapt into the driver's seat and started the engine. They shot out of the compound. Mackenzie glanced back unhappily towards the lab.

He wasn't expecting the roar, which deafened him, or the shockwave which rocked the truck and shattered the windows around them. Mackenzie shot round, his heart hammering wildly, and stared at the cloud of dust and flame billowing into the air behind them.

Col kept driving at rollercoaster speed through the empty industrial estate as a tidal wave of smoke enveloped them. Mackenzie started coughing. "Col." He could barely hear himself speak. "You need to slow down, man. If anyone sees us driving like that –"

Col slammed on the brakes and Mackenzie grabbed the dashboard to stop himself hurtling through the windscreen. The next thing he knew, Col's hand was wrapped around his throat. "What the fuck were you doing back there?" Col demanded. "You nearly got us both blown up!"

It was possible Col sort of had a point, but that didn't make him any less of an arsehole. Mackenzie shoved back at him. "Get off me. I'm not a robot. I didn't think there was going to be anyone in there!"

"Oh, that's right. I forgot you wanted to have your revolution without getting any blood on your hands. Lucky I came along to do the dirty work, eh?"

"You shot an unarmed woman in the head! Excuse me for not feeling completely okay with that!"

"Well? You were gonna blow her up."

Mackenzie hated him. And he had nothing to say.

"Oh, you were gonna help her escape? Yeah, I'm sure she'd have been dead grateful. She was a murderer, Mackenzie, just like all the rest of 'em. Don't you forget it."

But I'm not. He bit back the words.

Col gave him another disgusted look and let go of him. "If it were up to me," he said, "I'd have bloody well left you in there. The only reason I didn't is for some reason Angel seems to think you're not a completely useless piece of shit and I don't want to listen to her bitching at me if I don't bring you back."

Mackenzie mentally translated this as 'I know full well Angel could kick my arse with both hands tied behind her back.'

They drove on in silence through the dust and smoke.

44

HEARTBEATS

First came one siren, faint, in the distance. A moment later one more joined it; then another, and another, until the air was shrill with them.

Skyler closed her eyes against the burst of relief and slumped against Angel's shoulder.

"That'll be the lab, then," Joss said. "Now they just have to get back."

"They'll be okay," Angel said. "Anyone who sees the truck'll just think it's the army."

Skyler's fingers intertwined with Angel's, clung on tight. *Come on, Mackenzie. Come on.*

Please.

"How long since the sirens started?" Lydia said after a while.

Joss checked his watch. "Twenty minutes? Won't be long now, if they're coming."

An engine growled close by and then stopped. A car door slammed. Angel squeezed Skyler's hand and Skyler listened to the pounding of her heart in her ears. *You're alive. You're alive. You're alive.*

The back gate flew open and Mackenzie came hurtling in. Her knees buckled. "You made it!"

He nodded, breathless, and grabbed a box of tins. Col stalked into the yard behind him, looking murderous. "Filth are all over the place," he said, picking up a petrol can. "We'll be lucky to make it to the watchtower."

"The truck must look realistic enough if no one stopped you," Lydia said, and Skyler thought how strange it was to see people she thought of as much braver than her struggle to reassure themselves, in these murky, uncertain moments, that everything was going to be okay.

She tried to help the others as they hurried to load the truck, but when she lifted a case of water one-handed it felt like she'd been stabbed in the ribs. She dropped the case with a gasp and Lydia snatched it up, frowning at her. "You cut that out. We need you in one piece for the next bit."

Angel and Lydia squashed in the front of the truck with Col while Skyler, Mackenzie and Joss clambered into the back amongst the supplies. The truck jolted off and Joss started checking his weapons, holding a small torch between his teeth. Mackenzie's face was smudged grey with dust and smoky residue. His eyes looked hollow.

"How'd it go?" Skyler asked.

"Well, we blew it up."

"You did well."

He shook his head.

Don't go to pieces on me, Mack. Not now. "I mean it. You had the worst bit. You were really brave."

"We killed people." His whole body was limp with dejection.

"You saved a lot more. Remember that. Remember what we're doing here."

He just stared at his hands.

Skyler hesitated, and then leaned forward and caught his hand in hers. He looked up at her, startled.

"Keep it together," she murmured, so only he could hear her. "You and me – we're in this together, right? Since the beginning. We can do this."

He nodded and squeezed her hand. She squeezed back, and wondered when it was that she'd stopped thinking of Mackenzie as the person who'd delivered the worst news of her life to her, and started thinking of him as a friend.

*

The truck thundered northwest out of Birmingham. The streets were empty of pedestrians and cyclists but for once there were vehicles everywhere – the greycoats' shiny black cars, the army's camouflage trucks, more than Mackenzie had seen on the roads in years. Nobody seemed interested in their truck.

Out in the countryside west of the city a razor wire fence flanked the road leading North, hung with bright yellow signs. "Attention! You are entering a restricted area. Trespassers will be shot without warning." No buildings. No vehicles. All the Board's activity seemed to be focused on the city centre, as they'd hoped it would be.

Through the windscreen, Mackenzie saw the concrete bulk of the watchtower and, behind it, the Wall.

Early on in the planning, he'd really hoped they might be able to blow a hole in it. If he regretted anything, it was leaving that wall behind them intact.

Skyler caught his eye and grinned at him. "One day we'll come back and take it apart. Just you wait."

He managed a smile. "That's gonna be a good day."

They pulled up a few hundred yards from the watchtower – "If they come down to meet us, we need to be ready to go," Lydia had said. "Can't be faffing around trying to get out of the truck if they come at us with guns." The top of the tower was just visible, spilling yellow light into the darkness.

Skyler stretched her neck back and sighed. "Power's still up there. Good."

Angel turned to face them in the back. "Remember the plan. The twins and I go first. Col stays on the door. Sky – you let us cover you. Just hang back and stay out of sight until everyone's dead."

Skyler scowled. She'd had a brief go at using Angel's gun with her left hand that morning before Angel had swiftly taken it off her, professing that they would be lucky if she managed not to shoot any of them with it. She was having a hard time accepting that she couldn't fight for herself.

Mackenzie made a decision.

"Angel," he said, taking even himself by surprise. "You got a spare gun?"

He ignored Col's snort of derision. Angel cleared her throat. "Do you, uh, know how to shoot?"

"I'll figure it out."

Skyler poked him. "You don't have to do this, Mack."

"Yeah, I do."

Angel shrugged and handed him a small pistol. "Well – it's up to you. Cover Skyler, then. We need to move. Those guards'll be out to meet us in a sec."

The air outside the truck was cold enough to sting. As Mackenzie raised his head, tiny flecks appeared against the spill of light from the tower. Something icy landed on his face, soft as a kiss. It was snowing.

Angel, Lydia and Joss strode towards the watchtower through the thickening flakes as though they did this sort of thing every day. Mackenzie followed with Skyler. She must have been in agony, but she was keeping up and her face gave nothing away. He wondered if she was as scared as he was.

Col lurked behind them like a lump of rock, his presence unnerving even though Mackenzie kept reminding himself that he was on their side. Well, he wasn't exactly on Mackenzie's side – he'd made that perfectly clear – but he certainly hated the Board as much as rest of them did and that would have to be good enough.

The chill in the air had cut all the way through to his bones by the time they reached the base of the tower. Mackenzie thought it would be a miracle if he ever felt warm again.

Joss hefted the massive weapon in his hands, the one that made Mackenzie's gun look like a water pistol, and it erupted with a crashing boom. The door buckled. With the second blast, it burst open. At the top of the tower, the shouting began.

"Well," Mackenzie murmured. "If they didn't know we were coming. . ."

Angel disappeared into the tower and the twins thundered after her. A moment later, the shouting was drowned out by the rattle of semi-automatic gunfire and the answering bangs of Angel's hand gun, joined by a deafening barrage from the twins' weapons.

Mackenzie hovered with Skyler halfway up the stairs, hating how useless he was being. He trained the unfamiliar weight of the gun on the darkness, his muscles so tight he thought they might snap.

The gunfire cut off abruptly. Over the whine in his ears, Angel's voice echoed down the stairs: "It's done."

He climbed the rest of the stairs a little reluctantly. It wasn't the sight of blood that bothered him so much as the sight of actual chunks of person strewn across the floor, and sure enough, the scene at the top of the watchtower was enough to bring bile to the back of his throat. He swallowed hard and tried to avert his eyes from the dead guards, without much success. Skyler seemed to be working equally hard to ignore their surroundings and Mackenzie thought he might have been the only one who'd noticed her turn several degrees paler as she entered the room. She sat in front of the computer terminal and fixed her eyes on the screen.

The air was filled with the tang of gunfire and a sour, coppery smell. Lydia and Joss leaned against the glass, wearing identical deadpan expressions. They were both in one piece, although Lydia's face was flecked with blood which didn't seem to be hers.

Mackenzie glanced at Angel, who was leaning heavily against a table. He'd sort of assumed she would be fine – because of course she would be, she was Angel – and it took him a moment to realise that not all of the blood staining her clothes belonged to someone else.

He lurched towards her in alarm and she waved him off. "It's nothing."

"Doesn't look like nothing."

"Just a graze. Bit of a shock, that's all." She mouthed the next words at him: *Shut up. Don't distract Skyler.*

He pulled an agonised face at her. She rolled her eyes, beckoned him closer and lifted her shirt. "See?" she said under her breath as he squinted at the bloody gash below her ribs. "All fine."

He exhaled. She was okay.

"Skyler?" Joss said. "How're you doing?"

Skyler scowled at the computer screen, her fingers moving crab-like over the keyboard. Eventually, she lifted her right arm in its cast onto the desk and held it clumsily, jabbing at the buttons.

Joss' expression rapidly lost its neutrality. "Skyler!"

"If you could shut up, Joss," she said, her face etched with concentration, "that'd be awesome."

Joss opened his mouth and then seemed to think better of it. Skyler slammed her hand onto the desk so hard all of them jumped. "Shit!"

"What is it?" Angel said.

"The gates are locked down. I need to get into a separate system to override the command."

"How long's that gonna take?" Lydia demanded.

Skyler bent over the keyboard again. "By all means, keep asking me questions. That'll speed it up."

Silence fell. The clatter of her typing resumed.

Then – "It's not working," she muttered. "It's not *working*."

Mackenzie shared a glance with Angel. She stepped forward and laid a hand on Skyler's shoulder. "It's all right," she said, so low Mackenzie could barely hear her. "You've got this. Just take your time."

Skyler closed her eyes and nodded. Mackenzie stared out of the window to distract himself and tried to ignore the blood splattered on the glass.

Out in the dark, something caught his eye. The air disappeared from his lungs.

He beckoned Angel and the twins over. They all looked down at the two points of light speeding towards the tower. "Shit," Joss said.

"They might not be coming here," Lydia murmured.

The lights slowed. Angel sighed.

"How did they *know*?" Mackenzie moaned.

"Maybe there's a system to check in with each other if the comms go down," Angel said. "Doesn't matter now."

"C'mon, Joss," Lydia said. "Let's roll out the welcome committee."

The twins headed downstairs. Angel took a deep breath, reached over and picked up her gun again.

Skyler leapt to her feet, holding up a stopwatch. "Done! Gate's open for ten minutes." She looked at them, and her triumphant expression faltered. "Oh...what's the matter *now*?"

Outside, three dark figures climbed out of the Board vehicle. "Angel," Mackenzie said. "What do we –?"

She held up a hand. "Wait."

Evidently, the new arrivals hadn't been expecting an ambush. There was a lot of yelling, cut short by gunfire. Mackenzie held his breath and wished there was a ritual that would make all of this okay.

After what felt like a thousand years, a shout echoed up the stairs. "All clear!"

When they burst out into the open, Joss, Lydia and Col were waiting, the bodies of the guards sprawled in the snow around them. Skyler looked at the stopwatch again. "Seven minutes, guys."

As one, they ran for the truck.

Mackenzie didn't know why he threw that final glance over his shoulder when he should have been running for his life, but he did. He jerked his head back towards the watch tower, just for a second, and he thought one of the dark figures on the ground had moved, so of course he had to check again. The second time, he knew he hadn't imagined it.

As he tried both to keep watching and run in the opposite direction, the figure lifted an arm and Mackenzie, letting the instincts that had kept him alive all this time take over, spun and raised his gun.

He fired wildly and the bullet disappeared harmlessly into the night. An answering shot rang out. Mackenzie pulled himself together, aimed and pulled the trigger a second time.

The half-rising figure in the distance slumped back into the snow. He lowered his gun and turned to run again.

And then he saw her.

Skyler lay in the snow in front of him, her breath coming in short, sharp gulps, blood spreading from her abdomen into the snow around her.

"Sky! Nononono –" He scrambled over and knelt beside her, holding out his hands, but he didn't know what to do.

"Mack." It came out as a gasp. "I don't think I can get up."

Angel skidded towards them and dropped to her knees in the snow and the blood, her voice high and terrified like he'd never heard it before. "Skyler? Sky? Talk to me."

Skyler turned her head towards her. "Angel –"

"Hey. Hey. I'm here. It's okay. Does it hurt?"

"Not really. Feels. . . cold."

"Okay. That's okay. Listen, we need to pick you up, all right? We need to get you in the truck."

A choked breath. "Okay."

Angel's face was empty, like something had switched off behind her eyes. *If Skyler dies –*

She's not going to die. She's not going to die. She's not going to die.

"I'm going to take your shoulders," Angel told Skyler. "Mackenzie'll take your legs. It might hurt. Just hold on. Please."

The truck engine roared nearby and slammed to a halt in front of them. Lydia flung the back doors open. "Get in! *Now!*"

Skyler's eyes were half-closed now, her breathing shallow, audible, ragged. Mackenzie gripped her legs, and

Angel looked at him as though he was a stranger. "On three," she said.

They lifted her. Skyler let out a ragged, yelping sob and Mackenzie, hating himself, forced down a sob of his own. "I'm sorry. I'm sorry, Sky, hold on, please hold on –"

She was heavy, and he was terrified he was going to drop her, and her blood left a dark trail in the snow. In the back of the truck, Lydia shoved boxes aside and spread out a plastic sheet to protect her from the dirt on the floor.

They lowered her. Lydia slammed the doors, and the truck flew towards the Wall.

Angel crouched beside Skyler, scrubbing her hands with antiseptic wipes as Lydia held a torch over them. Mackenzie took the stopwatch from Skyler and took hold of her hand. Her fingers were freezing but when he squeezed them, she squeezed back. "Don't cry, Mack, for God's sake," she murmured.

He sniffed and wiped his eyes. "Sorry. Sorry."

"'S all right," she said. "I mean, I am pretty great." Mackenzie tried to laugh through his sobs. "Just. . . could you try not to look so much like I'm about to die?"

He gripped her hand. "You're not gonna die. You're gonna be fine."

"I've got a hole in my stomach, Mack."

"And? Anyone'd think it was something serious." He tried to grin at her. She gave a choking laugh and then cried out, her face screwed up with pain. Blood ran from the corner of her mouth.

Mackenzie's chest went tight. "Angel –"

Angel was frowning over a syringe full of clear liquid. Her eyes flitted towards Skyler's face, and he heard her sharp intake of breath.

"Angel?" Skyler whispered.

Angel laid a hand on her cheek. "I'm here."

"Am I going to die?"

"Absolutely not."

Skyler's breath caught. "Hurting a bit now."

"I know. I need to examine you properly, Sky. I need to stop the bleeding. I'm going to give you something for the pain first."

Skyler swallowed. "Is it... Will I go to sleep?"

"Yes."

"And I'm not going to die?"

"You're not going to die."

A tear trickled from the corner of Skyler's eye. "You won't leave me?"

"I promise I won't leave you."

Another ragged breath. "Okay."

Angel stroked the tear from Skyler's face. Then she swallowed hard, picked up the syringe and rolled up Skyler's sleeve.

Mackenzie looked up. They were hurtling towards the Wall at breakneck speed. Through the truck's windscreen he saw the square of blackness they were aiming for, the gateway that stood between them and their immediate survival, slowly getting smaller as the gate began to roll closed.

Lydia squinted at the stopwatch, abandoned on the floor beside him. "Thirty seconds, Joss."

Skyler's hand went limp in his.

Angel started cutting Skyler's top open with a pair of scissors, her face blank. "She's gonna be okay, right?" Mackenzie said. "Angel?"

She closed her eyes. "Clean your hands," she said. "I'm going to need your help."

He took the antiseptic wipes and glanced at the stopwatch. *Twenty seconds.*

The steel gate, inching closed as they tore towards it.

Eighteen seconds.

Skyler, pale and still and icy cold, her blood soaking his shirt.

Seventeen seconds.

Angel, trying to keep her voice steady. "Lydia, hold the light still. Mackenzie, pass me that bag."

Fifteen seconds.

He didn't know if they were going to make it through the gate or just smash into it as it closed.

Fourteen seconds.

They shot through into the darkness.

The gate clanged shut behind them.

THE END

ACKNOWLEDGEMENTS

When I started writing *Blackout* I hardly knew any other writers, had absolutely no confidence in myself, and had no idea what I was doing. There are a number of people without whom this book would be in no fit state for anyone else's eyes, and even more without whom I would never have had the courage to publish it.

So my sincere thanks to: Ash McKenna, for all the evenings playing word wars with me through the first (terrible!) draft; to everyone at West Oxfordshire Writers, Banbury Writers, Naomi's Café and River Exe Writers; to Judith Facer, Charlotte Facer, Julie Norris, Caroline Wills-Wright, Natasha Narayan, Sam Drury-Shore, Colin Smith (especially for the tough love!), Holly Snaith, Gwen Davies and Carl Blakey, for their invaluable critique on various stages of the manuscript; to Nick Frampton, Annie Filmer-Bennett and Katy Smart for helping to wrestle the blurb into shape; to Jess Cooper for cheering me on through all my angst and doubts.

To my dear friend Faith Dillon-Lee – I have so many things to thank you for I don't even know where to start. From reading and critiquing not one but two versions of the manuscript, to endless hours of discussion, advice on formatting, the geography of Bournemouth, publishing and a hundred other things; and most of all, for your unwavering enthusiasm and your belief in Sky, Mack,

Angel and me. It's no exaggeration to say that this book would not be out in the world without you.

Thank you to Ben Marwood for his permission to use the line "Outside There's a Curse", from his album of the same name.

Thanks to my brother Jason for his eagle eyes and technical advice – I bear sole responsibility for the inevitable errors in my understanding of encryption techniques and hacking.

Thank you to my lovely mum and dad, Carol and Chris, for believing in me far more than I believed in myself and for making sure I know that you always have my back.

And to Genevieve, for your unwavering encouragement, endless patience, and a thousand big and tiny acts of support over the years – thank you. I couldn't have done it without you.

ABOUT THE AUTHOR

Kit has been writing since she was old enough to hold a pen. She lives with her girlfriend in rural Devon and has a secret alter ego who works as a mental health nurse. She might have been a mermaid in a former life, and when she's not writing can generally be found in the sea or on the moors. *Blackout* is her first novel.

Lightning Source UK Ltd.
Milton Keynes UK
UKHW01f0636290518
323381UK00001B/120/P